'As we begin to comprehend that the earth itself is a kind of manned spaceship hurtling through the infinity of space – it will seem increasingly absurd that we have not better organised the life of the human family.'

Hubert H. Humphrey, Vice-President of the United States, 1966

✳ ✳ ✳

'Turned out nice again.'

George Formby

Praise for *Calling Major Tom*

The feel-good story everyone can't stop talking about:

'A book about loneliness, about bravery, about the walls we all put up to protect ourselves and about how it is never ever too late to try to change.'   Katie Marsh, author of *My Everything*

'A gorgeously quirky story about families, forgiveness and unexpected friendships - sheer joy.'
Lucy Diamond, author of *The Secrets of Happiness*

'...a pure pleasure to read, full of well-observed characters and hope, and a much-needed antidote for these worrying times.'
Julie Cohen, author of *Together*

'*Calling Major Tom* is blooming marvellous! Original, moving and mercilessly funny, this is an unashamedly feel-good story. I laughed, I cried and I cheered for the wonderful characters. Don't hesitate - fall in love with this book!'
Miranda Dickinson, author of *Searching for a Silver Lining*

'Brilliant, funny, heartwarming and exactly what everyone needs right now. I loved it.'   Rachael Lucas, author of *Wildflower Bay*

'A funny, moving, absorbing hot chocolate of a story - hot chocolate with chilli, that is, because there were bits were I laughed aloud! The pages just turned themselves - I can't wait for the next David Barnett.'
Daniela Sacerdoti, author of *Calling You Home*

'A bitter-sweet, original blend of social realism and sci-fi; funny, engaging and honest.'   Stuart Maconie

'I loved this book. One huge step for a man no longer in space.'
David Quantick

David M. Barnett is an author and journalist based in West Yorkshire. After a career working for regional newspapers he embarked upon a freelance career writing features for most of the UK national press. He is the author of the critically acclaimed Gideon Smith series of Victorian fantasies, published by Tor Books, and teaches journalism part-time at Leeds Trinity University. David was born in Wigan, Lancashire, in 1970 and is married to Claire, also a journalist. They have two children, Charlie and Alice.

By David M. Barnett

Hinterland
Angelglass
The Janus House and Other Two-Faced Tales
popCULT!
Gideon Smith and the Mechanical Girl
Gideon Smith and the Brass Dragon
Gideon Smith and the Mask of the Ripper

Calling Major Tom

DAVID M. BARNETT

First published in Great Britain in 2017 by Orion Books,
an imprint of The Orion Publishing Group Ltd
Carmelite House, 50 Victoria Embankment,
London EC4Y 0DZ

An Hachette UK company

7 9 10 8 6

A CIP catalogue record for this book is
available from the British Library.

ISBN 978 1 4091 6813 3

Typeset by Born Group

Printed in Great Britian by CPI Group (UK) Ltd, Croydon CR0 4YY

www.orionbooks.co.uk

To Claire, Charlie and Alice.

*When my head's in space you keep my feet on the ground
and my heart filled.*

*In memory of Malcolm Barnett,
1945-2016*

Part One

FEBRUARY 11, 1978

A long time ago in a cinema far, far away from where he is now, a boy and his dad are walking into darkness. The boy hugs a bag of Revels and a small popcorn to his chest, his dad steers him with a firm hand on the shoulder down the aisle, the carpet sticking to their feet. The film hasn't started yet but already the faces of those seated are turned towards the advertisements, painted with pale light. Tendrils of cigarette smoke weave and knot together in the black void between the screen and the audience. Rising from the packed rows there is a muted murmur of whispered conversation.

Thomas Major has never been happier. It is his eighth birthday treat, coming to the Glendale cinema to watch this movie he has been aching to see – as though it is already, has always been, part of his life, imprinted on his DNA. At home, carefully positioned on the desk in his bedroom are his presents from his actual birthday, a month ago; a *Star Wars* Cantina playset, which comes with action figures of the aliens, Snaggletooth and Hammerhead, whom you can fix to little stands that twist and turn as though the characters are fighting; and a recording of the movie's soundtrack by the London Philharmonic Orchestra, placed neatly next to his mum's old Dansette and the stack of her old 45s she has given him to play on it.

And now, Thomas and his dad are at the film. The actual film. The opening weekend. They have queued around the block to get in to Caversham's oldest cinema – and one of the oldest in Reading – and while they wait Thomas asks his dad if he would like to go to space.

'I bet when you're my age they'll have cities on the moon,' says Dad. 'Not for me, though. No atmosphere.' He guffaws and slaps

Thomas on the shoulder. 'You could go and live there. Be like that song. "Major Tom". Your mummy was about three months gone when that song was out. I think that's why she wanted to call you Thomas. She's about the same time along now.' Dad pauses, then looks at Thomas. 'Bloody hell. Is that "Figaro" still top of the hit parade? I don't fancy shouting that out of the back gate at teatime.'

'"Space Oddity",' says Thomas absently. 'It's not called "Major Tom", it's called "Space Oddity".'

As they queue to get inside, a beige car cruises past the cinema. Frank Major whistles. 'Look at that. Volkswagen Derby. Only came out last year. Quite fancy one of those myself.' He nudges Thomas. 'We'd look like a right pair of cool guys, riding round in that, eh?'

Thomas shrugs. He isn't really interested in cars. His dad continues, 'Maybe we'll get one this year. But I'd like to get a conservatory up this summer. Adds value to the house, does that. Maybe we could convert the loft as well. There's a house in the next street with a conservatory and a loft conversion, went for nearly twenty-three grand last year, can you believe that?'

It's only the afternoon but already the sky is deep blue, a full moon low on the horizon above the black rooftops. 'Like a ten-pence piece,' says Dad. Thomas closes one eye and puts his thumb and forefinger around the disc of the moon.

'I got it, Dad! I got the moon!'

'Put it in your pocket, son,' he says. 'You never know when you might need it. Come on, we're going inside at last.'

Thomas puts the invisible, weightless, ten-pence-piece moon in the breast pocket of his brown shirt with the wide collars. Thomas's belly is weighed down agreeably with the Wimpy he had for lunch, but he still has room for sweets and treats. His dad shakes his head and comments on his 'hollow legs' before handing over the money at the kiosk.

Now Dad is directing him to a single empty seat on the end of a row, next to a man and a woman with three small girls. Thomas feels something knot inside him, something he can't put a name to. He looks quizzically at his dad. 'But there's only one chair.'

'Wait here,' says Dad, and goes over to speak to the lady who sells ice creams. She has hair that looks as though it has been carved from granite and a face to match, which she turns towards Thomas, her pin-prick eyes peering at him through the gloom.

Dad gives her a pound note and she gives him two choc ices. She looks at Thomas again, then at Dad, who pulls a face and gives her another pound note. Then he walks back to Thomas with the lady behind him. Thomas has the popcorn balanced on his knees and the Revels in his pocket. Dad pushes the ice cream into his hands.

'Thomas, son,' he says. 'Dad's got to run an errand.'

Thomas looks at him, and blinks. 'What errand? What about the film?'

'It's all right. It's very important. It's . . .' He looks at the screen as though he might find inspiration there. 'It's a surprise for your mum.' He taps the side of his nose. 'Boys' day out rules, OK? Just between us.'

Thomas taps the side of his nose, too, but without much conviction. He feels a yawning chasm open in his belly. Dad says, 'This is Deirdre. She's going to keep an eye on you until I get back.'

The woman looks down her nose at Thomas, her mouth set in a thin, bloodless line, as though the sculptor couldn't be bothered to even try to make it human-looking.

'How long will you be?' says Thomas, feeling the weight of all that blackness in the cinema against his back, feeling very alone.

'Back before you know it,' says Dad, and winks. Then the music starts and Thomas turns to look at the screen as it fills with stars and words that begin scrolling away from him.

> **It is a period of civil war. Rebel spaceships, striking from a hidden base, have won their first victory against the evil Galactic Empire.**

Thomas looks back to see his dad, but he's already gone.

THE 22,000-MILE-HIGH SHED

5 Across: The Latin sun, one masticated, though sadly misspelled (8)

Thomas Major closes his eyes to think, and decides that the absolute best thing of all is the silence. No car horns blaring, no voices shouting, no engines revving, no telephones ringing, no beep-beep-beep of reversing bin wagons.

Nothing.

No doorbells, no shuddering bass of someone else's awful music, no slamming doors, no blasting televisions.

Just quiet.

No inane radio-host chatter, no incessant ping of incoming messages, no drilling of tarmac, no buskers murdering classic songs.

None of the things filed in his head under the label *aural menaces*.

Thomas Major has always wanted a shed. Cocooned and insulated, away from everyone else and their hateful noise, he taps the point of his pencil on the first page of *The Big Guardian Book of Really Hard Cryptic Crosswords*, and gets back to thinking. The tapping of the pencil is a good sound, an accompaniment to honest mental toil. And it's his sound, his noise.

As is the slurping he makes when he takes a mouthful of tea, hot and far too sweet. No one in here to tell him to mind his manners. He'll slurp if he wants to. He swishes the tea around his mouth until it's cool enough to loudly gargle at the back of his throat.

'Take that,' he says when he's swallowed it, to no one at all.

All his life he has wanted his own shed. He envied those men who could disappear to the bottom of their gardens and lock themselves away from everything and everybody. And now, here, on his forty-seventh birthday, he is finally alone, free to slurp tea, able to spend as much time as he likes doing his crosswords. He's been saving this book and its 365 fiendishly difficult puzzles. He taps his pencil on the page again. Masticated? Chewed. But misspelled? *Sadly* misspelled?

Because Thomas Major can do precisely what he wants in here, he decides he might like to have a bit of music to help him think. Proper music, mind, not the thud-thud-thud that issues from expensive cars driven by young men sweating arrogance. He would have liked to have his entire vinyl record collection with him, but there was the space issue. So he's got it all digitised, every album track, every single and B-side, every rarity, every flexidisc that was taped to the front of a music paper or magazine. Everything. Because it's his birthday, he thinks he might like to listen to something uplifting and jolly, perhaps The Cure. He fires up the computer terminal – grimacing at the laboured ticking and buzzing it makes – and decides on *Disintegration*. Magnificent return to gloomy form, 1989. The tracks start to shuffle, which Thomas doesn't like – an album should be listened to in the order the band intended – but he hasn't yet worked out how to stop it doing that. The first song it plays is 'Homesick'.

Thomas grunts, and expels air through his nose, and gives a wry smile.

Almost. But not quite.

Latin sun – that must be Sol, obviously. *One* masticated – number? Thomas sucks on the pencil thoughtfully until the next track comes on. Perhaps a look through the window might help. It serves only to take his breath away, and he wonders if he'll ever tire of this view, ever think it commonplace or lacking in wonder. He sincerely hopes not. Because here he is, all alone with his tea and his crossword and his music, and out there is everyone else.

The Earth fills the four-inch thick pane, blue and green and wreathed in cloud and quite, quite beautiful. So big he could almost reach out and touch it. He is in high earth orbit, 22,000 miles above the planet's surface, and very shortly he will catapult out into the void, travelling away from it at 26.5 kilometres every single second. Soon it will shrink to nothingness, a speck in the velvet blanket of space. He closes his eyes and listens to the music, and tells himself that of course he's done the right thing, that this is exactly what he wanted.

Thomas's world is a hexagonal tube thirty feet long and dominated at one end by his workstation and the other by a large hatch that leads to an airlock and then to the great, unending void.

Thomas doesn't go to that end of the capsule very often.

In between are banks and banks of electronics – Thomas knows what less than half of them actually do – a series of doors that open into storage compartments holding all manner of things – mostly dried – to keep him alive on his journey, and a treadmill, which he clips himself to in order to run and stop his muscles completely wasting away.

It is, for all intents and purposes, home. It even has its routines like home, too, but instead of commuting to a job and coming home to sit in front of a TV or listen to music while his dinner cooks, Thomas starts each day zipped into a sleeping bag on the wall. He's tried sleeping free in the microgravity but he just gets sucked towards the air vents. Then he cooks breakfast – some tasteless dried food, or a nutritious fruit bar – and then washes himself and uses the toilet, which is always fun. The morning is spent carrying out checks on all the systems, then there is exercise, then he's meant to read up on all the jobs he'll have to do once he reaches Mars . . . chief among them: keeping himself alive. This seems to involve a lot of potato farming.

The music stops and is replaced by a jarring, insistent pinging noise. He turns away from the window, from the world, and pushes himself off the wall, swimming in the zero gravity to the monitor bolted to the wall, his crossword book and pencil floating above it. The screen is displaying the words INCOMING COMMUNICATION.

'Bloody marvellous,' he whispers as the screen dissolves into a mess of pixels, which turn into a laggy image of a huddle of people in suits standing before rows and rows of technicians sitting at computer terminals.

'This is Ground Control to Major Tom!' says the man in the middle of the huddle, tall and thin with slicked-back dark hair. 'Come in, Major Tom!'

Thomas anchors himself in front of the monitor and a postage-stamp-sized image of his head appears in the bottom corner of the screen. He glances at it and wonders if he should have shaved; he can only use an electric thing up here and he hates it. He suddenly realises he'll probably never have a wet shave again in his entire life. His brown hair, flecked with grey, is sticking up comically, like fronds of seaweed waving in a tide.

'Hello, Ground Control. This is *Shednik-1*, receiving you loud and clear.'

There's a cheer from the technicians, though a very muted, polite, British one. The man in the suit – Director Baumann – glares at him through the camera. 'Are you going to keep calling the *Ares-1* that silly name, Thomas?'

'Are you going to say "this is Ground Control to Major Tom" every day for the next seven months?'

Director Baumann has hair so dark he must dye it. He is also never without a tie, top shirt button proudly fastened. Thomas is suspicious of anyone who wears a tie to work in this day and age. It's completely unnecessary. Ties are for funerals – of which Thomas has much experience – and weddings, of which he has a passing knowledge. Baumann's shirts are so neatly pressed he either has obsessive compulsive disorder or a wife chained to an ironing board in his basement. But what Thomas loathes most about him is, he realises, Director Baumann's love affair with clipboards. He is never without one. He consults the one he is holding now. 'All your systems are running A-OK from our diagnostics here. Have you completed your on-board checks?'

Thomas swats away the crossword book that's hovering incriminatingly in front of the camera and mumbles something non-committal. Baumann says, 'Your launch went perfectly, as I imagine you know. You're properly aligned with the Hohmann Transfer route and the engines are firing. You're on your merry way, Thomas. Three hundred and ten million miles to go. NASA tells us there's a bit of a micrometeoroid shower in your vicinity, but it shouldn't cause you any problems.'

Talking about the weather, even in space. How very British. 'I knew I should have packed my umbrella.'

There's more laughter from the technicians. A woman holding an iPad like it's a baby flicks her hair with her free hand. 'We're recording this session to release to the media. And we believe it's your birthday today . . .?' Her voice rises in a hateful sing-song effect.

This is Claudia who handles public relations. Thomas knows she detests him for what he did a year ago. She is tanned and toned and Thomas imagines that she spends all of her free time engaged in some form of highly costly exercise, punching leather bags, trying to focus and seeing only Thomas's wayward hair and pale face. Every day Thomas has seen her she has worn a different outfit, quietly imparting the name of the label or designer to anyone within earshot as though they're the secret passwords to her better and more expensively clad world.

'January 11. Same time every year. Don't tell me there's a cake in a tube somewhere? It's got to be better than that tea I squeeze out. Too much sugar. And certainly not Earl Grey like I asked for.'

Baumann waggles his eyebrows, semaphoring *for God's sake stop being such a grumpy bastard.* Claudia prods at her iPad. 'We've got someone *very special* here to talk to you, Thomas . . .'

He opens his mouth and closes it again. Really? Someone special? Has she . . . is it Janet?

✳ 3 ✳

134 FEET ABOVE SEA LEVEL

'That's Nan's phone,' shouts James.

Then: 'I haven't got a clean shirt.'

And: 'It's PE today, where's my kit?'

Followed by: 'And I hate ham sandwiches. Can't I have a school dinner?'

Gladys sits in her chair by the fireplace in the small living room of number 19 Santus Street, Wigan, admiring her long, pink quilted dressing gown. It's like the duvets they used to call Continental Quilts back in her day. She wonders why. Did they come over from the Continent? And why did they have them over there? Wasn't it always warm on the Continent? Or at least the places people used to go when they used to say they were going 'to the Continent'? Benidorm and suchlike?

James is standing in the doorway to the kitchen, no shirt, his white, bony elbows touching either side of the frame as he holds his arms out, as though imploring someone to do something. He'll catch his death, standing there with practically nothing on in the depths of January. Gladys thinks for a moment she might try to help. That is, after all, her phone ringing – James is quite right. Though it sounds very dull, like it's in a bucket down a well. It's amazing what they can do these days – James put an old song on the phone instead of a ringing sound. It's 'Diamonds and Rust' by Joan Baez, one of Gladys's favourites, though it makes her sad, and she often can't say just why that is. Maybe it's because it's about remembering things from a long time ago, and that's pretty much all that Gladys has these days. She remembers something then, quite unrelated to anything, but a fact worth remembering, she thinks. 'Wigan is one hundred and thirty four feet above sea level.'

James groans and stares at his elbows, his arms twisted in on themselves.

'Ellie!' Gladys calls from the chair. 'James needs . . . stuff. I'll iron his shirt.'

There's a muffled shout from upstairs. James – Gladys clicks her tongue at his hair, far too long and curly for a boy of ten – and hauls her thin frame up. The living room is small, only a chair and the sofa and the telly, a door into the kitchen where the stairs are. Behind the sofa is a plastic basket piled high with a teetering tower of washed clothes. The ironing board is already set up beside it, has been for months. For ever. Gladys rummages through the pile, finds a white shirt, and plugs in the iron.

'I'll give you a shilling for your dinner.'

James rolls his eyes and roots through the washing basket himself, pulling out a pair of shorts and a rugby shirt. 'Shall I iron that for you as well?' she says.

James stuffs it into his bag. 'Don't bother. It'll only be full of mud and probably blood by teatime. I don't know why we have to play rugby in January. We should do that in summer.'

'Your granddad was always good at rugby. He could have played for Wigan when he was younger.' Gladys peers at the buttons on the shirt she's spread out on the ironing board. The stitching's awful. They wouldn't have got away with that in her day. She peers at the label. Made in Taiwan, she shouldn't wonder.

'Nan!' Ellie has appeared in the kitchen doorway. Far too much eye make-up on, as usual. Hair looks like she's been dragged through a hedge backwards. And that skirt. Practically a belt. Not that Gladys has any room to talk. Liked a miniskirt did Gladys. Great legs. All the boys said so. That was the first thing Bill ever said to her, when they were outside the chippy near the Ferris Wheel pub. 'Tha's got great legs, lass.' She used to like the Ferris Wheel. Nice glass of stout on a Saturday night. She wonders if it's still open, then remembers that they knocked it down to build the big supermarket.

'Nan!' Ellie rushes over, squeezes between the sofa and the wall, and grabs for the iron, which has been laying face down on James's shirt.

'Oh, great.' There's a big, iron-shaped brown mark right over the breast pocket.

Ellie puts her hands over her face. 'He's only got three shirts.'

'Here, I'll do another one,' says Gladys. She holds up the shirt and inspects it critically. 'Stitching was very poor on this, anyway. I'll cut it up for dusters.'

'I'll do it,' says Ellie, gently steering Gladys away from the ironing board by her elbows. 'You sit down. Have you had any breakfast yet?'

'Piece of toast and a cup of tea would be lovely. Have you seen my phone? I heard it ringing.'

James is already climbing into a creased white shirt. 'It's fine,' he says, though in a voice that suggests it's anything but. 'I'm going to miss my bus.'

'Don't forget your butties,' says Ellie, rubbing at her earlobe. 'Has anyone seen my earring?'

'Has anyone seen my phone?' says Gladys. 'I plugged it in when you brought home the shopping last night. I was putting the food away. I remember now.'

James is standing at the fridge, staring into it as though it contains all manner of wonders. He reaches in and pulls out his clingfilmed sandwiches. 'It's here, Nan. Your phone. You've left it in the fridge. In the butter dish.'

James starts laughing and walks into the living room with the phone. Ellie shakes her head. 'Nan.'

Gladys rubs her chin. 'I could have sworn blind I plugged it in last night. Over there, on the sideboard.'

The sideboard is under the window, just a small, cheap thing. On it is a bowl with a couple of shrivelled tangerines in it, flanked by photographs of Ellie and James's mum and dad. James points and laughs again. 'Oh, Jesus. That's rank.'

Behind the fruit bowl is the snaking lead of Gladys's phone charger, the contact rammed into a block of Anchor that's begun to melt and spread over the varnished wood.

'I'll clean it up.' Ellie sighs loudly. She looks at her phone. 'James, you need to go.'

'See you,' he says, and Gladys watches him stuff a biscuit into his mouth before he leaves. She winks at him. *Our secret.*

Ellie looks at her phone again. 'Crap. I'm going to be late for school.' She rushes into the kitchen – she's always rushing around that girl – and Gladys hears the kettle hissing and the toaster going. Five minutes later Ellie is bringing her a cup of tea and a piece of buttered toast on a plate, a folded-up slice of toast hanging out of her own mouth.

'You're a good girl,' says Gladys.

Ellie squats down in front of Gladys and takes the toast from her mouth. 'Nan,' she says. Always serious. Rushing around and serious. 'Nan, promise me you won't go out today. And don't plug anything in. I've put a Tupperware bowl in the fridge with your dinner in it. It needs to go in the microwave for two minutes. I've written it all down and Sellotaped it to the lid. Follow the instructions exactly, OK? Are you all right making cups of tea?'

'Of course I am,' sniffs Gladys. 'I'm not a baby, you know. I'm seventy-one next birthday.'

Ellie nods. 'Don't answer the door and ignore any phone calls unless it comes up on the screen that it's me or James, you understand?'

Gladys gives Ellie a little salute and laughs. Ellie doesn't laugh. She looks around for her rucksack, locates it by the sideboard, and hefts it over her shoulder. 'I'll be back at four. James will be home at half three. OK? You just watch telly. Don't forget your dinner. I thought we could have fish fingers for tea. Then I'll have to go out to work.'

'Lovely,' says Gladys. 'Though I might like a pie, I think. Meat and potato. Do you know, they're not allowed to call them that any more? They have to call them potato and meat because there's more potatoes than meat. Be nice with a bit of gravy though. Have a good day at school.'

When Ellie's finally gone, Gladys heaves a sigh. Sometimes she can't hear herself think in this house. She looks around for the zapper and finds it on the mantelpiece, and she points it up close to the telly and jabs at the buttons until it comes on. News news news. Those idiots on that sofa. Some American rubbish. People going up into space. All this choice and nothing to watch. Gladys might read her book if she can find it. Or remember what it's called. Or even what it's about.

She picks her phone up and wonders who was calling earlier from the fridge. No, not from the fridge. In the fridge. While the phone was in the fridge. It might be her boyfriend, though he doesn't normally phone. Well, never phones. Email's his thing. Gladys peers at the screen that says ONE MISSED CALL followed by a number she doesn't recognise – well, one that doesn't have a name attached to it, anyway. Then she jumps, almost dropping the phone as it rings again.

'Hello?' Gladys listens for a moment to what the nice-sounding young woman on the other end has to say. She thinks about it and says, 'Why, yes, I think I do have payment protection insurance. How many loans? Ooh, six or seven I should think. Eight. Claim it back? That sounds interesting . . .'

WHAT IT'S LIKE IN SPACE

Thomas glances at his image in the corner of the monitor and tries to flatten down his hair, which just springs up again. He wonders if he can take a break to have a shave. What he doesn't wonder is why his ex-wife would be there, several months after she told him she would not be speaking to him again.

Then a man in a checked shirt and a small child shuffle into view. And no, not Janet at all. Claudia beckons at the girl. 'We ran a competition with your old primary school in Caversham for one pupil to get the chance to ask you a question.' She puts her arm around the child, who is perhaps nine or ten. 'This is Stephanie. And this is Mr Beresford, her form tutor. Go on, Stephanie, say hello, don't be shy.'

Thomas peers at the teacher. He looks actually young enough to conceivably be Thomas's son. The girl waves a shy hello and Thomas says, 'My form tutor was Mr Dickinson. Whatever happened to him?'

Mr Beresford says, 'Ah, is that Tony Dickinson? I think he retired some while back and died about a year ago. I remember seeing something on one of the newsletters.'

'Good. He was a hateful, sadistic bastard. He once caned me three times on the arse because I scratched my nose in class. I hope he died in agony.'

'Major Tom . . .' says Baumann through gritted teeth. 'Major Tom has a very . . . funny sense of humour, Stephanie. He doesn't mean that at all.'

'I bloody do. I think old Dicky actually got off on smacking boys.' He directs his attention to Mr Beresford, all trendy haircut and hipster beard. 'I suppose they don't let you do that sort of thing these days. Criminal background checks and all that.'

Claudia is elbowing her way in front of Baumann, who's tugging at his shirt collar. 'Anyway, Thomas, Stephanie has a question for you.'

'If this is going to be about how I take a shit in space, I can tell you now that it's time-consuming, awkward and undignified.' Thomas sees Baumann put his hand to his forehead.

The girl looks up at her teacher, then at Claudia, who smiles tightly and nudges her. She looks down at a card and recites in a tremulous voice, 'What's the best thing about being in space?'

Jesus Christ, was that really the best they could come up with?

Too late, Thomas realises he's said that out loud. The girl's face crumples and she starts to cry. Thomas closes his eyes. 'Okay. You want to know the best thing about being in space? It's the not being on Earth. I was probably about your age when I realised something, and that was that the world is shit and so is everybody in it. I've spent my whole life watching my ambitions wither and die. So when the opportunity came to leave it all behind – I mean literally bloody leave it all behind – I grabbed it with both hands. I've got the only thing I ever wanted. No people. I'm alone. Complete and total—'

Sol. One. Chewed. Sadly misspelled. Sad. Misspelled. Chewed. Tude.

'SOLITUDE!' Thomas yelps, opening his eyes and looking around for his crossword book. Then he realises the monitor is blank and dead. The bastards have cut him off.

His pencil is floating somewhere over by the window and he's just about to retrieve it when a shrill buzzing sound issues from a slab of grey plastic he hasn't noticed before. He picks it up cautiously, and realises it's some kind of telephone.

'Hello?'

'Thomas, this is Director Baumann,' says a voice, blanketed in hiss. 'We lost comms with you just before you started speaking. Don't worry though, we're on it at this end. Probably just a software glitch. But I might bone up on EVA procedures if I were you.

Bone up? Who says that these days? And Thomas lets the EVA comment slide in favour of a world-weary sigh. 'Serves you right for buying all the computer systems in the PC World sale.'

Director Baumann ignores him. 'We're all over it now. In the meantime, we'll have to use this system to stay in touch.'

'I didn't know I had a phone.' Thomas momentarily takes the slab of plastic away from his ear to inspect it. It looks like something from the seventies. Given that *Shednik-1* is a bastardised hybrid of bits of going-cheap Soviet space tech, it probably is. But at least it works.

'It's an Iridium phone,' says Baumann. 'It uses the satellites in orbit around Earth to relay a signal between us. The thing is, you're not going to be in range for very long. The technology is a little old and clunky, but there is something like sixty-six satellites which can bounce the signal, so we should be able to stay in touch.'

'There should be seventy-seven,' says Thomas absently. 'That's the atomic number of iridium.'

'It doesn't really matter,' says Baumann crossly. 'We anticipate having the main comms up and running again before you know it.'

'So you can't see me? At all?'

'Well . . . no, not directly. As such. Don't panic, though. The tech guys are all—'

'All over it, yes,' says Thomas. *Like a cheap suit.* He makes a grab for his hovering crossword book. 'Well, if you're sure you can't see me . . . I suppose I'll just do some, um, checks. And stuff.'

'Good man,' says Baumann. 'It's just visuals that are down so I'm going to email you some numbers that you can contact us on in an emergency from the Iridium phone.'

'Numbers? Ordinary phone numbers? That's how this thing works?'

'Yes. Ordinary phone numbers. We'll be in touch. And Thomas . . . you made that little girl cry, you know. Is there any chance at all you can stop being such a . . . a . . .'

Director Baumann can't seem to find just the right word.

'Miserable wanker?' offers Thomas helpfully.

He can't see Director Baumann, of course, but he can picture him all the same, hugging his clipboard to his chest, pinching the bridge of his nose between his thumb and forefinger, his eyebrows folding in on each other.

'Yes,' says Director Baumann with quiet resignation. 'Is there any chance you can stop being such a miserable wanker, especially when we have guests who want to talk to you?'

'Roughly the same chance as a snowball has in hell.'

'Thomas,' says Baumann again, in the tone of voice you would use to address a simple child. 'Thomas. We took rather a large risk in selecting you for this mission. Need I remind you that you made certain . . . promises? As regards your commitment to the mission?'

'I think you'll find my commitment to the mission is second to none,' says Thomas through gritted teeth. 'On account of the fact that I am currently on a one-way trip to Mars and will very likely be dead before anybody else from Earth gets their arses into gear to join me. Which, as we have all already established, is a state of affairs I am more than happy with. And if you cast your mind back a year you will no doubt recall that you didn't select me for this mission at all. I selected myself.'

Thomas hears Claudia's muffled voice in the background, saying, 'Yes, I aged five years on that day, and that's something I'll never bloody forgive him for.'

'Yes, Thomas, we are all fully aware of that. Of everything. But you must also accept that we all have certain responsibilities . . . it's a great honour for us all to be involved in getting the first human being on to Mars. There are conditions we must fulfil. We need to maintain a level of . . . presence. To that end—'

'No, I absolutely will not start tweeting. Get Claudia to do it. Just make up some rubbish every now and then about how breathtaking the Earth looks from space and how my thrusters are firing nicely. I'm sure they'll lap it all up. That should keep the sponsors happy, yes? You can tell them I'm showering in Coca-Cola and using Big Macs for pillows, if that helps.'

There's a hissy silence. Baumann sighs heavily. 'OK, Thomas. We'll be in touch.'

Then the connection goes dead. Thomas looks at the phone for a moment then says, 'Happy birthday to me,' and replaces it in its holder.

He gets back to his crossword, but he can't concentrate. He'd thought that they'd got Janet there. He'd thought she wanted to speak to him. How could he have been so stupid? After everything that happened, after getting the letter from her solicitor on his *previous*

18

birthday . . . well. After the final time he saw her he imagines she's the last person on Earth to feel the need to speak to him. But still. His birthday. He lets the pencil and the book float away and goes to find one of the self-heating toothpaste tubes of sickly sweet not Earl Grey. As he squeezes it into his mouth he looks at the Iridium phone and picks it up. It has buttons, and is connected to the control panel with a thick black wire. He wonders . . .

Thomas jabs in the number he had for Janet, burned into his mind, and listens to the clicks and hisses and the sudden, thrilling sound of a ringing phone.

✶ 5 ✶

GLADYS ORMEROD'S ADVICE TO THE NATION

Gladys watches the kettle boiling and thinks she should probably go and get dressed. It was a lovely chat she'd had with the young lady, though she hadn't seemed quite as nice as she had at first when she established that Gladys probably hadn't actually had any loans, ever, with payment protection insurance. Still, it was nice of her to take the trouble to phone up and ask.

Gladys weaves back to her chair with the tea and peers at the list of programmes on the screen. What side was *Pebble Mill at One* on again? She does like that. But it all seems to be people shouting at each other about who's the father of their unborn baby, or bailiffs, or people rushing around the countryside buying antiques. While she's pondering, Gladys hears the swing of the letterbox and the light slap of something on the mat. The living room opens straight on to the street, and Gladys goes over to the door where there's a brown envelope lying on the floor. Brown envelopes are never anything exciting. She bends down and hears her hips creaking. There's a little window in the envelope with her son's name on it. Well, he's not here. They should know that. On the front in big dark letters it says URGENT INFORMATION ENCLOSED. THIS IS NOT A CIRCULAR.

Gladys stares at the envelope for a while. Of course it's not bloody circular. It's oblong. She says it out loud, 'Oblong.' It makes her laugh. She's not sure they even use that word any more. *Rectangular*, they probably say. She thinks she prefers oblong. Isn't there a tea called oblong? Made in China? Or Taiwan, like James's shirt? Gladys wonders when they stopped saying oblong. Probably a European thing. Most changes seem to be, according to the news. They probably sent over the word *rectangular* when they started sending over the Continental Quilts. Which reminds her. She was going to get dressed. Looking at the letter one more time, Gladys goes upstairs to get changed into her skirt and blouse, and to put the brown envelope, unopened, at the bottom of the drawer where she keeps her tights and knickers, along with all the other unopened brown envelopes.

'Hello?' This time it's a young man. He says his name's Simon. She listens to him and says, 'Yes, actually, you're quite right. We have had an accident. When? Well, my husband was driving. Bill. It wasn't his fault, though. The cow just came out of the field. Well, yes, I do think someone's at fault. The cow, for a start. People don't think cows can move very fast but this one did. Straight out of the field. The gate? Yes, it was wide open. That's how the cow got out. No, I suppose someone must have left it open, you're right. Well, I don't think the cow would have opened it. They're not that clever, are they, cows? Well, this one certainly wasn't. I can't see a cow being clever enough to open a gate and then just stand in front of a car. When? Well, as I say, Bill was driving. It was the pale blue car. A Toledo, I think? Triumph? Yes, it is an old car. Well, it wasn't then. It was quite new. Not new new, obviously, but new to us. Made a bit of a mess. Of the cow. The car was all right. Bill? No, you can't speak to him. He's been dead for twenty years now. Hello? Simon . . .?'

The phone call upsets Gladys. It makes her think about Bill. She misses Bill terribly. Sometimes she forgets that he had the heart attack, expects that he'll be home at teatime like he used to be. Sometimes she can picture what she made for his tea thirty years ago better than she can remember what she ate today. The worst thing about it was they'd had that row the day he went off to work and never came back. If she could change anything in her life, she'd not have had that row with Bill that Thursday morning. If the Prime Minister came up and asked her what bit of advice she had for the nation, she'd say never let anyone you love out of your sight if you've had a row. You never know when you're going to get a phone call saying your husband has collapsed at work and been taken to hospital. You never know when you'll have to get two buses up to the hospital only to find out that he died almost instantly from a massive heart attack. You never know when you're going to be standing there at the side of your husband, who's all cold and white and doesn't look like himself, and that you're going to be saying *I love you* over and over again but he can't hear you and you wish you'd said it before he went out to work, because even if it was his time and nothing could stop him dying anyway, at least he wouldn't have died with the last words you'd said to him, all harsh and spiky.

It wasn't even a proper row. It was about wallpaper. She wanted to put some Anaglypta up in the bedroom but Bill hated Anaglypta.

Twenty years is a long time to be on your own. She looks around the empty living room, at the sofa and the chair and the sideboard under the window, and wonders where everyone went. Not James and Ellie; they're at school, she knows that. She's not *completely* stupid. But where did everyone else go? Why did Bill have the heart attack? What happened to all the people she used to work with at the sewing factory? Where is Mrs Mir from number 35? She hasn't seen her for ages. Lovely woman. Brought all those children up and not one of them, as far as Gladys knows, became one of those terrorists you see on the telly. Not one. That's got to be worth something, hasn't it? Got to *mean* something. People don't give mothers enough credit.

Gladys looks around the room again. This house is lacking a mother. How long has it been since Julie went? She can't remember. There's a lot she can't remember, some days. She often wonders if her memories are disappearing, popping like those bubbles the kids used to blow on sunny days, or if they're all there somewhere in her head but she's just lost the key to unlock them. She hopes it's the latter, that all her memories are there. It stands to reason that they are, because sometimes a memory just surfaces, like a trout on

21

a river, comes out of nowhere and makes her laugh, or sometimes cry. Maybe one day the doctors will invent a key that helps people like her unlock all those hidden memories. They can do wonders, these days. Help the blind to see and help the deaf to hear. There was a man on the news with what looked like bendy butter-knives for legs. Then she remembers that maybe he killed someone. Just goes to show. Mrs Mir can have umpteen kids and not a suicide bomber among them, but you give a man with no legs a set of butter-knives and he goes and shoots somebody through a door.

There's nothing on telly and Gladys can't find her book, so she thinks about Bill and has a little cry to herself, then decides that she'll just have a nap and then put that dinner in the microwave.

Then the phone rings again. It's not the payment protection and it's not the accident helpline people this time. It's not someone offering a loan or anyone wanting to fix her computer or a survey.

It appears to be – which surprises even Gladys – a spaceman.

✳ 6 ✳

JANUARY 11, 2016. DAVID BOWIE IS DEAD

The day Thomas turns forty-six begins with the news that David Bowie has died. Well, that's just great, thinks Thomas. And on my birthday as well. He spends some time pulling his vinyl Bowie records from the Ikea shelf in his living room, lingering over the sleeves, looking for a long time at the rather nightmarish illustration on the front of *Diamond Dogs*. In truth, Bowie always part-fascinated him and part-repelled him as a child – the psychedelic apocalyptic horror of the 'Ashes to Ashes' video, the science fiction craziness of Ziggy Stardust. He is surprised to hear that Bowie was sixty-nine when he died; he feels as though he should have been both older and younger. Bowie was timeless, like one of his created personas. Bowie shouldn't be able to die like normal people, he's more fictional than real.

Thomas realises he is quite sad about this. He would be sadder, quietly play some of Bowie's music before work, in reverence to his passing, but for the godawful sound of drilling from outside.

Thomas tears open the curtains on his flat and stares, uncomprehendingly, at the phalanx of men in high-visibility jackets cheerfully destroying the road. He puts Radio Four on as loudly as possible to drown it out, until the man upstairs begins to bang incessantly on his floor – Thomas's ceiling – which provides an equally annoying counterpoint to the drilling.

Then he discovers that the water is off. He can't have a shower. He just stands there in the tiny mildewed shower tray, staring with loathing at the silent shower head. He can't go for a run before work if he can't have a shower. He goes to the kitchenette – a grand name for a row of cabinets that wouldn't take up too much space in a caravan – and holds the kettle under the tap before he realises, in his bleariness, that of course the water is off. So he won't be having a cup of tea. He climbs into his bathrobe and storms down the stairwell to remonstrate with the workmen, only then noticing a pile of letters addressed 'to the occupier' on the electricity meter cupboard. They have a thin coating of dust, indicating they have been there a while. Thomas can't understand why he hasn't seen them before. He suspects that the woman in the ground-floor flat, who he sometimes sees rifling through rubbish bins for tin cans, which she then for some reason washes with water from a two-litre bottle she carries with her in a string bag, has been hoarding them and, for reasons best known to herself, has finally decided to return them to the lobby.

Thomas tears open the one addressed to his flat and finds a letter from the water company informing him that supplies will be switched off for three hours on that day while urgent works are carried out. The letter is three weeks old. He takes it and bangs loudly with his fist on the door of the ground-floor flat until the occupant, a wild-eyed woman of indeterminate age with a frizzy halo of grey hair and wearing, somewhat disconcertingly, a Motorhead T-shirt with a flowery skirt, peers round the security chain.

'Have you been hiding the letters?' says Thomas, waving the envelope.

She stares at it as though he's brandishing a dead sparrow at her.

'It's against the law to interfere with the mail.' The woman's head moves up and down as her eyes follow the angry wafting of the envelope.

'The water's off,' says Thomas.

'How am I supposed to wash the tin cans, then?'

'I don't care,' shouts Thomas, the woman blinking at each yelled word. 'How am I supposed to wash myself?'

She looks him up and down, critically. 'That's a nice dressing gown.'

Thomas stalks back to his flat, where he finds that not only is the water off, but so is the bottle of milk in his fridge. Even if he'd had the foresight to fill the kettle with water before the supply was cut – which he hadn't because he hasn't seen the letter – he wouldn't have been able to have a cup of Earl Grey because he couldn't abide tea without milk. Now he can't even have a glass of milk. Or any cereal. There is a splash of orange juice, barely a thimbleful.

Things get worse. As he sets off for work the postman comes and pushes a handful of envelopes through the door. None of them is a birthday card. Not that he had expected one. Thomas Major doesn't think about this very often, but he does sometimes wonder if he's part of a rather unique club on planet Earth. No family and no friends and a job where he consciously avoids human interaction as much as possible. He supposes, now he thinks about it, there are probably plenty of people like that. He occasionally sees adverts or articles in the newspapers about loneliness, especially in the run-up to Christmas. But they make it sound like having no one is a *bad* thing. However, one of the letters the scowling postman hands over is addressed to him, a chunky brown envelope with his name formally typed in the window. He opens it on the doorstep and spends a long time reading the typed pages, and the Post-it note written in his wife Janet's hand. Then he folds it up and puts it in his pocket.

As Thomas passes the workmen noisily digging through the road, he snarls, 'You could have given us a bit more warning about this, you know.'

'Naff off,' says a man in a high-vis jacket, cheerfully, a hand-rolled cigarette hanging from his lips. Thomas memorises the name of the sub-contractor so he can file a formal complaint about the man's attitude later.

His train from Paddington is overcrowded to the point of suffocation.

It begins to pour down on his walk from Slough station to BriSpA.

He leaves his umbrella on the train and by the time he gets to work he is sodden.

As soon as he gets through the door of the offices he is met with an atrium stuffed with people carrying notebooks and recording devices and cameras and furry sound booms.

And finally, when he reaches his desk he finds an email with the subject heading URGENT waiting for him from Director Baumann himself, with whom Thomas has exchanged no more than two words in his entire career, at the Christmas party two years ago which Thomas had, against his better judgement, been talked into attending.

Director Baumann: 'So . . . Thomas, isn't it? Are you enjoying working at BriSpA?'

Thomas: 'Not particularly.'

Thomas might have said more, and expanded upon that, but Director Baumann had waggled his eyebrows and moved on to swap platitudes with someone else.

If Director Baumann remembers their earlier meeting, he doesn't let on, as Thomas stands in his office which has what can only be described as the best possible views of Slough. Unlike the tiny booth in which Thomas spends most of his days, Baumann's office is designed to what Thomas believes are ergonomic principles – which largely means he has bought an expensive table in the shape of a teardrop and has his own espresso machine. The vast converted industrial unit which houses both Baumann's spacious ergonomic office and Thomas's rabbit-hutch booth is the headquarters of the British Space Agency – BriSpA. The rather clunky contraction, which often puts Thomas in mind of some expensive device that needlessly filters water, was originally meant to have been just BSA, which made more sense to everyone, but there were, as he understood, no shortage of organisations queuing up to object, including but not limited to the Broadcasting Standards Authority, the Building Societies Association, the well-known motorcycle manufacturer (which Thomas was surprised to find stood for the Birmingham Small Arms Company when he looked it up), the British Sandwich Association, and the Belarusian Socialist Assembly.

'What I don't really understand,' says Thomas, at this point beginning to suspect some kind of joke, 'is why me?'

Director Baumann's eyebrows do a little dance. Thomas idly wonders if they are sentient and controlling him like twin parasites while Baumann is trapped inside his own body, screaming silently. Thomas tries to think what their agenda is. Perhaps they're alien life-forms and they're controlling Director Baumann in order to get back into space. While Thomas has been thinking this, Director Baumann has been talking. The upshot, as far as Thomas can tell, is that he looks 'a bit sciencey'.

'Sciencey?'

Baumann waves his hand up and down. 'Yes, you know. The hair. The lab-coat. All those pencils in your pocket. You look sciencey. So few of our staff do, these days. I remember when scientists used to look like scientists.'

'Like on the Open University programmes they used to put on early in the mornings.'

Baumann looks at him curiously. Thomas wonders if the eyebrows are processing this, deciding to investigate the Open University as a potential alternative means of getting off the planet. Then Baumann picks up his mobile phone and jabs at it.

'What are you doing?' asks Thomas.

'Making a note to speak to HR,' says Baumann absently. 'More lab coats. More Open University types. Good call, Thomas.'

Thomas looks at the window. Rain is lashing down. Every morning he walks into work and mutters, 'Come, friendly bombs, fall on Slough.' The receptionist always looks at him like he's a bit funny, possibly even some kind of sleeper agent. 'So what do I have to do?'

Baumann sits back in his leather chair. 'This is a very big day for BriSpA, Thomas. Very big. The biggest. It's been under wraps, but we've got a big announcement.'

'Ah. The press in the lobby. I thought . . . well, for some reason I thought it might have had something to do with David Bowie.' As soon as he's said that he realises how stupid it sounds.

Baumann nods enthusiastically, or at least his eyebrows do. 'Yes, bit of a bugger, that.'

The director goes up a very slight notch in Thomas's estimation. Then he says, 'To be quite honest, I was worried this morning that it would put the mockers on the whole thing. You know what the press is like. Celebrity this, celebrity that. Thing is, we couldn't give too much away in advance. Claudia's been on the phones all morning talking to editors, trying to persuade them to get here, that it would definitely be worth their while.' Baumann stands up and wanders over to the window, watching the rain sluice off the glass. 'I mean, bloody hell, talk about bad timing.'

'He was only sixty-nine.'

'Precisely!' says Baumann, turning back to him. 'I'm glad we're on the same page here, Thomas. Only sixty-nine! He could have hung on for a bit longer, I'm sure. As it is, I'm not completely certain that we'll be able to knock him off the front pages. I mean, we *should* be able to, but you never know in this day and age, do you? You'd like to think what we're doing would be the most important news break of the decade, of the bloody century, but then someone like . . . like Justin Bieber goes and farts or something and that's all anyone's interested in. Don't worry, though, it should all be fairly simple for you.'

'What exactly am I supposed to do?' Thomas wonders if he has at some point in the conversation nodded off and missed a vital piece of information.

'Nothing much, just look after him until the press conference starts, then walk on with him and look a bit sciencey. Then walk off.' Baumann appraises Thomas for a moment. 'We'll get you a clipboard.'

'But look after who?' says Thomas.

*

The big meeting room has been set up for the press conference. Thomas is in a smaller room just down the corridor, sipping tea with a man who appears to be meditating in a padded chair with his eyes closed. Thomas, perching on a stool, watches him for a moment. 'So. You're going to be the first man on Mars, then.'

The man is fit-looking, with a shaved head, in his late thirties. He is wearing an orange jumpsuit, padded and with a black helmet ring, covered in pockets and BriSpA patches. A spacesuit. He opens his eyes and looks at Thomas.

'Yes. Yes, I am. It's a great honour.'

'Are you military?'

'Former RAF. Used to fly Westlands. Test pilot up until recently.' He holds out his hand. 'Terence Bradley. Wing Commander, as was.'

Thomas takes his hand, hating Terence Bradley, Wing Commander as was for the inevitable crushing grip.

'Six- or seven-month journey,' says Thomas. 'Depending on how the Hohmann Transfer Orbit stacks up. The same back, plus however long you have to wait for the alignment again – three or four months, probably. That's at least a year and a half, maybe more.'

Bradley looks into the middle distance. 'I'm not coming back.'

Thomas goggles at him. 'What?'

Bradley narrows his eyes. 'How much clearance do you have?'

Thomas waves his clipboard. 'All of it. To the highest level. That's why I'm here.'

Bradley nods. 'You know all these settlement missions? They're going to be years off yet, but they need the way preparing. That's my job. Set up solar panels, a few habitation modules, oversee irrigation trenches.'

'You're going to Mars to dig ditches? And you're not coming back?'

'I might survive until the first commercial missions arrive. Might. Depends on how well I set everything up and whether I can cultivate crops in the habitation modules.' He smiles. 'I know what you're thinking. Sounds dreadful, doesn't it? A suicide mission. But it's what I've trained all my life for.'

'Dreadful?' says Thomas. 'Going to Mars for ever? Away from everything on planet Earth?'

Bradley nods ruefully. Thomas shakes his head. 'It sounds bloody wonderful.'

There's a brief silence then Thomas says, 'Did you hear David Bowie has died?'

Bradley looks at him as though he's just told him that bread has gone up tuppence a loaf. He shrugs. 'Never a fan. More of a Chris Rea man, to be honest.'

Thomas loathes him just a little more.

A woman in an expensively cut suit lets herself into the room and flicks her brown hair out of her face. 'Hi.' She gives Thomas a cursory glance. 'I'm Claudia from PR. The press are assembled. We're going to give them ten minutes to build up the buzz. Timing is critical with these things. We were a bit worried, to be honest, with Bowie dying but we've got a full house by the looks of it.' She glances at the time on her iPad. 'I'll call you on the phone in this room when it's time to come through. I'm thinking you'll stand there looking . . . astronauty . . . for a few minutes, let them get some good pics. Try to perhaps look off into the distance. Towards space or something. And stand in front of the BriSpA flag. It's vital we get some good branding on the front pages. I'd imagine some of the press will want a few selfies with you. That's fine. That's good. They'll be all over Twitter by lunch.' She looks at Thomas. 'You. Walk Wing Commander Bradley up to the tables, then walk off. No grandstanding, all right?'

Bradley closes his eyes and meditates again when she's gone. Thomas says, 'Do you want a cup of tea? Might be your last one.'

'I'm not going for almost a year. Lots of preparation to do. Training at Star City in Russia.'

'Plenty of time for tea, then. If you can get a decent cup in Russia.'

Bradley winces, and frowns.

Thomas takes a slow sip of his tea and looks at him over the rim of his cup. 'Are you all right?'

Bradley meets his eyes. '*Glurrk*,' he says.

'Is that Russian? For tea?'

Bradley stares at him and puts a hand to his chest, then slides off the chair to the floor. Terence Bradley, Wing Commander, as was. Alive, as was.

'Shit,' says Thomas.

Bradley appears not to be breathing. Thomas does his best to roll him into what he thinks might be the recovery position, though it looks like he's arranged the astronaut as if he's a sleeping child, then runs for the door. He's looking for Claudia but he just sees a security man playing a game on his phone.

'He's collapsed. The astronaut. Bradley. I think he's dead.'

'Shit,' says the security man. He stows his phone and starts to shout into his walkie talkie.

Two men carrying a green first aid bag run down the corridor and elbow Thomas to one side. They look down at Bradley, then at each other, and say in unison, 'Shit.'

One of them picks up the phone on the wall and shouts into it. The other one starts to strip the orange spacesuit off Bradley.

Then Thomas is forced even further back in the small room as a man and a woman in paramedic overalls burst in. The man interlocks his hands and starts compressions on Bradley's chest. The woman breaks open a plastic case and pulls out a defibrillator. The man pauses and leans in to cover Bradley's mouth with his own and give three sharp breaths. He looks at the woman and says, 'Shit.'

'Clear,' says the woman as the man rips open Bradley's white vest. The defib charges and his body judders as she applies the pads, which whine electrically. Both paramedics hold up their hands for silence, then look at each other.

'Shit.'

Two more paramedics arrive with a stretcher and then Bradley, the four paramedics, the two first aiders and the security guard are gone, leaving Thomas alone with the crumpled orange spacesuit that makes it look as though the man who was going to be the first human on Mars has somehow just evaporated.

Thomas stares at it for a moment. He feels as though he should say something, but all he can think of has already been said, several times, by everyone else.

Then the phone on the wall rings. It's Claudia.

'Um,' says Thomas.

'We're ready. Bring him through now.'

Thomas feels he should tell her what has happened but he just blurts out, 'David Bowie's died.'

'Yes,' says Claudia testily. 'Haven't we already had this conversation?'

Then phone goes silent. He looks at the spacesuit on the floor.

'Dreadful? Going to Mars for ever? Away from everything on planet Earth?'

He reaches into his lab coat and pulls out the envelope that came this morning, his only birthday post. It's from Janet. Well, her solicitor at least. Divorce papers. There's a scrawled Post-it note in her handwriting. *I hope you're not going to be difficult, Thomas. I've met someone. It's time to move on. Time to explore new horizons.*

He'd known it was coming, of course. They'd been separated for five years now. Barely talking for three years before that. The first couple of years of their marriage had been rocky as well. In fact, now he comes to think about it, there was probably one year, right in the middle of all that, when they were anything approaching what someone might loosely call *happy*. He'd always known she would find someone else. She deserves to be happy, he thinks, then deletes the thought. No, no she doesn't. Nobody *deserves* to be happy. People deserve food and water and shelter and those sorts of basic human rights, but not happiness. It isn't vital to survival. He's done well enough on a dearth of happiness, pretty much since he was eight years old.

The telephone rings again. Thomas ignores it. He stuffs the letter back into his lab coat then begins to strip to his underwear and to climb into the orange spacesuit. Then he quietly leaves the room and walks down the corridor to where a young woman is waiting by the door.

'What. The. Actual—?' she says, and before she can say anything else Thomas brushes past her and opens the door, stepping out into the expectant hum of the conference room.

Flashbulbs start popping and there's an audible hum of conversation as Director Baumann announces from the row of tables at the front, 'And it gives me great pleasure to introduce to you all the first human who will set foot on Mars—'

Thomas stands by the tables and waves at the press. 'Thomas Major,' he calls loudly.

There's a momentary silence. Thomas glances at Claudia who's gone pale. Baumann's eyebrows are wrestling on his brow. There are three other people in suits, who Thomas recognises vaguely from their photos on the wall of the lobby. On the wall behind the panel are the Union Flag and the BriSpA standard.

Claudia stands up and waves at everyone. 'Ah, if everyone could just look this way . . . we've got some animated infographics of the projected, um, the flight plan and the . . .'

But the press are turning their attention on Thomas. He flexes his arm muscles in the suit. It feels good. Then one of the reporters on the front row says, 'Thomas Major? Major . . . Tom?'

And then the cameras are flashing and everyone's shouting questions all at once and Thomas can hear, very quietly but very clearly, Director Baumann saying, 'Is this someone's idea of a joke . . .?'

✳ 7 ✳

THE SNIPER RIFLE OF TRUTH

All happy families are alike, but all bug-fuck stupid dysfunctional families are bug-fuck stupid dysfunctional in their own way, thinks Ellie as she sits on the benches outside the bank, sheltering from the desultory, spotting rain beneath some spindly trees, on the lookout for happy families. She imagines she's a sniper, like the ones in Stalingrad. They did Stalingrad in History. The average lifespan of a Red Army conscript sent to Stalingrad was twenty-four hours. Ellie squints and sweeps the square with her invisible sight. Every time she spots a happy family – there's one, a clean-cut guy with long legs pushing a buggy with all-terrain wheels, his wife or partner hauling a couple of designer brand-name bags as she talks urgently into her phone – Ellie's Sniper Rifle of Truth hits them with her magic bullet.

Blam! *She* hides vodka behind the bleach and antibacterial spray under the sink. *He* stays up late pretending to watch *Question Time* but really he's gambling in online casinos.

Ellie's sight moves on, settles on a couple repeatedly swinging a toddler between them, shouting 'one . . . two . . . three . . . wheeee!' as they move forward like some three-legged beast with an awkward but rhythmic gait.

Blam! *She* goes to work and can't help herself stealing bits of money and trinkets out of her co-workers' handbags and jacket pockets. *He* has feelings he can't really understand for the postman, a hirsute Welshman called Bobby.

All bug-fuck stupid dysfunctional in their own way. *Anna Karenina*, from where Ellie has adapted her new mantra, weighs heavily in her rucksack. This is the middle of Wigan, and everyone seems to be going somewhere, and quickly. The big municipal Christmas tree hasn't been taken down yet and it looks a sad, wilted sight, ignored now the festive season is over. People weave around it, wanting to be getting on with the normality of life. Everybody has a destination, an appointment to attend, a pointless thing to buy, a meal to eat, a job to be done. Everyone but her. This book, this *Anna Karenina*, might actually be interesting, but when has she got time to read it? She's already flicked through the plot summary on Wikipedia. And she can probably get hold of one of the films made of it from the library. Ellie gathers her bag and weaves through the thronging shoppers towards the dentists. The receptionist checks her records online and agrees to a check-up the following week. The appointment card she hands over is Ellie's alibi for missing the morning's classes, and she gets to do it again next week. Ellie heads down to the Galleries shopping centre, past the shops with their January sale signs plastered on the windows, pausing outside Waterstones. She stops before going into the shop, looking at her reflection in the window. It's an odd sort of reflection, smoky and ghostly, like she's only half a person. Spotty chin, hair tied up, school uniform that should have been replaced at the start of term, shoes scuffed. Not that she stands out much at school; most of her classmates come from what they call 'disadvantaged backgrounds' when they're being polite; *scummers* under their breath or behind their hands when they're not. She's glad they managed to get James into the better primary school, even if it does mean a bus ride for him rather than the five-minute walk to the little school she used to go to. He's a bright kid, if a bit weird. He deserves the chances she couldn't have. Ellie stares at her reflection a while longer. More than anything, she looks *tired*. Fifteen-year-olds shouldn't look so tired, not unless they've been up partying all night. Chance would be a fine thing, of course. She wonders why people say that? Chance would be a fine thing. Her entire life has been built on *chance*, and it's been anything but fine. It was chance, you could argue, that took Mum and Dad away. Was it chance that meant Nan started to lose the plot pretty much as soon as Dad was put in jail? Or was that just chemistry, or biology, or whatever caused dementia? Was it chance that James's potential was spotted and he was pushed to go to a better school, where it was just assumed Ellie – twice as bright as him, she scoffed to herself, ten times as bright – would go to the same old primary and same old comprehensive as everybody else from her street? Whether all that was chance or not, it was very rarely a fine thing.

Ellie wanders the aisles, running her fingers along the spines of the books. She loves books, loves the way they quiver softly with the weight of the words inside them. She just wishes she had time to read them. She trails her bag behind her, finding herself at a shelf lined with *York Notes* guides. There's one on *Anna Karenina*. She cracks it open and there's a full chapter on the quote at the front of the book (the *epigraph*, it says), which is: *Vengeance is mine; I will repay*. Ellie rolls the words around her mouth, trying them out softly.

'Vengeance is mine, I will repay.'

A pensioner with bleached hair who's wearing a tracksuit pauses and looks at her. 'Did you say something, love?'

'Vengeance is mine,' says Ellie again, though she knows it isn't, and never will be.

The woman peers at her white shirt and tie. 'Do you work here, love? I'm looking for *One Hundred Years of Solitude*. We're doing it for our book club.'

Ellie shrugs. 'I've never heard of it.'

'Me neither. Sounds a bit heavy.' She nudges Ellie hard in the arm with her bony elbow. 'I mean, *One Hundred Years of Solitude*, it's like that every night at our place. *He* falls asleep in the chair by seven. I mean, it's not like I *want* him awake when I'm trying to watch the telly, asking me what's going on and who's who every five minutes. Those Swedish things are the worst. With the big jumpers, where everybody is bloody miserable and serial killers are all over the parish. I mean, I like a bit of a crime drama, me, but it's those subtitles. He can't keep up. Every five minutes it's *who's she* and *what's he doing in this?* Are you sure you've never heard of it? By some Spanish bloke I think. Spanish sort of name, anyway. I wanted to do *Fifty Shades of Grey*. I don't get *that* at home.' She cackles. 'It's OK, love, I'll go and ask at the desk.'

The woman moves on and Ellie stares at her back for a minute, then looks at the book in her hand. She could go and get it out of the library. Instead, she bites her lip, opens her bag and shoves the book inside. Then she heads for the doors, head held high, looking every member of staff square in the eye and silently challenging them to stop her, to take her into the staff room, to call the police, to blow her whole life wide open.

Chance would be a fine thing.

✳ 8 ✳

THE PHONE CALL

Gladys is watching the news when the phone rings. There's a report about a man in space who has been talking to a little girl back on Earth. It appears he made her cry, but another man with black hair and a suit and tie from the space people says she probably got over-awed at the idea of talking to an actual astronaut. They have a couple of people sitting on the sofa, and the man from the space people on a big screen behind them. He doesn't half have bushy eyebrows.

'The thing is, in a post-Tim Peake world we expect our astronauts to be more than what they are,' says a blonde-haired woman in a beige suit, sitting to the left of the news presenter. 'We expect them to be celebrities.'

The man on the other side of the presenter has thick glasses and wild hair. He looks more like a scientist. 'But he's not a celebrity. He's up there to do a job. He'll spend the best part of half a year flying to Mars with a strict pattern of work to do every single day. He's not there to entertain us.'

'But try telling the sponsors of his mission that,' persists the woman. 'Try telling the schoolchildren whose hopes and dreams he carries in the *Ares-1*. We have a British man about to be the first human being on Mars. We should get the astronaut we deserve, not a . . . a *curmudgeon*.'

The man from the space centre on the big screen waggles his eyebrows.

Gladys is sitting in her chair by the fire, trying to decide how many Hobnobs she's had and whether she wants another one.

'Who's *that*?' She squints at the phone's display. It's a string of numbers, longer than the usual ones that call her. Must be from abroad. She likes talking to people from abroad.

'Hello,' says Gladys into the phone, loudly and slowly, just in case they are calling from abroad.

There's a hiss and a pause, and then a man's voice says, 'Uh. This is the last number I had for . . . is that . . .? No, it's not but . . . is that Janet's phone? Is she there . . .?'

'Who is it?'

'Well, who's *this*?' says the voice.

Gladys isn't sure she particularly likes his tone. 'You go first. You phoned me.'

'Look, is this Janet's phone or not?' Ooh. He sounds like he's got, as Bill would say, a stick up his backside.

'Janet.' Gladys searches her memory. 'Yes, I know Janet. Who's calling, please?'

The man's voice gets rather excited, then seems to try to calm itself. 'Well, this is . . . it's Thomas. Can I speak to her?'

'I've just been watching a man called Thomas on the telly.' Gladys decides to have another Hobnob after all. 'He's in space. He was talking to a little girl.'

'Yes!' says the man. 'God, that's me! Thomas Major! I'm the man going to Mars! I'm Janet's husband. Is she there?'

Gladys frowns. 'You made that little girl cry.'

'No, I didn't. Well, she did come on asking the most *banal* question . . . We lost comms while we were talking . . . who is this, anyway? Can you get Janet for me?'

'You're really calling from space?' Gladys holds the Hobnob up and squints at it. Imagine if the moon was a giant Hobnob. She takes a bite out of it. It's waning, now. The Hobnob Moon. That's what they say when it's getting smaller, isn't it? Waning.

'Yes, I'm really calling from space,' says the man. Thomas.

'And you say you're Janet's husband?' She could really do with a cup of tea to wash the biscuit down. 'You're not telling me porky-pies, are you?'

There's a brief silence. 'Well, if we're going to do this to the actual letter of accuracy, if you're a member of some kind of accuracy police who Janet's got answering her phone, then yes, I suppose you're right, I'm not actually her husband. I suppose I'm her ex-husband. Well, what I mean to say is, yes, I'm her ex-husband.'

'I *thought* you were telling porky-pies!' says Gladys triumphantly. 'Janet was married to that other bloke. Can't remember his name now.'

'Ned, you mean?' says Thomas across the miles of space and air. 'The man she was living with? Wow. That must have been . . . Wait, what do you mean, she's not married to him any more? She got married and divorced? Just who is this is, by the way? Seriously?'

'She's not divorced, she's widowed. He died. Emphysema, I think it was.'

'Emphysema. Bloody hell.' There's a long pause. 'Look, I'll ask you one more time. Who is this? I thought you might be the mother of Ned but you're obviously not. Why do you have Janet's phone? Do you work with her?'

'This is not Janet's phone,' says Gladys coldly. 'It's mine. I doubt Janet Crosthwaite even knows how to use a phone like this, let alone owns one.'

'Janet . . . Crosthwaite?'

Gladys begins to speak loudly and slowly again. This is much worse than the phone calls that come from abroad. 'Janet Crosthwaite. I used to work with her at the sewing factory. I thought you had to be clever to be a spaceman. Why are you phoning here asking about Janet Crosthwaite, anyway?'

'Oh, for God's sake. This number used to belong to my wife. My ex-wife. Janet Major. Or Eason, I suppose, if she's gone back to her maiden name. Are you telling me you don't know her at all?'

'Did she used to be the lollipop lady at St Michael's Infants?'

'No.' He sighs. 'She's a lawyer. Why would she be crossing bloody children at a school?'

'Then they're the only two Janets I know, so no, I don't suppose I do know her.' She could really do with that cup of tea now.

'Oh,' says Thomas. 'Oh. Well. I . . . I'm sorry to bother you, then, I suppose.'

'I should think so, too. You're quite rude, you know. Are you really calling from space? I mean, really? Or is that another one of your porky-pies?'

'Yes,' says Thomas. 'I'm calling from space.'

'What's it like?'

'What?'

'Space. What's it like?'

'Cold. Lifeless. Dark. Pretty much as you'd expect.'

'Sounds like Morecambe,' sniffs Gladys.

'Well,' says Thomas. 'Thank you. Ah, could I ask that you don't mention this? I'd probably get in trouble. Not that there's much they can do to me, now I think about it.'

'Your secret's safe with me,' says Gladys. 'Mum's the word. What did you do, by the way?'

'Do?' What do you mean?'

'For her to leave you. For you to get divorced. From the other Janet. Men always *do* something. Was it the porky-pies? Or just the general rudeness?'

There's a hissing silence that lasts so long Gladys thinks Thomas has put the phone down. Then he says, 'I think it was more about what I didn't do.'

'Well, you've done something now,' says Gladys. 'You've gone to space.' She points the zapper at the telly. 'Anyway, *Loose Women's* about to start. Have a good trip.'

She jabs her finger at the phone and kills the connection, then thoughtfully inspects her Hobnob.

Well, that was different.

She'd have to tell Ellie not to get the dark chocolate ones next time.

* **9** *

#CALLINGMAJORTOM

Two days after Terence Bradley, Wing Commander as was, tragically died, the name on everyone's lips is Thomas Major. Director Baumann thinks how much simpler life would have been had it been the other way round; if Thomas Major had suffered a massive cardiac arrest due to a hitherto undetected congenital heart condition (and Baumann would be composing a very strongly worded missive to the Director of Health – a square-jawed man with the fascistic bearing of a PE teacher, who is at that moment sitting alongside him at the oval table in the meeting room – about just exactly why the congenital heart condition in question was undetected) and Terence Bradley was being feted as the first human being to be sent to Mars.

As the rain lashes against the windows Director Baumann sits at the head of the table in SOMBRERO. It is actually generally called the more prosaic Meeting Room A, which pretty much looks like all the other meeting rooms – blue carpet tiles, white suspended ceiling, one white tile stained by the obligatory leak, wide windows overlooking car parks and roundabouts and grass verges. But this is not like the other meeting rooms, because Director Baumann has for some time privately re-designated it for use in an emergency situation and has come up with SOMBRERO, which means Special Operations Meeting Board Room, Exceptional Representatives Only. It is, he admits, a rather clunky acronym and after emailing everyone to tell them that a special meeting had been called in SOMBRERO that afternoon he had to take a call from every single one of them to explain what SOMBRERO was. But he is quite convinced they will get used to it and, obviously, it adds a bit of gravitas and – yes, he admits it – some James Bond mystique to the whole affair. So he sits and regards in turn the faces of each of the department heads of BriSpA, all the people under his command who are responsible for the running of the British Space Agency. The assembled brains who, singularly or together, will come up with a solution that will pull BriSpA's – and Director Baumann's – arse out of this particular fire.

'Can we have a quick roll-call? Help us get used to the new titles I handed out last month.'

Claudia, the PR woman, obliges by rolling her eyes.

'Employee Engagement Officer?' The former head of HR, a short, plump woman with a steely stare, nods.

'Chief of Multi-Platform Safeguarding?' The former head of security, a broad man with a buzz-cut, glares at Baumann.

'CommSat Facilitation?' A bearded man who wishes he was still just 'IT' waves a hand.

'Head of Mars Insertion?' Everyone snickers and a curly-haired woman who has worked hard for twenty-five years to be part of the ultimate in British space exploration scowls at the stupid *Carry On* film name she's been landed with.

Baumann looks up. 'And . . .'

Claudia raises a hand. 'Head of PR. I can't even remember what ridiculous string of random words you assigned to my job, but forget it. I'm Head of PR. And I'm here.'

'So,' says Baumann with as much brightness as he can force. 'We are rapidly floating upstream on Shit Creek and paddles have not yet been invented. Any thoughts?'

The manager of the electronic communications team raises a hesitant hand. His team is situated in the basement and appears to consist of a huddle of hirsute men constantly catching bits of sandwich and pie in their beards, and which no one at all apart from Director Baumann refers to as CommSat Facilitation.

Baumann nods. 'Yes. You.'

'Strictly speaking, would we be floating upstream if we didn't have a paddle? Wouldn't we be drifting downstream?'

'Get out,' says Baumann.

The man sits there and looks around uncertainly. Baumann sighs. 'Well, stay, then, but shut up. Anyone have anything constructive to say about the Thomas Major problem?'

The Chief of Multi-Platform Safeguarding runs a hand over his buzz-cut and raises one eyebrow. He's piggy eyed and has a proud history with various law enforcement and military organisations. His name is Craig. Baumann is unsure whether it's his first name or last name, but it's what everyone calls him. Baumann gives him the floor and Craig carefully looks everyone in the eye. 'Accident. Might happen.'

Baumann stares at him. 'You're suggesting we . . . what? We *kill off* Thomas Major?' He waves frantically at the young man taking the minutes. 'For Christ's sake don't put that down.'

The piggy eyes narrow. 'No. I said an *accident*.'

Baumann pinches his nose with his thumb and forefinger. 'Claudia. You of all people must have something sensible to say.'

'I do,' says Claudia, flicking her hair and swiping at her iPad.

'Thank God,' says Baumann. 'What's the solution?'

Claudia smiles. 'We let him go.'

Baumann opens one eye. 'We *fire* Thomas Major? We can do that? On what grounds?'

'No. We don't sack him. We *let him go*. To Mars.'

Baumann shuffles some papers on the table in front of him, not because they particularly require shuffling but he feels he needs to distract his hands from gravitating towards the nearest neck and squeezing very hard. 'I'm sorry,' he says with as much jollity as he can, 'for a minute there I thought you said that Thomas Major, a lowly chemical technician who on the spur of the moment decided to put on a dead astronaut's spacesuit and present himself to the world's press as the first man to go to Mars, should actually get to be the first man to go to Mars.'

'Precisely.' Claudia points one perfectly manicured finger at the blank screen behind Baumann's chair. 'Do you mind if . . .?'

He waves his assent and Claudia wirelessly connects her iPad to the screen and motions for the lights to go down. Her fingers play over the tablet, her nails *skritting* on the touch-screen like tap-dancing insects, and the first thing that appears is a clip from the BBC coverage of the press conference. Baumann groans as she dials up the volume. He hears his own voice: 'And it gives me great pleasure to introduce to you all the first human who will set foot on Mars—' and then the camera is panning to the right and flash-bulbs are going off and Thomas Major is standing there, looking somewhat shocked himself, then waving shyly and saying his name.

The camera cuts back to Huw Edwards in the studio, who is almost looking impressed. 'And there you have it . . . the first human on Mars will be a Briton . . . English, of course . . . Name of Thomas Major. The press already calling him Major Tom . . . unveiled on the day that the news came out that David Bowie of course had died . . .' Edwards looks critically at a piece of paper, as though weighing up whether to believe what's written on there. 'All of which is purely coincidence, according to the British Space Agency . . .'

Then Claudia minimises the clip and brings up a series of front pages of the day's newspapers. Most of them are variations on a rather obvious theme.

The *Mirror*: CALLING MAJOR TOM

The *Sun*: GROUND CONTROL TO MAJOR TOM

The *Guardian*: BRITISH EXPEDITION TO MARS PAYS TRIBUTE TO LEGEND BOWIE

The *Telegraph*: THERE'S A STARMAN WAITING IN THE SKY—AND HE'S BRITISH

With, of course, the expected deviations.

The *Mail*: WILL LIVING ON MARS GIVE MAJOR TOM CANCER?

The *Express*: TOP TORY SAYS SEND MIGRANTS TO MARS

The *Star*: WHY DOES MAJOR TOM LANDING SITE LOOK LIKE PRINCESS DIANA?

'The hashtag #CallingMajorTom is still top-trending in the UK,' says Claudia, checking her phone and showing the screen around the table to prove it. 'We're all over Facebook. BriSpA's mentions on social media are through the roof and every single news website has a picture from the press conference on its front page. We're getting calls from the world's media wanting interviews.'

'So we're deciding British space policy now on the say-so of a few Facebook and Twitter notifications?' says Baumann.

Claudia swipes her iPad again and the screen is dominated by the photograph of Thomas Major from his company file. 'No, I'm not saying that. But, to be clear, we're not talking about a "few" updates here. We're talking record amounts of internet chatter. Thomas Major is already embedded in the nation's psyche as the first man on Mars. The Major Tom brand has traction like nothing else. They're already talking about who should play him in the movie. It's just the whole Bowie thing . . . it's actually worked in our favour like we could never have anticipated.'

Baumann pinches his nose again. 'But this is like . . . it's like choosing an astronaut on *X Factor* or something. It's practically like dragging someone off the street and sending them to Mars.' But he can tell, already, that somehow he's lost this battle.

'He's a chemist,' says Claudia. 'He's healthy' she looks pointedly at the Director of Staff Robustness – 'with no medical conditions, congenital or otherwise. He runs every day. He's no ties – he's divorced, no children, both parents dead, no siblings . . . well, he had a brother, but he died when he was very young. Also . . .' here, Claudia bites her lip. 'I did a straw poll, very unscientific, of women in the office.'

'And?' says Baumann.

'And,' says Claudia, dropping her voice to a conspiratorial whisper. 'He's *fanciable*.'

Baumann does a double take at Thomas's photograph. 'Fanciable? You're telling me this curmudgeonly, forty-odd-year-old chemical technician with unruly hair and a collection of Biros in the pocket of his lab coat is the . . . what? The Casanova of BriSpA?'

'Well, no one's actually got off with him or anything. And I don't think they would have even considered it before all this happened. But there's something indefinable about him. A vulnerability, perhaps. He's excessively grumpy, true, but people can see a bit of their husbands or boyfriends or even fathers in him . . . and the fact that he's going on a one-way trip to Mars makes him unattainable . . . they can fancy him without having to worry that they'd actually have to sleep with him.'

Baumann rubs his chin, looks at the photo and then back at Claudia. 'Do *you* fancy him?'

For the first time she appears slightly flustered. Baumann's never seen that in her before, thought she was some kind of ice queen. She waves away the question, 'I said it wasn't a very scientific poll, didn't I?'

The Employee Engagement Officer leans forward and taps her pen on the table. 'The fact is, Major has dumped us in a rather difficult position. No one out there has even heard of Terence Bradley, no one even knows he existed. But everybody loves Major Tom. If we backtrack, issue a statement saying it's all been a terrible mistake and he isn't going to Mars after all, we'll look incredibly stupid and on top of that we'll still need to find someone else to go. It's essentially a suicide mission, remember.'

'Not at all,' interjects the Head of Mars Insertion. 'The plan is for the astronaut to set up habitation modules and prepare the way for the first settlement flights. Our projections are that, everything being equal, they could survive up there for ten years. Twenty, if they get the infrastructure in place quickly and efficiently.'

'He'll need training,' says Baumann, defeated. 'He's going to have to go to Russia. And we'd need full psych evaluations before we even start.'

'Already on it,' says Claudia. 'He had a preliminary evaluation yesterday. You want to know the sweetest thing? He says one of the defining moments of his life was being taken to see *Star Wars* by his father when he was eight years old.'

✳ 10 ✳

FEBRUARY 11, 1978, AGAIN

During the battle, Rebel spies managed to steal secret plans to the Empire's ultimate weapon, the DEATH STAR, an armoured space station with enough power to destroy an entire planet.

Pursued by the Empire's sinister agents, Princess Leia races home aboard her starship, custodian of the stolen plans that can save her people and restore freedom to the galaxy . . .

For more than an hour, Thomas is entranced by the film, mechanically shoving popcorn and Revels into his mouth until the treats are all gone. It is only when the ghostly voice of Obi-Wan sounds in Luke's cockpit, Darth Vader hot on his heels, that Thomas is ejected from the warm, enveloping fantasy of the movie. Obi-Wan is like a replacement for the dad Luke never knew, and the thought of that makes Thomas think of his own dad, and just as the rebel X-Wing fighters are going in for their final run on the *Death Star*, Thomas starts to wonder just where his dad has gone.

He is halfway up the sloping, sticky carpet to the doors when the ice-cream lady collars him. 'Where are you going?' she hisses, shining her plastic torch in his face as though she's interrogating him. Thomas thinks about a film he watched where soldiers were caught by the Germans and all they will give their captors is their name, rank and serial number, and he considers doing that, but Deirdre is still an adult, still an authority figure, and he doesn't feel confident cheeking her like that at eight years old. So he lies instead.

'I need the toilet.'

Deirdre clucks her tongue, evidently wondering whether the two pound notes (minus the price of one choc ice) merits a toilet visit too, then a child is tugging at her sleeve asking for a Rocket lolly and her decision is made; she's a job to do and that job isn't babysitting on behalf of errant fathers. Thomas slips out of the doors into the lobby. The film must be about to finish because they are already starting to let people queue towards the ticket office for the next showing. He wonders if Luke blows up the *Death Star*, wonders if he'll ever find out. He's shocked to see it's dark outside and wonders how long he's been left on his own. Putting his head down he pushes through the crowds of people getting ready for the teatime showings and shoulders his way outside into the cold, biting evening air.

He wonders what the surprise is for Mum that took Dad away for the whole of the film. He wishes Mum could have come with them, but she's sick every morning, hobbles around the house with her hands on her belly or pushing at the small of her back. Everyone says that they bet Thomas is hoping for a little brother, someone to play with. All he thinks is a brother will probably want to chew on his *Star Wars* toys and ruin his records. But perhaps, unlike Thomas, a brother might be more interested in football. Perhaps if Thomas knew more about football his dad wouldn't leave him on his own in the cinema. But he doesn't. He's tried, but the names of the players and the teams just don't stick in his head.

What does, is music. Effortlessly, it finds a place in his mind, artists, songs, labels, chart placings, producers, B-sides. He reads liner notes on gatefold album sleeves like his dad scrutinises the league tables in the Sunday papers. Music, and the Periodic Table of the Elements. He can't remember when he first saw it; probably in the dusty old set of encyclopaedias his granddad had given him, intended for Dad but shown no interest by Frank Major as a boy. It has always fascinated him, the ordered ranks of chemical elements, like Lego bricks for building the whole universe. He's memorised them all, from hydrogen to nobelium, cross-referencing them within the encyclopaedia to find out what they do, what they are for, when they were discovered, how they reacted with other elements. He has learned to deftly stack up a pile of singles on the old Dansette, dropping one after the other, songs from his mummy's childhood and teenage years, which he listens to while staring at the Periodic Table drawing-pinned to his wall.

Strictly speaking, Thomas shouldn't cross roads on his own but the car park is across a road and besides, it's only a small one and there aren't any cars. It's dark, though, and Thomas starts to get scared by the blank windows of the rundown shops. He feels as though they're dead. It reminds him of a film he watched about the last man alive on Earth, after everyone else had got sick and either died or been turned into vampires with white hair and milky eyes. The streets looked like this, deserted and empty, though with monsters hiding behind the windows. The same actor was in *Planet of the Apes*, which was also about the world ending, though you didn't know that until the end of the film when the man found the Statue of Liberty buried in the desert. Turning the corner on to the patch of land where the car was parked, Thomas wonders what would be the absolute worst end-of-the-world thing? If the car park was full of apes from *Planet of the Apes* or the vampire people from the film that he's just remembered was called *The Omega Man*?

But he doesn't have to worry about it because there, right where they left it, is dad's car, vibrating as it chugs exhaust fumes out into the chilly night air, the dim bulb in the ceiling above the rear-view mirror illuminating the interior of the car with pale, thin light. His dad has returned. Thomas glances up at the night sky. The full moon is high now. That can't be right, though. Because he has the moon in his pocket. Thomas runs over to the car across the frozen ridges of dirt, sees his dad in the driving seat, and just as he clamps his hands on the passenger window, which is already slick with a frosting of ice, he realises someone is already sitting in the front seat. It's his Mum. That must be the surprise errand. Dad is leaning over and covering her face with his and he has one hand pressing at her chest. But then Mum screams and pushes Dad away and shouts, 'Jesus, Frank, it's a kid.'

And Thomas realises it isn't Mum.

And he knows that his dad has lied. Thomas doesn't have the moon in his pocket at all.

And then he knows what is the absolute worst end-of-the-world thing to find in the car park. It isn't vampires with white hair and milky eyes. It isn't apes with guns and horses who enslave humans. It's this, he thinks, even as hot tears come and his stomach convulses and expels a stream of ice cream, chocolate and popcorn on to the solid earth.

It's this.

11

THE PEASANT'S REVOLT

James slams the door behind him and heads straight for the stairs, ignoring Nan's calls from the kitchen enquiring who it is. He is halfway up the staircase when the tears come again, and he stops to force his fists into his eyes. Nan appears at the bottom of the stairs and looks up.

'Oh. It's you.'

James ignores her, sucking back his sobs, kneading his eyes until he sees stars and blobs of colour. She tuts. 'Look at your blazer. Ellie won't be happy.'

'Stuff Ellie.' James carries on up the stairs. He hears Nan creaking up behind him. For God's sake, can't she just leave him alone? James heads straight into his bedroom and throws the door closed, leaning on it. His dressing gown is hanging on a hook from the door, and behind it a thick woollen jumper of his dad's. He buries his face in the jumper, absorbing the scent, the mustiness, the slight tinge of cement, the stale sweat. It makes him feel worse.

'James?' says Nan with a tentative, thin-knuckled knock at his door. 'What do you want for your tea?'

'Cabbage. Broccoli. Do we have any kale?'

Nan laughs. 'Kale. That's a funny word. And I never heard a child actually ask for cabbage for tea before.'

'I want to encourage the generation of methane in my gut,' mumbles James into the jumper.

'Lovely,' says Nan, a little uncertainly. She pushes tentatively at the door. 'We might have some Christmas cake left, if that helps. Can I come in? If you give me your blazer maybe we can get that mud off before Ellie gets home.'

'I don't care what Ellie thinks!' shouts James, moving away from the door and throwing himself on his bed. Nan comes in and leans on the doorframe. He shouts again. 'She's not my mum! And you're not my mum either!'

'No, silly,' says Nan softly. 'Julie's gone, isn't she? Your mum.'

'Thanks for that, I feel much better now,' says James into his pillow.

Nan chances another step in her slippered-feet into his bedroom. 'How'd you get your blazer so muddy anyway? Did you play rugby in it?'

James wriggles out of it without lifting his face from his bed and tosses it on the floor. 'That's nothing. Look at this.'

Across the back of his white shirt, written in black marker pen, is the word PEASANT. Underneath someone has drawn a sad face behind a series of vertical lines, a rough but evident portrayal of someone supposed to be in locked up in a cell. James chances a look at Nan. She's frowning. Then she says, 'I'm not the pheasant plucker, I'm the pheasant plucker's son; I'm only plucking pheasants 'til the pheasant plucker comes.' She smiles broadly. 'I can say that after three bottles of stout.'

'Oh, God. Can you please go away?'

Nan scoops up the blazer. 'I'll go and get your cabbage on. And see if we have any . . . what was it? Kale? Does it come in packets?'

'Go away!' shouts James and buries his face in his pillow until she does.

It is the usual mob. The ones who shoot balls of spit-enhanced paper at him through empty Biro casings, who trip him up in the corridors, who shoulder him out of the way in the lunch hall, who grind his face into the mud in rugby. The ones who think they are better than him, the ones who object to some poor kid being bussed in with a better brain than they have. They corner him on the way to the buses.

'Oh, look, it's the peasant.'

'Gaylord.'

'The science nerd.'

'Going home to your shed, gaylord? On the peasant bus?'

'Can't your dad pick you up?'

'His dad's in jail, innit. Jailbird.'

'Probably being all gay in prison. That's what they do in the showers. Be gay, innit.'

'What about your mum, nerd?'

Then the inevitable tuneless chorus of 'Where's Your Mama Gone?' from *Chirpy Chirpy Cheep Cheep*, and – emboldened by James's sudden, furious tears – they're tugging off his blazer, stamping it into the mud, and scrawling on his back. It's a picture, he sees now for the first time as he takes off the ruined shirt, that's meant to be someone in prison.

James hears the front door bang and Ellie saying, 'Oh my God what is that *smell*?'

She's right; the house stinks of drains and old socks. Nan shouts, 'It's cabbage for James's tea. For the methane. Do we have any kale? Or broccoli?'

'*Methane*?' shouts back Ellie, then he hears her thundering up the stairs. He doesn't bother telling her not to come in. She stands in the doorway and stares at him, stripped to his trousers and lying face down on the bed, then she sees his shirt.

'Oh. My. God,' she says, squatting down to scoop it up. 'Oh my God. That's two shirts you've ruined in a day.'

'Actually, I haven't ruined any shirts. Nan burned one and this one . . .'

He sits up and looks at Ellie, crouching down in her own school uniform, looking narrow-eyed at the pen marks. 'Did somebody do this? At school? James, are you being bullied again?'

He nods sadly, then feels his mouth turning downwards of its own accord, and the tears are coming again. Ellie is by his side, enfolding him in her arms, the scent of her cardigan almost as comforting as Dad's jumper. 'Can you do something?' he says snottily into her shoulder.

'Ssh, it's OK,' she whispers. 'We just have to hang on . . .'

'But I want you to *do* something.' He's angry now. 'Go to school! Tell them!'

'We can't,' says Ellie soothingly. 'And you can't say anything yet . . . you've seen Nan. She's getting worse, right? You know what'll happen if we draw attention to ourselves . . .'

James nods. 'They'll say she can't take care of us. They'll put her into a home and they'll put us in care.'

'Split us up,' agrees Ellie. 'I'm not going to let that happen.'

'But she's not looking after us anyway. You are.'

'But I'm not *supposed* to be. I'm only fifteen. Nan's meant to be the responsible adult,' says Ellie.

They both think about that for a while.

'I hate Dad.'

'No, you don't,' says Ellie. 'You're angry at him, we all are. He was an idiot. But we just have to hang on . . . he'll be out soon. Just a few months.'

'Why can't we go to see him?'

Ellie sighs. 'Because they've got him down in Oxfordshire, they can't find a place for him up here. And if we want to organise a visit Nan'll have to come, and the way she's been the last month or so . . . we just can't risk it, James.'

James pulls away from her. 'I wish we were a normal family.'

Then Nan, carrying a steaming, stinking dish, pushes into the room. 'Cabbage!' she announces proudly. 'I couldn't find any broccoli or kale, so I put a tin of marrowfat peas in it.'

James puts his head in his hands. 'Oh God.'

Nan sets the dish down on his bedside table. 'Ooh, this'll cheer you up. Guess who I had a phone call from today?'

'Father Christmas?' says James.

'No! That spaceman! The one on the news.'

James blinks at her. 'Major Tom? Who's going to Mars?'

'Yes!' says Nan happily.

'But why?' says James, wiping away his tears.

'I don't know! He wanted to speak to Janet Crosthwaite.'

'Jesus!' shouts Ellie, standing up and throwing the balled-up shirt at James. 'Jesus Sodding Christ! She didn't speak to Major Tom! She doesn't speak to anyone who isn't in her head apart from me and you!'

Then Ellie storms out and her own bedroom door slams. Something breaks, distantly and tinnily, and Ellie is shouting again. James can't quite make out her muffled words, but they sound something like 'bug-fuck', 'stupid' and 'dysfunctional'.

*

12

GLADYS ORMEROD WAS HERE

Gladys Ormerod isn't stupid. She knows what is happening to her. Knows that what she has is an actual disease – a thing that is attacking her brain, not just bouts of forgetfulness or lapses of concentration. Some days that makes it easier for her, knowing that it's an illness and there's nothing she could have done to avoid it. Some days that gives her hope that they'll eventually find a cure for it. But then, they can't even cure the common cold, can they? On her laptop Gladys frequently googles her condition and reads all about proteins and things called plaques and tangles. Tangles make it sound not too bad, like the lugs she used to have ferociously brushed out of her hair by her mam when she was a little girl. It's a good way to describe what goes on in her brain, everything getting tangled up. She imagines a normal brain runs in straight lines from the moment a person is born until they die, with the earliest memories receding into the distance like train tracks. With people like Gladys, the lines are all knotted and weaving in on themselves. An incident from forty years ago can shine as bright as a new penny, while something that happened this morning is murky and far-away. Plaques are like those blue signs they put on famous people's houses. *Gladys Ormerod's mental faculties lived here, 1946–2015.*

That was when she knew for sure she had it. 2015. Just two years ago. It had probably been creeping up on her before that, like one of those old villains from the pictures with a black cloak and a moustache to be twirled between long, thin fingers. It had been hiding, until one day it leapt out at her and she couldn't remember what she'd had for her breakfast, even as she was washing up the plates. She knows it's only going to get worse. In a way, she almost looks forward to it, to the time when she can live completely in her memories until the end. She's never been one for God and all that malarkey, Gladys Ormerod, though her mam used to drag her to church every Sunday morning when she was a girl. She has to admit that lately she's been hedging her bets . . . half-heartedly telling people off for blaspheming, that sort of thing. To be on the safe side. But sometimes she wonders if that's what heaven really is, being lost in your memories, just the nice ones, the lovely ones. That's where Bill is, not in a cold, dirty grave at Wigan Cemetery. He lives in her memories. He's there, waiting for her.

But she knows she can't go, not all the time, not yet. Not until Darren gets home. She made a promise that she'd look after young Ellie and James until he did. Silly sod that he is, getting himself in trouble like that. And such a shame about Julie. Mind you, there were those that said they'd never last. Too much of a dreamer was her Darren, while that Julie always had her feet planted firmly on the ground. What was it some folk said, though? Opposites attract. What was that answer on that quiz show the other day, which she had to look up on the Google? Yin something. Like two tadpoles. Big Yin. Or was that the Scottish comedian, the one with the beard? Gladys remembers a thing he did on telly once, banana boots or something. She smiles at the thought of it. Then she looks down at the envelopes laid out on her bedspread, and bites her bottom lip, and stops smiling.

THIS IS NOT A CIRCULAR.

Tentatively, Gladys slides a thumbnail under the gummed flap of one of the brown envelopes and tips out the letter inside. There's red writing on it. She winces and closes her eyes. The phone calls have been coming, too. She pulled the wire out of the wall a week ago, and the children don't seem to have noticed. Too busy with all their mobile phones. Gladys opens one eye and the word EVICTION leaps at her like a pink salmon. She turns the letter over so she can't see it. But the damage is done. The pink salmon of a word wriggles into her brain and gets knotted up in the tangles and plaques.

'Oh, Bill,' says Gladys. 'What am I going to do?'

My dearest Prince Aluysi,

How are you? I do hope all your troubles are getting near to being sorted out. You see, I have a few troubles of my own at

*the present moment. It does seem to have been a long while
since you first got in touch with me to tell me about the difficulties you have been having and to be honest I did not think
it would take quite so much time to resolve. It may well be
that you are not in a position to transfer the whole $4 million
to me right now, but maybe you could send me a little something? Say about £5,000? It would be preferable if this was in
English pounds, please. You have my bank account details.
Please give my regards to your lovely wife, the princess.
With my best wishes,
Gladys Ormerod (Mrs)*

The problem with kids today is that they have no confidence in
what older people can do. And they probably think anyone over
twenty is an 'older person', in the same way that Gladys thinks of
people in their fifties as 'that girl' or 'that lad'. It was different when
Gladys was a girl, of course. You had respect for your elders. Mainly
because they could fetch you one up the back of the head with the
flat of their hand without anyone running around and calling the
social services or Esther Rantzen. But it wasn't *just* that. Gladys's dad
fought in Burma, and her mam worked in the munitions plant up
Beech Hill. And even as a kid, you had to respect that. It rubbed off
as well. People of Gladys's generation, they just got on with things.
She closes her eyes and it's the May Day bank holiday weekend, back
in 1972. Darren was just in his pram then, and Gladys and Bill's
sister, Winnie, walked it the five miles to Bickershaw to look at the
hippies in the rock festival they were putting on. It was something
to do with that man off the telly who died, the one with the funny
beard and one hand smaller than the other, who used to do the
practical jokes. That was much later, though. Gladys had never heard
of him back in 1972, but she liked some of the bands. They went
on Saturday and Sunday; on Sunday The Grateful Dead were on for
five hours straight, but they didn't stay that late to catch it all, not
with little Darren in his pram. They'd had a hell of a time dragging
that buggy over the fields. Wet through it was, pouring down with
rain. Like a bog. When she got back, soaked to the skin, Bill thought
she was as daft as a brush. He'd been working all weekend at Heinz.

Brought home a bag-full of soup in bashed tins from the staff shop. She sat in front of the fire – three bars on, though it was May – and he made her a big bowl of chicken and mushroom.

'You daft apeth,' he'd said, rubbing the steam off her glasses with the corner of a tea towel. 'And taking Darren as well. Anything could have happened.'

'I don't think them hippies eat children,' said Gladys, sipping soup from the spoon. 'They were quite nice. A lad in a pair of dungarees and a top hat tried to give me and your Winnie some of that dope.'

Bill had said nothing, staring into the orange glow of the electric fire. 'Do you think you'd rather have got married to one of that sort? More exciting than boring old Bill Ormerod who works nights at Heinz.'

Gladys made a show of thinking about it for a bit. 'Happen it would have been. But I'm not sure I'd really like to go down the Swan on a Thursday with a bloke in dungarees. Besides, boring old Bill Ormerod, it's like them Kinks sang yesterday: you really got me. Now come and give us a kiss while Darren's sleeping.'

The memory shines like a star in the night, but Gladys can't remember why she was even thinking about that. She was thinking about how kids today don't know what older people can do. What they *have* done. What lives they've led. Gladys was only, what, twenty-five when she marched off to Bickershaw with a one-year-old in tow to watch the bands and the hippies smoking their dope. She was capable. She *is* capable. She looks at the pile of brown envelopes. Bill's not here and Darren's not here and Prince bloody Aluysi's not here. It's down to Gladys. Ellie has told her not to go out, but she's seventy-one next birthday. Gladys is supposed to be the one in charge. What's the worst that can happen? She's lived in Wigan all her life. She's not a child. She can sort this out. She *will* sort this out.

Gladys goes to get her coat. It's mild and wet for January. That summer she went to Bickershaw was mild and wet as well. People say that summers always used to be hot and winters always used to be cold. But people only remember the very good times, and the very bad times. In between, things are just mild and wet and ordinary, unless something very remarkable occurs.

13

1,800 DEGREES FAHRENHEIT

The summer of 1988 is wet and miserable, but Thomas Major doesn't care. School is over, A-Levels are finished. He is eighteen years old, he is going to university in Leeds in September. The long holiday is crawling by at an agreeable snail's pace.

And Thomas is in love.

But, more than that, to his constant amazement and slight bemusement, he is loved right back.

Her name is Laura and they have been inseparable since Christmas when, full of Bacardi and Coke, she dragged him on to the dance floor at the sixth-form festive do, which Thomas attended completely against his better judgement. They danced to 'Stop Me If You've Heard This One Before' by The Smiths – well, Laura danced, crouched low, her cardigan hanging off her arms and down her back, the cuffs bunched up in her fists, while Thomas swayed arrhythmically. After the song finished she insisted he bought her a drink, then railed at him for half an hour about Thatcher. She is fierce and intelligent and funny and quite, quite beautiful. Even now, in summer, Thomas is wondering when the scales will fall from her eyes and she will look at him, frowning, unable to work out how one drunken night that ended in a kiss in a shuttered shop doorway could have lasted so long. But it hasn't happened yet; indeed, they have both applied to and been accepted at Leeds University, Thomas to study chemical engineering and Laura to read history and politics.

It is raining when Thomas gets up, as it has been raining all summer, but he doesn't mind at all. In the kitchen diner his mother is washing the dishes and listening to the tail-end of the Radio One breakfast show. Thomas slumps at the kitchen island and watches his mother at the sink, her orange skirt rendering her bottom half almost invisible against the dark pine cabinets that run around the space. The breakfast show is presented by Simon Mayo, who mum doesn't like all that much; she can't understand why they got rid of Mike Smith. But Thomas secretly likes Mayo, though he tacitly understands through Laura that listening to Radio One is strictly *verboten* until John Peel's show starts in the evening. Simon Mayo is playing 'Heatwave' by Martha Reeves and the Vandellas. Thomas doesn't know it yet, but it is a song he will never be able to listen to after that day.

'Chance would be a fine thing, a heatwave,' says Thomas' mother. Theresa Major is only in her early forties, but she looks old and shrunken to Thomas, has done ever since his dad died two years ago. At the funeral she took him to one side and said, 'What happened between you two? You always used to be such pals when you were small?'

Two years earlier, in the summer of 1986, they are standing outside the domed building of the crematorium at the Henley Road Cemetery in Caversham, on a bright sunny day. A fair-sized crowd is gathering; Frank Major would have been satisfied with the turnout. Thomas scowls and scans the faces. Is *she* there? The woman who was in the car that afternoon at the cinema? Most of the people here he doesn't even recognise. There are many women, and Thomas wonders if Frank Major has been through them all like a forest fire, if he collected affairs throughout his marriage like he chalked up new cars, conservatories, loft conversions.

'I don't know what you mean,' says Thomas. He is wearing black jeans and a black T-shirt, and his Army Surplus jacket.

'Yes, you do,' says Theresa Major. She is gripping Peter's hand tightly, and has dressed him up in a little black suit, white shirt and clip-on tie. Peter's eyes are red-rimmed from crying. Theresa looks washed out and pale. 'You were such pals when you were small.'

Thomas says, 'Look, Peter, Auntie Margaret's there with the cousins. Why don't you go and say hello?'

Peter nods sadly and wanders away. Theresa looks at him. 'Why did you do that?'

'Because he doesn't need to hear what I have to say.' For a moment he thinks he's going to do it, going to tell her about that dreadful day, that *Star Wars* day. Instead he says, 'I was never what dad wanted in a son.'

Theresa looks shocked. 'That's a terrible thing to say. He doted on you.'

'He did until Peter came along. Peter's more like him. He's into football and climbing trees and cars and all that *boy* stuff. Dad never understood me. Never got anything I was into. Never understood the science, never liked music, never read books. He thought I was weird. He thought I was soft. I think he probably thought I was gay.'

Theresa looks at the crematorium building. 'He wouldn't have cared if you were. He loved you.' She pauses. 'Are you?'

Thomas laughs, though without humour. 'How would I know? I'm sixteen. I haven't had a girlfriend, but I haven't had a boyfriend either. So don't worry.'

'I'm not worried,' says Theresa quietly. 'Not about that, anyway. I just worry about . . . well, you and Peter. Growing up without a dad.' She gazes into the blue sky. 'And I worry about me, too. In a couple of years you'll be off to university. I know it's selfish but I'm scared of being on my own.'

'You'll always have Peter. He's only eight. He won't be going anywhere for a long time yet. And by the time he's ready to leave home . . . well, you never know. I might be married with children and living back in Caversham.'

Theresa smiles, it's the first time he's seen her do that in a week. 'Do you really think so?'

Then the vicar is appearing at the door of the crematorium and signalling to Theresa. She says, 'We're ready.'

Thomas takes her hand and she grips it tightly. She looks old now, empty, withered. He is guilty that he doesn't feel that way, that he feels . . . nothing. Not relief, not sadness, not bereavement. Not even a sense of a weight lifting. Because now he knows that Frank Major didn't take his secrets to the grave with him, he just passed them on to Thomas, burdened his son with his infidelities.

'Thanks, Dad,' mutters Thomas.

Theresa looks at him and manages half a smile. 'I knew you'd come round.'

The crowd waits respectfully until Theresa, Thomas and Peter have filed hand-in-hand into the crematorium then follows them inside, where they listen to a eulogy about the love and esteem in which Frank Major was held by friends and family until his body is burned at 1,800 degrees Fahrenheit.

Thomas hates his father a little bit more. He should be here now, in 1988, not in his grave. He should be there for his mum, they should be growing old together. Now all she's got to look forward to is her children growing up and leaving her. Thomas knows that it will be a wrench for her when he has to go away at the end of the summer. But that's what children do; they go away. That's what you want for them, surely. To succeed. To be happy.

Theresa turns and smiles at him, wiping her hands on the tea-towel. Rain lashes against the window, blurring the view of the garden beyond. 'Morning, sleepyhead. You're going to have to start getting up earlier when you go to university, you know.'

Thomas nods, looking in the fridge for breakfast. Whether she's intentionally trying to make him feel bad or not, guilt gnaws at him at the thought of leaving her on her own with Peter. He wishes she wouldn't mention it.

'What are you doing today?'

'Meeting Laura,' says Thomas into the fridge. 'Probably go to the record shop. Hang about a bit.'

'What time are you going out?'

Thomas pulls his head out of the fridge. 'Don't know. Lunchtime. Why?'

'I need to take Peter to the dentist. He's over at that pond with his friends. Could you go and get him in about half an hour? I told him to be back but he's left his watch on the sideboard.'

Thomas puts two Pop Tarts in the toaster and pours a glass of orange juice. He goes and gets the watch and pockets it. 'I'll go and find him straight after breakfast.'

When he looks back on that moment, which will be crystal clear and preserved in the amber of his memory for ever, he will wish he could scream across time, reach back over the years, shake himself and furiously yell, 'Go! Go now! Run! Don't stop!'

14

THE LETTER

James is home first, ramming his shoulder against the door to push it open and saying, 'Ow' as the bone comes up against unyielding wood. Nan must have put the latch on. He hammers on the door and waits, then flips open the letter box with his thumb and shouts, 'Nan! It's me, James! Open the door!'

When she doesn't come he sighs and fishes in his bag for his keys, unlocking the door and letting himself in. She must be asleep upstairs, or sitting in Dad's room thinking it's nineteen-zero-plonk or something. One time he caught her twisting the dial on the radio and getting increasingly frustrated, eventually slapping it hard on top and saying to him, 'Can you help me find Dick Barton?' He had no idea what she was talking about.

Nan isn't in the kitchen, so that's where James stays for a bit. The lino floor is curling at the edges and the fridge makes a juddering noise. The walls are an awful yellow colour and the table is rickety and almost as old as Nan. He likes the kitchen, though, likes the window that looks out on to the narrow yard, piled high with bits and pieces – his dad's tools and lumps of wood and bags of cement. Perhaps that's why James likes the kitchen. He can see remnants of his dad's old life here.

He had some trouble with the gang today while he was talking to his friends at break, but after that . . . He takes the envelope out of his bag and smoothes out its contents on the little table. He can't wait to tell Ellie. James opens the fridge and stares inside, as though hypnotised. He's not sure he can wait for tea. He finds a tin half-full with beans, covered in cling-film, and a lump of cheese. James slaps the cheese in a dish, pours the beans on top and sticks it in the microwave, sitting at the table and reading the letter again and again until he hears it ping.

One day, thinks James, as he swirls the melted cheese and beans together with a fork to make a yellowish sticky goo, he's going to be a famous scientist. He'll have lots of money and an apartment somewhere like Manchester. Or maybe even New York. Dad will be home and Ellie won't have to work every night and James will look after them all. He'll probably write a book that's as popular as Stephen Hawking's *A Brief History of Time*, which James has read three times, though he barely understands the concepts. And they'll interview him on the TV and they'll ask him how he came to be such a brilliant scientist and he'll say to the interviewer – Jonathan Ross or Graham Norton or somebody – that it wasn't easy for him, not at all. He went to a good school but everyone thought he was some poor kid and he got terribly bullied. But one day his life changed when he was given a letter at school . . .

James reads through the letter again. This is it. This is going to be the day everything changes for him. He hears the door bang Ellie shouts, 'Hello?'

'In here,' says James through a mouthful of cheese and beans. Ellie pops her head around the kitchen door. She looks tired. She looks older than she is, but not in a good way, not like some of the girls he sees when he's at the bus stop, with their skirts rolled up and thick make-up on their faces. They're trying to look like they're in their twenties; Ellie just looks as though she's always staying up all night. Which, he supposes, she is. She works at the burger joint, and at the welding place and at the Polish shop. He doesn't know when she finds time to do her schoolwork, doesn't even know if she does any. But it'll be all right; he's going to be a famous scientist and save them all.

'Where's Nan?' She looks at the bowl of gunk in front of him. 'Is that what you're having for your tea?'

'I got a letter from school,' says James. For some reason he feels weirdly nervous now.

'Where's Nan?'

James shrugs. 'Upstairs, I think. I've got a letter.'

Ellie shrugs off her jacket and throws it over the sofa then comes into the kitchen. 'They don't want money for anything, I hope. Is she asleep?'

James holds out the letter and Ellie takes it, scrutinising it as she rubs her forehead with one hand. She looks at him blankly. 'What is this?'

'Read it again,' says James. 'Read it out.'

To the parent/guardian of James Ormerod

Each year the finals of the National Schools Young Science Competition are held at the Olympia Exhibition Centre in London. Schools may enter teams or individuals to the competition and finalists are selected via a series of local and regional heats.

Due to a government initiative to encourage young people who, through one reason or another, might find themselves in circumstances that are unfavourable due to social or economic factors, we are pleased to say we have been selected to fast-track one pupil or team direct to the final stages of the competition. This competition brings with it not just prestige and a great opportunity for future career development, but monetary rewards for both the school and the team/pupil.

Due to James' excellent performance in science lessons we would like to put him forward for this initiative and select him for a place in the finals of the National Schools Young Science Competition, which take place this month.

Obviously, you will have questions about this and I would like to invite you to attend a meeting in my office at your earliest convenience to discuss this and allow us to set the wheels in motion for James to attend the event.

It will be a great opportunity for him and we are certain he will shine in the competition. You can contact me through the school office at any time to set up a meeting, though I would impress upon you the need for some speed given the rapid approach of the competition and the need to work with James on a suitable entry for the finals.
Yours, Mrs S Britton, headteacher.

'Isn't it absolutely brilliant?' says James.

Ellie just stares at the letter. 'Um. Wow, I suppose.' She looks at him for a longer time than James is comfortable with, then drags a chair from under the small table and sits at it. 'But we know you're brilliant. You don't need to go to some competition to prove it.'

James can already feel hot tears pricking the back of his eyes. 'But I *want* to go.'

Ellie taps the letter with the backs of her fingers. '. . . *young people who, through one reason or another, might find themselves in circumstances that are unfavourable due to social or economic factors* . . . James, it's the bloody sympathy vote. They're doing this because it makes them look good, and they think we're some sort of pond life. We're not scum. We're better than this. You're better than this. You can make it on your own without someone patting you on the head and feeling sorry for you.'

James stands up, his chair falling backwards and clattering on the lino. 'But I WANT to go! I WANT to do the competition.'

Ellie's face hardens. 'James. They want your parent-slash-guardian to go in and talk about it. How are we going to do that, eh?'

'Send Nan,' says James in a sullen mumble. 'She's our guardian, isn't she?'

'And risk her blowing everything? You want them to put her in a home? Want them to split us up in foster families or in care?' Ellie looks around. 'Where is she, anyway?'

Ellie walks out of the kitchen, still holding the letter, James following at her heels like a puppy dog. They run upstairs, but Nan isn't in her room. She isn't in the bathroom. She isn't anywhere.

'Crap,' says Ellie. 'She's gone out.'

Ellie runs back downstairs, James close behind, and digs in her jacket pocket for her phone. She dials Nan's mobile number and waits, then angrily breaks the connection and tries again. Her eyes fix on James's. 'Line's busy. Where the hell is she and who's she bloody talking to?'

Ellie stalks up and down the small living room, re-dialling and aiming an angry kick at the pile of laundry behind the sofa. 'Nan,' she says urgently into the phone. 'Where are you? Why is your phone engaged? Ring me back as soon as you get this.'

'Maybe she's just gone to the shop,' suggests James.

Ellie rubs her hand over her eyes. 'She's not supposed to go anywhere. James, if she talks to the wrong person . . .'

'Ellie, about the competition—'

'James. Not now. We've got to find Nan. Maybe we should go and look for her . . .'

There's a sharp rap at the front door. James and Ellie look at each other.

'Oh, God,' says Ellie. 'Who's that . . .?'

James goes to open the door but Ellie pulls him back. 'Let me deal with this. And you don't say anything, right?'

She takes a deep breath, closes her eyes for a moment, then opens the door.

Standing there is Nan, her phone clamped to her ear. 'Yes, yes, it's fine now. I'm home. Thank you very much.'

'Nan!' says Ellie. 'Where have you been? Who are you talking to?'

Nan bustles in, the palm of her hand on her chest. 'Oh, Ellie, I've had a right time of it. I went out to sort something out but I got a bit confused. I couldn't remember where I was or how to get home. I think I left my keys, too. But he helped me get back.'

Ellie looks at the phone. 'Who did? *Who* helped you get back?'

'The spaceman!'

James watches as Ellie turns to him, her face twisted in fury. 'You see?' she says through her teeth. 'You see why she can't go to see your headteacher? You see why you can't do this stupid competition?'

Then Ellie screws up the letter and throws it across the room towards the waste-paper bin by Nan's chair and storms towards the stairs as Nan continues to smile and says, 'It was the spaceman. The spaceman got me home.'

* 15 *

IT'S GLADYS!

Earth is even farther away now. It is five hundred million miles to Mars, by virtue of the Hohmann Transfer Orbit. Thomas quickly learned that going to Mars isn't just a case of pointing a rocket at the planet and letting it go. By the time the rocket gets there Mars will have gone. So you point the rocket at the place Mars will be in – according to the *Ares-1* flight plan – two-hundred and eighteen days. So the ship is heading out into the void, towards nothingness. Thomas doesn't really know how he feels about this. There's a vague sense of vertigo, of falling away from the world, but without the sort of fear you'd have if you fell, say, from the top of Blackpool Tower. The falling would be quite nice, like flying; it's the hitting the ground that would hurt. And Thomas isn't going to hit any kind of ground for the next seven months.

He floats at the window, watching the Earth recede imperceptibly. To be honest he feels like there's a yawning gap inside him, as though he should be either terrified or sad or happy or excited. He feels none of these things. Oh, he'll occasionally think about sun-lit meadows or the glittering of the sea or conkers on the damp ground beneath a tree or the clink of milk bottles on an electric dairy float or the hiss of a needle on a vinyl record or the smell of a new book or the gentle pressure of another person's lips on the nape of his neck, and feel a distant sense of loss, but largely he just feels . . . nothing. The blankness you have in a long queue at the bank, your documents in hand, waiting with a vacant mind for the line to trudge forward. It's as though he's in the process of being *born*. It's as if the world has nurtured and grown him just as much as it can and now it's time for him to be pushed out and away, along this seven-month airless birth canal, into the place where he'll see out his days.

Then he thinks, what a load of old hippy bollocks, and goes to answer the Iridium phone that's buzzing angrily on the control desk. It is, of course, Director Baumann.

'No comms yet,' he says cheerfully. 'We've got someone coming in from ESA this morning.'

The European Space Agency. Obviously the budget won't stretch to flying someone over from NASA, or indeed the Russians who built the bloody spaceship in the first place. Thomas says, 'Are you sure you've paid the phone bill?'

'Ha bloody ha,' says Baumann. 'I'm pretty sure we'll be up and running today. In the meantime, we're emailing you up some diagnostic checks you can do on the habitation modules in the cargo hold.'

'I can't wait. How long will this phone be in range, anyway?' He wonders if he should mention that weird phone call to the old lady, then decides against it. He's sure he shouldn't be using the Iridium network to try to call his ex-wife, much less having conversations with complete strangers who now own the number which Janet has evidently given up. To stop him calling her?

'In range for a couple of weeks, tops,' says Baumann. 'But that's not going to be an issue when we get the comms up.'

There's a ping from the monitor. 'That'll be your habitation diagnostics.' Thomas reaches over to wake up the computer by running his fingers over the keyboard. 'Oh, my mistake, it's someone trying to sell me Viagra. Not that I've much use for it up here.' *Not that I had much use for it down there, now I think about it.*

Baumann pauses. 'How do you do that? Appear to be grumpy and jokey at the same time?'

'It's a gift. I'll show you how to do it over a pint sometime. I'll let you know when I've got the pub up and running on Mars and you can come up for a few jars. On second thoughts,' he says hollowly, 'there probably won't be much atmosphere . . .'

When Baumann's gone, Thomas spends thirty seconds reading enough of the email to allow him to make the decision to completely ignore the rest of it. He brings up his music library, contemplates it for a moment, then chooses *Gold Mother* by James. Digitised from the original 1990 pressing. It annoys him intensely that the band re-released it after a year to accommodate a remix of 'Come Home' and two extra tracks; an album should stand or fall on its original line-up. It annoys him so much he considers not listening to it at all, but it is a good album, so he relents and hits play. Then he pulls his crossword book out of its new home in a Velcroed pocket by the control desk; the booklet that was housed in it originally is floating around somewhere. Something about closed-system irrigation networks. He'll give it a flick through when he's in orbit around Mars. Chewing the end of his pencil, Thomas studies the next clue.

18 Down: If put off, can encourage angina, say – proverbially (4)

He ponders it for a moment, floating horizontally around the module, absent-mindedly pushing himself off the wall with his toes. Angina? Proverbially? He sighs as the phone buzzes again. What can Baumann want now?

'Yes?' he says, suspended upside down, still contemplating the crossword puzzle.

'Major Tom!' says a voice, breathless, panicked. 'Major Tom! It's me! It's Gladys!'

16

EVERYTHING IS GOING TO BE ALL RIGHT

Earlier: 'Who would win in a fight between Iron Man and Batman?'

In the playground of St Matthew's Primary School, sheltering from the damp, cold wind behind the Trim Trail and climbing wall designed to encourage physical activity among sedentary young people, James and his friends Carl and Jaden stick their hands in their pockets and ponder the question.

'First thing you've got to accept is that such a battle would never happen,' says James. 'On account of them inhabiting completely different universes.'

'Yes, yes,' says Jaden. 'We all know Iron Man is Marvel and Batman is DC.'

'So why not have . . . Iron Man and Iron Patriot?' says Carl. Carl's dad is an engineer and he says he's going to build him his own Iron Man suit. Jaden, whose dad is a lawyer, says that would be a breach of copyright and would get him sued. James, whose dad is a builder currently residing at Her Majesty's pleasure, does not contribute to that conversation, but tries to steer this one back on track.

'There's no point in that because both suits of armour are designed by Tony Stark. Iron Man versus Batman is a good match, because they are both non-superpowered humans who rely on technology to fight crime.'

None of them have noticed they have company until there's a snigger and four boys appear from around the wooden climbing wall. James's heart sinks. It's Oscar Sherrington.

'All right, Stig of the Dump?' he says, nodding at James.

'What's that?' says one of the other boys.

'Telly show my mum used to watch when she was a kid. About some swampy who lives in a tip. Bit like Ormerod here.'

'He's cleaned his shirt,' says another of the boys.

Oscar Sherrington, who is bigger and meaner than any other ten-year-old at St Matthew's and who already has a speckle of acne on his chin, puts a hand inside his blazer. 'Great. Blank canvas. What shall we write on it today?'

Then James is quite literally saved by the bell, and the cries of the lunchtime supervisors calling everyone in.

Oscar puts his pen away. 'Another time, maybe.'

Carl and Jaden are staring at their feet, trying to become invisible. James says, 'Why do you only pick on me? Why do you leave everybody else alone?'

Oscar sneers at him. 'Because everybody else would tell the teachers. You won't because my dad says you're looked after by your gran and she's round the twist, and if anybody found out they'd come and put you and your sister in a children's home.' He smiles, not a pleasant sight. 'Maybe I'll tell the social services myself. Might be doing my duty and all that.'

When Oscar has taken his coterie off, James glares at Carl and Jaden. 'You were no help.'

'Sorry,' mumbles Jaden. He brightens. 'Do you want to come round for dinner tonight? Carl's coming. We could carry on talking about Iron Man and Batman.'

Dinner, to James, is what you have at noon. Tea, which you have at five o'clock, is what Jaden is referring to. 'That would be brilliant.'

Jaden gets out his iPhone 6, which James regards enviously, and punches in a text. James's old Nokia vibrates in his pocket, but he doesn't get it out. 'I've messaged you with my address and our house phone. Get your gran to call my mum to say it's OK. We eat at six-thirty.' Jade pauses. 'Oh. What Oscar said about your gran. Is it true?'

'It's fine,' says James. 'It's all fine. I'll see you after school.'

*

After disappointing James with the science competition, Ellie feels somehow obliged to agree to the play date he'd set up with his friends from school. She looks at the address of his friend's house; posh. And a bus ride away. She calls the number and asks to speak to Jaden's mum.

'Oh, hello,' says the woman. 'Jaden said he'd invited James over for dinner. It's no problem of course . . . does he have any allergies?'

Only to common sense, Ellie wants to say, but instead she agrees she'll get him there as soon as possible. James is quiet on the bus ride, and she knows he's sulking about the science competition. But it's the last thing they need right now; attention. Jaden lives in a detached house with a huge gravel drive and a double garage. It's dark by the time they get there. Shrubs with fairy lights wound through them dot the large garden.

Jaden's mum answers the door, a woman with hair that looks as though it's made of candy floss and a dress that Ellie thinks would be more suited to a night out than a tea for some boys. She looks Ellie up and down. 'Oh. Are you . . .?'

'Ellie,' she says. 'James's sister.'

'Ah. I spoke to your mother . . .?'

Ellie smiles tightly. 'That was me. Our mum's . . .'

A small boy appears at the woman's side and gives James a little wave. He says, 'Their mum's gone.'

'Oh,' says Jaden's mum. 'Well. I am sorry to hear that. Then you're looked after by your father . . .?'

'Their dad's in jail,' says Jaden.

His mother makes no move to let them in the house. She looks as though there's a bad smell on the air. 'Oh. I see. So who . . .?'

'Their gran,' says Jaden. 'But she's gone a bit loopy. Are you coming in? Carl's upstairs. We've been talking about Batman.'

Ellie and Jaden's mum look at each other for a moment. Eventually the woman says, 'Loopy. That's not nice, Jaden.' She taps a finger on her chin. 'Well. I see.' She looks back at her son. 'Jaden, I really think . . . perhaps if you'd mentioned this earlier . . . maybe could have bought more food . . .'

'It's fine,' says Ellie through gritted teeth. 'I fully understand.'

The woman looks relieved. 'You do . . .?'

'I do. You're a posh cow who thinks the poor kid with the jailbird dad will either clean your lovely house out of valuables or turn your son on to a life of crime.'

'Ellie . . .' says James.

Jaden's mum puts a hand to her chest. 'Well. I'm sure I never . . .'

'You didn't need to.' Ellie takes James's arm. 'Come on. We're going home.'

'But Ellie . . .'

She drags him back along the gravel drive and towards the bus stop.

'THANKS A LOT!' he shouts.

'Why did you have to tell them about Mum and Dad? And Nan?' she shouts back. 'How many times have we talked about this?'

'I didn't tell them!' protests James. He pulls his arm out of Ellie's grip. 'You've ruined it. You've ruined everything. Do you know how many friends I've got? Two. And they're both in that house. And now I've not got any. It's bad enough you saying I can't do the science contest. Are you just trying to ruin my entire life?'

Ellie grabs his arm again and pulls him towards her. He struggles but eventually allows her to embrace him at the bus stop. 'Ssh,' she says. 'We don't need science contests. We don't need friends. We're fine. We're fine. We're on our own, like we always are. Everything is going to be all right.'

✳ 17 ✳

L-O-S-T

The voice on the phone is some unintelligible gabble, northern he suspects. Thomas says, 'Who is this? Is this Mission Control?'

There's a ragged sob then a deep breath. Thomas can hear the swish of traffic. 'It's me. Gladys.'

Thomas pinches the bridge of his nose tightly. 'Gladys. Look, Gladys, you've got the wrong number. I'm going to have to hang up.'

70

'I know I've got the wrong number,' says Gladys, her voice rising. 'I thought I was calling Ellie but I did that last number thing and I got you. The spaceman.'

'I'm hanging up,' says Thomas. He adds loftily, 'I have to keep this channel of communication open.'

'I'm lost,' wails Gladys.

'Hanging up. Don't call this number again.'

He presses the button to disconnect the call and replaces the handset.

If put off, can encourage angina, say – proverbially. Four letters.

He looks at the handset again.

Four letters. Four letters.

She said she was lost.

He lightly pencils in L-O-S-T. It fits the space, but it doesn't feel right. He smiles wryly.

She sounded old, Gladys. Confused. Thomas thinks about his mum, how she was at the end. Frightened. Desperate. Lost.

Sighing, he picks up the Iridium phone again and studies the buttons. There's one with two arrows turning in on each other like snakes eating each others' tails. He presses it and listens to the clicks and whirrs of the signal bouncing off the network of satellites and then the hissy ringing tone. It's picked up almost immediately.

'Ellie?' shrieks the same voice.

'Gladys?' says Thomas cautiously. 'You just called me?'

'I don't know where I am,' she says. 'I went to the Town Hall to sort everything out but when I got to Rodney Street they'd demolished it. I didn't know where to go. So I got on a bus to get home but there's another family living in the house. I think they're Polish. I forgot. I went to our house, where me and Bill lived. I forgot we didn't live there any more. I forgot Bill was dead.' She dissolves into thick, choking sobs.

'Right. I'm going to need you to calm down. Do you know who this is?'

There's a sniffling noise then the alarming blast of a nose being blown. In a small voice Gladys says, 'You're the spaceman. Major Tom. You called me yesterday asking about Janet Crosthwaite.'

Thomas pinches his nose again, tight enough to leave indentations in the skin. This woman is evidently insane. 'Yes,' he says slowly. 'This is Major Tom. Now, do you think you can ring someone? Ellen, did you say? Is she your daughter?'

'Ellie. She's our Darren's girl. But I just want to get back. I need to make their tea. James will be home by now.'

Thomas can see that getting her to ring another number is going to be next to impossible. 'Look, I can call people at Mission Control. They'll be able to help if you give me your phone number.'

'No!' says Gladys, horrified. 'No! Nobody can know! Ellie was quite definite about that. I just need to get home.'

Cradling the phone in the crook of his neck, Thomas anchors himself to the desk and calls up Google on the computer, swiping away the Twitter feed of the account Claudia had set up for him with annoyance. He brings up Google Maps instead, and says, 'Now, do you know where you are?'

'I'm on Poolstock. I need to get to Santus Street. Number 19.'

'What city is that?'

Gladys says something like *Wussly Mains*. Thomas says doubtfully, 'Is that a town?'

'It's in Wigan.' She sounds calmer now.

'OK.' Thomas taps in the street name and 'Wigan'. The map centres on a warren of avenues in an area called, according to the plan, Worsley Mesnes. He shakes his head. How do you even say that? 'I think I've got you.'

'Oh! You can see me, from space? Do you have a telescope?'

'Of course not!' scoffs Thomas. 'I'm using . . .' He pauses, and considers whether he's got the time and patience to try to explain the internet to this woman who's obviously not so much a sandwich short of a picnic but *sans* an entire loaf of bread. He sighs. 'Yes, a telescope. A really special telescope. Now, can you give me that address again where you *actually* live, as opposed to where you used to live God knows how many years ago?'

There's a brief silence, then Gladys mumbles, 'Santus Street.' Thomas taps it in and scrutinises the dotted line that appears between the two streets. 'You're about ten minutes away. You need to go straight up that road you're on, take a left at the end, cross over, take the second right, then the first left. Then you're home. OK?'

Gladys repeats the directions back to him, or at least, something approximating a set of instructions utterly unlike the ones he has just given to her. She says, 'Can you stay on the line until I get there?'

'Not really. On account of me being in space and everything.'

Gladys starts to cry again, and Thomas says under his breath, 'Jesus Christ.' Then with as much brightness as he can muster, 'All right. Start walking now. To the bottom of the road. Quick as you can.'

'I'm seventy-one next birthday, you know,' she grumbles.

'Are you at the end of the road yet?' says Thomas after five minutes.

'I was just looking at number 29. They've put cladding up all over the front. I don't like it.'

'Jesus wept.' He doesn't even bother to mutter this time.

'I won't have talk like that,' chides Gladys. 'Taking the Lord's name in vain.'

'I'm sorry!' yells Thomas. 'I'm just trying to get you home so I can get back to flying my spaceship! Have you crossed the road yet?'

'Give me a chance,' says Gladys. 'I'm sev—'

'Yes, you're seventy-one next birthday, I know. Can you get a bit of a wriggle on, though?'

A message notification flashes up over the map, from Baumann with the subject header ARE YOU ON THE PHONE?! Attached is a pdf of the EVA protocols. Thomas deletes it. Gladys says, 'Did you say first or second right?'

'Second. Then first left.'

There's more traffic noise and huffing and puffing, then Gladys exclaims, 'Yes, yes, it's fine now. I'm home. Thank you very much.'

'Brilliant. I'm going to go now. Can you get Ellen or whatever her name is to delete this number from your phone? I really can't have you calling here every time you get lost.'

73

His thumb hovers above the button on the phone, as he listens to Gladys and a babble of other, younger voices. 'It was the spaceman,' he hears Gladys say happily. 'The spaceman got me home.'

Thomas finally kills the connection and stares for a long moment at the handset, ignoring the insistent ping of incoming emails from Mission Control.

∗ 18 ∗

STAGNATION

'When faced with a challenge, Tolstoy's characters have three choices,' says Miss Barber. She is perched on the corner of her desk, holding the paperback of *Anna Karenina* with one hand, her thumb keeping the book open. She scans the room. 'Anyone?'

Ellie sinks into her chair. *Not me, not me.* She glances around the class. Half of them are surreptitiously playing with their phones or texting beneath their tables, the rest are gazing into space or exchanging whispers. 'Anyone?' Miss Barber is in her late twenties, quite pretty, with dark hair she scrapes back into a ponytail. She wears tight skirts and blouses open at the neck. Ellie has seen the boys looking weirdly at her, their minds on things darker and more secret than Tolstoy.

Miss Barber smiles. 'Delil.'

Ellie looks over her shoulder at the boy sitting at the back of the room. He has a frizzy afro and black-framed glasses that are too big for his face. Delil Alleyne. The idiots sometimes sing 'why, why, why, Delilah?' at him in the corridor. She vaguely remembers being shocked, a few years ago, when they were in year seven or eight and a hatchet-faced dinner lady called him Man Friday to his face because he was loitering inside at lunchtime. With a sudden burning in her cheeks, Ellie remembers that she just put her head down and walked on. Most of the time she doesn't even notice him, doesn't notice anyone.

'Well, the first choice is to overcome the challenge, rise to it,' says Delil.

Someone throws a rubber at him and it lodges in his hair, and everyone laughs. 'Swot,' calls a cracked male voice, viciously.

'Sshh,' says Miss Barber. 'Good, Delil. And which character typifies this approach?'

'Konstantin Levin. With all the farming and everything . . . he just cracks on with it.'

Miss Barber smiles again. 'So, triumph. Good, Delil. Now, anyone else?' Her gaze settles on Ellie, who tries to fold herself into the chair. 'Ellie?'

'Don't know, miss,' mumbles Ellie.

'I know,' says Delil. There's a chorus of boos from the class. Ellie has never noticed before how sweaty it smells, all these boys and their testosterone. 'They give up, and die. Like Anna.'

'Spoilers!' shouts a boy, and Delil ducks from a hail of pen-tops, chewing gum and balled-up paper.

'Quiet down!' shouts Miss Barber. Then, 'Excellent Delil. And well done for reading ahead.' She looks down at her book. 'So. Tolstoy's characters tackle challenges by meeting them head on, or dying trying. One more? Not Delil, this time.'

There's silence, punctuated by the occasional beeping of a phone, or subdued belch.

'Stagnation,' says Miss Barber eventually. 'Doing nothing. Compromising. Like Karenin. Like Vronsky.' She sweeps the room with her eyes, and settles on Ellie. 'Like some of you.'

Someone says, 'Charming.' Miss Barber goes to her desk and bends over her computer. There's a sharp intake of breath from most of the male pupils. On the whiteboard their week's assignment appears.

'Why do Tolstoy's characters have to come to terms with death in order to understand life?' she reads. 'One week today. And I want you working in pairs for this one.'

The class starts shuffling itself into natural groups. Ellie sinks further into her plastic chair. With a bit of luck Miss Barber won't notice her not pairing off with anyone and she can just do it on her own. But the teacher says, 'Ah, no, for this one I'm going to decide the groups.' There's a groan from the class as she starts reeling off names. 'Ellie Ormerod and Delil Alleyne.'

'Safe,' says Delil.

Ellie scowls at Miss Barber, who raises an eyebrow at her. 'Problem, Ellie?'

'He's a weirdo, miss.' Ellie folds her arms and stares out of the window.

The knot of boys in the corner start to chant, 'Weirdo! Weirdo! Weirdo!' and throw things at Delil. When Miss Barber's got them under control, she glares at Ellie. 'You can see me after class.'

'I expected better of you, Ellie,' says Miss Barber. The classroom is empty now, everyone having scrambled out as soon as the bell went. The chairs and tables are haphazardly abandoned, and Miss Barber has done her best to encourage learning by Blu-Tacking quotes from her favourite books onto the peeling paint of the walls.

'Sorry,' mumbles Ellie. 'I didn't mean it.'

'Hmm. That almost makes it worse. How do you think Delil feels about that? He gets enough hassle from this lot' – she waves her hand in the direction of the empty chairs – 'without you egging them on. He's not weird. He's a bit different. I'd have thought you'd have been able to empathise.'

Ellie's eyes flash. 'What do you mean? Are you calling *me* weird?'

'I'm saying you're not like the rest of them.'

'You don't know anything about me,' pouts Ellie.

'How are you getting on with *Anna Karenina*?' asks Miss Barber, changing tack.

Ellie tries to remember what she read in the York Notes book she nicked from Waterstones, though she's barely had time to glance at it. She looks at her shoes – scruffy, falling apart – and something pops into her head. She says, 'It's a novel of unparalleled richness and density, isn't it, miss?'

Miss Barber smiles tightly. 'Yes, Wordsworth Classics do write quite succinct blurbs on the backs of their books, don't they? Well remembered, though.'

Ellie looks out of the window, trying to ignore Miss Barber scrutinising her. Eventually she shrugs, 'I haven't really had time to get too far into it, miss.'

When she looks back at the teacher, she's staring intently into her eyes. 'I hope you don't mind me saying this, Ellie, but you look tired. I know you're fifteen, you're not a small child, but sleep's important. Are you getting to bed early enough?'

Ellie shrugs non-committally. Miss Barber nips her bottom lip with her teeth, hesitates, and then says, 'Are you having any problems? You know you can talk to me in confidence at any time. I know what it's like being young. I know there are temptations. The urge to experiment. And I know that . . . that drugs can be easily obtained in our communities . . .'

Ellie closes her eyes and sighs. As if it was so easy to explain. Sometimes she wonders if she shouldn't go and score some drugs, some heroin, something that'll blast her out of it all, even for just a few hours. Miss Barber seems to take her silence as encouragement to go on.

'Ellie . . . last year I'd have said without hesitation that you were a straight A student in English. In fact, I'd have put money on it. A lot of money. Now . . .' She leaves it hanging there, in the silent air of the empty classroom, between them. 'I know what it's like, being young.'

Ellie stares at her. 'Stop saying that. You might know what it's like to be young but you don't know what it's like to be *me*.'

Miss Barber leans forward, staring at her intently. 'Then tell me.'

She's kept it bottled up for so long. Had no one to talk to. Imagine if she just let it all go now, let the dam break. The words tumble out of her in a rush.

Ellie says, 'My mum's gone. My dad's in prison. My brother's being bullied. My nan's losing her mind. I'm holding down three jobs on top of school just to make ends meet. I have no friends. I never go out. I'm trying to keep the family together but I wonder if it's even worth it. I just want to go to sleep for a day. A week. For ever.'

But she says none of these things. Instead she looks at her scruffy shoes again and just mumbles, 'I'm fine, miss.'

Miss Barber sighs and pats her hands on her thighs in surrender. 'Okay. You can go.'

Ellie drags her bag towards the door and turns when Miss Barber says, 'I'm always here. I wish you'd give me something. Anything. Just say what you're thinking.'

Ellie looks at her critically for a moment, then says, 'You might want to think about doing up another button on your top if you don't want every boy in this room wanking themselves to sleep over you every night.'

Then she walks out and heads to another class she can sleepwalk through until it's time to go home.

✳ 19 ✳

SIX BILLION YESES AND ONE NO

The *Shednik-1*, which Thomas will never stop calling this heap of junk, keeps to Greenwich Mean Time, but of course it's all the same to him, in the little section of the cabin where he sleeps, eats, goes to the toilet and works. There are other small spaces off the main cabin, used for storing supplies and electronic panels that hum and blink. He has now broken out of Earth orbit and is on the Hohmann Transfer Orbit, which means he doesn't go in a straight line from Earth to Mars, he swings out in a loop. He's going to the Red Planet by the scenic route. Of course, Thomas knows he mustn't look directly at the Sun, unfiltered by the atmosphere of Earth, save through one particular heavily tinted window, but he sometimes likes to glance at it quickly from the corner of his eye, to reassure himself that it's there, blazing away in the endless night, casting no shadows in the dull winter of England.

Director Baumann calls. 'Are there problems on the line? We've tried calling you a few times and you've been, well, engaged.'

'Sounds find to me.' He really doesn't want to get into a conversation about Gladys from Wigan. 'Must have been . . . solar flares.'

'Well, I have good news and some . . . other news,' says Baumann with an overly cheery demeanour that immediately puts Thomas on his guard.

'Give me the bad news first.'

'I didn't say *bad* news. Thomas, we've got a rather exciting opportunity.'

Opportunities are never exciting when someone else puts them to you. A lifetime of work has assured him of that. He says with a resigned tone, 'Go on, then.'

'I've got someone here to speak to you. Ideally we'd have liked to do this on video link but . . . anyway.'

'Is this that kid again? From my old school? Has she got a better question this time?'

'You'll see. I'm handing over the phone now.'

There's a pause and then a familiar voice says, 'Thomas. This is a huge, huge honour.' Thomas is wondering who he thinks the honour is for, but the man goes on, 'Do you know who this is?'

Thomas knows exactly who it is. He makes a point of avoiding the TV shows the man has his fingers in, but him and his influence are like the tentacles of some insidious octopus on a mission to poke every corner of the world with an insincere celebration of mediocrity. 'Simon Callow. You're one of my favourite actors.'

There's the minutest of pauses then the man laughs. 'Ha ha. They told me you were a bit of a joker, Thomas. They also told me you were something of a music fan . . .?'

'Yes. Proper music.'

'Precisely. Proper music. Which is what I want to talk about, Thomas. How would you' – here the man takes a deep breath as though he's mentally unfurling a red carpet for Thomas – 'how would you like to record for us, from space, a cover version of the absolute classic "Space Oddity"?'

Thomas takes a moment to remember to breathe. 'You are kidding me.'

There's a laugh. 'Oh no, I'm not, Thomas. I'm deadly serious. You. Sitting in your tin can. Singing "Space Oddity". I can cast-iron guarantee you that it would be number one all over the world by Christmas.'

'No.'

'Oh, yes,' says the man. 'And not just one yes, *six billion* yeses. Everyone in the world will buy this, Thomas. I am *one million per cent* sure of it. It will be a winner. An absolute, gold-plated, in-at-number-one-with-a-bullet winner.'

'No.'

'Yes, yes, and a thousand times yes. We're going to make you a star, Thomas Major. I am, right here, right now, giving you my Golden Buzzer. If I had a trillion Golden Buzzers, and a trillion hands to hit them with, I would be hitting them all now at the same time. You are not just on a one-way trip to Mars, you're going straight to the top on a rocket made of stardust and *yeses*.'

'Two things,' says Thomas, securing the phone in the crook of his neck and pushing himself over to the computer. 'One, you can't have one million per cent, so you really need to stop saying that. Two, when I said *no*, I wasn't speaking in some kind of disbelieving but ultimately enthralled manner. In other words no, *nein*, *nyet*, *non*, negative, no way and bugger off and die.'

Finding the song he's looking for on the computer – 'Spend Spend Spend', three minutes eighteen seconds of caustic low-fi discordant anti-consumerism from The Slits' 1979 debut album – Thomas puts the receiver right up against the speaker, and plays it down the line until he's sure that odious man has gone.

Thomas wonders briefly about Director Baumann's two pieces of news, just as another message pings into his inbox. PREPARING FOR EVA, is the subject header. Thomas deletes it quickly and looks for his crossword book.

20

HERE'S WHAT YOU COULD HAVE WON

A gale is blowing as Ellie shuffles out of the school gate at the end of the day, pulling her too-tight coat about her. She feels bad about what she said to Miss Barber. She didn't deserve that. She was only trying to help. But something about Miss Barber makes Ellie feel angry, all knotted and hot in her gut. She bet Miss Barber never had to struggle like this. Miss Barber had it all handed to her on a plate. Good school, time to do her work, university, teacher training. Everything Ellie will never have.

Her phone beeps and there's a Snapchat notification. Ellie wonders why she still bothers signing up to them, it's just her friends – her old friends – organising dates and shopping trips and petty, inconsequential things for which Ellie just doesn't have the time, energy or inclination any more. They are constantly posting pictures of the things they've bought, places they've been. Ellie looks at them with a vicious fury, *makes* herself look at them. *Here's what you could have won. Here's the life you could be leading. Look at it.* The message is from Alex. Ellie used to be such good friends with Alex, all the way from primary school. But when you stop going out, stop responding to invitations, it's like you become a ghost, always on the outside looking in. It's like people forget you and with each passing day you become as insubstantial in real life as their memories of you.

Want to come 2 Manchester on Sat? Bit of retail therapy?

With a shock Ellie realises the message is for her. The phone beeps again and another old friend joins the conversation. Maisie.

Yeh Ellie hvnt seen u 4 ages.

And just like that, Ellie feels ever so slightly less insubstantial. Maybe they haven't forgotten her completely at all. Maybe there is life out there. It's nice to be asked, but she can't go, of course. She types a quick message back with her thumbs.

Soz 2 much on but nxt week maybe xx

Ellie puts her head down against the cold wind and almost walks into Delil Alleyne, who appears to be lurking by the railings. He beams at her. 'Hello, study buddy.'

Ellie pushes past him. 'Have you been waiting for me?'

'Yep,' he says. 'Do you want to come round my house and we'll plan out the assignment?'

Ellie pulls a disgusted face. 'Urgh, no, thanks.'

'Well, shall I come round to yours?'

Ellie walks on. 'I don't think so.'

Delil keeps pace with her in long, loping strides. 'We could do the library, then? Tomorrow dinner break?'

She stops, the wind whipping her hair across her face. 'Look,' she says, 'you're obviously into all this Russian crap. How about you do the assignment and we'll say we did it together, right? Leave a space at the top for my name and I'll write it in.'

Ellie heads off without waiting for an answer, putting her head down as she feels the first spots of rain. She thinks that's the end of it, until he shouts, 'So shall we grab a burger after school tomorrow to talk it through?'

'Can we afford it?' says Julie. She is still in the two-piece suit she wears to work at the car dealership, sitting on the sofa with a glass of pinot. Darren stands in front of her, his work trousers caked with dried plaster and paint, brandishing the brochures.

'I just think the kids are at the right age. Ellie's eleven; she's going to be interested in boys and make-up and stuff soon. James still believes in Father Christmas.'

Julie takes a sip of the wine. 'Hmm. Well, Ellie's bright, you know. She's got more prospects than just being a bloody Barbie doll.'

He squats down in front of her. 'You know I didn't mean that. And yes, we can afford it. I've been working every hour God sends these last few months. I've got so much work I don't know how to fit it all in.'

Julie takes the brochure and glances at it. 'Disneyland Paris. I suppose it could be fun.'

'It will be,' says Darren. 'We haven't had a holiday for ages.' He looks around. 'Where are the kids, anyway?'

Julie pulls the bobble from her brown hair and shakes it out. 'Upstairs. James is playing with his chemistry set. Ellie's probably online looking at Urban Decay.'

Darren frowns. 'What's that? Some legal high site? Do we need to have a talk to her?'

Julie throws the brochure at him. 'It's a cosmetics brand, you clown. And I was joking anyway.' She takes another sip. 'Did you call in at your mum's at dinnertime?'

Darren nods. 'To be honest, I'm a bit worried about her. I think she's losing it. She kept going on about Dad, like she'd just been talking to him that morning.'

'It's tough for her, on her own,' says Julie. 'I know this house is small, but we have got the box room . . .'

Darren pulls a face. 'She's too independent. That's her problem. She thinks she can do everything herself. That phone I bought her? She'd put it in the butter dish. In the fridge. God knows where the butter is.'

'Do you think she'll still be able to mind the kids over the summer holidays?'

'She's not loopy. Not yet. It's just . . . Anyway. Shall I shout the kids?'

Ellie and James troop downstairs at the sound of their dad's voice. Ellie will start high school in September, and Julie thinks how much she's grown up just this last year. One summer and she'll be blossoming into a young woman. So bright, and so pretty. Julie worries about her, worries about those teenage years, and thanks God she'll be able to give her the benefit of her own experience to guide her through those stormy waters. James . . . well, James is James. So long as he's got a test tube and some copper sulphate solution, he'll be happy. It was Darren who insisted he go to St Matthew's, to give him a better chance. He does seem to be flourishing. The kids stand in front of them, Darren hiding the brochures behind his back.

'What have we done?' says Ellie, looking warily from Mum to Dad.

Darren adopts a stern face. 'You tell me.'

Ellie and James exchange guilty looks, then James cries, 'It was Ellie! She put the cup of water with woodlice in it in the freezer to see what would happen to them!'

'You lying little geek,' says Ellie, swiping at him with her fist.

'That sounds like something that deserves punishment,' says Darren. 'How about a trip to Disneyland Paris?'

The kids stare and then whoop, James running to hug Julie, who holds her glass out of the way to stop him spilling it. Ellie puts her arms around Darren, extracting the brochures from his grip.

'I'll go and book it tomorrow on my break,' says Julie. 'There's that big travel agent on the retail park.'

'Now can we have some tea?' says Darren. 'I've got to go back on that gable end job tonight while the weather's dry.'

'There's some pizzas in the freezer.'

They consider this, and the frozen woodlice, then say together, 'Takeaway.'

'If you don't like burgers there's always the Kentucky Fried Chicken place,' shouts Delil. 'Well, it's not a proper KFC. I think it's called Southern Style Chicken. Up near the park. It's probably the same thing, though. I once heard they put rats in those things, because it tastes just like chicken. But then everything is supposed to taste like chicken. They even say human flesh tastes like chicken! Whatever you want, that's safe with me!'

Ellie keeps walking. Invitations to shopping trips? Offers of fast food study dates? What do people think? That's she's *normal* or something?

21

A SINGULAR, HIGHLY STRESSFUL ENVIRONMENT

From 'Preparing For Space', European Space Agency Bulletin 128, November 2006:

> During Extra-Vehicular Activities (EVAs – spacewalks), astronauts venture from their protective spacecraft in autonomous spacesuits to work on, for example, the International Space Station (ISS) or the Hubble Space Telescope.
>
> EVAs are among the most challenging tasks of an astronaut's career. They are complex and demanding, placing the astronauts in a singular, highly stressful environment, requiring a high level of situational awareness and coordination while working at peak performance. Careful and intensive preparation of the astronaut is key to safe, smooth and successful EVAs. Water is the best environment for EVA training on Earth, substituting neutral buoyancy for microgravity. Preparation is therefore centred on special facilities such as the Neutral Buoyancy Laboratory (NBL) at NASA's Johnson Space Center (JSC, Houston), the Hydrolab at the Gagarin Cosmonaut Training Centre (GCTC, Moscow) and now also at the Neutral Buoyancy Facility (NBF) of ESA's European Astronaut Centre (EAC, Cologne).
>
> During their Basic Training, all astronauts undergo a scuba diving course as a prerequisite to EVA training. For NASA and ISS partner astronauts undergoing Shuttle Mission Specialist Training, this is followed by a general EVA skills programme at JSC that also helps to identify the most suitable EVA crewmembers.
>
> A successful EVA requires psychomotor, cognitive and behavioural skills. Psychomotor skills range from the ability to move in the suit, move along the Station using handrails and pass obstacles, to operating courses, briefings and in-water exercises, scripted to challenge the trainees to think and perform as if they were conducting actual EVAs.

'Bollocks.' Thomas flips to the front of the leaflet. 'From 2006?' He starts to compose an angry email to Baumann, suggesting that if BriSpA does expect him to actually go outside into space they might have given him some literature that wasn't more than a decade old. But then he can't be bothered and instead carefully tears up the leaflet into small pieces and throws it above his head, where it hangs like confetti.

And that just makes him think about Janet all over again.

Inevitably, the Iridium phone buzzes again. Probably Baumann taking him to task for playing punk to that horrible man. He picks it up and yells down it, 'I'm not sorry!'

There's a brief silence then a voice says, 'Um. Hello? Is that Major Tom?'

It's a child. Thomas sighs. 'Is that . . . look, I can't remember your name. Sharon? Stephanie? The kid from my old school? Have you got a question?'

There's another pause, then, 'No. It's James.'

'What sort of name is that for a girl?'

'It's James. J-A-M-E-S. And I'm a boy.'

'Oh. Sorry. It was your squeaky little voice. But James who? What have they got *you* doing?'

'James Ormerod,' says the child. 'They haven't got me doing anything. Nobody knows I'm calling you.'

Thomas takes the phone away from his ear and stares at it for a moment before replacing it and saying, 'Christ, has someone posted this number on Facebook or something? I'm getting more unsolicited calls than when I was on Earth.'

The boy sniffles. Oh, God, please don't start crying. He's had enough of weeping children. 'My nan said she'd been speaking to you but Ellie just thinks it's because of the dementia. She's having a sleep so I got her phone and redialled the last number she called. It is you, isn't it? You're really Major Tom?'

'Yes,' sighs Thomas. 'I'm really Major Tom. But I'm not actually a major and my name is Thomas. Your nan? Is that Gladys? The old woman who was lost?'

'Yes. Thank you for bringing her home. She could have got us in a lot of trouble. Not that she hasn't already.'

Thomas rubs his temple. 'Look. James. You can't call me again. I need you to do something for me. Delete this number from your nan's phone, OK?'

'I just wanted to talk to you,' says James in a small voice. 'I read on Wikipedia that you're a chemist.'

'A chemical technician. I was, anyway. Now I'm an astronaut. A very busy one.' He wonders vaguely where his crossword book is. 'And I've got to go. You'll delete this number, yes?'

'I want to be a scientist. I've won a place in the finals of the National Schools Young Science Competition. But Ellie says I can't go.'

'Well, that's very . . . well done.' He pauses, despite himself. 'What do you mean, you can't go? Who's Ellie?'

'My sister. She's a cow. But I think it's because we're in trouble. I think my nan's done something bad but I don't really know what.'

Thomas shakes his head. No. No no no. He will not get involved in this. 'Well. That's a shame. Right. Going now.'

'You don't know what it's like. Wikipedia said you didn't have a sister or a brother. You don't know what it's like.'

Thomas says nothing. But he doesn't hang up. He just sits there, thinking of the lump of a digital watch in his jeans pocket, a damp summer long ago. Eventually James says, 'Can I ask one question? Then I'll go. I promise I won't bother you again. I just wanted to see if it was true what Nan said. One question.'

'What is it?' sighs Thomas.

James clears his throat. 'What would happen if you set fire to a fart in a spaceship?'

Thomas opens his mouth and closes it again. He feels blood rush to his head, prickling his scalp. He puts one hand over his mouth, then without a word quietly puts the phone down in its holster, killing the connection.

22

WE'RE GOING TO BE RICH!

The last thing Ellie needs is a shift at the convenience store after the day she's had. But they need the money, and she needs to get out of the house, as tired as she is. Besides, Mr Woźniak needs her. One frozen ride on a bus with no heater later she's pushing through the door of the Polski Sklep where Mr Woźniak is standing by the three tills in his usual smart suit, his hair Brylcreemed down.

'Good evening, Eleanor,' he says. Mr Woźniak is very formal and always uses her full name. He says that is how to get ahead in business, especially for a Pole. Mr Woźniak was frightened that he would be deported after Britain voted to leave the European Union but that hasn't happened. Just as well, as his empire is on the increase; he has three Polski Skleps now, selling a variety of Eastern European fare and catering for both the immigrants and the indigenous population. That is the key to success, says Mr Woźniak; being all things to all people. He plans to be the Polish Morrisons. 'All things to all people,' Mr Woźniak is fond of saying.

Ellie knows just how he feels.

'Evening, Mr Woźniak,' says Ellie, shucking off her coat and going to hang it in the staff room. The shop is quite large; big enough to employ about a dozen people on any one shift. She checks the rota and is glad she's on stockroom and shelf-filling; she's not sure how well she'd cope on the tills tonight. She stops at the noticeboard where Mr Woźniak lets customers put up index-cards with things for sale and notices about lost cats. There's someone offering baby-sitting shifts not too far from Santus Street; she keys the number into her phone. Every little helps.

'Has the day been tolerable to you, Eleanor?' asks Mr Woźniak when Eleanor returns to the shop floor with a wire cage of dairy products to be stocked on to the shelves.

She tries her best to smile.

*

When Ellie gets back to Santus Street after eleven she's surprised to find both James and Nan still up. She throws her bag near the washing pile. 'Oi, bed, you. This is far too late for a school night. Besides, I want to talk to Nan about just where she went off to today.'

Then she sees the look on his face. He's kneeling up by Nan's chair, and Nan looks like she's been crying. On the little coffee table in front of the fire are a pile of brown envelopes.

James says, 'Promise me one thing, Ellie. You won't blow your top. Promise.'

She feels the colour draining out of her face. 'I'm not going to be able to promise that, James, am I? You know I'm not. What's going on? Is this to do with why Nan went out this afternoon?'

He nods solemnly. 'I went in to see her tonight and she was crying on her bed with all these letters round her.'

'You don't have to talk about me as though I'm not here,' says Gladys, crossly.

'You're going to wish you weren't in about five minutes,' mutters James.

Ellie sits on the sofa and takes the envelopes, shelling them like peas until a sheaf of letters sits on her lap. They are all from the housing association that owns their house. She reads through them, one by one, feeling the tension rise from James and Nan. She takes a deep breath and forces down the boiling rage that is threatening to erupt and blow the top of her head off.

'Nan,' she says as evenly as possible. 'Why hasn't our rent been paid for the past six months?'

Gladys covers her face with her hands and shakes her head.

'Nan. Six months. This was on a standing order. What happened?'

'I cancelled it on the internet thing,' wails Nan through her fingers. 'I was on the bank thing and I didn't know what it was and it seemed such an awful lot of money and I cancelled it. I only had to press a button.'

Ellie rubs her temples and looks at the top letter. 'And you've been hiding these?'

Nan nods sadly.

'But I don't understand why they haven't phoned or been round, even.'

'They have,' says Nan. 'I kept putting the phone down. A man's been round three times. The first time I told him we didn't live here any more. The second time I pretended I was foreign and didn't understand him. The last time . . .'

James hands over a letter he's been clutching. 'The last time he pushed this through the door.'

'Oh, Jesus,' says Ellie. 'They've been to court. They're going to evict us in . . .' She reads the letter again. 'Jesus. In less than three weeks.' She looks at James, whose face has crumpled up and is starting to cry. She looks at Nan, who's as white as a pint of milk. 'Three. Weeks.'

Ellie stands up and paces up and down the small living room. She drops the letters to the table and puts her hands to her head. 'OK. Think. Think.' She snatches up the eviction notice again. 'This says that if we pay the full arrears before the eviction date they'll stand it down.' She balls her fist and taps it against her forehead. 'We can do this. We can sort this out.'

She squats down beside James, who's crying freely now. 'It's OK,' she says softly. 'We can sort this out. Nan, we're going to have to go on to your online banking. The payment details are on this letter. The money's there, it's just not been paid, right? So we just need to pay six months' back rent and set the standing order up again. I'm sure we can just do that online. If we can't, I'll ring the bank tomorrow and pretend to be you. You've got all the passwords and memorable information written down some-where, right?'

Gladys is just looking at her. Ellie shakes her head. 'What? What?'

'About the money . . .'

'Yes,' says Ellie, trying to speak as evenly as possible and doing her level best to ignore the feeling that she's standing on a very high, very thin pole. 'The money. All the money that was from Mum's insurance policy. The money that they paid out when she died. The money that Dad put into your account before he went to prison. The same account where he set up all the standing orders to pay all the bills. That money. All those thousands of pounds.'

Gladys brightens. 'Oh! It's all right! I almost forgot!'

Ellie closes her eyes and breathes a ragged sigh. 'You've just moved it, right? Into a savings account or something? You can get it back?'

Gladys laughs. 'I can get it back and more! Much more! I've *invested* it!'

And Ellie is on top of the pole again, teetering in the wind. 'Invested it,' she says numbly. She picks up the letters and stares at them as though she can change the words on them through very force of will.

'Yes!' says Gladys. 'A guaranteed return. A lovely man emailed me. A prince. From Nigeria. We've become quite the pals.' She giggles. 'I call him my boyfriend. But that's just a joke. He's married. But he's had some troubles, you see. I'm not sure I really understand it but he's got all this money that he needs to get out of the country but they won't let him. Someone won't let him. So he needs to put it into another account in a different country.'

Ellie feels faint. She might black out. 'Please tell me you didn't—'

Gladys holds up her hand. 'Wait! Let me tell you. So I gave him my bank numbers and he just said I had to transfer some money to him so he could get things moving over there. I've been doing that for a few weeks now.'

'How much?' says Ellie weakly.

'Well, all of it.' Gladys stops and frowns. 'Most of it, anyway. But the best thing is, guess how much we're going to get back?'

Ellie says nothing. She can only stare at Gladys. James has buried his face in his arms and is sobbing his heart out.

'Four million dollars!' says Gladys triumphantly. 'Four million! We're going to be rich, Ellie, rich!' She starts singing, 'Who wants to be a millionaire? I do! Who wants to be a millionaire? We do!' James is sobbing and sobbing and Ellie is just standing there, the letters falling from her hands like autumn leaves. Gladys gets up and starts to do a little dance, singing and singing away. James lifts his head and looks at Ellie with red-raw eyes.

'We're not going to be millionaires, are we?'

'Who wants to be millionaires! We do!' sings Gladys.

'No. She's been scammed. Completely scammed. I never even knew people actually fell for this.'

'Ellie?' says James. 'Ellie, what's going to happen?'

Ellie doesn't look at him. She just stares at the photograph of her mum and dad's wedding that sits on the mantelpiece. She doesn't even recognise her own flat tones as she starts to speak.

'What's going to happen? In less than three weeks some men are going to come to the house. They'll take our keys off us and put all our stuff out in the street. We'll have nowhere to live. But that won't matter, because social services will be down on us like a ton of bricks. And when they see what state *she's* in, they'll commit her. Cart her off somewhere. And we'll be put into care. Maybe foster parents. Maybe a care home. If we're lucky we might be together, but don't count on it. And that's the way it'll be until Dad gets out of jail.'

James wails and sobs. Nan dances around him, singing. Ellie just continues to stare at the picture of her mum and dad. She feels weirdly calm.

'We're fucked,' she says softly. 'Absolutely, utterly, royally fucked.'

Part Two

23

SUMMER 1988. THE POND.

The pond, or to give it the name used by generations of children, courting couples and recreational drug users, The Pond, is a twenty-minute walk from the Major household. It is the third house Thomas has lived in, each one larger and more grandiose – on a middle-class scale – than the one before, the result of his father's consistently improving performance in climbing the ladder at the large insurance company where he worked until his death. Always in Caversham, always improving. Keeping his family upwardly mobile was a way for Frank Thomas to ensure that no one stood still long enough to look too closely at the discrepancies in the patchwork quilt of his personal life. *Where was I on Friday night? Never mind that, look at this! A new house! A new car! A leather Chesterfield sofa!*

Before he sees them, Thomas hears Peter and his friends. The rain has let up but the grey clouds hang oppressively over him as he navigates the short, thin path through tall, glistening grasses that weave towards a copse of trees ringing The Pond. It's nothing grander than a rather wide ditch really, but deep. It sits on the edge of a housing estate, a red telephone box squatting on the pavement, marking the entrance to the place beloved of generations of small boys.

Had Thomas not got Laura, and the promise of meeting her later, he might feel a pang of jealousy at the easy way that his younger brother, only turning ten this coming August, makes friends. Peter might be no genius at school, but he charms people in an effortless manner that is a complete mystery to Thomas, engages strangers immediately, can pick up a conversation with anyone. Thomas is studious and academic and clever, but general social skills are on a list of things that he finds either difficult or downright impossible, along with football, skimming stones across water and unfastening a bra with one hand. That he has even tried and failed on the latter makes Thomas feel like some kind of hero.

When Thomas pushes through the trees he sees Peter and four or five friends – they never stand still long enough for him to count them properly – stripped to their underpants and dripping wet. A tatty thick rope is tied to a tall branch that overhangs The Pond, the water dark and deep but only thirty feet across. They have been swimming, against all adult advice. The Pond is rumoured to hold all kinds of dangers, traps and perils in its black depths; shopping trollies, bicycles, even an orange Lada car. But now they are gathered around Peter, who is sitting with his bare back against a tree, his feet in the air, his legs spread wide. Thomas pauses in alarm.

'Here it comes!' shouts Peter, and one of his compatriots strikes a match from a box of Cook's Matches stolen from a mother's kitchen, and holds it close to the sagging wet gusset of Peter's Arsenal underpants. Peter clenches his face and lets loose a loud fart. It blows out the match and everyone groans.

'Come on, you,' says Thomas. 'Mum sent me to get you. You've got the dentist.'

Peter pulls a face. 'Why didn't my fart light, Thomas? Come on. You're a scientist.'

Thomas puts his head on one side and considers. 'Hydrogen sulfide, which also makes your farts stink, by the way – and yours really do stink – is combustible.'

The kid who held the match, who is now pulling on a T-shirt over his thin, white torso, says, 'They don't half hum, he's right, Pete. Your huffs are the worst ever.'

'Methane is flammable, too. As is oxygen. The rest of your fart is mainly made up of nitrogen, carbon dioxide and hydrogen.'

'But why won't it light, Thomas?' says Peter. He watches as another boy takes a swing on the rope, letting go over the water and plunging into its depths with a slash.

'Maybe your underpants were too wet. Blew water and put the match out. What you need is a high methane content; that'll give you a nice blue flame. Now, come on, the dentist.'

'Do you think a fart would light on the space shuttle?'

'Who knows?' says Thomas. 'Come on. I'm meeting Laura in a bit.'

'One more swing.' Peter hares off before Thomas can stop him. He grabs at the rope, pulls it back up the bank, and leaps into the air, wrapping his pipe-cleaner legs around the frayed knot at the bottom, crying 'Geronimo!' as he throws his body into a star shape, leaves the rope, and flies out in an arc over The Pond, at the last minute making himself arrow-thin and cleaving the surface of the water feet-first and with barely a splash.

Thomas feels a sudden stab of envy at the way Peter is so carefree and fearless, so opposite to him. Thomas would never have risked a rope swing over The Pond at that age, would never have had the nerve to throw himself so freely like that. Thomas wonders if that's why dad always liked Peter better. Perhaps because Peter is a proper boy, a haring, tearing, harum-scarum boy who gets his face dirty and throws himself into peril. Perhaps Frank Major saw something of himself in Peter, something that he never saw in Thomas. A recklessness. It was so easy for their father to transfer his affections from Thomas to Peter. He was more aligned with his youngest son, less wary of him. Peter didn't tack up the Periodic Table on his wall, didn't lose himself in old music. He could talk about football with confidence, was already *one of the lads*. And since Frank died, the relationship between Thomas and Peter has shifted, so now he feels the age gap is even wider than eight years, feels as though more and more often he's sliding into the role of surrogate father, a situation their mother seems happy to allow. I'm only eighteen. I'm not ready to be a dad. He vaguely wonders if he'll have to at some point have The Talk with Peter, tell him about the birds and the bees. Oh, God, he hopes not.

Thomas feels the lump of Peter's digital watch and pulls it out of his pocket. For some reason it makes him think of that old song that was on the radio this morning. He glances at the time and starts to whistle, thinking about Laura. He looks at the watch again. He looks at the tangle of boys trying to sort their jumpers and jeans out from a pile that's refusing to give up its booty without a fight.

Peter surfaces and shouts, 'One more!'

Sighing, Thomas decides he will call Laura to tell her he might be late. He jogs back along the short path to the telephone box and digs in his pockets for change.

The line is busy. He stands there listening to the engaged tone for a moment, half in and half out of the red box. He spots through the trees the lean shape of Peter flying through the air again. Sighing, Thomas hangs up and as he's pushing back through the foliage he realises he can't see Peter.

Thomas glances at the watch in his hand. He tries to remember how many seconds have passed since he saw Peter on the rope.

How long can you hold your breath?

Thomas looks out at The Pond, Sargasso-calm. He frowns.

He tries to remember how long he's ever been able to hold his breath underwater at the swimming pool. The seconds have ticked on. Perhaps Peter has already emerged on the other bank.

From somewhere very distant Thomas hears a dog barking.

The smell of burning coals drifts over the water, a hopeful barbecue lit in one of the nearest gardens, a family seizing their chance at the cessation of the rain.

He taps the nearest boy on the shoulder. 'Where's Peter?'

The boy glances around and shrugs and continues forcing wet feet into unforgiving socks. Thomas can feel pressure rising, somewhere inside him.

Peter hasn't come out of the water. He's sure of it. He would have seen him. Unless he's playing a game. Unless he's slid out of the water, reed-thin, and is hiding behind a tree, laughing at him.

Thomas looks at the watch again.

A dragonfly hovers over the still waters of the pond, its wings moving too fast to see, its iridescent blue body shining in a shaft of sudden, unexpected sunlight that spears through the overhanging branches.

'Peter!' he shouts. 'Peter!'

He saw him go in. He's sure of that. Straight and true as a knife blade, barely a ripple.

He didn't see him come out.

'PETER!' he cries, his voice cracking.

Attracted to his distress, the boys gather round him like dogs.

'Pete's not come out!'

'Pete's in The Pond!'

'He's drowned! He's drowned!'

'He's got to go in!'

'Why's he not doing anything!'

'He's got to get him.'

As though he's been flying away from his body but unable to escape, Thomas now feels him twang back into himself like he's connected by invisible elastic. He realises they're talking about him.

He's got to go in.

He's not doing anything.

He's got to get him.

Thomas knows what he should do but he can't move. He just stares at the water, black from the reflection of the clouds overhead, and watches a single insect flying lazily and erratically over the millpond-calm surface.

'Get help,' he whispers, his entire body frozen but for his dry, cracked lips. 'Get an ambulance.'

The boys, as a single entity, scarper into the trees, leaving Thomas alone with the water, the silence, and the digital watch that damns his every second of inactivity with its grey display. At last he moves, wading into the cold shallows, the rope swinging above his head, swishing his hands ineffectually in the water as though he will somehow find Peter right beneath his feet. Then the ground drops steeply away and Thomas loses his footing, his feet pumping against just the gentle resistance of pond water. His head goes under and he closes his eyes, his cheeks bulging with trapped air, and he scrabbles about beneath him, his hands closing on fabric. Thomas starts to pull just as he feels strong hands grip his own shoulders. Pond water and weeds obscure his vision but he can see a crowd of adults wading into the water to help.

'I got him,' he gasps when he remembers to breathe, his hands still gripping what he now looks down to see is just an old cloth, a thing, a submerged, cast-off robe. And not his brother Peter at all.

*

When they pull him out of the water and the police divers eventually bring up Peter's body, pale and bloated with water and blue with cold, they tell him that there was nothing more he could have done. There was indeed an old Lada at the bottom of The Pond, and Peter's foot had become caught in a broken window, fifteen feet down. Not quite the bottomless pit of local legend, but a watery, silt-muddied grave for his brother nonetheless. There is an inquest, of course, and Thomas has to give evidence, along with the small boys who had been there with Peter. Thomas is praised by the coroner for sending the other boys to raise the alarm and for attempting to rescue his brother. But when the evidence is pieced together and it is determined that it was a full two minutes from Peter disappearing under the water to Thomas attempting to get into The Pond to find him, Thomas feels the weight of his mother's stare on him as he stands in the polished wooden witness box. Peter could have survived perhaps a minute in the depths of the pool. There was no chance that anyone could have done anything.

Why didn't you go in sooner?

It is a question he has asked himself a hundred times, a thousand. It is a question that he feels projected at him in the unwavering, red-rimmed gaze of his mother from the public gallery.

Why didn't you go in sooner? You could have saved him. Why did you go to the phone box?

'Pete's not come out!'

'Pete's in The Pond!'

'He's drowned! He's drowned!'

'He's got to go in!'

'Why's he not doing anything!'

'He's got to get him.'

Thomas has been allowed a small plastic box of personal items of sentimental value to bring with him, which is fastened to the underside of the bunk where he straps himself in for his few hours of sleep a night. He swims through the zero gravity to it now, and unclips the lid, sliding his hand in quickly to stop the few trinkets floating out. His fingers fasten around one piece and he pulls it out, refastening the lid and replacing the box. Thomas looks at the item for a long moment, then slides it over his hand, the flexible metal strap sitting snugly on his wrist. He looks at the face of the digital watch, still inexplicably keeping the correct hour. Peter's watch.

Why didn't you go in sooner? You could have saved him. You were too late.

The watch has been marking the passage of time since Peter's death, the march of seconds and minutes and hours and days. Weeks and months and decades. Thomas stares at it. But what if time is no longer moving away from one tragedy? What if it is instead heading towards another?

And what if, he wonders, what if this time, he isn't too late?

* 24 *

FIVE THOUSAND POUNDS

Ellie has made some notes on a piece of A4 paper and has called an emergency house meeting. She has taken Nan's chair by the fire; Gladys and James sit expectantly on the small sofa, like children waiting to see the headteacher.

'Item one. In fact, the one and only item. Can we get ourselves out of this mess, and if so, how?'

'So,' says James slowly. 'If we pay back all the money we owe, we'd be all right?'

'I've gone through the letters,' says Ellie. 'Yes. If we pay back the arrears before the eviction date, then we'll be fine. Plus some costs they've added for the privilege of taking us to court and sending us lots and lots of letters.' She looks pointedly at Gladys. 'Any thoughts?'

'Could we get a loan?' says James.

Ellie is pleased that he's at least been thinking about it, but says, 'No. Who would give us a loan? You have to be able to prove you can pay it back.'

'What about one of those they advertise on the telly? Payday loans?'

101

'No. They're the work of the devil. The interest rates are . . . Well, we'd be in an even worse mess than we are now. Also, the clue's in the question. They're called payday loans because you have to pay them back on payday. None of us have a payday.'

'You have three jobs,' points out James.

Ellie sighs. 'And with the money from that we have to buy, y'know, food and stuff. And pay the gas and electricity. And, if we even find a way out of this, we have to be able to pay the rent in the future. As of now we're on a strict budget. No sweets, no comics, no nothing.'

James groans and flops back on the sofa. Gladys says, 'I tried to go to the council to sort it out. Do you think I should try again?'

'Absolutely not. That's the *last* thing we want to happen. Look, we have a choice. We should vote on it now. We can either just give up, go to the social services, let them split us up right away, or we can fight on for the next three weeks, see if we can find a way to get this money and keep paying the rent until Dad gets out of jail. So . . . who's for giving up?'

She looks around the living room. James sits resolutely on his hands. Gladys crosses her arms defiantly. 'OK. So we try to sort this. Does anyone have any more suggestions?'

'Ellie,' says James. 'What about the science competition?'

She rubs her forehead. 'James. Love. Look, I think it's great that they asked you, but we really have other things to worry about right now. I think you should just put it out of your head.'

'But—'

'James. No. I said no.'

'But—'

Glady's's phone bursts into life, that old song 'Diamonds and Rust'. Ellie shoots her a warning glance. 'If it's anyone asking for money, hang up and block the number.'

Gladys says politely into the phone, 'Hello? Gladys Ormerod speaking.' She listens for a moment then hands over the phone to Ellie. 'He wants to speak to you.'

'Who does?' says Ellie.

'The spaceman. Major Tom.'

'Jesus, Nan,' says Ellie. 'We really don't have time for this.'

'It's true!' blurts out James. 'I called him myself. Before you got in. It's really him.'

Ellie glares at James and takes the phone. 'It's a stupid prank. Probably those kids who are bullying you at school.' She glances at the string of numbers on the phone's display and puts it to her ear. 'Look, I don't know who you are but this really isn't a good time, all right?'

'Is that Ellie?' says a man's voice.

'Who *is* this?' She looks around at the others and puts the phone on loudspeaker.

'It is me. Thomas Major. The one the papers call Major Tom. I'm on my way to Mars.'

'Ee, it sounds like he's in the next room,' says Gladys wonderingly.

'I'm not convinced this isn't some wind-up,' says Ellie. 'And we've had our fill of wind-ups in this house, I can tell you.'

'It's not a wind-up,' says Thomas. 'I helped your grandmother – your nan – get home when she was lost. I phoned her by accident the other day. This used to be my ex-wife's number.'

'So what do you want?' says Ellie.

'Um.' It sounds as though he's searching for words he's not used to using. 'I think I want to help.'

Ellie looks around the room. 'What have you been telling him? What have I told you about talking to people?'

'Nothing!' says James. 'I just said . . . I just said I thought we were in trouble. That was even before I knew about all this stuff with the rent. It was just a feeling I had. But that's what I wanted to say about the science —'

'Hush,' says Ellie. 'OK, spaceman. What do you want to know?'

'Everything,' says Thomas.

And Ellie, against her better judgement, because finally, *finally* she has someone to talk to who isn't her brother or her nan, tells him everything. The words come hesitantly at first, then tumble out in a rush, and once the dam's broken she can't stop, telling him about the rent arrears and the Nigerian scam and why Mum's gone and about Dad going to prison and the fact that everything, every single thing, is well and truly screwed.

Nan tuts. 'Language, Ellie.'

When the words have dried up, the tears come. Ellie puts her hands over her face and sobs quietly into them. When she's composed herself she says, 'So that's it. Have you got a magic space wand you can wave?'

'Why's your dad in prison?' asks Thomas.

'Does it make a difference?' says Ellie. 'Are you going to change your mind because our dad's a convict? He's in jail because he's an idiot. He's a builder, or he was. He was struggling to get work. He was in the pub one night and some blokes he knew asked him if he wanted in on a job. It was only because he had a van. They were burgling some cash and carry place and he was the driver. They were loading up loads of booze into his van. He probably wouldn't have gone to jail but the other blokes were disturbed by a security guard and one of them hit him over the head with an iron bar. Then they got themselves all caught. Idiots. The lot of them. Idiots.'

'Why can't you just ask someone for help?'

'Because,' says Ellie, sick to the back teeth of explaining this, 'Dad left Nan in charge of us. I'm fifteen and James is ten. The trouble is, she's going downhill rapidly. She's got dementia. The minute anyone finds out it'll be social services for us, and then we'll all be split up. So nobody finds out, OK? You don't tell a soul about this. You have to promise.'

'I promise,' says Thomas. 'And how much do you need to pay the rent arrears?'

'About five grand,' sighs Ellie. She pauses. 'Are you going to give it to us? They must have paid you some money to go to Mars.'

'They did pay me. I gave most of it to my ex-wife. Well, I sent a cheque to her solicitor. She didn't even write back. The rest I sent to the Royal Society for the Prevention of Accidents.'

'Why?' asks Ellie.

'Why what? Janet or RoSPA?'

'Has he been sending Janet Crosthwaite money?' says Gladys suspiciously.

'Ellie,' says James. 'The science competition . . .'

'Hush, Nan,' says Ellie. 'And be bloody quiet, James. The accident, thing. RoSPA.'

'It's . . . my brother,' says Thomas. 'It's a long story. But I don't have any money. I didn't think I'd need it up here. I could ask Mission Control to help . . .? They'd want to know why, though. They'd want to know the whole story.'

'No,' says Ellie firmly. 'We'll just have to find some other way to find the money.'

'Ellie!' shouts James. 'I've been trying to tell you all day! Why won't you listen to me! The National Schools Young Science Competition!'

'James!' yells Ellie back. 'Will you shut up about that stupid competition! You're not going and that's final!'

'Wait!' says Thomas. 'Wait. James, what about the competition?' 'THE PRIZE MONEY IS FIVE THOUSAND POUNDS!' he screams, then sits back on the sofa, closing his eyes. 'I've been trying to tell you.'

Everyone is silent. Ellie says, 'Five thousand pounds?'

'What do you have to do, James?' asks Thomas.

'An experiment. An original experiment. That's it. Something that's going to wow everybody. I'm already through to the final because I'm a working-class peasant with crap shoes. Now all I need to do is come up with an experiment that can win.'

There's a moment of quiet, then Thomas says, 'Look, I've got this routine . . . I'm supposed to spend a couple of hours every evening reading up on how to grow potatoes. To be honest, that fills me with dread. Maybe I could use that time to talk to James, about science. About his experiment. Maybe I could . . . you know, maybe I could help.'

And Ellie, who has for the past few days felt darkness closing in around her, the future made of formless static that she can't pierce, sees in the distance a very small but very bright pin prick of light.

'Yes,' she says slowly, picking up the phone. 'Yes, maybe you bloody well could.'

25

EXTRA-VEHICULAR ACTIVITY

When Thomas puts the phone down he feels . . . strange. It takes him a while to identify the prickling at the back of his neck, the buoyancy in his brain, the way his mouth involuntarily curves upwards. Surprising himself, he performs a quick somersault in the cramped cabin.

He's feeling good about himself, he realises in awe.

He doesn't know how this is going to work – *if* this is going to work – but he feels a renewed sense of purpose. It is something Thomas Major is unused to. The feeling that he is *needed*. That he could actually help someone. The Iridium phone buzzes. Thomas picks it up, almost breathless, and shouts, 'Hello! This is *Shednik-1!*'

There's a pause and Director Baumann says, 'Ah. Thomas?'

'Of course!' yells Thomas. 'Who were you expecting? Buck Rogers?'

'Have you been on the nitrous oxide?' says Director Baumann suspiciously.

'We have nitrous oxide?'

'Yes. As an oxidiser for the landing pod's rocket thrusters. Never mind. I need to speak to you. Remember I said there was good news and *other* news?'

'Yes! What's the good news?'

'What?'

'The good news. I presume the insane request to get me to sing "Space Oddity" was the *other* news. The *bad* news.'

'That was the *good* news,' says Baumann in an exasperated tone. 'This is the *other* news. It's about the comms link. We've had experts from the ESA all over it. They've found the problem. Do you remember when I told you there was a micrometeoroid shower in your vicinity?'

'Vaguely.' He can feel his good mood dissipating. 'I remember you saying it wouldn't cause me any problems.'

'Yes. Well. It did, unfortunately. It's taken out the comms dish. We think it's knocked it for six and just needs recalibrating.'

'So do it,' says Thomas.

'We can't do it remotely. You're going to have to do it.'

Thomas sighs. 'Is it in one of these instruction booklets? You know half of them are written in Russian, don't you?'

'Thomas,' says Baumann. 'You're going to have to conduct an EVA.'

Thomas says nothing. Baumann goes on, 'That means—'

'I know what it means.' *Extra-Vehicular Activity.* He looks to the window, at the inky blackness stretching out to infinity. A spacewalk. They want him to go out *there*. Just looking at it brings him out in tremors. He can almost feel the weight of the empty vacuum pressing down on him, folding him into nothingness. He imagines himself, floating off into the blackness, watching the spaceship recede to a tiny dot before blinking out for ever. He will be buggered if he's going out there.

'If you think I'm doing this you're insane,' says Thomas, just before he slams down the phone. 'Director Baumann, you can take your EVA and stick it right up your shiny, corporate arse.'

✳ 26 ✳

THE BEATING HEART OF MULTICULTURAL WIGAN

Ellie's favourite job at the burger place is working the grill. There's a rhythm she gets into that almost makes her feel disassociated from her own body, a mechanical process that allows her mind to wander even as she's slapping down double rows of frozen beef patties then flipping the burgers that are already on the grill, scraping the fat and burnt meat from the next section of the hot plate, sprinkling salt and onions, flipping the half-cooked beef as the timer flashes, then laying down another row and sliding the row of patties that are ready on to the waiting buns.

She can do this all day, hunched over the grill, surrendering to the automation of her own body in concert with the rest of the finely tuned equipment in the busy kitchen. And it's hard work as well; by the end of a shift the muscles in her forearms are bulging and sore.

Ellie's least favourite job is working the tills, especially at night when groups of men weaving between pubs stop off for some sustenance to soak up their beer, jostling at the counter, making lewd gestures, asking her what size her buns are. Company policy is that staff are not allowed to answer back, and in the evenings a security guard is stationed in the restaurant, keeping a watchful eye for high spirits spilling over into something more serious, but usually turning away from what he evidently considers harmless banter.

Somewhere between is what's grandly called on the staff rota 'lobby hosting', and that's what Ellie finds herself marked up for as she starts her evening shift. The job always puts Ellie in mind of well-groomed men with Poirot moustaches standing attentively in the foyers of posh hotels, but it's nothing like that. It's generally just emptying tables of the piles of half-empty drinks cups and crushed cardboard burger boxes, wiping down the smears of sauce and abandoned pickles from the Formica surfaces. She gets to hide in the toilets sometimes, under the pretence of filling up the tissue or soap dispensers, and can stretch out a trip to the storeroom for black bin liners or drinks straws for half an hour.

The problem with lobby hosting is the anxiety she feels constantly while working the tills – that she'll see someone she knows; specifically, someone from school. As with the convenience store job, Ellie has lied about her age to work at the burger place, using the same pile of forged documents James made on the computer. Her third job, spot-welding wire shopping baskets in an industrial unit where she's paid cash in hand along with the dozen or so assorted people who turn up every Sunday for a ten-hour shift, has never asked for proof of age and she's never volunteered it. She doubts the motley workforce is even on the official books of the unshaven man who always has a self-rolled cigarette dangling from his dry lips. He only seems to possess one T-shirt which he wears in all weathers and which has a crude drawing of a naked woman on it and the word HOOTERS. But she lives in constant fear of someone from school – especially a teacher – spotting her working behind the tills. She can't afford to lose her job – especially not now.

Ellie is rubbing at a stubborn stain of dried ketchup on one of the upstairs tables and thinking about Major Tom. If she had time to stop and consider it properly, she might think how weird it all was. But she hasn't got time. Between her three jobs, trying to stay awake in school, looking after James and Nan . . . how does she have time for anything but keeping moving? She once saw something on TV about sharks and how if they stop swimming they drown. That's what Ellie feels like. If she stops, she'll drown. They all will. She jumps at a light tap on her shoulder.

'Hello. I thought it was you.'

It's Delil. He's wearing a burgundy V-neck jumper over a crumpled shirt, and skinny black jeans. He actually looks kind of cool out of his school uniform, though she guesses that's more by accident than design. Just as Delil's smile starts to falter she gives him a tired one back and says, 'Oh. Hiya.'

Delil has a tray of food debris in his hand. He looks around the almost deserted top floor and says, 'I didn't know you worked here. I didn't know we were old enough to get jobs here. Do you think they'll give me a job?'

'No,' says Ellie brusquely and returns her attention to the ketchup stain. He still stands there expectantly and she turns back to him and says quietly, 'I'm not supposed to be here. Please don't tell anyone.'

Delil nods and taps the side of his nose with a long finger. 'Safe.' He looks around again but makes no sign of moving. 'Have you read much of *Anna Karenina* yet?'

Ellie narrows her eyes. 'Has Miss Barber asked you to check up on me?' Even as the words leave her mouth she realises how crazy it sounds.

Delil's eyes blink behind his glasses. 'What? Why would she do that? I just wondered if you'd read it. I'm quite enjoying it. Do you not read much?'

'I . . . well, I love reading,' says Ellie, feeling disarmed and on the back foot. 'I just don't get as much time as I'd want to. Do you like it, then? *Anna Karenina*?'

'It's great. I love reading, me.' He puts his head on one side and considers her for a moment. 'You look surprised.'

'Well. It's just . . . well, not many people in that class pay much attention. And you don't say much to anybody.'

Delil shrugs. 'I open my mouth and somebody usually jumps down my throat. When you look like me it's best to not stick out too much. That's one thing I have learned at school. We're not exactly what you might call the beating heart of multicultural Wigan, are we?'

Ellie gives a little laugh despite herself. 'Where'd you get that from?'

'The *Guardian*. I read it every day. Quite fancy being a journalist when I leave school. Or maybe write a book myself.'

'Oh,' says Ellie. 'Bit creative, are you?' She takes the tray from him and puts it on the table.

'Thanks. We all are in our family. My brother Ferdi's in a grime crew. He MCs. They're doing a big party in town next weekend.'

'I'm impressed.'

Delil looks at his watch. 'I've got to go. Here.' He tears a corner off one of the burger boxes and scrawls something on it with a pencil he fishes out of the pocket of his shirt, hidden behind his jumper.

Ellie takes it. 'What is it?'

'My number, stupid. I don't expect you to actually talk to me at school, but give me a call.'

'What for?'

'Well, one, we still have this project to do. To be honest, I've done most of it. But I thought you might want to at least show willing. Two, so I can give you details of the party my brother's playing at,' says Delil as though talking to a child. 'See you.'

Ellie watches him head towards the stairs, and looks down at the number, shaking her head. What just happened? She screws the piece of cardboard up and tosses it on the tray, then heads towards the nearest rubbish bin.

NOBODY ELSE HERE

'Is that Major Tom?' says James.

'There isn't anyone else here, you do realise that? And you don't have to call me Major Tom all the time. In fact, I'd prefer it if you didn't. I'm not actually a Major. My name's Thomas.'

'Oh.' Nan is dozing in her chair and he's copied Major Tom's number into his own pay-as-you-go phone – an old Nokia, handed down from Ellie. Something else for him to get bullied about at school. 'I like calling you Major Tom, though.'

'You know it's from a song, don't you?'

'Yes,' says James. 'That guy who died last year.'

'*That guy?*' says Thomas, his voice dripping with what James imagines is contempt. 'That guy? You mean David Bowie, one of the greatest musical geniuses that Britain has ever produced?'

'Yeah. Him. He sung "Major Tom", didn't he?'

The sigh echoes down the connection. 'It's not called "Major Tom". It's called "Space Oddity". It's not that difficult a concept to get your head around.'

'Fine!' shouts James. Nan grumbles in her sleep and starts to drool. 'Fine. I only called to say thanks for saying you'll help me with the science experiment. I don't know why you have to be so cranky.'

There's a silence so long that James thinks the connection has been lost, but eventually Thomas says, 'All right. Well. Thank you for calling. It's polite of you. Not many kids your age are polite. In fact, most of them are little sodding nightmares, in my experience.'

'And have you got much experience of ten-year-old kids?'

'Not since . . . not since my brother. Well, no. As it happens. Not recently.'

James takes a breath. 'Well, you're probably right anyway. Most of them are sodding nightmares. Especially the ones at my school.'

'Are they giving you trouble?' asks Thomas. 'Do you get bullied?'

'I'm fine!' shouts James. 'If you're just going to go on and on like a bloody adult we don't have to even bother with this!'

'I am an adult!' shouts Thomas back. 'And watch your language!'

'You're not a bloody adult! You're a bloody astronaut!' says Thomas. 'Adults do boring stuff like go to bloody work and have no time for you and then get sent to jail like bloody idiots! You get to go to bloody Mars!'

'Stop saying *bloody* or the deal's off, you foul-mouthed little wretch!' shouts Thomas.

'Fine!' James takes a deep breath. 'So how are you going to help me win this competition?'

'Well, I can't actually *help* you win, you know that? I can't do it for you. You've got to do it yourself or it's cheating.'

'So what's the point?' wails James. 'I can't come up with an experiment that's going to wow the judges by myself. I'm nobody.'

'Surely they wouldn't have asked you to enter if they didn't think you could do it,' points out Thomas.

'It's because we're disadvantaged. That's why I get to go to the final. It makes the school look good. That's what everybody thinks.'

'Hmm.'

'What does *hmm* mean?'

'It means *hmm*,' says Thomas. 'Which means, I don't know how we're actually going to do this unless you actually do some work yourself. What sort of thing were you thinking you might do?'

'I don't know! I don't know anything! I just want to do something big! Dramatic!'

'OK. Right. What's your house number?'

'What? Why?'

'Because I'm coming round for dinner! Just tell me your house number.'

'19.'

'OK, what element has the atomic number 19?'

'What? Oh, God . . . Argon?'

'Not bad. Close,' says Thomas. 'That's 18. So the element with the atomic number 19, which is the number of your house, is potassium.'

'Great,' sighs James. 'That's me first place in the contest, then, no problem.'

'Stop whining. Now, tell me what happens if you put potassium in water.'

'How the bloody hell should I know?'

'Don't they teach you anything at school?' shouts Thomas. 'And enough with the bloody! Seriously!'

'I still don't know. What's that got to do with anything, anyway?'

'I just want to see how much you know and where we're starting from,' says Thomas. 'What do you know about potassium?'

James wipes his nose with the back of his hand. He does remember something about potassium. 'Is it an alkali?' he ventures.

'An alkali metal. Very good,' says Thomas. 'What else?'

'It's got one electron. Which . . . which it can give up easily. I remember now. It, what do you call it, oxidises quickly.'

'See, you do know. Very good. Here endeth the lesson.'

James frowns. 'Is that it? What's the point of that?'

'That's it for now,' says Thomas. 'And the point is to get you thinking. Thinking about *reactions*. Because that's what science is all about – reactions. How one thing and another thing combine to make something else, one way or another. What you've got to work out now is what reaction you want to create, why you want to do it, and how it's going to happen.'

'Can't you just tell me what to do?' pleads James.

'No, I can't,' says Thomas. 'And now I've got to go. Call me again tomorrow when you've thought about it some more. Isn't it time you were in bed, anyway? Where's everyone else?'

'Ellie's working and Nan's asleep. I can call you tomorrow?'

'Yes. If you've got something to say. Now go to bed. Over and out.'

'Over and bloody out,' says James, and quickly presses the button to end the call.

28

CAN'T SLEEP NIGHTS

Gladys shouldn't have had a sleep because now she's wide awake, sitting in her chair and wearing two cardigans because Ellie says they have to save money and not put the heating on or the fire if they can help it, even though it's the depths of winter. Gladys contemplates putting just one bar on the fire, but it makes a racket when it's warming up and Ellie has only been in bed half an hour, though she looked exhausted after her shift. It's gone midnight and Gladys wonders what the spaceman is doing. She supposes he'll have to go to sleep sometime, like everyone else, but if he's up there on his own, who'll be driving the spaceship? Maybe he just parks it up for a bit while he has a nap. On one of those asteroids or something.

She's flicking through the telly channels looking for something that might send her off when she hears the creak of footsteps on the stairs.

'I haven't got the fire on,' she calls out. 'Though God knows it's cold enough to freeze the doo-dahs off a brass monkey in here.'

But it isn't Ellie who emerges from the staircase, it's James, his hair sticking up and his eyes heavy, dragging a fleece blanket with him.

'I can't sleep.' He stifles a yawn.

'Come here, I'll hutch up a bit.' Gladys pats the cushion of her chair. James climbs on with her, throwing the thin blanket over both of them. 'Now, what's to do?'

James yawns again. 'I just can't sleep.'

'You can't fool me. I know there's something up. Usually I could peg you out on the washing line and you'd go to sleep. What's to do? Is it those bad lads again?'

James nods and looks miserably at the telly. 'What's this film?'

Gladys squints at the screen. 'Ooh, *Taxi Driver*. I've not seen this for years. I went to the pictures with your Granddad Bill watching this. Your dad was only a babby. Bill's sister minded him while we went. First time we'd been out since he was born. He cried all night. Colic.'

James watches the car pull away in the opening shot, leaving a cloud of exhaust fumes and the title of the film. 'Who's that?' he asks of the dark-haired man with the nose. 'Is he the taxi driver?'

'That's Robert De Niro. He *was* handsome.'

'He looks like the dad in *Meet The Fockers*,' says James. 'But younger.'

'I'm not sure you should be watching films called that,' says Gladys, scandalised. 'Did you watch it on the internet?'

So whaddya wanna hack for, Bickle? says the guy with the moustache and glasses.

I can't sleep nights, says Robert De Niro.

'Just like you!' says Gladys giving James a hug.

'Is it just about a guy driving a taxi? It doesn't sound very exciting.'

'Oh, it is,' says Gladys, then sucks her teeth. 'Not really one for kiddies, though. He doesn't like what he sees so he starts to shoot people, robbers and stuff. He's a, what you call it, a vigilante.'

'Like Batman? Does he wear a mask?'

Gladys ponders. 'No. No, I don't think he wears a mask. He gets a haircut, though.'

'Vigilantes should really wear masks,' says James. 'What's he called? Does he have a cool name?'

'Not really. He's called Travis Bickle.'

James yawns. 'That's a funny name. I wish I had a Travis Bickle, though. Sort those idiots out at school. They found out today about the science competition. They say I'm only in the final because I'm a scumbag.'

'They're the scum,' says Gladys. 'Someday a real rain will come and wash all this scum off the streets.' She closes one eye and points her fingers at the telly. 'Pshoo! Pshoo!'

James watches the screen for a bit, but his eyes start to droop. 'Come on,' says Gladys. 'Bed. If you're going to win this contest you need your sleep.'

James gives her a sleepy kiss on her cheek and drags his blanket back upstairs. Gladys watches the film for a while longer, until Travis Bickle says *I got some bad ideas in my head*, then she takes herself thoughtfully off to bed.

29

SLOUGH, WE HAVE A PROBLEM

Thomas is pondering over his crossword. *If put off, can encourage angina, say – proverbially.* The rest of the grid is filling up nicely but he'll be buggered if he can work this one out. Come on, come on. Four bloody letters. That's all. Four letters. Encourage angina. Proverbially. He screws up his face. Four. Letters.

There's an unfamiliar sound from the computer, and when he waggles his finger on the mousepad a grainy, jerky image appears on the screen. Mission Control. Baumann and Claudia, with the rows of technicians behind them. There's a half-hearted cheer which Thomas suspects only happens because people think that's what's expected of Mission Control whenever anything goes vaguely right. They've watched too many movies.

A mess of pixels resolves itself into Baumann's face. Thomas hides his crossword book in its Velcroed pocket and says, 'Ah, so you've fixed the comms dish from there, then? No need for the spacewalk. Some good news at last.'

'No, we haven't,' says Baumann crossly, his mouth not in sync with his words, like a badly dubbed foreign film. 'We're Skyping you.'

Thomas nods. 'I wondered when you'd come up with that idea.'

Baumann looks at Claudia then back at the camera. 'What? You knew we could Skype you but didn't say anything?'

Thomas shrugs. 'Stands to reason. I've still got internet connection, presumably on the same comms link the Iridium phone is using. It did occur to me but I didn't bother mentioning it as you have the finest minds of BriSpA working for you so I imagined someone would have already thought about it and discounted it. Besides, I like using the telephone. It means I don't have to look at you.'

Baumann straightens his tie. 'Um. Well. We have thought of it now. But it's only an interim measure, because you're going to be out of range in' – he consults his clipboard – 'maybe two weeks, maybe less. So you're going to have to do the EVA. Thomas, I can't stress the importance enough of this. This is a three-line whip. It's of utmost urgency. You're going to lose contact with us . . . with Earth. If something happens out there, we won't be able to do anything about it. There's a network of satellites in orbit around Mars and you could piggy-back on them when you make Mars orbit but that would leave a rather large six-month hole in communications. It's simply vital. You're going to have to do it.'

'No.'

'Yes.'

'Sod off,' says Thomas. 'I'm not going out there.'

Claudia elbows Baumann out of the way. 'For God's sake, you're like a couple of children in the playground.'

Thomas leans forward to scrutinise the screen. There's something different about her since the last time they had a video link. He says, 'Have you done something to your hair . . .?'

Claudia pauses and self-consciously pats at her head. 'Er, yes, I had it cut yesterday, in fact. I wouldn't have thought you'd have . . . Do you like it . . .?'

Then it's Baumann's turn to push Claudia back. His eyebrows are doing overtime. 'What is this? A bloody coffee advert or something?'

Claudia raises an eyebrow and Thomas, despite himself, smiles. Is that a little jealousy he's detecting in Director Baumann? How interesting. So he's holding a torch for Claudia. Feeling suddenly mischievous, he says, 'I do like it. It suits you. Have you had it coloured as well?'

'For God's sake.' Baumann's eyebrows waggle some more. 'Claudia, tell him the news.'

'Tell me what news?' says Thomas, narrowing his eyes.

Claudia looks at her iPad. 'We're informing the media you're going to do a spacewalk over the next week. We've told them that there's a problem. Ramped up the drama a little bit. It's all going to be very exciting publicity.'

'Well you can bloody well un-tell them. I'm not doing it for anybody.'

Baumann fiddles with his tie again. 'Thomas . . . do you want the world to think you're a . . . *coward?*'

Thomas almost laughs. 'This isn't *Back to the Future* and I'm not Marty McFly. That's not going to work on me. Because, as it happens, yes, I am. A coward. It's how I got where I am today.'

Thomas just has time to see Baumann looking quizzically at Claudia and saying '*Back to the Future?*' before he clicks off the window and kills the link.

'Hello, Major Tom.'

'Hello, Gladys,' says Thomas, cradling the phone receiver between ear and shoulder. 'You're not lost again, are you?'

'No more than usual. Anyway, I've been wondering. When you go to sleep, where do you park the spaceship?'

'Park it?' says Thomas. 'It's not a bloody camper van, you know. They don't have lay-bys in space. It just keeps going. It's not going to stop until I make Mars orbit in two hundred days.'

'Right,' says Gladys. 'I was just thinking about it. Have you had your dinner yet?'

'I've squeezed some gunk from a tube into my mouth, so yes, I suppose I have.' He feels like he should reciprocate. 'Have you?'

'I can't remember! But I could really go chips, pea wet and scratchings.'

'The only thing I understood in that sentence was chips. What the blazes is *pea wet*?'

'It's the juice from peas,' says Gladys as though he's stupid. 'And scratchings are bits of fish batter. The best thing is, you pay for the chips and you get the pea wet and scratchings for free. It's lovely. You should try it.'

'I probably won't get the chance now, unless the catering team who put my supplies together happen to be from Wigan.'

'Well, I'd better be off,' says Gladys.

'Wait . . . I don't suppose you're any good at crosswords, are you?'

'Crosswords . . . I do like a good puzzle. Use to buy a puzzle book for my holidays every year. Sat on the beach at Southport once, couldn't see the sea, tide goes right out there. It was drizzling. Got the page all wet.'

'Lovely,' says Thomas. 'Anyway, four letters, *If put off, can encourage angina, say – proverbially.* I'm not actually holding out any hope but, you know, maybe your mind works differently . . .'

'Reminds me of Sunday School, that. We used to walk at Whitsun. My mam always made me a dress and a little bag for people to put pennies in when you walked past. My Bill died of a heart attack, you know.'

'Right,' says Thomas. 'I hope you don't think me rude when I say I wish I'd never asked.'

'You *are* rude. Very rude. But you're helping James, so that's a nice thing. That reminds me. I know he's only ten but he should really be thinking about the future. I think he'd be a dead good spaceman, like you. Can you put a word in for him?'

'Well, not really. It doesn't work like that. It's not like getting a job for someone at the local factory or something.'

'Oh, that's a shame,' says Gladys. 'I think that would have given him something to look forward to. But he's good with the science stuff. If he wins this competition, might they give him a job then?'

'Well, maybe when he's older.'

'How did you get to be a spaceman?'

'The man who was supposed to go had a heart attack.'

'Well I never. So it is a business of Dead Man's Shoes. Just like a factory. You said it wasn't. But there must have been something else. They wouldn't let any old Tom, Dick or Harry just go to space. There must be another reason.'

'Funnily enough, there was,' says Thomas.

✳ 30 ✳

PRIMARY OBJECTIVE

Before Thomas could be properly presented to the media again following the rather disastrous press conference – well, disastrous for Terence Bradley, at the very least – there were more SOMBRERO meetings in a shorter space of time than anyone at BriSpA could ever remember having before.

119

'The thing is,' said Director Baumann at one of these meetings, 'we still need to justify Major, not just to the press but also to the shareholders and backers. And Star City in Russia is asking what kind of experience he has had prior to starting training. Does he have any flying hours at all?'

The Employee Engagement Officer looks over her notes and says, 'Only on Ryanair, to be honest.'

Baumann perks up. 'He's flown for commercial airlines?'

'No,' she says. 'He went on holiday once. Hated it, by all accounts.'

Baumann rubs his temples. He's been doing that a lot lately. He wonders if he's about to have a brain haemorrhage. At least that would get him out of this mess.

'There must be something,' says Claudia. 'Something we can slot into the PR narrative that chimes with our mission objectives.'

There's a brief silence and then Employee Engagement says, 'There might be one other thing. What's his primary objective on Mars?'

'Aside from being weirdly fanciable?' Baumann can feel his temples bulging again. He is starting to hate Thomas Major. Really, really hate him. He wonders how he would feel if the *Ares-1* hit an asteroid or just blew up. Is there some kind of self-destruct mechanism? Some red button in Mission Control. He wonders if he could get away with pressing it.

Claudia says, 'Calm down, Bob. I really think you should leave this. You're beginning to sound mildly obsessed. Are you sure you don't have some suppressed feelings you need to talk through . . .?'

Baumann has a sudden vision of Claudia wearing stockings and a basque, beckoning him towards a bed in a dimly lit room he's pretty sure is in a Travelodge. He pushes it away – perhaps to examine in more detail when he's alone – and says, 'OK. Major's primary objective on Mars is to prepare the landing site for the eventual manned missions that will travel to the planet sometime in the next decade.'

Claudia taps her nails on the table. 'Well, that's something that will chime quite well with the public. Major is the great pioneer, the settler. He's being parachuted into this harsh environment, where no human being has set foot before, to pave the way for the eventual colonisation of Mars by Earth. There's something of the . . . Old West about that, right?'

'Clint bloody Eastwood is he now?' mutters Baumann.

Employee Engagement shakes her head. 'Yes, yes, but he doesn't have that background, does he? He's not exactly Bear Grylls. I'm sure there was something in his files that rung a bit of a bell with me . . . Director, what will his main tasks be?'

'Setting up a series of interconnected habitation modules, planting and tending a variety of plants and crops, conducting some experiments, monitoring and logging weather patterns, and organising the installation of an irrigation network to pump fresh water in and waste out of the habs.' Baumann grimaces. 'More Bob the Builder than Clint Eastwood, really.'

'There,' says Employee Engagement. 'That last one. That's where we're in luck.'

'Irrigation?' says Baumann. The throbbing in his temple subsides. 'Really? He has experience?'

'He spent a summer digging ditches for the water board,' she says, scanning her notes. She looks up. 'Close enough for me, to be quite honest.'

* 31 *

SUMMER 1988

The day after Peter's funeral Thomas meets Laura in the Dreadnought, on the banks of the Thames. It's a surprisingly sunny day, dry enough for the students, bikers and outsiders who frequent the pub to sit outside, leather jackets splayed out on the damp grass as makeshift blankets. Thomas and Laura sit at a table, sipping snakebite and black. She wears black Dr. Marten boots, striped black and white tights, and a paisley vest over a purple bra. Thomas looks at her for a long moment.

'You've coloured your hair.'

She tugs at her bangs. 'Just a darker shade of pink. How was it?'

Thomas shrugs. 'As you'd expect. You could have come.'

It hangs in their air between them. Thomas says *you could have come* but what he means, and what Laura hears, is you *should* have come.

She looks away, at the people on the grass. 'It was for the family. You needed to be looking after your mum. Not looking after me.'

Through the speakers fixed to the outside wall of the pub a howling guitar rages over a thudding garage beat. Laura starts to rock side to side. 'I love this.'

Thomas frowns. He's never heard this song. How does she know it? 'Who is it?'

'Nirvana,' says Laura, closing her eyes. 'It's called "Love Buzz". They're from Seattle. The lead singer's a bit dreamy.'

They have tickets to go to the Reading Festival in late August. Iggy Pop is playing, and the Ramones. Thomas and Laura have been listening to his LPs in his room, kissing urgently, Thomas's hands burrowing under the layers of vests and T-shirts that Laura always wears, until she gently pushes his hands away. 'Not here,' she always says. 'Not at your mum's.'

There is always Leeds, looming on the horizon for them in autumn. Leeds, when they will be together. Leeds, where Thomas's roaming hands will not be stayed by the presence of his mother in the living room. Or rather, there *was* Leeds. He is about to speak when two students come over, shaking a bucket. 'We're raising money for the families of the Piper Alpha disaster.' Thomas digs into his pocket and pops a twenty-pence piece in the bucket.

'Mum wants me to stay at home for another year,' Thomas blurts out when they've gone, because there's no other way to broach it. 'Now she's on her own. With Dad gone, and Peter . . .'

'I understand,' nods Laura, her eyes still closed, as though the music is just as important as what Thomas is saying, as though it's more important.

'I've been on to Leeds,' says Thomas. 'I can defer for a year. Just do the course next September instead.' He pauses and bites his lip. 'They say you can, too. Defer.'

She looks at him now, her eyes flashing momentarily. 'What? You asked them about me deferring for a year?'

Thomas nods. 'I thought . . . well, we'd want to go together . . . it's just a year. We could have fun, yeah? Maybe get jobs.'

'I love you, Thomas,' says Laura.

'I feel a *but* coming.'

'I need to get out of Reading. I thought you did too. I thought us going to Leeds was going to be perfect, us, together, no families. A whole new place. An adventure.'

'It can still be an adventure,' presses Thomas. 'Just next year . . .'

Laura looks away again. She sips her snakebite. 'I don't want to defer, Thomas. And I know you've been going through hell so I'm not going to have a row with you but you had absolutely no right to ring Leeds and even talk to them about me. It's nothing to do with you at all.'

'Have you met someone else?'

She frowns, and smiles, and touches his cheek with the palm of her hand. 'No. Of course not, silly! But I want to meet someone else. I want to meet *me*. And I don't think I can do that in Reading. I need to go. And I need to go now.'

'So you're going to Leeds? This year?' says Thomas numbly.

Laura gives the minutest of shrugs. 'Yes.'

He looks at his pint. 'But we can still see each other? You can come home at weekends? I can come up there on the train?'

'Course,' says Laura, sounding to Thomas as though she's agreeing to something vague that will never happen. She finishes her pint. 'Right. I need to get off. I'll give you a call, right?'

Thomas feels as though the ground is shaking and cracking, fissures are opening up and that everything is falling into them, the tables and leather jackets and students and pints. He tries to scrabble for purchase but can't find any. Only Laura seems unaffected, unmoved. He says, his voice sounding tinny and faraway, 'Where do you need to be?'

She leans forward and gives him a chaste kiss on the cheek, throwing her bag, the black cloth one inlaid with a hundred shards of Rajasthani mirror, over her shoulder. 'It's you. You need to be with your mum, remember? I'll call you.'

He watches her walk away before letting himself fall into the black hole beneath his feet.

✳ 32 ✳

TO BOLDLY STAY

In August there are plenty of black holes beneath Thomas's feet as he gets a job with the water board. It will be another year before Margaret Thatcher privatises the regional water authorities and they are hived off into a multitude of suppliers providing the same water through the same pipes. For now, Thomas is a public servant, albeit one as far down the chain as possible, a casual worker assigned to a gang of men who dig trenches along the roads, repair leaks and patch up pipes, then fill the trenches in again. Thomas's role largely involves pushing wheelbarrows full of hardcore and dirt to and from the repair sites. Sometimes he gets to operate the stop-go sign on busy roads, which gives him a feeling of power hitherto missing from his life. The rest of the gang, a mixture of veteran water board workers, other casuals and the occasional clipboard-carrying supervisor, christen him Spock as soon as they get a whiff of his intelligence and plans to go to university.

Over the summer and into the autumn, Thomas finds his body changing, toughening up, becoming leaner and more toned as he works through all weathers and becomes adept at handling a pick, digging into tarmac and hard earth.

'Who do you fancy to win the league, Spock?' asks a wiry man with a leathery face who Thomas knows only as St Ivel – because he is guaranteed to either start a fight or get off with a woman after five pints of beer.

Thomas has no idea which league St Ivel is even talking about. He hazards a guess. 'Erm. Spurs?'

124

St Ivel nods thoughtfully as though this is a serious consideration, for which Thomas is grateful. He takes a sip of tea from the plastic cup of his flask. 'You'd like to think so after what they paid for Stewart from Man City. But I've got my eye on Arsenal after Spurs at the weekend.'

Thomas shrugs noncommittally. 'Well, it's early days yet,' he says, praying that's the right thing to say.

'Yup,' says St Ivel, tossing the dregs of his tea in the gutter and screwing the lid back on his flask. 'I'm even thinking of putting a fiver on Chelsea to go up to the First Division this year. What do you reckon?'

Thomas hefts his pick. 'Well, I reckon that'd probably be a good bet.'

St Ivel narrows his eyes. 'Right. Well. I will. But if they don't go up you'll owe me a fiver.' He shakes his flask. 'I'm out of tea. Spock, go and get some brews in from that caff over the road. Come on, you might be Mr Clever where you come from but here you're the bottom of the heap, son.'

By the following May Thomas is no longer working for the water board as all casuals have been laid off prior to the impending privatisation. His mum has reluctantly accepted that Thomas is going to university in September. However, he is not going to Leeds, and declines his deferred place. Thomas is gratified to learn that Chelsea do indeed get promoted.

He has not seen, or spoken to, Laura since she left for the north. The night before her father drove her to Yorkshire, they make quiet, unremarkable love in his bed. It is, he knows even as he gasps and comes and collapses on her, a farewell shag. The next morning she says she will send him a letter as soon as she is settled.

No letters ever come.

Because of his lateness in applying, Thomas has very few options when it comes to choosing where to attend university. He wants somewhere he can go and hide, study chemistry, and not think about Laura. In fact, he wants to be as far from Leeds, and Laura, as possible. He comes home from work one day to find his mother hovering in the kitchen with brochures. For the University of Reading.

'I know you wanted to go away,' she says. 'But I was thinking . . . you could still live at home if you went to Reading. Or, if you wanted to live in halls, you could come home at weekends. Some evenings, even.'

He looks dully at the brochures. 'I don't even know if they do chemical engineering.'

'They do. I phoned them today.'

Thomas exhales sharply in what might be a laugh. Oh, the irony. Is this his punishment for daring to call Leeds about Laura deferring? She was right. It's not very nice when someone takes control of your destiny.

Unlike Laura, though, Thomas merely nods. 'Yes, I'll give them a call.'

And a week later he has a place.

Before he finishes at the water board, the gang take him and the other laid-off casuals out for a beer. In an uncertain world, it is some measure of comfort to Thomas that some people are true to themselves and others, and St Ivel exemplifies this like nobody else.

Thomas, his tongue loosened and his head fuzzied with beer, doesn't even know what he's said to offend him, but he evidently has said something, as no sooner has he swallowed the last mouthful of his fifth pint of lager, than St Ivel punches him solidly in the face.

'No hard feelings, Spock,' says St Ivel as Thomas sits heavily on the floor, blood running down his shirt. 'And it's your round if I'm not mistaken.'

☆ **33** ☆

THE DOORBELL

Ellie has no work this evening, which is both alarming – as every penny counts at the moment – and a source of guilty pleasure. She is exhausted and is looking forward to sitting on the sofa and doing nothing, perhaps even picking up *Anna Karenina* and getting on with what she's supposed to be doing – schoolwork. In fact, what she wants to be doing is what all her friends will be doing: avoiding homework and just vegging out in front of *Coronation Street,* and then talking about it on social media. She wants to be thinking about clothes and boys and make-up and Netflix and friends. What she doesn't want to be thinking about is the impending eviction of the Ormerod family. She needs a plan, but she can't wrap her head around one, not yet. Give it a week. See how James is going with this science competition. See if they win the lottery. See if Nan has a period when she's actually lucid enough to contact the bank and try to get the money back that she's sent to these scammers. But Ellie has been looking into it and knows it's unlikely without the involvement of the police. And if they go down *that* road, then the break-up of the family will only be quicker. The first thing the police will do is get the social services snoopers in.

'Ellie,' says James, running downstairs. 'I need some potassium.'

'Have a banana.' She is curled up on the sofa, her book open, pages down on her lap. Nan is watching some sit-com or other, but not laughing, rather staring at it intently as though it's some kind of anthropological documentary she must study. Ellie has relented and allowed the heating to be put on for an hour, just to warm the house through.

'Not that sort of potassium,' says James, then pauses, his hands on the back of the sofa. 'Actually, I suppose it is that sort of potassium. But not in that form. Can you get some?'

'Where do I get it? Can I get it at Aldi?'

'Jesus, Ellie. You'll have to get it from school. We don't have any at ours. I've asked. They'll have it at big schools though. You might have to nick it from the science block.'

'Neither a borrower nor a lender be,' pipes up Nan, not taking her eyes from the screen.

'That's a bit rich coming from her,' mutters James.

'I'm not nicking anything from school.' Ellie turns her book right way up. *All happy families are alike, but all bug-fuck stupid dysfunctional families are bug-fuck stupid dysfunctional in their own way.*

'So you won't get me any potassium?' says James. 'It's for my experiment. Don't you want me to win to get us out of the crap?'

'Language, James,' says Nan.

'Crappity-crap.'

'Give it a rest,' sighs Ellie.

James leans over the sofa and snatches at her book. Ellie growls at him and gives chase, James screeching with laughter and running round the sofa, diving into the kitchen where Ellie corners him by the fridge.

The bing-bong of the doorbell sounds. James and Ellie look at each other for a moment, then Nan calls, 'I'll get it!'

'Shit,' says Ellie. James pushes the book into her hands and they both fight to get out of the kitchen and into the living room. Every time that doorbell rings Ellie feels her heart miss a beat, feels the colour drain out of her face.

It's the social services.

It's a teacher come to check up on her.

It's someone who's seen Nan wandering about the streets.

It's any number of people who can bring their world crashing down around them.

Nan's already at the door, turning back to them with a foreboding look on her face.

'It's for you, Ellie.'

'Oh God.' Is Nan together enough for the Ormerods to pass themselves off as exactly what they claim to be?

'There's a lad at the door,' says Nan. 'And—'

'And what?' says James.

Nan makes an exaggerated effort to enunciate the words without actually saying them, writhing her lips and tongue until she's pretty sure she's got her message across through a hybrid of pantomime and mouthing.

HE'S. BLACK.

WHAT? mouths James back.

Nan rubs her hands over her cheeks, as though putting on moisturiser. BLACK. HE. IS. BLACK.

'I think she's saying it's Jack,' says James to Ellie. 'Do you know a Jack?'

Ellie edges round the sofa to the door, gently moving Nan to one side. Nan's shoulders slump and she says loudly, 'For God's sake, what's wrong with you two? I'm trying to tell you there's a boy at the door for Ellie—'

Ellie pulls open the door again to see Delil on the doorstep, in his school uniform and leaning against a pedal bike, an old racer with dropped, curved handlebars and thin wheels.

'Hiya,' he says, smiling broadly.

'—and he's black,' finishes Nan loudly. 'He's a darkie.'

✳ 34 ✳

WHERE JULIE ORMEROD WENT

'I am so sorry,' says Ellie for the fifteenth time. Her, Delil and James are sitting around the tiny kitchen table drinking supermarket-own-brand cola. Gladys has been banished to the living room with strict instructions to sit and watch telly and not interrupt them under any circumstances.

'It's safe.' Delil looks around the kitchen. 'I've had worse.'

'She's old,' says James. 'And a bit . . .' He waggles his forefinger around his temple.

Ellie glares at her brother. 'James. Don't say that.'

'It's true,' protests James, then he says, 'Ow,' when Ellie kicks him under the table.

'She's a woman of her generation,' shrugs Delil. 'They didn't have many ethnic minorities in Wigan when she was growing up. I've looked at the demographics. There weren't many black faces in Wigan even in the 1980s. Apart from the market traders.'

'Do you read demographics for fun, then?' says James.

Delil shrugs and glances at Ellie. 'We did it in geography before Christmas. Don't you remember?'

Ellie says, 'So . . . what are you actually doing here?'

Delil slides a piece of paper across the table at her. 'My phone number. So you can call me about the party next week. I saw you accidentally screw up my number and throw it in the bin at the burger joint.'

Ellie's face reddens and James stares at her. 'You're going to a party?'

'My brother Ferdi's MCing,' says Delil. 'He's very good. I think you're a bit young to come though.'

'I'm not going to any party. But how did you know where I live?' Her face turns to a scowl. 'You didn't follow me home, did you?'

Delil laughs, a deep, rich sound. 'Oh, God, no, nothing like that. I got your address from the school office files.'

Ellie blinks. 'What? You broke into the school office just to get my address?'

'Nah,' says Delil, taking a swig of cola. He burps and winks at James. 'I work there some lunchtimes. Filing and stuff.'

Ellie pulls a face. 'Work there? At the lunch break.'

Delil nods enthusiastically. 'If you've noticed me at all in class, which you obviously haven't, you might also have realised that you never see me around at break or lunch. That's because I'm always doing something. I don't really have many mates at school. Well, any, in fact. So I volunteer to help out. School office, art department, English block, science labs . . . I just tidy stuff and re-organise and file stuff and hang about. It's funny what you learn. I can get pretty much anything from the files and nobody even notices I'm looking. In fact, most of the teachers forget I'm there, sometimes. You should hear the conversations I listen to.'

Ellie puts up her hand. 'Wait. You got my address from the school office. That's a bit stalkery, isn't it? What do you actually want, anyway?'

Delil shrugs. 'I don't actually know. I just wanted to see you again. Did you not feel me staring at you in English today?'

Ellie shifts uncomfortably. 'Um. What are you trying to say, Delil?'

'I don't know!' he beams. 'I think it's my hormones. They're all over the place. I was a bit of a late developer. I thought I might be gay for a while, until I realised I didn't actually fancy men. But I can't stop thinking about you.' He holds out his palms. 'So, there you have it.'

'Hang on a minute,' says James. 'Did you say you have access to the science labs?'

'Yep. I'm there tomorrow lunchtime, in fact.'

'Can you get me some potassium?'

'James!' says Ellie, shocked. 'You can't ask Delil to steal for you!'

'Sure,' says Delil nonchalantly. 'I can get you potassium. They wouldn't miss it. That science lab's chaotic. What do you want it for?'

'My experiment. I'm entering the National Schools Young Science Competition. I'm through to the final.'

Delil slaps his hand on the table. 'That sounds worthy enough. It's a deal. I'll bring it round tomorrow.'

'Wait,' says Ellie. 'I didn't say you could come round after school. In fact, I'm still angry at you for getting our address from the school office. I could report you.'

Delil sits back. 'You could, but you won't.'

Ellie glares at him. 'And how are you so sure about that, Mr Hormones?'

He finishes his glass of cola. 'I don't know for sure. But I think there's something . . . weird about this set-up. Weird enough that you don't want to draw attention to yourself.'

Ellie screws up the piece of paper that Delil has pushed across the table to her and throws it at him. It bounces off his glasses and she says, 'Get out.'

Holding up his hands in surrender, Delil scrapes his chair back and stands up.

'What about my potassium?' says James.

Delil opens the door and Gladys almost falls into the kitchen, hunched over. She looks up at him and enunciates loudly, 'I wasn't listening at the door.'

Delil raises one eyebrow at Ellie as she puts her face in her hands and mutters, 'Oh, God.'

James tugs at Ellie's sleeve. 'Is he still getting my potassium?'

Gladys straightens up and looks Delil up and down. 'WHERE ARE YOU FROM?' she shouts.

'OFF GIDLOW LANE,' shouts back Delil.

'THAT'S FUNNY!' yells Gladys slowly. 'WE HAVE A GIDLOW LANE IN THIS COUNTRY. IT'S NOT FAR FROM HERE!'

'I KNOW,' says Delil. 'THAT'S WHERE I'M FROM.'

James says, 'Nan, why are you shouting at him?'

'He's foreign. It's how you talk to them.'

'Nan, he was born in Wigan. He goes to Ellie's school. He understands you perfectly, don't you, Delil?'

'Oh,' says Gladys, at normal volume. 'Delil. What sort of name's that?'

'My grandparents came from Barbados. Back in the 1950s. They wanted to integrate so they called my mum and her brothers proper British names. But they all gave their kids old Barbadian names. Getting back to our roots and all that, I suppose. I'll probably call my children Alf and Mabel.'

Gladys laughs and says to Ellie, 'Ooh, he is funny.' She looks at Delil. 'Are you coming back?'

He puts the back of his hand to the side of his mouth and stage-whispers in a fake American accent, 'I've got a shipment of potassium coming in tomorrow, but you ain't seen me, all right?'

Nan laughs and Delil heads towards the door. At the sideboard he stops and picks up the photo of Darren and Julie. 'Is this your mum and dad?' he asks Ellie.

She looks away. 'Yes.'

'Where are they?'

Ellie says nothing. James says, 'Dad's in prison.'

'Right,' says Delil, replacing the photo frame carefully. 'That must be rough. What about your mum?'

Ellie carries the cutting with her everywhere. It is brittle and yellowed now, and every time she gets a new purse – which is not frequently – it is the first thing she transfers from her old one. She takes it out and hands it to Delil.

Mum-of-two killed by drink driver

Wigan Evening Post, July 13, 2013

A mother of two died from appalling injuries suffered when her car was hit by another motorist who jumped a red light after drinking four pints of strong lager, an inquest heard.

Julie Ormerod, 41, of Worsley Mesnes, Wigan, was driving home from her job as an administrator at a car dealership firm when the incident happened in June.

Trevor Blackman, 52, an accountant, had finished work early and gone to the pub with some colleagues before driving home. He told police in an interview following the accident that he had failed to notice that the traffic lights on Poolstock Road were on red and had continued across the carriageway.

His BMW was travelling at 43mph in a 30mph zone and he was found to be almost three times over the legal drink-drive limit.

Mrs Ormerod's Vauxhall Corsa was crushed by the impact and she was declared dead at the scene by paramedics after fire crews fought for half an hour to free her from the wreckage.

She leaves a husband, builder Darren Ormerod, and two children, Ellie, 11, and James, 6.

Wigan Coroner Howard Smith said at the inquest that Mrs Ormerod had everything to live for and had just that lunchtime been to book a family holiday to Disneyland Paris.

Blackman has been charged with causing death by dangerous driving and is due to appear at court next month.

Ellie says nothing while he reads it. He nods thoughtfully and hands it back. It is the first time she has seen him apparently lost for words. Eventually, Delil says softly, 'Not safe.'

'No,' says Ellie, walking him to the door. 'Not safe at all.'

✳ 35 ✳

IN SEARCH OF THE BLUE ANGEL

'Why were you so horrible to him?' asks James after Ellie has supervised him cleaning his teeth. He feels like he needs to go to the toilet, but has been holding it in all day. His tummy is aching a bit. He feels like he needs to do a massive trump. Which is good.

'He found our address from the school office and came here uninvited, duh,' says Ellie, leaning on the frame of the bathroom door. 'That sort of attention we can really do without.'

'He seems all right.'

'Only because he said he'd nick you some potassium. What do you want it for, anyway?'

'An experiment. Is he your boyfriend?'

'No, he is not! Even if I wanted a boyfriend, if I had time for a boyfriend, I wouldn't pick him. He's a weirdo. A stalkery weirdo.'

James wipes his face with his flannel and dries it on the towel hanging off the radiator. 'I like him.'

'Because he's nicking stuff for you,' says Ellie again, wearily. 'Now go to bed.'

Once Ellie has given him a kiss on the forehead and he hears her bed frame creaking as she climbs into it, he throws back his blankets and digs beneath his mattress for the disposable lighter he's hidden there, between the pages of a small notebook. His tummy is really hurting now, and he throws back his legs as far as he's able, sticking them up into the air. James has been saving up scraps of money all week to afford a school dinner. He could get a free lunch, but Ellie's too proud to sign them up for it. She says people would ask too many questions. So he presented his handful of coppers and ten piece pieces at the canteen and asked for the biggest plate of cabbage they could give him, which they cheerfully did, surprised by the novelty of a ten-year-old boy willingly asking for cabbage.

Of course, James has an ulterior motive. Methane. He's been stewing it and boiling it in his gut all day, praying he's generating enough for the ultimate in *flatus ignition*: the blue angel.

He looks at his notebook while he's waiting for it to boil up in his colon. His last entry was a week ago, when he managed to produce a seven centimetre flame, approximately, though not the blue colour he was looking for. Not enough foods rich in sulphur to generate methane. But he's gorged himself on cabbage, held it all in since lunchtime. His guts are in turmoil. It's like the Large Hadron Collider down there.

'Preparing to launch,' says James quietly to himself. He reaches under his raised thigh and clicks the lighter until it catches, and puts it as close as he dares to the seam of his Captain America PJ bottoms.

Reactions. That's what Major Tom said. Science is all about reactions. Chemistry is about reactions – potassium in water. Physics is about reactions – how a light comes on when you flip a switch. Even biology is about reactions – how Ellie said one thing with her mouth when he asked if Delil was her boyfriend, but the subtle physiological changes, the reddening of her cheeks, the momentary dilation of her pupils, said another. Reactions.

James feels his thumb burning, and with a gasp lets loose his gaseous load. Craning forward, he sees the lighter flame flare for a moment, the yellow dancing along the spectrum and not quite reaching blue, but further along than he'd ever seen before.

James falls back on the pillow, spent. He nearly had it. Nearly had the mythical blue angel. It is a good omen. He is going to do it, going to nail this competition. Win the five grand and save the house. Stop the family breaking up.

He smiles, and notes the results of the experiment in his book, then shoves it and the lighter back beneath the mattress. He sniffs the air.

'Ugh,' he says. 'That's actually rank.'

James jumps when Ellie says, 'You're not wrong, you disgusting little freak.'

He turns on his bedside lamp and sees her leaning on the wall just inside the door. 'How long have you been there?'

'Long enough.' She perches on the end of his bed. 'Please tell me this is science and not some weird pervert thing.'

'It's science. Did you know people have different gas signatures? Depending on their own biochemistry? And that if I lit your farts they'd probably be a different colour to mine?'

Ellie runs a hand through his hair, and for once James doesn't flinch or push her away. She says, 'Can you do this? Really? The competition?'

'I think so.'

'Because I've been thinking about this, I've been thinking of nothing else. And I can't see another way. You winning this contest is the only way we can save ourselves. And that frightens me, James, because I'm not used to relying on other people. Not since Dad went to jail. I've done it all myself. I look after you. Look after Nan. Work. Go to school. And I can't do any more, James. I can't

135

do anything other than hope that you can make this work. And that makes me feel angry and sad and terrified all at the same time.'

He begins to snore gently. Ellie pushes her fingers lightly through his hair one more time, then quietly stands up, smoothes down the blankets where she was sitting, and lets herself out of his room. James was asleep the whole time. She was talking to herself. She's doing it all alone. As usual.

That Delil was a nice lad for a foreigner, considers Gladys as she examines her reflection in the full-length mirror on the inside of her wardrobe door. She is wearing her black cardigan, a pair of James's tracksuit bottoms, and her little zip-up boots with the fur round the top. Not real fur, mind. Fake fur. Around her mouth and nose she has wrapped that scarf that Ellie bought her from the market for Christmas, and pulled over her eyebrows is a black hair net.

'Who are you blathering on at?' she asks her reflection. She pauses and looks around her bedroom. 'There's nobody else in here. Are you blathering on at me?'

Her left forearm bulges alarmingly and she taps her chest with the forefinger of her right hand. 'You talking to me?' She looks around again. 'You talking to me? Well, who the blinking flip else are you talking to?'

She is wearing the scarf and hair net because James was rather insistent that vigilantes should wear masks, but she can't find anything that remotely resembles a mask in the house. This will have to do. Even Bill wouldn't recognise her.

She smiles, though the effect is somewhat lost beneath the scarf. Then she shakes her left arm and out of the bulging cardigan slides the rolling pin, falling snugly into her hand.

Listen, you fuckers, you screw-heads, says Robert De Niro in her head. *Here's a nan who will not take it any more.*

Gladys pushes the rolling pin back up her sleeve and tries the manoeuvre twice more, until she's satisfied that it slides out and into her palm with a smooth motion. Then she takes off the outfit, folds it all neatly, places the hair net and rolling pin on top, then slides it under her bed, puts on the Winceyette nightie she's had since 1973, and climbs beneath her sheets.

36

AT HEART A GOOD MAN

When Ellie gets home from school she is only mildly surprised to see Delil sitting in Nan's chair. James is on the sofa cradling a number of white containers. She says, 'So you came back.'

'Bearing gifts,' says Delil.

'He's got loads of stuff!' says James. 'Potassium, hydrogen peroxide, lithium . . .'

Ellie tuts. 'You'd better not get us in trouble, Delil.'

'They'll never miss it.'

'Can I go and do some experiments?' begs James. 'Please?'

'Only if you're careful.' She looks at Delil. 'Is this stuff dangerous?'

'How should I know?' says Delil. 'But they wouldn't have it in schools if it was, surely.'

'Where's Nan?' says Ellie as James gathers up his bottles.

'Asleep. I popped my head round her door but she's spark out.'

As James hares upstairs, Ellie dumps her bag in the corner. Delil says, 'Cup of tea?'

'You can go now,' she says, not looking at him. Then she adds, 'Thank you for bringing that stuff for James. But I don't want anyone to get in trouble.'

Delil looks at her for a moment. 'Are you already in trouble?'

'What's James been telling you?'

'Nothing. Well, nothing I believe. He says he's been talking to that guy who's going to Mars.' Delil shakes his head. 'Kids and their imaginations, eh?'

'We're absolutely fine. How did you get here, anyway? Is that your bike propped against the wall?'

'Yep. Quicker than the bus on that, me.' He runs a hand through his hair. 'But why do you work at the burger place so much?'

'Not just there. I also work at the Polish shop. I'm going there tonight. And tomorrow. And on Sunday I do the welding.'

'It's like you're looking after everybody,' says Delil. 'Your nan . . . she's a bit . . . she's losing it, right?'

'It really is none of your business.'

'Why's your dad in jail?'

James thumps downstairs and heads into the kitchen, emerging a moment later with a mixing bowl half-filled with water. Ellie says to him, 'You need to learn to keep your mouth shut.'

James looks at Delil. 'Can I borrow your glasses?'

'He's just going.'

'Sure,' says Delil, taking off his spectacles and passing them to James. 'What for?'

'Goggles,' says James, and disappears back upstairs.

Delil squints at Ellie. 'You're quite pretty when I don't have my glasses on.'

'Piss off.' She sits down on the sofa. 'My mum died in a car accident. My dad's in jail. That's all there is to tell.'

'But *why* is he in jail?'

Ellie has made James go to school but she makes Nan phone in for her to say she's sick. Their dad is being sentenced at Liverpool Crown Court for his part in the robbery on a cash and carry warehouse out near Skelmersdale. There has been no jury trial, because all five of the men involved admitted their parts in the crime when they were arrested the day after the offence. That was the morning that Darren Ormerod called Ellie and Nan together in the living room.

'Something's happened,' he says. 'I don't want to say too much, but I've just transferred all the money in my account to your bank, Mum, and I've set up some standing orders to pay the rent, the bills, and other stuff. Just leave them as they are. There's enough money in there to cover everything for . . . well, for a good while. With the insurance money.'

'What are you talking about?' says Ellie. 'What's happened?'

'I'll tell you later. Go to school. It might all be something and nothing.'

'Are you going to work today?' says Ellie. Darren's van is parked outside the house. His builders' tools are stacked up in the kitchen. Work has been sporadic recently.

'I'll talk to you tonight.'

When Ellie comes home from school, Nan is sitting in her chair, crying. 'The police came for him,' she says, her eyes red. 'They've taken him away. Your dad.'

The judge at Liverpool Crown Court puts on his glasses and considers his notes. From the public gallery Ellie looks at her dad, who has been remanded in custody ever since his arrest four weeks ago. It is July, almost the end of the school year. Darren Ormerod looks pale and frightened, standing in the dock with four other men who Ellie does not know.

The judge clears his throat. 'It is quite clear from the evidence presented at this and earlier hearings that this is an endeavour that went horribly wrong from the outset. You five men had it in your minds to burgle a premises and steal a quantity of alcohol, which you planned to sell on and make for yourselves a tidy profit. Had you properly researched your target you might have had the realisation that the warehouse from which you were intending to steal employed a security guard who was patrolling the premises throughout the night. However, it is evident that the presence of the guard came as something of a surprise to you, and you were barely minutes into loading the stolen items on to your vehicle when you were found out.

'Had you abandoned the burglary there and then you might not be standing in this courtroom today. However, upon being confronted by the guard, Mr Stephenson, one of your number, the defendant Gary Wilkins, attacked him with a hammer causing him most serious injuries.

'A disagreement broke out between you, as is often the case in these poorly planned escapades, and you fled the scene with what few stolen goods you had managed to place in the van. You fitted false number plates to the vehicle, but badly; although seriously hurt, Mr Stephenson managed to note down the true registration of the van as you departed, where one of the false plates had slipped.'

The judge looks over his glasses at each of the men in turn, then says, 'You, in short, bungled the burglary, gentlemen. But not only that, thanks to the vicious attack the defendant Wilkins carried out on Mr Stephenson, this became a much more grave offence, that of robbery. To your credit, you have all pleaded guilty at the earliest opportunity, and the court will take that into account when passing sentence.'

The judge clears his throat, and considers his papers for a long moment. Ellie feels as though she is going to burst, or faint. Nan holds her hand tightly. The judge says, 'First, I will take the case of Darren Ormerod. You, Mr Ormerod, can rightly be considered to be a junior partner in this crime. You were approached by the other men, with whom you had the merest passing acquaintance, because they knew you possessed a suitable vehicle, which you use in your trade as a builder, and because they understood you had suffered some financial difficulties recently and that work was not as plentiful as you needed it to be.'

The judge takes off his glasses and looks directly at Ellie and Gladys, then back at Darren. 'I understand that your wife died some time ago, and that you look after your two children alone. I appreciate that times are difficult, Mr Ormerod. But that is no excuse for being tempted into criminal activity, even to better the situation of your dependents.'

Ellie has never been religious, but now she finds herself praying to a formless god, a vague figure dredged from childhood. *Please, please, please. Please don't let them send my daddy to jail.*

'You gave a full and frank confession to the police, and I am firmly of the opinion that you were subjected to not a little coercion with regards to your involvement in this matter,' says the judge. 'However, that is merely my instinct and opinion; you have not given evidence against your co-accused, showing that there is indeed honour among thieves, no matter how misplaced. But while this court deals with facts and evidence, I cannot help but consider my instinct and opinion. You were bullied into this, Darren Ormerod. Your co-accused knew that work was thin on the ground and that you needed to make enough money to keep your two children and your mother, who is helping you out with childcare while you work long hours, provided for. They took advantage of your desperation and made you an offer you felt you could not refuse. You *should* have refused, because you are at heart a good man, Mr Ormerod. But you didn't. And thus you embarked upon this criminal enterprise, and even if that was done for the best reasons and with the welfare of your family at heart, it was severely misguided.'

Please, please, please, thinks Ellie. I'll go to church every Sunday.

The judge shuffles his papers and lays them flat. 'For those reasons outlined, I am inclined to be lenient.'

Ellie realises she has stopped breathing, and allows herself to exhale slowly.

'But that does not mean the law must be seen as doing anything other than upholding the protection of the public and providing a deterrent to others who may be tempted into such a course of action. Darren Ormerod, I sentence you to two years in custody.'

Ellie breaks into violent tears.

'And when was that?' says Delil. 'Surely he'll only serve half of it.'

'Last summer,' says Ellie. 'Which means he could be out in maybe six months.'

Delil smiles. His eyes look small without his glasses. 'Safe. Not too long to wait, then.'

'Too long. What's all this *safe* business, anyway? You say it all the time.'

Delil shrugs. 'It's *Bajan* slang. And Bajan is slang for Barbadian. Which means from Barbados. My granddad used to say it all the time. Safe. It means cool, or good. I like it. It's like . . . protective. Inclusive. Safe. We can learn a lot of stuff from old people.'

'Not my nan,' says Ellie.

Delil looks at her thoughtfully. 'Is she OK to be looking after you?'

'We don't have a choice,' says Ellie, standing up. 'She only started going downhill after my dad was jailed. You don't tell anybody about this, all right? You don't talk about her to anybody . . .' She looks around, frowning. 'Nan shouldn't be asleep at this time, really.'

Ellie heads for the stairs, Delil following. She gets to Nan's bedroom and pushes open the door. Delil stands behind her. She can feel his breath on her neck. Nan's curtains are closed and she can see the shape of her beneath the blankets.

'Nan,' she whispers. The shape doesn't move. She says more loudly, 'Nan.'

'Do you think—?' says Delil quietly.

Panic grips Ellie. She feels the same way she did when Dad went to prison. Hot and cold and like she's going to black out, her head banging. 'Nan?' she shouts.

Then she's in the bedroom, pulling back the blankets from the bed, and that's when the house shakes and there's the sound of something exploding and Ellie thinks this is it, her world had finally collapsed in on itself, it's all over.

But Delil is gripping her hand; he's heard it too, felt it too. She looks down at the bed. Two pillows are laid lengthways along the mattress, covered up by the blankets. The oldest trick in the book. Then James emerges from his room across the landing and Ellie and Delil turn to look at him, buoyed out of his room on a white cloud, plaster crowning his hair, Delil's glasses coated with pale powder.

'That. Was. AWESOME!' he grins.

Then the front door goes and Nan shouts gaily from downstairs, 'Hello! Anybody home?'

* 37 *

FREEFALLING

'I'm in the crap,' says James into his phone. He is lying in bed, staring up at the hole in the ceiling.

'Watch your language,' says Thomas. 'And what have you done?'

James outlines how he positioned the bowl of water on his bedroom floor and threw in a spoonful of potassium.

'What?' shouts Thomas. 'Jesus Christ! It could have taken your face off! What on earth possessed you to do that?'

'You told me to!' shouts James.

'I did not!' shouts Thomas back. 'I asked you if you knew what would happen if you put potassium in water! I didn't tell you to do it. Christ. You could have blown the house up.'

'I nearly did. But how am I supposed to know what happens if I don't do it myself?'

'It's called theory,' says Thomas levelly. He sings in a staccato voice, 'Albert says ee equals emm see squared.'

'What the hell's that?'

'Einstein's Theory of Relativity,' sighs Thomas. 'God, don't you know anything?'

'I know what E=mc² means,' shouts James. 'I mean that stupid song you were singing.'

'Oh. "Einstein A Go-Go". Landscape. I wouldn't expect you to know that one.'

'I listened to Maj—I mean, "Space Oddity". By David Bowie. On YouTube,' says James. 'It was pretty good. But it's a bit sad. I liked that other one, "Starman". And "Life on Mars". Did he always do spacey stuff?'

'It was a phase he was going through. Have you heard *Diamond Dogs*?'

'A phase? Like puberty? Ellie says I'm hitting puberty early, which is why I'm so cranky. I told her she should speak to you more often if she wants to know what cranky is.'

James hears Thomas take a deep breath. He thrills slightly to think of Major Tom up there, sitting in his tin can, far from the world, just like the song. Before Thomas can say anything else, James quickly puts in, 'How did you train to be an astronaut?'

Thomas pauses, then says, 'I went to Russia. A place called Star City.'

'Did you go on the Vomit Comet?' asks James.

'I knew you'd want to know that,' tuts Thomas. 'What is it with small boys and bodily functions?'

'Does anyone know Russian for "not a buggering chance"?' says Thomas.

'No need for Russian,' says the big man with a shaved head and a bushy moustache, his eyes laughing. 'I speak the English no problem. And there is every buggering chance if you are going to the Mars.'

The big man's name is Sergei but he likes to be called The Meerkat ever since a previous trainee astronaut told him he looked like the character from the insurance comparison TV ads in Britain, the popularity of which Thomas considers to be one of the contributory factors to the decline of Western civilisation. The Meerkat has described in detail the weightlessness training which is going to occur this morning at Star City near Moscow. Thomas is spending the next six months here in preparation for his historic journey to Mars. Providing he gets through the training in one piece.

It is bitterly cold and an icy wind whips across the tarmac of the airstrip in the middle of what used to be called Closed Military Townlet No. 1. In front of them is the colossal blunt shape of the *Ilyushin Il-76* aircraft, fuelled and ready for take-off. The Meerkat says proudly, 'The Vomit Comet. Let's go.'

The belly of the former commercial freight airliner has been stripped bare, resembling a corridor out of some seventies science fiction movie. Rails run at waist-height and above head level; Thomas is wearing a green flight suit and The Meerkat instructs him to put on his helmet as the engines hum and then roar into life. Thomas shouts over the noise, 'Why does your helmet have a face shield and mine doesn't?'

The Meerkat grins as the plane lurches forward and Thomas hangs on to the rail. 'That you will see.' He puts down the plastic face-shield. 'We are going to fly high at an angle of forty-five degrees in a parabolic curve. When we hit the top of the climb we get the weightlessness. Just for a few seconds, but just like being in space.'

As the plane thunders upwards, Thomas gripping the rail to arrest his slide down the cabin, The Meerkat hits a button on an old CD player chained to the wall. "Dancing On The Ceiling" by Lionel Richie emerges tinnily from the tiny speakers just as the aircraft hits the zenith of its climb. Thomas feels himself lift and rotate in the air. He grips the rail as The Meerkat laughs throatily. 'Space! Weightless!'

Then the plane begins to descend and Thomas's stomach lurches and he lets loose a stream of sick which hits The Meerkat squarely in the helmet. 'Now you see why the faceplate!' he laughs, wiping off the vomit with his sleeve.

'Jesus Christ. How many more times do we have to do that?'

The plane starts to climb again. 'Until no more vomit!' yells The Meerkat.

Thomas finds the next track on The Meerkat's CD, Tom Petty's 'Freefallin', a little more palatable than Lionel Richie, but that doesn't stop his stomach whining in protest again as they begin their descent for the second time.

It's not until the seventh bout of weightlessness – which Thomas is rather beginning to enjoy – and of course David Bowie's "Space Oddity" that Thomas manages to keep whatever's left of his breakfast inside him. The Meerkat embraces him in a huge bear hug and bellows, 'See? Simples!'

'That is awesome,' says James. 'Man, I'd love to do that.'

'Sign up for the astronaut programme at BriSpA and they might let you.'

'Really? Do you think so?'

'Well, anything's possible. Especially if you win this competition. Now, what ideas have you had?'

James thinks about it. 'Apart from blowing stuff up, not much. Can't you just tell me what to do?'

'No. Because then I'll have won the competition, and not you.'

James stares at the hole in the ceiling. 'I can't do it. I can't have an idea that nobody else has had. It's impossible.'

'Then you're not a scientist,' says Thomas. 'Sorry, but it's true. If you're giving up, let me know because I've got a crossword to do.'

'You don't care!' shouts James. 'We're nothing to you! We're just some peasant family in Wigan! You're probably laughing at us from up there in space!'

There's a long pause, then Thomas says, 'I'm not laughing at you.'

'But you don't care.'

'What do you want me to say?' yells Thomas. 'It's nothing personal. I don't care about anyone. Caring doesn't get you anywhere. Science doesn't *care*. It just does. It solves problems. Now think about it. Science solves problems. What problem can science solve for you? What one thing would make your life better, right now?

Think of a problem, then solve it like nobody else has thought about solving it. What would make your life better?'

James continues to gaze at the hole in the ceiling. Then he says in a small voice, 'My dad coming home.'

✳ 38 ✳

MAYBE YOU'LL BE THE FIRST MAN ON MARS

When Thomas is sure his father isn't coming home again, he goes to visit him in hospital. Frank Major is shrunken and wasted in his bed. The cancer had started in his lungs, born of thirty Woodbines a day and ripening over the years, colonising the rest of his body until he is more cancer than man.

Which is something that Thomas has thought for some time, in the dour, glowering, poetically bad way that only sixteen-year-olds can muster. Thomas has not brought flowers, or chocolates. He has simply brought himself, armoured in tatty jeans and an Army Surplus jacket, hunched on the plastic chair by the bed, turning his hooded gaze on his father. The hospital smells of disinfectant and toilets, death and fading hope.

'I'm done for,' wheezes Frank, every breath a trial, every word an Everest to climb. 'This is it.'

'Yes,' says Thomas.

'Is that it?' says Frank. 'Is that all?'

Mum took Peter to say goodbye this morning and they came home red-eyed and sobbing. She begged Thomas to go. It is his last chance to see him. 'To sort things out,' she says, though she has no idea what needs sorting out. Only that for the first half of his life, Thomas doted on his dad, loved him as though he was the only boy in the world with a daddy. And then, for the second half of his life, seemed to hate him.

Thomas pinches his bottom lip with his finger and thumb and stares at the green blanket covering his father's stick-like frame. He would rather be anywhere else than here. Would rather it was tomorrow, next week, a year in the future. Would rather it was all over.

'We . . . we used to be such good . . . pals.'

'Did we?' says Thomas carelessly. 'I can't remember.'

Anguish dulls the faint light in Frank's eyes for a moment. He reaches for the mask lying loosely on his thin chest and puts it to his face, inhaling raggedly the oxygen it delivers. Thomas looks around the tiny room and for the first time realises the drip stands that feed a constant cocktail of drugs into his father's system are absent.

Following his eyes, Frank takes away the oxygen mask and says, 'I told them to stop giving me the medication.'

Thomas meets his gaze, finally. 'Why?'

There's the smallest of shrugs. 'It was making me feel awful.'

'But it was prolonging your life.'

Frank takes another blast from the mask. 'Delaying . . . the inevitable. What's the point of a few more days?'

Thomas thinks back to this morning, to what his mum said when she brought Peter home from the infirmary. *He's going, Thomas. Fast. If only we had a few more days with him. That's all I'd want.*

He says to his father, 'It's your decision.'

Frank lays a bony hand on Thomas's jacket sleeve, and Thomas flinches. Frank says, 'You have to tell me . . . while I've still got time. What happened between us?'

Thomas sneers. 'Are you really asking me to believe you don't know?'

'Tell me,' says Frank, his grip tightening slightly. 'Please.'

Thomas closes his eyes. '*Star Wars*.'

Frank releases his hand and uses it to take another lungful of oxygen. 'Oh. That. I didn't . . . I didn't think you remembered that.'

Thomas's eyes widen. 'You didn't think I'd remember? Not remember being left on my own in the cinema? Not remember coming out into the dark to find you? Not remember seeing you with your . . . with your hands all over that woman?'

Frank is silent, just watching his son as he inhales deeply through the mask. Thomas says, 'On the drive home, you said

147

it was just a friend and you were wrestling with her in the car. Because that's what friends do. Wrestle. Just for a joke. Did you think that worked? Did you think I was slow or something?'

'You were just a kid . . .' says Frank. 'I thought . . .'

'You thought you could palm me off? "Don't tell your mum," you said. "It's a surprise. She doesn't know I've been practising my wrestling without her." I mean, really, Dad? Really?'

'You didn't . . . tell her though,' says Frank. 'Why not?'

Thomas throws his hands up in the air. 'Because even when I was eight I knew you were wrong and you were a lying, cheating bastard and I knew what that would do to her. So I kept my mouth shut and . . . what? You thought I'd bought all that bollocks? Wrestling. For Christ's sake.'

Frank doesn't say anything. Thomas holds out his hands. 'Your turn. Why? Why did you do it?'

Frank shakes his head sadly. 'I don't know. I can't explain it. Your mum . . . she was pregnant with Peter. Things weren't . . . Well, I don't . . . expect you to understand yet. You might do when you're . . . older. You might understand me a bit more when you have children . . . of your own.'

Thomas laughs, a dry, barking, humourless sound. 'Have children? Me? I don't think so.'

'You're sixteen. You're young yet . . .'

Thomas leans forward, puts his face as close to Frank's as he can bear to. He says through gritted teeth, 'You think I'd ever have children when there's a danger I might turn out to be the sort of father that you've been?'

'Thomas . . .' says Frank, but Thomas has already stood up.

'I'm going now, Dad.'

'Thomas.' Frank's breath comes sharp and urgently. 'You've got to . . . you've got to look after your mum. Promise me that?'

Thomas shrugs. 'What are promises worth to you? And I don't need you to tell me to do that anyway.'

'Keep up with the science stuff,' says Frank. He tries to smile. 'Maybe you'll find a cure for cancer one day.'

'Maybe,' sneers Thomas. 'Or maybe I'll be the first man on Mars. Miracles happen, I suppose.'

'Your mother . . . she wants me to carry on taking the medication,' says Frank.

'Do whatever you want. You usually do.'

'I will if you say so,' whispers Frank. 'If you'll say you'll forgive me, or at least talk to me some more. If you'll listen . . . to me. Let me . . . explain.'

Thomas turns away. 'I think we've said everything we need to say.'

As he's passing through the waiting room he sees his mother. She stands up and grabs at his arms. 'How is he? Did you speak to him?'

Thomas looks around. 'Where's Peter?'

'Mrs Jenkins at number 12 has him. I said you'd pick him up when you get back. Did . . . did your dad tell you he's stopped the medication?'

Thomas nods, and his mother says, 'I've begged him to carry on. Just so we can have a few more days with him. I know it makes him feel bad but . . . Did he mention anything about it to you?'

'It's his decision,' says Thomas bluntly. He can't meet his mum's frantic stare. He knows all he has to do is go back in there and tell his father he'll listen to him, and Frank Major will take the medicine, though it makes him feel dreadful, and his mum will get what she wants. Instead he says, 'I'd better go and get Peter.'

His mother nods and puts a hand to her mouth. Thomas walks quickly to the hospital entrance, and when he gets to the concourse he breaks into a run, straight across the car park, through the gates, on to the main road. He has never run before, not like this. But he can't stop. He feels the guilt and the sadness peel away, as though it can't keep up with him. And he knows if he stops running he'll go back into the hospital and tell his father to keep taking the medication, to give his mum what she wants. But Thomas doesn't want that. He wants Frank Major gone and forgotten. So he keeps running, leaving it all behind in his slipstream, feeling the never-before experienced joy of endorphins flooding his system, driving him on in his jeans and Army Surplus jacket through the pain of the stitch in his side, through the fire in his lungs. He could run for ever, if this is what it does, strip away all the horror. So, he decides, that's what he'll do. He'll run for ever. From everyone.

*

149

'He made one mistake,' says James. 'He shouldn't have to pay for that for ever, should he? Everybody else shouldn't be punished for it as well?'

'No.' Thomas is silent for a long moment before he realises James is talking about Darren Ormerod, not Frank Major. He shakes his head to loosen the memories, to dislodge them, and says, 'OK. Let's work with this. You want your dad to be at home, but he's in prison. How is that going to work?'

There's a pause, then James says, 'Maybe I could get a helicopter to fly over the jail and it's got big guns and I blow a hole in the wall and he gets out and I drop a rope ladder—'

'That's a film not a science experiment!' shouts Thomas.

'Fine!' shouts James back. 'Have you got any bright ideas?'

'No,' says Thomas more calmly. 'But you have. You've had a bright idea. You just need to develop it. Come on, think. Let's unpack this a bit. Your dad's in jail, but he's basically a good man, is that what you're saying?'

'He's a brilliant man!' says James. 'He's the best dad ever. Apart from when he's being an idiot and I hate him.'

'OK. So he's in jail. But . . . what? You don't think he should be punished for what he did?'

'No,' says James quietly. 'I mean, no, I don't think that. He should be punished. But maybe he shouldn't have to be in jail. Not all the time, anyway.'

'Why not?' presses Thomas. 'Talk this through.'

'Because how can he show he's a good man if he's in jail? He's mixing with all kinds of robbers and murderers and stuff. Nobody cares whether he's a good man or not. They just want him to eat bread and water and stare through the bars at the sunshine outside.'

'So, if the authorities could see that your dad was a good man, perhaps . . . what?'

'Maybe they'd let him go free quicker.'

'And how would your dad show that he's a good man?'

'By doing all the things he does to be a good dad!' says James, a note of exasperation in his voice. 'We're just going round in circles here.'

'No, we're not. We're moving in a linear fashion from a problem to a solution.'

'He shouldn't be in jail,' says James again. 'They should . . . what's it called when they put you in jail but you stay at home?'

'House arrest, maybe?'

'That's it. They should put him under house arrest. That way he could still be a dad and they could see he was a good man. He could . . .'

There's a pause and Thomas smiles. James, he knows, has hit something. Thomas feels a slight prickle at the back of his neck. James says softly, 'Oh, my.'

✳ 39 ✳

TWICE AS MUCH AT THE VERY LEAST

It's a blazing hot day when they bury Julie Ormerod. James is just six years old. People keep talking over his head, in hushed voices, tearful friends and distant relations keep grabbing him and rubbing his hair and saying what a shame it is, and how he doesn't understand.

James understands fully. A bad man crashed into his mum's car and now she's gone.

'She's in heaven now,' says a woman wearing a fur coat despite the heat, stood alongside the parched earth where they've dug a rectangular hole for Julie's coffin. 'She's an angel.'

James looks at her curiously. 'I don't believe in God,' he says. The woman's hand flies to her mouth and she nods.

'I can understand that. I can understand you're angry.'

James shrugs. 'I'm not angry. Earth was created four and a half billion years ago. Not in six days by God. I believe in science.' He goes forward to pick up a handful of dirt – so dry it's just dust really – and throws it on the coffin. He looks back at the woman, whose name he doesn't even know. 'I'm not angry. I'm just sad.'

Ellie has cried nonstop since Mum died. She is standing with Dad as the procession of mourners walks past them away from the

151

grave in single file, patting Darren on the shoulder, kissing the top of Ellie's head. They are all going back to Santus Street where Nan has made some sandwiches and they will all drink from warm cans of beer and tell stories about Julie and they'll laugh and they'll cry until after midnight. James goes to stand with Ellie and Dad and Darren puts his arms around both of them.

'I want my mum back,' says Ellie.

Darren's strong arms hold them both tight. 'I want your mum back as well. But as long as we remember her she'll still be with us.'

James brushes the dry dirt from his hand. 'It'll not be the same though.'

'No,' says Darren. 'No, it won't. But we have to try to get through this and we have to get through it together. It's just us now. Me, you and Ellie.'

James thinks about it. 'Who's going to make our tea when we come in from school? Are you going to stop working?'

'I wish I could. I'm going to have to work harder. I was thinking . . . how would you feel about Nan coming to live with us?'

'Will she make us drink flat Coke like she does when we go round hers on Boxing Day?' asks James.

Darren smiles. 'No. No flat Coke. I promise.'

Ellie looks up at him and says, 'Why do you have to work harder?'

Darren kisses the top of her head. 'There's only one wage coming in now. I'll have to work twice as hard. But don't you worry about that. We'll be fine.'

The last of the mourners is walking through the gravestones towards the road. James says, 'If you have to work twice as much because we've got no mum now, does that mean you have to love us twice as much as well?'

And Darren Ormerod sags, and steadies himself on his children, and in a cracked voice says, 'Yes, that's exactly what it means. Twice as much. At the very least.'

'I need some stuff,' says James to Ellie as she comes downstairs in her convenience store outfit. She has work this morning and is per-turbed to see James bouncing up and down on the sofa.

'I've done it,' says James. 'I've come up with an experiment. It's awesome. I'm going to need some stuff.'

'I hope you're not going to blow the house up again,' says Nan from her chair.

Ellie scowls at her. Gladys has not given a satisfactory explanation for why she went missing yesterday afternoon, just saying that she 'wanted to go for a walk'. Ellie is highly suspicious but nothing bad seems to have come of it, and Nan did in fact turn up again. The dummy made of pillows in the bed is cause for concern, but Gladys just says she needed some air and didn't want the kids to worry.

'She's right,' says Ellie to James. 'No explosions.'

'I just need some plasticine,' says James. 'And some boxes. And LED lights. I bet Delil can get the lights from the science labs.'

'I can get the boxes from the shop,' says Ellie. 'And I'll get you some plasticine from the toy section as well. What's the idea?'

James outlines the plan and Nan says, 'That sounds absolutely lovely.'

'Actually,' says Ellie, 'that does sound like a pretty good idea.' She's been reading the website of the competition, which suggests that the winning experiment will have 'practical and social applications'. James's idea does seem to tick a lot of boxes. 'And Major Tom came up with this?'

'No!' says James. 'It's my idea! He just put me on the right track.'

Ellie ponders it for a minute. 'It is brilliant, actually. Well done, James.' She bites her lip. 'Bloody hell, we might be in with a chance of doing this, you know.'

'We still need to tell school I'm entering,' says James. 'They wanted to meet our parent-slash-guardian.'

Ellie nods. 'I'll go in on Monday morning. We'll get Nan to write a letter giving her permission and I'll tell them that she's busy doing . . . doing some charity work or something so can't go in to see them.'

Nan gives a little cheer from her chair and starts to sing, 'We are the champions, my friends! We'll keep on fighting to the end!'

Ellie laughs and joins in, nudging James. 'We are the champions, we are the champions!'

153

'No time for losers!' shouts James, pumping his fists in the air.

'Because we are the champions of the world!' they all finish, Nan hitting and holding a warbling vibrato on the final note that is only ended by a sharp, official-sounding rapping on the front door.

Ellie and James look at each other. Nan says, 'I wonder who that could be?'

James pokes his head cautiously around the curtain, first seeing the car parked behind their dad's van on the street, then the shape of the figure standing at the door. He looks back at Ellie and swallows.

'It's the police.'

✳ 40 ✳

PERSONS UNKNOWN

The policeman is tall and middle-aged, and when he takes off his cap and tucks it in the crook of his arm Ellie sees that his hair is grey and thinning. She knows him, or at least by sight. He dominates the small living room as he stands by the door and looks around in turn at Ellie, James and Gladys.

'Do you mind if I sit down?' He nods towards the sofa.

Gladys screws up her face. 'I know you. You were the one who arrested our Darren.'

That's where Ellie recognises him from. He gave evidence at the court case, just briefly, to say that Darren Ormerod had immediately admitted his part in the robbery and had co-operated with the police from the very beginning. But what is he doing here now?

Then the colour drains from her face. 'Oh, God. Has something happened to Dad?'

Visions of fights, of crude, homemade knives being shoved into stomachs, of beatings in the shower block, of Darren lying bruised and bloodied in his cell, all tumble over each other in her mind. She puts one hand against the sideboard to steady herself.

What exactly will happen if he's dead? What will happen to them? They'll be put in care for ever. Not just until he comes home. Thoughts wrestle for attention. Is there insurance? Would they pay it out to them? Will the shock kill Nan? And oh God her dad will be dead. There'll be a funeral. Will they bury him in the prison grounds? Will they bury him with Mum? *Who* will bury him? Will that be down to her as well? Ellie can't cope with any more of this. She might just collapse on the carpet right there and then, and give up.

'Can I sit down?' the policeman says again. Ellie remembers his name. PC Calderbank. Shouldn't he be telling *me* to sit down? she thinks. Isn't that what they do on the telly when they deliver bad news? PC Calderbank smiles at Gladys. 'Cup of tea would be lovely, too.'

Gladys settles back in her chair. 'James, go and put the kettle on.'

PC Calderbank peers at James. 'Aye, lad, put the kettle on. But I'll need to speak to you in a minute as well.'

'What's happening?' says Ellie. 'Is it Dad, or not?'

PC Calderbank clears his throat and pulls out a tiny black notebook. 'We've had a complaint. Quite a serious complaint. I've come round to see if I can get to the bottom of it.'

Oh, God, thinks Ellie. The chemicals that Delil stole from school. They've got him and he's grassed them up. PC Calderbank looks at Gladys and then at Ellie. 'It's an allegation of assault.'

'What?' says Ellie, wrong-footed. 'Assault? Who's saying that?'

He flips through his notebook. 'The complainant is a Mr Neil Sherrington. It regards his son, Oscar.'

'Oh, God,' says James, standing at the kitchen door.

Ellie looks at him sharply. 'James,' she says, trying to keep her voice as level as possible. 'What have you done?'

'Nothing! I swear! But Oscar Sherrington . . .' He bites his lip and looks at Gladys. 'He's the one who's . . . he's the boss of them.'

PC Calderbank narrows his eyes. 'Boss of who?'

'The gang that's been bullying me,' mumbles James. The kettle starts to whistle on the hob and he ducks back into the kitchen.

'What's James done?' She feels as though the floorboards are creaking, as though they're going to snap and separate, and they're all going to be swallowed up. How could he? How could James be so stupid? Just when they had something to grab on to, just when it looked like they might be in with a chance of saving themselves.

'Well . . .' PC Calderbank draws out the word while he studies his notes. He puffs out his cheeks and exhales slowly. 'Well, the complaint isn't directly against James. In fact . . . it's Ellie, isn't it?'

She nods and James emerges with a tray of cups. 'I didn't know if you wanted sugar so I put three in,' he says, laying it down on the little table in front of the fire.

'Lovely,' says PC Calderbank, lifting the cup at which James has pointed. He takes a sip of the boiling tea and says to Ellie, 'In fact, Ellie, the complaint might be about you.'

Ellie stares at him. 'Me? *Might* be about me? What does that even mean? *Might* be? And I haven't done anything! I don't even know this . . .'

'Oscar,' says PC Calderbank. 'Oscar Sherrington. He goes to St Matthew's Primary School, the same as young James, as we've just established.'

'Ellie,' says James, staring at her with something that could be admiration, or could easily be fury. 'Ellie, what have *you* done?'

'Nothing!'

PC Calderbank nods and says, 'The nature of the complaint is that around three-fifteen yesterday afternoon Oscar Sherrington and three of his friends were approached just outside the school gates by a person unknown, who the complainant has reason to believe is connected with this household. Said person unknown—'

'How can they be a . . . a *person unknown*?' says Ellie desperately.

'Said person unknown,' continues PC Calderbank, 'was wearing some kind of face covering and dressed all in black. It was evidently female, though given the time of year and the weather yesterday Oscar Sherrington says he didn't get a good enough look at them, and they disguised their voice in a—' PC Calderbank looks at his notes again and raises one eyebrow. 'In an American accent, possibly New York.'

Ellie shakes her head bewildered, and looks at James. James is staring aghast at Gladys. PC Calderbank says, 'The masked assailant then, according to the complaint filed by Mr Neil Sherrington, assaulted Oscar with a blunt instrument.'

'Oh, rubbish!' says Gladys at last, crossing her arms and sticking out her bottom lip. 'It wasn't a blunt instrument. It was my bloody rolling pin. And it was only a tap.'

They all stare at Gladys, PC Calderbank raising both eyebrows this time. James looks as though he's catching flies, his mouth hanging wide open, and Ellie pinches her nose tightly. 'Nan,' she says. 'What on earth have you done?'

* 41 *

THANK GOD FOR THE RAIN

What Gladys has done, after placing her pillows lengthways in her bed and pulling the covers over them, is close her curtains and then quietly get into the clothes she had hidden under her bed. She looks at herself critically in the mirror then she packs the scarf and black hairnet into an old plastic carrier bag, along with her rolling pin, gets her coat and umbrella, and lets herself out of the house into the gloomy January afternoon, the sky already darkening and heavy with the prospect of rain.

It is a ten minute walk and then a bus ride and another ten minute walk to get to St Matthew's. Gladys doesn't know why he can't go to the school round the corner from them – Ellie went there, after all – but it was some big plan Darren had. Send James to a better school where they'll be able to encourage his gifts. In Gladys's opinion, she was quite on the side of Ellie, who is just as bright – more so – but was never singled out for chances like that. James gets his intelligence from Julie. She was awful clever, and though she'd never have said it to anyone else, she never really knew what she saw in her Darren. Ellie's more like Darren – a grafter. Hard-working. Does what it takes to get things done. A bit impetuous sometimes. She's good with words and feelings, not science and maths like James. Darren was always good like that. Never really, what did they used to say on his school reports? Never really applied himself. But he used to write those most wonderful stories at school. Could have been a writer, she supposes, but she doesn't know if anyone actually does that for a job, if they make money from it. There is that Harry Potter woman who was on the telly, she seems to be doing all right for herself. Though Gladys supposes that's all to do with them making films of her books.

The bus driver waits patiently at the stop as Gladys carefully steps down on to the pavement, which is now wet with a sheen of rain. It is only mid-afternoon but the lamp-posts are fizzing into life and she likes how the dull purple turns to orange, like embers from the fire. She misses a real fire. Those electric ones aren't the same. Though she doesn't miss cleaning it out every morning. That was always her job when she was a little girl, and Mam wouldn't give her any breakfast until she'd done it.

On the street where James's school is there is already a line of cars, nice posh ones, waiting for the children to come out. In each car there is a rectangle of white light illuminating the face of a parent, staring at their phones, updating their statuses, she shouldn't wonder. It's all about status these days. Why else would they turn up in these fancy cars to pick their kids up from school? What's wrong with getting the bus, like James does, or even walking? Gladys used to walk everywhere when she was a girl. That's why she got such good legs, why she looked so nice in a miniskirt, how she got Bill's attention.

The cars only go halfway up the street, though, and there's a line of cones along the kerb, presumably to stop people parking there. It's probably so that the kids don't run out between the parked cars and get knocked down, like that rabbit or squirrel that used to be on the adverts when Darren was little. Taffy? Toffee? Tufty, that was it. She remembers one where he ran into the road and his little ball got squashed flat by a car.

There's a streetlamp by the main gate, though it isn't working. It's getting really dark, thanks to the clouds that roll overhead.

Good weather for revenge. She takes out her plastic bag and puts her scarf around her face and pulls down the hairnet to her eyes. She slides the rolling pin up her sleeve.

There's a bus turning circle at the end of the cul-de-sac and she sees a knot of boys in padded anoraks lurking by the metal barriers. Lurking. That's exactly what they're doing. She knows instinctively it's them. James said they always wait for him at the bus stop before going off to their mums and dads in their posh cars, pretending that butter wouldn't melt. Gladys sets her thin shoulders as squarely as possible and walks up to them.

There are four, and one's bigger than the others. Bigger than Gladys by a good head. He turns and looks at her from beneath his hood, raising one eyebrow. 'All right?' he says.

'You looking at me?' she says, hissing the words, trying to sound like Robert de Niro. She looks around. The other boys are laughing and elbowing each other. 'I don't see anybody else. Are you looking at me?'

'I don't know what I'm looking at,' says the boy. 'They don't put labels on hoboes.'

The boys guffaw and one says, 'Sherro, leave it. It's some mad woman.'

Gladys looks up as there's a rumble of thunder and a sudden downpour. 'A real rain,' says Gladys, talking out of the corner of her mouth in her de Niro voice. 'Come to wash the scum off the streets.'

'Who are you calling scum?' says the boy, his eyes flashing.

'Sherro, let's go and get a teacher, she's nuts,' says one of the others.

Sherro leans back on the railing. 'Naw. We've not had our fun with the peasant yet.'

'You leave him alone!' says Gladys shrilly. 'You're horrible boys and you have to leave him alone!'

Sherro laughs, an ugly sound, right in her face. 'Or what?'

Gladys shakes her arm, twice, until the rolling pin drops snugly into her hand. The boy's eyes widen, and he doesn't even try to move as she lifts it up and bops him sharply on his forehead.

'Ow!' shouts Sherro. 'That hurt!'

Then Gladys hears a shout and turns to see a wave of children passing through the gate. She turns on her heel and hobbles away as quickly as she can, pulling down the scarf and taking off the hairnet. She is going to get home after James and Ellie; she will have to come up with some excuse. She'll say she wanted to go to Bill's grave. A woman in a high-visibility vest is standing in the road, ushering the children across to the bus stop. She looks curiously at Gladys.

'Everything OK, madam?' She glances over at the gang. 'Those pupils weren't bothering you—?'

'Not at all, love,' says Gladys sweetly.

As she waves the tide of children across, the rain plastering her hair to her forehead, the teacher looks again at Gladys. 'Foul weather.'

Gladys nods, and leans in to the woman, and says in her best de Niro voice, 'Thank God for the rain to wash the trash off the sidewalk.'

The policeman says, 'Mrs Ormerod . . . are you admitting to me that you hit Oscar Sherrington over the head with a rolling pin?'

Gladys shrugs and holds out her hands, wrists towards PC Calderbank. 'It's a fair cop. Take me away.' She looks at Ellie. 'They might put me in the next cell to your dad. That'd be nice, wouldn't it?'

PC Calderbank makes a note in his book, then says, 'Mrs Ormerod, do you mind if I ask how old you are?'

'I'll be seventy-one next birthday.'

He nods, thoughtfully taps his pencil on his chin, then closes his book. Ellie grabs the sleeve of his black tunic. 'Are you going to arrest her? For assault?'

'What I'm going to do,' says PC Calderbank, 'is go back and visit Mr Sherrington at his home. I don't know if you know anything about Oscar's family, James, but his father is a former Lieutenant Colonel in the Army.'

'Oh, God.' Ellie puts her face in her hands. 'They're going to press charges, aren't they?'

'He is very by-the-book,' agrees PC Calderbank. 'The complaint arose when one of the other boys in the group told their father what happened, and he told Mr Sherrington, probably at some golf club or other, who got it out of the boy and then made a complaint to us. The thing is . . . well, let's just say that Oscar's story suggested that the masked assailant was a lot larger, a lot younger and a lot more violent than appears to be the case.'

Ellie looks at him from between her fingers. 'So . . .?'

'So I'm going to go and tell former Lt Col Sherrington that the person who appears to have assaulted his son is a seventy-year-old granny who stands four-foot-two in her fur-lined boots and weighs about six stone wet through. Furthermore, if this does indeed result in a charge then there is likely to be some serious discussion about the nature of the bullying that Oscar and his friends are responsible for.' PC Calderbank smiles. 'I think, somehow, that this isn't going to go any further.'

He drains his tea and stands up. Ellie surprises herself by hugging him. 'Oh, thank you! Thank you!'

PC Calderbank adopts a stern face. 'Mrs Ormerod, you don't need me to tell you that this is not the way to deal with problems. There are proper procedures to go through, and if James is being bullied the school has systems in place to deal with it. You're James's guardian while Darren's inside, yes?'

Gladys smiles benignly. 'I am.'

'Well, I might suggest a visit to the school, have a meeting with the head. They can stop this at the source. It's not like in the old days. They're very hot on bullying now.' He puts on his helmet. 'Though, somehow, once I've had a word with Mr Sherrington, I have the feeling that young Oscar won't be bothering James again.'

PC Calderbank nods at James and Ellie, and says, 'I'll see myself out.' At the door he pauses, and turns back to Gladys. 'And just remember, Mrs Ormerod, no more vigilante stuff, right? No more real rain washing the scum off the streets. We all know how that film ends.'

Gladys nods soberly, and as PC Calderbank pulls the door shut behind him Ellie collapses back on the sofa, staring at the ceiling. 'Oh. My. God.'

Gladys leans forward in her chair. 'I'm sorry. I shouldn't have done it. But it just got me so annoyed when James was telling me about those bullies, and I was watching *Taxi Driver*, and . . . oh, Ellie, I'm so sorry.'

Ellie looks at her. 'Did you really hit him over the head with a rolling pin?'

Gladys nods, her eyes laughing. 'You should have seen his face.'

Then Ellie is laughing too, and it feels so good, liberating. She's laughing and laughing and tears are rolling down her cheeks, but this time they're not sad tears, which feels really strange and new. It's like she'd forgotten how to laugh, and now she's remembered she can't stop.

Until James, standing by the kitchen door, shouts, 'Are you all stupid?'

Ellie drags in a deep breath and says, 'What?'

'I said,' yells James, 'ARE YOU HAVING A LAUGH?'

Gladys says, 'James, love, it's all right, they're not going to arrest me.'

'You think this is over?' says James, hard tears springing from his eyes. 'You think they'll stop now, just like that policeman says? You don't know them, Ellie. They'll never stop. And if Oscar Sherrington gets a bollocking from his dad, who do you think he's going to take it out on?'

James rushes towards the stairs. Ellie calls out his name and he pauses, one foot on the bottom step, and glares at Gladys. 'You've just made it all worse, Nan. Thanks a lot. You've just made it all a million times worse.'

Part Three

42

THOMAS MAJOR IS MADE OF KITTENS

When BriSpA's Chief of Multi-Platform Safeguarding, Craig, was in the Royal Navy he was generally known as Hammerhead due to his habit of smashing his head against doors, walls and other heads after too much drink. Those days are in Craig's past, as is the nickname, though he sometimes uses a variation of it when he frequents certain online forums that require a certain level of anonymity. At least until an assignation is organised in a dark nightclub, or sometimes on a moonlit heath, where for the purposes of identification he carries a dog lead though, of course, he owns no dog. Craig does own two cats, named Ethel and Frank. He will know he has found true love when he meets someone who knows that those are the names of the parents of Judy Garland. He is still waiting.

Although his head-butting days are behind him, Craig has considered reviving them purely for the benefit of Bob Baumann. Craig is a great believer in discipline, and in all his Hammerhead days never head butted a wall, or door, or man that didn't deserve it. He is also, being a military man, a great respecter of hierarchy. He was, however, so appalled when Bob Baumann and his stupid eyebrows re-branded Craig's role from Head of Security to Chief of Multi-Platform Safeguarding that for one brief and glorious moment he almost went full Hammerhead. Everyone knows what the head of security does. Chief of Multi-Platform Safeguarding sounds as though he is in charge of safety nets at a circus. Which, considers Craig, might not actually be that bad a description of his job at BriSpA on some days.

All of which are reasons why Craig has not contacted Director Baumann with his news, but rather Claudia, the head of PR.

Claudia has never been to the security office before Craig sends her a cryptic email telling her he has something he thinks she should see. Craig always wears a vaguely non-specific military outfit and his square jaw and close-cropped hair give the impression of a man in possession of so much testosterone he has to siphon off the excess and store it in barrels in his basement. Claudia has the idea that the security office will be a broom cupboard that smells of socks and jock-straps where unspeakable self-abuse occurs, aided by top-shelf literature and grim non-BriSpA-approved websites.

'Oh,' she says as she lets herself in to a wide, airy office where half a dozen mainly young, mainly good-looking men sit at computer desks engaged in a variety of tasks. There's a glass-walled ante-room at the far end, from where the head of security gives a little salute, framed in the doorway. There is music playing quietly; Claudia scrunches up her face and listens. Erasure?

'This is not what I was expecting,' says Claudia as Craig closes the door of his office behind her and indicates a chair facing his desk. There's a vase of cut flowers on a table where a pot of coffee bubbles and gently steams. Craig grunts as, with his back to her, he hurriedly hangs a BriSpA-issue calendar on the wall near the door. Over his wide shoulder she catches what might be the black-and-white Adonises of a Herb Ritts calendar being hidden by the far more prosaic BriSpA-issue merchandise.

'I know fourteen different ways to kill a man,' says Craig, going over to the table and teasing one of the blooms. 'Just so you know. Coffee?'

Claudia points through the window at the rows of desks in the main office. 'Why do I never see these gorgeous men anywhere in the building?'

'Because they're security operatives.' Craig pours two cups of coffee. 'They're not . . . not *eye-candy*. We are the British Space Agency after all. We're a *target*, you know. Potentially.'

'You're a dark horse, is what you are.' She sits down and sips at the coffee. 'So what was so important and secret?'

'It's a . . . potential security breach. And it involves Major.'

Claudia raises an eyebrow. 'And Director Baumann has asked you to bring me in on this?'

'I haven't told Baumann yet.'

Claudia sits back. 'But I'm just the head of PR. I think—'

'I'm not going to him with this, I'm going to you. I don't trust him. He makes me want to go full Hammerhead.'

'What?'

'Never mind. The point is, I've got this stuff and I don't know what to do. But I trust you and I think you should hear it first.'

'Hear it? What is it?'

Craig beckons her round to his side of the desk and gives up his seat. He plugs a set of earphones into his monitor and passes them to her. 'Hit play when you're ready,' he says, pointing at the media player on the screen. 'I'll get you another coffee. You'll need it.'

Two hours later, Claudia takes out the earphones. 'Bloody hell. Can you email me copies of those files?'

Craig nods. 'What do you think we should do?'

'I'm not sure what we should do at all. Do you know who it is?'

'Yes. I've called in some favours and got the number traced.' He reaches around her and opens his desk drawer, pulling out a piece of paper and handing it to Claudia. 'That's the address. Are you going to go to Baumann with this?'

'I think,' says Claudia, looking at the paper, 'that Director Baumann doesn't need to be bothered with this at the moment. This is gold. Pure, public-relations gold. He wouldn't know what to do with it.' She looks back to Craig. 'What do you think's going on?'

Craig shrugs. 'I think he's trying to make amends in some way. To achieve closure.'

'To who? For what?'

'Have you read his file?' Claudia nods. He goes on, 'His brother. His mother. His father. The girl who went to university. His wife. Especially his wife. And the baby.'

They both look at each other for a moment then simultaneously their brows crinkle and they bite their lips and they both say, 'Awwwww,' as though they have just discovered that Thomas Major is, in fact, made of kittens.

43

NEW YEAR'S DAY 2000

Thomas wakes without a hangover on New Year's Day, because he didn't go out on New Year's Eve. So he does what he always does; he runs.

He is this year turning thirty; he is leaner and fitter than many of his peers who work at the bio-chemical research facility just outside of the M25; his colleagues of a comparable age are either balding and tending to fat, or pale and owlish through lack of sunlight and proper nutrition. Thomas is working with a large team who are employed on a vast and open-ended experiment to introduce enzymes and proteins into the gene-structure of papayas from Hawaii (which Thomas feels should be a song in a Busby Berkeley musical) with the view of extending their life-span, plumpness and hardiness. On some days there are people wearing tie-dyed T-shirts and shapeless jackets – knitted from what Thomas can only surmise, due to their texture and smell, must be yak hair – who gather outside the chain-link fence with placards daubed with words such as 'Frankenfood' and 'No to GM crops' but Thomas thinks they are in a minority, which will shortly lose interest and fade away. After years of stuffing processed food and chicken burgers made from the sweepings up off takeaway floors down their necks, he's pretty sure the British public won't turn up their nose at food that's had a bit of scientific help to grow bigger, tastier and hardier.

One day as he drives his battered, old-style Mini into the site, his car held together largely by webs of rust and chugging out black smoke from its rear end, he thinks he spots Laura among the protesters, but when he looks again she's gone and he decides it can't have been her anyway. Or rather, he doesn't want it to have been her. He cannot abide the thought of seeing her again.

The site has closed down for two weeks over Christmas and New Year, it being the turn of the Millennium and all. Thomas is sick and tired of pointing out to everyone that the 1990s doesn't actually end until the end of the year 2000, but no one wants to listen. They do, in fact, want to party like it's 1999. Thomas stays indoors, listening to his David Bowie on vinyl and going to bed at 10 p.m., his head under the pillow, praying fervently for the much-prophesied Millennium Bug to do what everyone fears and switch of all the computers, plunging the world back into the stone age and meaning Thomas could, finally and irrevocably, piss off somewhere remote and find a cave to live in and never have to see any other living soul again for the rest of his life. Unfortunately, when he wakes up on New Year's Day, society has hatefully declined to end. So Thomas resolves to spend the next week running, reading, listening to music and generally avoiding people.

Thomas, jogging along a pavement in front of the small gardens of a long avenue of semi-detached townhouses, is motivated to crank it up a gear. His Walkman is clipped to the waistband of his shorts and he knows this is the last track on this side of the tape; if he maintains a sprint for the duration of the track he will get back to his flat agreeably out of breath and ready for a shower. Then some lunch, and the rest of the day to read and see what the dog-end of the Christmas TV schedules have hidden among them in terms of movies.

Thomas already has one foot off the kerb to cross a side street when he notices the black Fiat Punto out of the corner of his eye; the next instant there is a screech of brakes and he feels the cold kiss of the vinyl bumper on his leg just below his knee. Thomas skids and staggers, the earphones falling from his ears, and glares into the windscreen at the woman who is sitting hunched over her steering wheel, staring at him with big round eyes.

'You . . . you *idiot!*' shouts Thomas, his voice ringing and echoing off the walls of the houses.

The woman kills the engine and winds down her window. '*You* idiot!' she shouts.

Thomas limps round to her side of the car, pulls off his headphones and says, 'You nearly ran me down.'

The woman screws up her nose and frowns. 'You ran in front of me!'

Thomas plants his fists on his hips, only now realising how out of breath he is. 'Look,' he says.

'Here we go,' says the woman, rolling her eyes. 'Every time a man begins a sentence with "look" it means a woman is in for some patronising explanation.'

Thomas ignores her. She is trying to put him off. 'Look,' he says again. 'I'm not sure when you passed your driving test . . .'

'Like I said' – she pulls up the handbrake and folds her arms –'Patronising git.'

'*But*,' says Thomas, trying to ignore her, 'perhaps you might have a passing acquaintance with the rule that says a car turning right into a side street must give way to a pedestrian that is already on the carriageway—'

'Ah-a,' says the woman triumphantly.

Thomas shuts his mouth mid-sentence. 'What do you mean, ah-a? That sounds as though you somehow misheard me and you do, in fact, think you are in the right and not the wrong.'

'I *am* in the right. I had already started turning while you were still on the pavement. *You* should have given way to *me*.'

Thomas gives a little laugh. Another car is trying to turn in behind the woman and the driver beeps his horn. Thomas gesticulates at him and shouts. 'We're trying to sort out a highways issue. There's a potential legal action here.'

The woman is looking at him with a humorous twinkle in her green eyes, which disarms Thomas even further. 'Legal action, hmm?' she says. Thomas sees her left leg – slim, pale, wrapped in a black skirt – depress the clutch pedal and she puts the car into gear. He is momentarily disarmed by her pale face with its constellation of freckles across her nose and cheeks, her copper hair cascading on to the shoulders of a black business jacket. 'In that case you'll need a lawyer.'

She dips into her jacket pocket and pulls out a card, handing it to him through the window. 'Call me tomorrow afternoon.' She guns the engine. The man behind beeps again.

Thomas looks at the card. *Janet Eason. Junior Partner. Kirby Chambers*. A telephone number. A mobile phone number. A fax number. He looks back at Janet Eason. 'Why?'

'So you can tell me where you're taking me for dinner tomorrow night,' she says, and Thomas almost forgets to jump back as her car moves forward and heads down the street, closely followed by the man in the next vehicle who glares at him as he passes.

But Thomas is oblivious. He stands in the middle of the road, his breath pluming in the mild-for-January air, and stares at the card. Janet Eason. Dinner. Tomorrow night. His first thought is that of course he won't go, he never goes to things like this, he doesn't know what to say, what to wear, whether to pay the bill or split it, if he's expected to make a sudden lunge while they're waiting for a taxi.

And then he supposes it's better to regret something you have done than to regret something you haven't done, and for the first time in the new millennium Thomas considers that it was possibly not a bad thing at all that the world didn't end as advertised.

✶ 44 ✶

MAD TO BE SAVED

Ellie sits on the benches outside the parish church, wrapped up tight in the scarf Nan knitted and the coat she's had for two years – tight across her back, the cuffs halfway up her forearms. Later, she might go and look in the shop windows at new coats she'll never be able to afford. She hugs her rucksack to her stomach and draws an imaginary bead on a couple in their thirties, briskly walking through the small gardens in the shadow of the clock tower, holding hands as though they're shipwrecked survivors bobbing in the sea, afraid of letting each other go.

Blam! *He* stays up late drinking and watching old movies because he can't bear to climb into bed with her.

Blam! *She* has twice in the last month almost booked a single ticket to somewhere hot and distant, only baulking at the final moment, putting away her credit card and killing the webpage. But she'll do it. She'll leave him. She'll run away.

It's cold today and the sky is black and heavy with the threat of snow, or would be if it were a degree or two colder. Ellie has her scarf pulled up around her ears so consequently does not hear the approach of Delil, who makes her jump when he sits down beside her in his padded anorak.

'Do you always do this?' he says conversationally, inspecting a sausage roll he's holding in a folded-up Gregg's paper bag. 'Pretend to shoot people, I mean. It's not really normal. Do you want a bite of this before I do?'

Ellie takes the sausage roll and bites a chunk from it before handing it back. She says through a mouthful of processed meat and flaky pastry, 'I'm not pretending to shoot people. I'm using my Sniper Rifle of Truth on them. It shows that people who think they're happy are just pretending. They're living a lie. Nobody's happy really.'

'I'm happy,' frowns Delil. 'Or at least I was until you ate half my sausage roll.'

'No, you're not,' says Ellie. 'Nobody's happy.'

Delil thinks about it. 'No, I'm pretty sure you're wrong. I am happy.'

'You only *think* you're happy,' insists Ellie.

'But if I *think* I'm happy, then surely I *am* happy,' says Delil, taking a bite of the sausage roll. 'Descartes, innit?'

'You can't be happy.' Ellie hugs her bag closer to her chest. 'Because that wouldn't be fair. The Sniper Rifle of Truth is all I've got. The only thing that stops me going mad. I have to believe that nobody's really happy, because if that's not true then that just makes my unhappiness worse.' She looks at him with pleading eyes. 'Don't take that away from me.'

He shrugs, pops the last of the sausage roll into his mouth and rolls up the paper bag. 'You're right,' he says, chewing the pastry. 'I'm desperately unhappy. Especially because you won't come to the party on Friday night.'

'I can't,' she sighs. 'You know I can't. James has to go to London at the crack of dawn on Saturday morning. I've got work on Friday at the Polish shop and that's even more important now.' Ellie looks at Delil. 'I lost my job at the welding place.'

*

172

'Bit of a problem,' says Hooters, roll-up dangling from his dry lips as he wipes the grease from whatever he's had for breakfast off his hand and on to his T-shirt, the pneumatic, vacant-eyed line drawing of the naked woman grinning inanely in thanks for his attentions. He has all the Sunday morning workers lined up inside the unit on the industrial estate, around the electric heater that is Hooters' one concession to trying to make the place a little more comfortable in the depths of winter. It's a vast, echoing chamber of concrete and corrugated steel, benches lined up around the edges. Ellie's job is to assemble wire cages and slide them into a spot-welding machine, stamping on a pedal with her foot to seal the joints together and make panels for shopping trolleys. It's hot, dirty work and her arms are always pocked with burns, her face smeared with oil, her fingers sprouting splinters from the rough wood of the pallets that are piled next to her work-station bearing the lengths of wire to be welded. She works all day Sunday and gets a brown envelope with twenty pound notes in it at the end of the day. She has a feeling that the days of cash-in-hand welding are probably numbered.

There is a radio playing *Steve Wright's Sunday Love Songs* in the far end of the unit. Hooters rubs his nose and shouts, 'Turn that ponce off for a minute.' Ellie looks around at her fellow Sunday workers, a motley crew comprising a few middle-aged men in shabby overalls who talk about football and beer and their wives; a few studenty-types, though their numbers have thinned out after the Christmas holidays, and various factions of immigrant workers who huddle together in their national groups, apart from a tall, blond Australian who will talk to anyone within earshot, but who has resolutely failed to ever return Ellie's admiring gaze.

'Got the bloody DWP sniffing round,' says Hooters. At the far end of the unit "Lady in Red" starts to play. Hooters shouts, 'I said, turn that ponce off! And that goes double for this ponce!' Then he turns to a knot of Latvians who all wear leather jackets. 'Dee-double-you-pee,' he enunciates. 'Department for Work and Pensions. Bloody snoopers. Trying to stop good, honest businessmen from making a few bob.'

Hooters pats his pockets for a lighter and tries to coax his roll-up back into life. He coughs drily twice and says, 'So. Going to have to lay some of you off. The foreigners, mainly.' Hooters looks at the Latvians and waves his arms. 'Lay. You. Off. No papers, see? No National Insurance. Us no friends with Europe any more. Cash in hand.' He pulls a face. 'Very, very naughty of me. Apparently.'

The Australian waves a hand. 'Had we better get out of the way now? Are they spying on us?'

'Not you, lad,' says Hooters. 'I think it's just the foreigners that need to bugger off for a bit.'

'I'm Australian.'

Hooters frowns. 'That's not *foreign* foreign, though, is it? Not like this lot is foreign.'

'I don't have a work visa, though,' says the Australian cheerfully.

'Bloody hell.' Hooters shakes his head. He looks at Ellie. 'What about you? Never even heard you speak. Don't tell me you're from bloody Uzbekistan or somewhere?'

Ellie shakes her head. Hooters says, 'Good. That's something then, love. Just need your National Insurance. Have you got a card and stuff?'

Ellie shakes her head again. Hooters squints at her. 'Driving licence? You are seventeen aren't you, love? Sure I put that on the advert. Seventeen and above.'

Ellie shakes her head, again.

'Christ. At least tell me you're sixteen.'

Ellie shakes her head.

Hooters slaps his hand against his head. 'Go. Latvians. Australians. Bloody jail bait. Useless, the lot of you. Piss off before you get me banged up.'

'Rough,' says Delil. 'Doesn't sound like it was that much of a great job though.'

'That's not the point,' says Ellie, hugging her bag. 'I need the money. We need the money.'

'Why are you always so worried about money?' says Delil. 'Ooh, look, there's one.'

'One what?'

'A happy couple. Over there. Shoot them with your imaginary gun.'

Ellie scrutinises the big man enveloped in a quilted jacket, a woollen hat pulled over his ears, walking on in front of the woman who hauls a brown paper Primark bag with both hands. She looks away. 'They aren't even pretending to be happy.'

'Like you think I am? Pretending to be happy, I mean?'

'There's only one way to find out.' Ellie raises the Sniper Rifle of Truth between them on the bench. She peers down the invisible sight at him through one eye.

'Well?' Delil has his eyes closed, bracing himself for the *blam*.

Ellie puts the rifle away. 'It won't work on you. On account of you being mad.'

'The only people for me are the mad ones,' says Delil, jumping to his feet.

'Sit down, idiot.'

Delil begins to flap his arms as though he's trying to take flight. 'The ones who are mad to live, mad to talk, mad to be saved, desirous of everything at the same time.'

'Delil,' hisses Ellie. 'You're drawing attention to us.'

'The ones who never yawn or say a commonplace thing,' he says, throwing back his head.

'We're supposed to be in school,' says Ellie through gritted teeth.

'But burn, burn, burn like fabulous yellow roman candles exploding like spiders across the stars,' Delil shouts, his arms cartwheeling. An old lady dragging a shopping trolley stops to stare at him. Delil takes an exaggerated stage bow, doffing an invisible cap to her.

Ellie is just shaking her head. 'What the hell was that?'

'Jack Kerouac. *On the Road*. You read it?'

'No I haven't read it. What are you doing here, anyway? Apart from embarrassing me?'

He digs into his jacket pocket and gives her a folded envelope. 'I got the LED lights for James.'

Ellie takes them and stuffs them into her rucksack. 'How did you know I'd be here?'

'Followed you, didn't I?' says Delil. 'I saw you go get your coat at break. You never get your coat at break. You don't go outside if

175

you don't have to. You always sit in the canteen or in the library. So I knew you were up to something.'

'Regular little Sherlock, aren't you?'

'I observe people. That's why I'm going to be a writer. Might be a detective as well, now you mention it. That would be safe. Hey, we could fight crime together. Like *Hart to Hart*. I saw that on UK Gold. Brilliant. Have you watched it?'

'I don't get much chance to watch telly.'

He looks at his watch. 'Hadn't we better get back? We've got PE after dinner.'

'Not me. I'm on my period. Got a note from my nan.'

Delil nods. 'Then I'm skipping PE too. I'm coming out in sympathy with you because you're my best friend. Belly ache, headache, the works. I'm really cranky as well.'

Ellie aims a kick at him which he deftly dodges. 'If men did have periods there'd have been a cure for them centuries ago.'

She stands up. Delil stands up too. 'Where are we going?'

'I'm going to my brother's school. You're going back.' She looks at him for a moment, head on one side. 'You're clever, Delil. Clever enough to do stuff. Proper stuff. Don't let me drag you down. Go back to classes.'

He shrugs. 'They can't teach me anything any more. Not about anything I'm interested in. I bet Miss Barber's never even read Jack Kerouac. What are we going to James's school for?'

Ellie sighs. 'You're like a rash. Can't get rid of you. Come on, then. We have to get ready.'

✻ 45 ✻

PLAYING AT GROWN-UPS

Half an hour later Ellie and Delil are sitting in the reception of St Matthew's Primary School. There are notices on the wall warning about not taking photographs of children and having suitable identification, alongside framed paintings and drawings celebrating everything from the Queen's birthday to football tournaments to one that shows children of all colours and creeds holding hands around the globe.

'Look.' Delil points at a white girl with dark hair and a beaming black boy on the latter poster. 'It's us.'

'Shush,' says Ellie. Before catching the bus to James's school she had gone into the bus station toilets and emerged in a pair of black trousers, a blue shirt and her hair piled on top of her head. She had done her make-up, dark red lipstick, eyes smouldering with kohl. Ellie had instructed Delil to take off his school tie and his blazer and had stuffed them into her bag along with her uniform, inspecting him critically.

'Who are we supposed to be?' he had said.

'I'm James's sister, but older,' Ellie had replied.

'And who am I?'

'I suppose you'll have to be my boyfriend or something.'

In the reception, Delil peers through the fronds of the fern on the side table between their chairs. 'Safe. We're undercover,' he says happily.

'Stop it,' hisses Ellie. A smartly dressed woman with greying hair cut short is approaching them. Ellie looks up and smiles. 'Mrs Britton?'

The woman nods. 'Ms Ormerod? And . . .?'

'Delil Alleyne,' says Delil, standing up and taking Mrs Britton's hand. 'I'm Eleanor's fiancé. We're getting married in summer.'

How wonderful,' says Mrs Britton. Ellie stands too and kicks Delil in the ankle, but he doesn't flinch. 'Please follow me to my office.'

The office is bright and airy, with a wide desk and more children's artwork on the walls, alongside framed certificates of Mrs Britton's extensive qualifications. Ellie and Delil are invited to sit down in two comfortable chairs facing the head, who leans forward on her desk and steeples her fingers together.

'So,' she says. 'We're hugely excited about James being invited to participate in the final of the National Schools Young Science Competition. *Hugely* excited. And he's been talking us through his proposals for his entry. I must say, he's put a lot of thought and effort into it. We think it certainly ticks a lot of boxes *vis a vis* the socially aware requirements of the competition.'

'Yes, well.' Ellie forces a laugh. 'James is nothing if not socially aware.'

Mrs Britton assumes a serious face. 'Indeed. We do realise there have been some . . . difficulties with the family.'

'You could say that, yes.'

'What with your mother . . . passing. And your father . . . your father—'

'In jail?' adds Ellie helpfully.

'Yes. In . . . incarcerated,' nods Mrs Britton. 'Though I must say, James doesn't seem to have allowed that to unduly affect his school life.'

'No,' smiles Ellie. 'Despite the best efforts of some of his classmates.'

Mrs Britton's smile falters. 'There have been some minor . . . issues, yes. I was going to raise that with you today, in fact. But it seems to have been sorted out as of this morning.'

'You mean Oscar Sherrington's dad has withdrawn his complaint that his son was attacked by some kind of . . . of ninja outside the school?'

'Why, yes. Yes, that is exactly the case. I had the police here this morning. Obviously, you understand that we had to investigate, but it appears that the boy in question seems to have admitted to making it all up. I'm not sure where he got it from. No one else saw this masked person. I'm sorry if you have become involved in this. I'm not sure why this happened . . .'

'Possibly because Oscar Sherrington and his mates have been bullying James.'

'Well, we'll keep an eye on that,' nods Mrs Britton. 'But it's probably something I should be taking up with James's officially designated guardian.' She glances at her computer monitor. 'Mrs Gladys Ormerod? I would have thought she'd have been here today.'

'My grandmother is somewhat . . . incapacitated at the moment,' says Ellie, smiling. 'Which is why she has asked me to come along and discuss the competition.'

'Incapacitated?' Mrs Britton frowns.

'Nothing serious. She has merely sprained her ankle. While doing some charitable work. She . . . makes soup. For the homeless.'

'She slipped on a potato skin,' says Delil. Ellie kicks him again under the chair.

'Ah,' says Mrs Britton.

Ellie delves into her bag, being careful to keep her school uniform out of sight. 'I have had to take time off my job as an account manager at an insurance company to be here. I do have a letter from my grandmother, though.'

She hands over the envelope to Mrs Britton. Delil pushes his glasses up his nose. 'I'm a journalist. I work for the *Guardian*. You can search for my name on their website, if you like.'

Mrs Britton smiles and opens the envelope, reading the hand-written letter that Ellie has dictated to Gladys. 'Well, this all seems to be in order. But I think we do need to speak to Mrs Ormerod personally, as James's guardian. Perhaps I could come round to your home if she cannot get out? Maybe after school today?'

'I don't think that's a good idea,' says Ellie quickly.

There is a short silence, which Delil fills. 'Actually, do you think you could tell me more about this masked assailant who is attacking children outside school?'

Mrs Britton blinks at him. 'Sorry? What? Sorry?'

'Yes,' says Delil. 'I think it could be a good story. "Masked Ninja on the Loose at School Gates".'

'But we already established that was just some fantasy made up by a boy . . .'

Delil smiles. 'No smoke without fire, though. What sort of mask was the man wearing?'

Mrs Britton frowns. 'I don't think the *Guardian* would be inter-ested in something like—'

'I also write for the *Daily Mail*,' says Delil, beaming at the teacher. 'And the *Sun*. I'm sure I could interest someone . . .'

Mrs Britton frowns. 'Are you sure you work for the *Guardian*? You seem awfully young . . .'

Delil puts his face in his hands. 'I have a condition. It's a congenital growth-hormone deficiency. I was just getting to terms with it. But then you mentioned it again. I'll probably have to go into therapy now.'

Mrs Britton looks stricken. 'Oh. I didn't mean to—'

'It's fine!' says Delil through gritted teeth. 'But can you imagine what it's like being a thirty-four-year-old man in the body of a fifteen-year-old? It's hell. It's a curse.'

Mrs Britton looks from Delil to Ellie and back again. 'I'm sure I didn't—'

Delil holds up his hand to silence her and pinches his nose, taking a deep, ragged breath. 'It's fine, I said. Please don't mention it again. I'd rather talk about the School-Yard Ninja. Is that what we're calling him?'

Ellie leans forward. 'I'm sure none of this will be necessary.' She points at the letter in Mrs Britton's trembling hands. 'So that note from my grandmother is fine . . .?'

Mrs Britton looks at Delil then back at the letter. 'Erm. Yes, yes, I suppose.'

Delil sits back in his chair. 'Then maybe you're right. It probably isn't a story at all.'

Mrs Britton folds the letter and puts it back in the envelope. 'So. Right. Fine. We're planning to set off for the competition early on Saturday morning. Myself and the deputy, Mr Waddington. We have train tickets booked. We can pick up James at home . . .?'

'We'll get him to school,' says Ellie. 'I think that would be best. Thank you.'

'Could he bring in his experiment on Friday?' Mrs Britton looks a little confused as though something has just happened that she can't quite account for. 'If he needs more time to finish it, we can allow him that, either at home or in school.'

'That would be useful,' nods Ellie. 'Well, I think that's everything. Thank you for your time.'

Mrs Britton hands Ellie an envelope. 'Here are all the details of the event. James's age group is on at 11 a.m.' They all stand and shake hands, Mrs Britton glancing at Delil somewhat mistrustfully. 'And you're sure you won't . . .?'

Delil smiles broadly. 'I'll be back in touch if I think I need to be. But hopefully I won't.'

*

'That was genius,' says Ellie, leaning back on the gates outside the school. 'I thought she was going to insist on coming round to ours. That would have been a disaster. But I did think you might have overdone it a bit with that hormone stuff.'

'Are you going to tell me what's going on, though?' says Delil. 'What's this masked attacker thing? And why are you so desperate for money, really? Why does this competition mean so much to you? It's not just for James, is it?'

Ellie looks at him. 'I can't really say. Not yet. But thank you for everything you just did.'

'Are we going back to school? I like playing grown-ups.'

Ellie looks at the sky, clouds gathering blackly. 'Nah. Can't be bothered.'

'So, what are we going to do, then? We could go to the library.'

'You know how to show a girl a wild time,' says Ellie, digging in her bag. 'Hang on. My phone's buzzing.'

'The library is a wild time,' says Delil. He waves his hands in front of him, a magician unveiling his finest illusion. 'It's the gateway to a million different worlds. It's—'

'Don't tell me, it's safe. Look, I have to go home,' says Ellie, staring at her phone.

'I'll come with you.'

Ellie stands up and puts a hand on his chest. 'No. No, Delil. You can't.'

'I'm coming.'

'You. Are. Not,' says Ellie and turns on her heel, heading towards the bus stop. She checks just once to make sure Delil isn't following her, then looks again at the message from Gladys. Ellie's breath comes sharp and shallow and she looks desperately around for a bus. Can she afford a taxi? She runs through the change in her purse. Just coppers. Please don't let them in, she says to herself. Please don't say a word. She's going to have to ring Gladys, coach her through what to say, tell her to pretend to be out. Ellie starts to run through her pre-prepared speeches for the inevitable visit of the police or the social services or some other authority figure who's bent on splitting them up. At last the bus arrives and Ellie leaps on, looking at her phone again, her hand shaking as she reads the text message one more time.

STRANGE WOMAN AT DOOR WHAT SHALL I DO?

✳ 46 ✳

I'VE BEEN TO WIGAN

18 Down: If put off, can encourage angina, say—proverbially (4)

The crossword grid is filling up, and those four blank squares in the middle are taunting him, those letters around it offering no clues at all as to the missing word. Thomas sits cross-legged, floating in the white-lit space of the main cabin like some levitating yogi, the book in one hand and the pencil gripped between his teeth. He cannot, for the life of him, get this. It is beginning to consume him. He closes his eyes and tries to allow his mind to go blank, like an endless black lake, in the hope that if he casts out his line he will pluck the errant word from his memory, like a fisherman flicking out a fly.

But all he catches is the insistent, irritating pinging of an incoming Skype call from his monitor. Thomas squints at the digital clock display at his workstation; gone 10 p.m., GMT. Usually too late even for Baumann to harangue him about how desperate the situation is regarding the EVA. Which suggests there's probably more dreadfulness. What fresh hell is this? He pushes himself over to the workstation and anchors himself to the chair. The delicate thrum of the engines sounds the same as it always does, and none of the instruments are indicating dangerously low or high levels of anything. For a piece of old Soviet junk, *Shednik-1* is performing pretty nicely.

Thomas accepts the call and is surprised to see Claudia's face fill the screen. Even more curiously, she doesn't seem to be at Mission Control, unless Baumann has had a brain-fart and allowed her to redecorate it with soft furnishings, scatter cushions, an IKEA

182

bookcase and . . . yes, what appears to be a framed film poster dominating the low-lit wall behind her.

'Claudia.' Thomas adjusts himself in the chair so he fills the smaller screen in the corner of the monitor that shows him what she sees. For a brief second he wishes he'd brushed his hair, then puzzles at why he should even think that. 'It's late. I take it there's some PR crisis? Have the papers found out about the body under the patio?'

Claudia starts to laugh, then pushes back her dark hair with one perfectly manicured hand, and her plump, red lips turn down in a frown. 'Um. Is there a body under a patio?'

'Probably,' says Thomas. 'But not one I've had anything to do with.'

She sighs and visibly relaxes. 'Even if there was, it's not as if anyone could do anything about it now.'

'You're not kidding. I had an attempted break-in at my flat last year. It took a week for the police to come. I doubt they'd have the resources to chase me to Mars if I had put a body under the patio.'

'Which you haven't, of course . . .'

'I like how you're not quite sure.' Thomas peers over her shoulder, though the image is fuzzy and starts to break up into constellations of coloured squares. 'Is that poster . . . *It's A Wonderful Life*?'

Claudia glances back. 'Hmm? Oh, that. Yes.'

'My favourite movie.' He has no idea why he's having this conversation. If he didn't know better, he might think he was actually *flirting* with Claudia. He looks over at the instrument panel again; maybe the air levels are screwy after all. Perhaps there's not enough oxygen in the mix, or too much nitrous oxide.

The image sharpens and Claudia narrows her eyes. 'Your favourite movie? I thought you science-y types were only into films like *Independence Day* or *War of the Worlds*. Isn't this a bit sentimental for you? Why, Major Tom, you want to be careful. People are going to think you have a heart.'

There's a brief – but not uncomfortable, thinks Thomas wonderingly – silence, while he and Claudia regard each other. 'You're calling me from home, I take it? Your house?'

'Flat. Well, room in a flat that's been divided up to accommodate six people. You know what it's like. Trying to get somewhere nice in London.'

Thomas opens his mouth and then closes it again when he realises he was about to ask if she had a boyfriend or husband. What's that got to do with him? Why would he even think about that? Instead he says, 'Why are you calling me, Claudia?'

She looks at him for a long time.

'Claudia? What have you done?'

She says, 'I've been to Wigan.'

Craig pulls his Audi in behind a battered white van on a narrow street of red-brick terraced houses, darkened with decades of soot, front doors facing straight out on to the pavement. 'Here we are,' he says, hauling up the handbrake. 'Number 19, Santus Street. Do you want me to come in with you?'

Claudia wipes the condensation from the window and peers through it at the house. The curtains are open and there is dim lamplight within. She says, 'I think I'll be all right. I'll shout if I get any trouble. But as far as I can tell, we're dealing with a seventy-year-old woman, a teenage girl and a ten-year-old boy, right?'

'Northerners, though.' Craig nods sagely. 'Once served with a logistics officer from Lancashire. Preston. Guild Hall Gary, they called him. Very unpredictable. Drank a bottle of vinegar while we were on our way to Belize. For no reason.'

'Right,' says Claudia. 'I'll keep an eye for them getting the vinegar out.'

Outside on the pavement, Claudia smoothes down her suit skirt and risks a glance in at the window. There's a woman in an easy chair, her face lit by the glow of afternoon TV. She catches Claudia looking at her and stares back. Claudia smiles and waves, and points to the door. The woman looks startled and scrabbles on a small table by her chair for a phone.

Claudia moves towards the door and consults her iPad while she waits. This must be Gladys Ormerod, the woman Thomas Major called seemingly by accident. Apparently Gladys now owns the number that used to belong to Thomas's ex-wife. Claudia wonders why she changed her number – to avoid Thomas's calls?

There's no movement behind the green wooden door, so Claudia raps smartly on it. She takes a step back and looks to the window, in time to see Gladys ducking back behind the curtains. Claudia looks at Craig in his car, but he's engrossed by his magazine. She knocks again and eventually she hears the rattle of the lock. The door opens an inch, Gladys Ormerod peering through the crack from behind a heavy security chain.

'We don't want none,' says Gladys, and makes to shut the door.

Claudia quickly but gently puts the palm of her hand against it. 'Mrs Ormerod . . .?'

'No. They've moved out. They've gone to . . .' She appears to think about this for a moment. 'Bolton. Aye, they've gone to Bolton. You'd be better trying them there.'

'Mrs Ormerod,' smiles Claudia. She looks at the van parked outside the house. On its dirty white flank is written *Darren Ormerod, Building Contractor*. 'It's all right. I'm not here to cause you any trouble.'

'Are you from the housing association? The cheque's in the post.'

She tries to shut the door again but Claudia sticks her toe into the crack, wincing as the wood scrapes against her shoe. She knew she shouldn't have worn the Blahniks to come to Wigan. 'I'm not from the housing association. I just need to talk to you for a moment. My name is Claudia Tallerman. I'm from BriSpA.'

Gladys looks blankly at her. 'Are you selling something? Because we've got no money.'

'No, no.' Claudia pauses. 'Well, I'm always selling something, that's sort of my job, but I'm here from the British Space Association. You know, Thomas Major? Major Tom?'

Gladys breaks into a wide smile. 'Major Tom! Why didn't you say so! Are you a friend of his?'

'Yes!' says Claudia happily. 'Yes, I am! I'm a very good friend of Major Tom's! Now can I come in?'

'No.' Gladys kicks Claudia's shoe out of the doorway with the toe of her slipper. 'You'll have to wait until Ellie comes back.' Then she slams the door in Claudia's face.

'That went well,' says Craig as Claudia lets herself back into the car. 'I could get you in there in five minutes, you know. And have the old bird singing in three.'

'I don't think that'll be necessary, Commander Bond. We're just waiting for Ellie.' She looks at her iPad. 'That's the fifteen-year-old. Who obviously wears the trousers in this house.'

Claudia nudges him and he looks up through the windscreen. A slim girl with her dark hair pulled in a careless ponytail, a rucksack hanging from her shoulders, is running up the street. Craig says, 'She doesn't look fifteen. She isn't wearing a school uniform. And look at that make-up.'

'That make-up is *exactly* how a fifteen-year-old girl who's lost her mum would do it.' Claudia gathers her bag again. 'I think the boss is home.'

As the girl fumbles in her pocket for her keys Claudia hurries from the car and calls out, 'Ellie? Ellie Ormerod?'

The girl turns with suspicion and fear in her eyes. She could be quite pretty if she had someone to give her some proper advice. Ellie says, 'Who are you? What do you want? The eviction notice isn't until—'

Claudia holds up her hands. 'I'm not here to evict you. I just want to talk.'

The door opens inwards as Ellie tries to sort her keys. Gladys stands on the doorstep. 'She's called Claudia. She's a friend of Major Tom's.'

Ellie regards Claudia with narrow eyes. She looks at the Audi, and Craig, who gives her a wave. 'You're from BriSpA?'

Claudia nods. 'I've got ID in my bag if you want to see it.'

Ellie sighs. 'You'd better come in.' She nods at the car. 'Is he coming in as well?'

'He's fine in the car,' says Claudia, following the old woman and the young girl across the threshold of 19 Santus Street. 'Between you and me, he's a bit scared of northerners.'

47

DAMAGE LIMITATION

Claudia perches on the sofa while Gladys makes a pot of tea, looking around the living room at the sideboard, the table by the window with its photographs of what she assumes are Ellie's parents, the TV, Gladys's easy chair. She feels Ellie looking at her, and the girl says, 'You probably think we're northern and quaint.'

'It's lovely. And about twice the size of my place in London.'

'I wish I lived in London,' says Ellie, sitting down beside her. 'In my own flat.'

'It has its moments.'

Gladys emerges from the kitchen with a tray bearing a teapot snuggled in a brown knitted cosy, and three cups. Claudia says, 'But I don't live in a flat; I live in a room. And it can get lonely sometimes. Besides, you're only fifteen. Too young to live on your own.'

Ellie's eyes narrow. 'You seem to know a lot about me.'

Claudia nods, glancing back at the photographs. They're a nice detail. She'll remember that. She was good on what the editors used to call 'colour' when she worked as a journalist for the magazines, before she jumped to what her fellow hacks called the 'dark side' of public relations. While mentally composing an opening paragraph for an article she says, 'Yes, I do. You're Ellie and you're fifteen. Your brother James is ten, and quite the little scientist. And Gladys here is seventy-one next birthday. And you're all in a little bit of trouble.'

Gladys beams as she pours the tea. Ellie says, 'It sounds like Major Tom has been talking. He promised us he wouldn't.'

'Oh, he hasn't. But we do have access to recordings of the telephone conversations he's been having with you all. I'm surprised no one thought of that. We are the British Space Agency, after all.'

'Are you here to help us, love?' says Gladys, settling into her easy chair.

'I suppose I am.'

'We need five grand,' says Ellie quickly. 'If it's going to be a cheque write it out to Gladys Ormerod.'

Claudia laughs lightly, and takes a sip of her tea. Gladys has heaped sugar in it. She's going to have to do an extra session at the gym when she gets back to civilisation. 'Oh, I wish I had five thousand pounds to give you. PR doesn't pay that much, I'm afraid.'

'Surely BriSpA can afford it.'

'Probably,' shrugs Claudia. 'But I'm not sure why they would.'

She catches Ellie and Gladys sharing a look, then the girl says, 'So why are you here?'

Claudia puts her cup down on the coffee table. 'Well, it seems to me that Major Tom has been doing a marvellous thing, helping James with his experiment for this competition. A marvellous, wonderful, selfless thing. Just the sort of good news we need.'

Ellie shakes her head – she doesn't understand a word of what Claudia is saying. 'Good news?'

'Well, between you and me, Major Tom hasn't quite fulfilled the media promise he had when we first announced him as the astronaut who was going to Mars. He's . . . well, he's a bit *grumpy*. The press haven't quite taken to him as much as we'd hoped. Especially after that incident with the schoolgirl . . .'

'He made her cry,' nods Gladys. 'I gave him what for over that.'

'Precisely. He made her cry. It isn't good PR. So we need to do some damage limitation. Increase his stock. Turn things around.'

Ellie's eyebrows raise. The penny is finally dropping. 'And you think we're the way to . . . to *increase his stock*?'

Claudia smiles warmly. 'I'm glad we're all singing from the same hymn sheet on this one. I can see it now.' She waves a hand in the air, unveiling an imaginary headline. 'Major Tom helps stricken family keep their home. The *Daily Mail* will love it. And I'm thinking for the *Guardian* we can do something about the difficulties of coping in modern Britain with one parent dead and one in prison. I think the BBC would probably do an extended feature on it as well. Or we could go for an exclusive with one of the women's mags.' She raises her voice towards Gladys. 'You'd like that, wouldn't you, Mrs Ormerod? Your lovely family in one of the nice magazines?'

Ellie stares at her. 'But if you've listened to the tapes you'll know . . . nobody can find out about this. If they do they'll decide Nan can't look after us. She'll be put in a home. Me and James will have to go into care. They'll split us up.'

'I'm sure it won't come to that. And as soon as it's out there, you'll be swimming in donations from do-gooders. We can probably get a decent fee from whoever we give exclusive rights to.'

Ellie stands up. 'It won't matter!' she shouts. 'The money won't matter! Social Services will have to get involved and they'll split us all up.'

Claudia considers this. 'Well, perhaps. But only until your dad gets out of jail. It's only a few months, isn't it?'

Ellie balls her fists in fury. Claudia remembers what Craig said about northerners being unpredictable. She wonders if she should call him. Ellie says, 'No. Absolutely no chance. We're not some bloody zoo animals to be put on display while everybody prods and pokes us and says how awful it is! You don't have the right! You don't own us!'

'But we do own Major Tom. And by extension, we own you too, I'm afraid. Or at least, we own your interactions with Major Tom. I have the recordings to prove it.' She stands up. 'I'm not going to make you agree to anything right now. Think about it. I'll call you before the weekend. But there really is only one way this is going to go, you know.'

'You bitch!' screams Ellie. 'Get out!'

'I'm going.' Claudia smiles at Gladys. 'Thank you for the tea.'

Thomas sits silently for a moment, staring at the grainy image of Claudia on the monitor. 'She's right, you know. You are a bitch.'

Claudia shrugs. 'I'm just doing my job.'

Thomas resists the urge to give her a Nazi salute. 'The Ormerods haven't called all day. Is this why?'

'I told them that it wouldn't be a good idea to make contact with you again, until this was sorted out. I told them if they did, I would go straight to the press.'

189

Thomas puts his head in his hands. 'Why? Why would you be so horrible? Just when I was getting to think you weren't utterly dreadful.'

'It's not my job to be liked,' says Claudia tightly.

'I wasn't going to go so far as "like",' mutters Thomas. He looks up at her again. 'So . . . what now? You're obviously going to do this. Even though you know what it'll do to the family. I won't give any interviews, you know.'

'You won't have to. We have the full recordings of all your calls. We can edit some lovely transcripts from them. But . . .' She bites her lip. 'Maybe I won't have to do it at all.'

Thomas frowns. 'What do you mean?'

'Maybe you have a better story,' muses Claudia. 'Maybe, if you give me something juicier, I can go with that instead. Everyone's a sucker for a tragedy, Thomas. They lap it up out there. I can see this, one of the women's magazines perhaps, or run over five days in one of the nationals . . . the heartbreak of Britain's loneliest astronaut.'

'You really are a piece of work.'

'Not as much as you are, Thomas. Your files hint at all kinds of sadness. I want to know the stories behind those notes. We can start right now.'

Thomas lets out a sigh. 'A story a night, to save the lives of the Ormerods? You're a regular Shahryar, you know that?'

Claudia adopts an innocent air. 'Does he play for Chelsea?'

Thomas thinks about it, then grunts. 'All right. What do you want to know?'

Claudia sits back. 'Let's see . . . why don't we start with something easy? Why did you break up with Janet?'

Thomas rubs his chin, then nods. 'OK.'

Claudia smiles. 'In your own time, Scheherazade.'

Impressed despite himself that Claudia had actually got his *One Thousand and One Nights* reference, Thomas gathers his thoughts for a moment, and begins.

48

LAURA'S LETTERS

Before he can talk about the end, Thomas has to talk about the beginning, and how he surprises himself by calling the number on the card Janet Eason gives him, and arranging to take her to a not-very-expensive Italian restaurant. There he learns that she is three years younger than him, is originally from near York, likes to do yoga, would love to have a cat but the lease on her flat forbids it, is an admirer of all the Brontë sisters, hates people who slurp their tea, and is a fan of Motown.

Janet Eason, in turn, surprises him by insisting on paying for the meal – at which Thomas is careful not to slurp drinks of any kind – and then instructing the taxi driver who is taking them both home that there will be just one stop, and that will be at her flat.

And the biggest surprise of all is that when she takes Thomas to bed and instructs him to first undress her and then himself, he finds that he is not at all dreadful at the sex and Janet Eason rather seems to enjoy herself.

So it only seems natural that, after a year of not-very-expensive meals, not dreadful sex, and the rather unexpected adequacy of another person's company, Janet asks Thomas if he's ever going to get around to proposing, because she's almost thirty and not getting any younger, and if he was to ask she'd almost certainly say yes. So, on that basis, he asks. And she says yes.

The wedding is planned for a year after the proposal, but three months before the nuptials Thomas's mother contrives to have a stroke. When he receives the news he cannot see it any other way than as a last-ditch attempt to keep him close, to try to stop herself from losing Thomas as well as her husband and youngest son. Thomas is mentally preparing his speech as he gets a cab to the hospital. He's getting married, not dying, and he will still be around, can visit her as often as she wants him to. He knows Janet will not even entertain the idea of his mother living with them, even if they could buy a house that would accommodate her, so he never bothers to raise the idea. He will tell his mother that nothing will change, he will still see her as much as he always has.

But when he gets to the hospital his speech is forgotten. This is no maternal cry for help. She lies in her bed, shrivelled and dead-eyed, one side of her face drooping, her hand a claw curled in on her thin chest. Thomas has even brought flowers and grapes. She stares at them, glassy-eyed, and he kisses her paper-dry forehead and goes to find a doctor, who gives him the news: she is not expected to recover.

Thomas sits by her bed, not knowing what to do. His mother beckons him close, a thin rope of saliva dribbling from the corner of her downturned mouth. He wishes Janet was with him. She is tied up with an important trial. He tells his mother this, saying Janet would want to be there but she simply cannot get away. Theresa stares dully at him; she never took to Janet.

'Home,' she whispers.

'Yes!' says Thomas, forcing jollity. 'We'll have you home in no time!'

She shakes her head. 'Home.'

Thomas tries not to let his smile falter. This isn't the time to tell her that he will never be coming home. 'Have to get you up and about for the wedding.'

Even saying the word *wedding* makes Thomas feel a little queasy. And it's not just the thought of being the centre of attention. It's the thought of being married. Although he loves Janet fiercely, he does wonder how it came to this. He feels somewhat like a chess piece that has been moved into position by a grand master.

Thomas's mother points with her claw at her handbag on the side table. He fetches it for her and she haltingly digs in it, emerging with a tiny brass key.

'Home,' she whispers. 'Drawer.'

Thomas has to go to his mother's house to get her some fresh nightwear and in her bedroom he pauses at a chest of drawers. He gathers underwear and pyjamas, though he knows that she is unlikely to see out the week. One small drawer at the top right of the vintage chest remains locked, and he fishes in his pocket for the brass key. The key does, of course, fit, and he opens it to find a small stack of envelopes, bound by an elastic band.

They are all addressed to Thomas. He takes off the elastic band. All the envelopes have been opened. He takes out the first letter, though he of course recognises the handwriting on the address.

They are from Laura.

There are nine letters, and Thomas sits on his mother's bed and reads them all. The first one is dated just a week after Laura left to go to Manchester. *Hi Tom*, it reads. *Just wanted to let you know that I'm settled in my digs – the address is at the top of this letter. I'm sharing with four other girls and they all seem really nice. We don't have a phone and the nearest phone box is always vandalised so I thought it would be nicer to write to you. I wish you could have started this year, but there's always next year – by then I'll know all the best pubs to go to! I was wondering if you wanted to come over, maybe the weekend after next? I could show you the sights of Leeds – but bring an umbrella ha ha. Write back to me will you? I feel like we parted in a bit of a weird way and I've been pretty upset. I'm sorry if I kicked off a bit about you asking if I could defer – I know you didn't mean anything bad by it. It just came as a bit of a surprise. Missing you like crazy. Love, L.*

Thomas reverently lays the letter flat on the bedspread and reads the next one, dated a week later.

Hi Tom! I'm not sure if you received my letter – maybe you did and you're too busy having a whale of a time without me ha ha. More likely it's got lost in the post. Anyway, just wanted to let you know I've settled OK in Leeds. It really is a buzzing place – I think you'd love it here. So many great gigs and pubs. My address is at the top – it's not exactly a palace, and Soozi (one of the girls I share with, she's really nice!) saw a cockroach in the kitchen the other day. She screamed fit to bring the roof down! Beth (who is a lesbian) used my boot to crush it – ew, thanks, Beth! But it's nice enough and pretty easy to get to the city centre. I was hoping you might come over to stay for a weekend – and kill some cockroaches for us ha ha

– maybe not this weekend now, as I promised the girls we'd go out to a Happy Mondays gig, but what about the one after? Even if you can't make it send me a letter to let me know how you're going on. Hope your mum's OK. Love, L.

In the third letter, Laura wonders if Thomas has perhaps gone on holiday.

In the fourth letter, she asks that if he really doesn't want to speak to her, could he do her the courtesy of just sending a quick note to say so.

In the fifth letter, she says that she's telephoned his house twice from a telephone box that stank of urine and spoken to his mother, who was very friendly and asked how she was getting on and promised to get Thomas to write to her.

In the sixth letter she says, well, fuck you.

In the seventh letter Laura says that she understands that Thomas might be hurting but she needs some sort of closure and could they meet, even if it was just to talk over coffee?

In the eighth letter, which runs to four pages, Laura writes in awful detail about the sex she's had with a rugby-playing medical student. The words burn themselves into Thomas's eyes, not least the line which says the energetic bedroom athletics with an enviously endowed paramour have left her 'walking like John Wayne'.

The ninth and final letter, dated two months after the start of the university semester, says:

Thomas. Firstly, I apologise for that last letter. I was drunk when I wrote it and drunk when I posted it. And angry. So very angry with you. But I'm not angry now. I've written, I've telephoned, I've done everything I can short of getting on a train and coming to see you. But you know what? I'm not going to do that. You've obviously moved on, and I'm going to do the same. Life's too short not to, and I've got to enjoy the time I'm here in Leeds. I had hoped that we could rekindle what we had, and failing that at least be friends, but it looks like that's not going to happen. Obviously I can't stop you taking up your deferred place at Leeds next year, but I really don't think it would be good for us to run into each other. Not yet. Not for a long while. This is really sad and heartbreaking but it is what it is. I did love you, you know. I just wish you could have shown me a bit of the Thomas Major that I fell in love with. So I suppose this is goodbye. Have a nice life, Thomas. Laura.

Each and every letter is a hammer to his heart, each word a kick to his groin, the final full-stop on the very last letter a veil drawn over his eyes. He feels he might faint, but instead he just sits on the bed and stares at them. His impending wedding feels even more indistinct and strange in the face of this. It is as though he is a character in a ghost story, suddenly visited by a long-forgotten phantom with unfinished business. Then he gathers up the letters, puts the elastic band around them, and puts them in his jacket pocket, filling a bag with clothes that his mother won't wear before she dies.

✳ 49 ✳

LIVE LONG AND PROSPER

Theresa Major has shrunken and withered even more since Thomas was last there. He wants to hate her the same way he hated his father, but all he can do is take a muslin cloth from the side table and gently wipe away the web of drool from her chin. She looks at him with eyes he's not even sure see him properly.

'I found the letters,' he says flatly.

His mother seems to deflate, as though the weight of her deceit has been something she has been carrying around inside her like a poison gas for fourteen years. She opens her mouth and Thomas brings his ear close to her.

'Sorry.' Her voice is as fragile and insubstantial as dandelion clocks.

'Why?'

'Didn't . . . want . . . lose . . . you.'

And she has lost so much, he realises. He wants to shout and scream, to hurl the letters at her like the confetti she will never throw at his wedding, but instead he sits beside her on a hard plastic chair, and holds the hand that isn't gnarled and bent by the stroke, and reads the letters to himself one more time. Why has she done this? Why now? Is it some final salvo to throw his marriage to Janet into disarray? At some point he nods off, and is startled into wakefulness by a nurse. It is dark outside and his mother is sleeping.

No, not sleeping. 'She's gone,' says the nurse softly. 'I'm sorry.'

'Yes, she has.' But Thomas is looking at the letters, not his mother. 'I'm sorry, too.'

It takes the better part of two months, but through a combination of Yahoo, AltaVista, MySpace and Friends Reunited, Thomas finally tracks down Laura. She is living in the North East, where she is working as a researcher at the Labour Party headquarters. Consequently, Thomas schedules in the stag weekend he is appalled to find is expected of him to take place in Newcastle. The only attendees are three people from the GM foods research lab, the nearest he could summon up to actual friends – on the basis that he's spoken more than two words to them – and Janet's brother, Robert, who has obviously been instructed to attend and who makes no bones of the fact that he'd rather be just about anywhere else in the world when it becomes evident that no one is going to engage him in conversation about football.

What makes things worse is that Kevin, who is going to be Thomas's best man by dint of the fact that they have actually exchanged more than a handful of sentences, has decided that the stag party is going to have a theme.

Robert holds up the red long-sleeved top with black detailing on the V-neck that Kevin has handed him from his hold-all in one of the two Travelodge rooms they are sharing between the five of them and says, '*Star Wars*? Are you having a laugh?'

'*Star Trek*,' corrects Kevin. 'And it's highly appropriate.' He is slight and has receding hair, slightly bulging eyes, and a girlish giggle which he emits now. 'Thomas once told me that when he worked in some job digging ditches they all called him Spock.'

'Also,' says Rajdeep, peering over the rims of his thick glasses, 'Spock says *Live long and prosper*. Which is also very appropriate for a wedding.'

Kevin passes a blue shirt to Thomas and a large, tent-like charcoal grey one to Jeremy. 'Starfleet Academy. The only one I could get in XXL.' Jeremy nods agreeably, and continues to eat his doner kebab.

'Hang on a minute,' frowns Robert. 'Doesn't the guy wearing red always get killed by the bug-eyed monster? What colour have you got?'

'Gold.'

'That's Captain Kirk, right? We're swapping.'

'No!' says Kevin, horrified.

'I'd let him if I were you,' murmurs Rajdeep.

Robert snatches the gold top from Kevin and pushes the red one at him. 'Captain Kirk does all the shagging, doesn't he? Be wasted on you, pal.' He nods at Thomas. 'Right, Doctor Spock, let's go and get changed. The Three Amigos here can have this room, we'll take the other so I can keep an eye on you. Don't want you having a final fling when you're marrying my big sister, ha ha.'

Thomas sighs and grabs his bag and follows Robert out of the room, as Kevin says plaintively, 'It's *Mister* Spock, not Doctor.'

Thomas had half an idea that the stag do would involve sitting in a quiet pub until last orders and hoping the conversation wasn't as stilted as it was at work, but Robert is having none of it. Growing up in York he is familiar with Newcastle and has plotted them a route through the pubs and bars of the Bigg Market that ends up at a nightclub housed on a decommissioned cruise ship docked at the Tyne. The evening goes in a blur of beer and whisky chasers, Robert displaying an incredible talent for spotting groups of mini-skirted girls and following them into bars.

'Set phasers to *stunning*!' He grins. 'Oi, ladies, want to see my sonic screwdriver?'

'Did you hear that?' says Kevin with barely contained fury. 'Sonic screwdriver! The man knows *nothing*.'

Rajdeep drinks so much he is practically comatose, apart from an hour-long weeping session over a girl he once knew in Delhi, Jeremy conspires to have some item of food in his hand at every stop and says not a single word, and Robert and Kevin manage to have a fight right at the end of the night. Thomas is so drunk he is past caring, but it seems to revolve around Robert's demands that Thomas is stripped naked and tied to a lamp-post, as stag night tradition dictates, while Kevin is having none of it.

The fight, such as it is, involves Kevin flapping his hands at Robert's broad chest and Robert pushing him over into a puddle.

'You're a bunch of arseholes,' fumes Robert. 'At least let me put him some proper Doctor Spock eyebrows on.'

The last thing he remembers is Robert looming towards him with a black marker pen and Kevin protesting loudly that it is *Mister* Spock, not Doctor, until Rajdeep throws up into Kevin's lap.

Thomas rises early the next morning, and can barely open his eyes because of the noxious cocktail of alcohol swilling around his body and the jackhammer going off in his head. After a desultory wash he heads out via tram, train and bus to a small former mining village some fifteen miles out of Newcastle. It is a pretty place, with a village green and a duck pond, and cottages with long gardens at the front. It is not the sort of place he can imagine Laura living in, with her stripy tights and Dr. Marten's and pink hair. He has the address written on a piece of paper, and he takes three turns around the duck pond, decides he is just going to go back to Newcastle for a drink and the inevitable conflict with Janet's brother, and then takes the plunge and finds the cottage. It has an arch covered with white and blue flowering sweet peas over the small garden gate. His heart hammering, Thomas unlatches the gate and walks down the cracked stone path to the door, inset in a brick-built porch with a little slate roof. Even as he knocks on the door, he is sure he has the wrong address.

Until she opens the door. Her hair is blonde, not pink, and she is wearing black three-quarter length leggings, a white vest and Birkenstocks. He drinks in the sight. It is her.

'Laura.'

She looks puzzled at him for a mere instant, then says, 'Thomas.'

And he realises he has not the faintest idea what to say.

Laura says, 'Um. What are you doing here?'

He reaches into his pocket and pulls out the sheaf of envelopes. 'I got your letters.'

Laura raises an eyebrow. 'Yes, you would have done. I sent enough.'

'No,' he says. 'I mean I *just* got your letters. Like, two months ago. My mother . . . well, she hid them.'

Laura raises her other eyebrow. 'Oh. How is she?'

'Dead.'

Laura nods. 'Right.' She pauses. 'Well. I'm sorry to hear that.' Then she squints at him. 'Um, Thomas. Your face . . .'

'Oh, yes.' He remembers Robert with the marker pen. He licks a finger and rubs at his eyebrow. 'It got a bit messy last night. *Star Trek* theme.'

Then Laura smiles and Thomas feels his heart fill, so much that he thinks it's going to burst. He starts to speak, and his voice cracks. 'I should have come with you. To Leeds.'

Her smile falters. 'Thomas. That was a long time ago.'

He nods. His mouth quivers. He cannot trust himself to speak. She looks at him curiously. 'Did you come all this way to tell me that?'

Thomas nods again. 'Well. I was in Newcastle anyway. For my stag do. But I only came to Newcastle because I found out you live here.'

Laura blinks. 'Your stag do? Then you're getting married?'

'In three weeks,' says Thomas. 'But . . .'

And that *but* hangs there in the still air between them, buoyed on the heady scent of the flowers in Laura's garden, threaded with the lazy flight path of droning bees, suspended from brittle, drifting spiderwebs.

The door behind Laura opens and a man looms over her, short hair, wearing shorts and a football shirt, wiping his hands on a dish-towel. He peers at Thomas and frowns, and says, 'Everything all right, love?'

He's Welsh and for a second Thomas wonders if this is the rugby-mad medical student whose prodigious member Laura wrote such a poetic ode to all those years ago. For the first time he notices the engagement ring and wedding band on her finger.

'Fine,' says Laura. 'This gentleman is selling insurance. I told him we have everything we need.'

'Everything we need,' nods the man – Laura's husband – and puts a hand on her shoulder. He looks curiously at Thomas, 'Thanks for popping by, though.'

'Yes,' says Thomas as Laura's husband steers her back inside. 'I can see that. Everything you need.'

Just before the door closes, Laura looks at him one more time, and says, 'You are aware you have a penis drawn on your forehead in marker pen, aren't you?'

'Bloody hell,' says Claudia. 'And what would you have done if she'd been single? What about Janet? Is that why you split up? Did you meet Laura again? Did you have an affair?'

'I think that's enough for tonight.' Thomas stifles a yawn. 'The rest is a story for another day. You promise you'll not do anything with the Ormerods?'

'Promise,' says Claudia down the hissing line. 'I want to see how this ends. I'll call you again tomorrow, Scheherazade.'

'I still think you're a bitch, Claudia.'

There's a static pause. 'Thomas? *It's a Wonderful Life* is my favourite film, too.'

He listens to the dead air on the line for a while, not quite knowing what to make of that, then pushes himself away from the desk towards his sleeping bag, pausing only to take a long look at the distant Earth, now no larger in the window than a football.

* 50 *

GREEN LIGHT

Ellie calls a family meeting and outlines the current situation. James looks as though he's about to burst into tears. Gladys seems content to sing 'Jesus Wants Me for a Sunbeam' under her breath throughout.

'But why can't we call Major Tom?' says James, his bottom lip trembling.

'Because,' says Ellie patiently, 'if we do this woman Claudia will be listening in on our conversations. She wants to turn us into some sort of freak show for the media. And if that happens . . .'

They both look at Gladys. 'Nan, can you stop singing for a minute? This is serious.'

Gladys smiles broadly at them. 'Sorry, love. I can't stop thinking about Sunday School. Ever since Major Tom asked me if I knew that crossword clue. I might have to ring him to ask what it was again.'

'No.' Ellie squeezes the bridge of her nose hard. 'No. We can't ring Major Tom again. Not yet.'

'But the experiment . . .' says James. 'I can't do it without him.'

Ellie twists on the sofa to face him and puts a hand on each of his thin shoulders. 'You can. You can do it without him. You came up with the idea. You just need to make it work, all right? I went in to see your headteacher. We need to get to school dead early on Saturday. They're going to take you down to London on the train. That'll be exciting, won't it? I'll make you a packed lunch.'

'Why can't you come?'

'Because I wasn't invited. And besides, I couldn't leave Nan here on her own . . .'

'We used to sit cross-legged in a big circle,' says Gladys. 'Mr Trimble used to read from the Good Book. Proverbs. I remember that one.' She pauses and whistles a little bit more of 'Jesus Wants Me for a Sunbeam'. 'That's what put me in mind of Sunday School. Something something angina something proverbially. That was it. That was the clue. Proverbially. Proverbs.'

Ellie shakes her head. 'How are you doing with the experiment, anyway?'

'Nearly finished.' James wipes his nose with the cuff of his school shirt. 'Do you want to see it?'

In his room James has swept everything off his desk on to the floor to make way for a cardboard crate which Ellie brought home from the fresh produce section. Instead of cabbages it now holds card walls subdividing the box up into a floor plan of their house on Santus Street, the left side downstairs and the right side the upstairs. Ellie has to admit he's done a great job, painting the outside of the box like red bricks and the interior in a fair approximation of the tired decor in each room. He's even fashioned furniture from pieces of cardboard, coloured to look like the sofa and their beds, an entire recreation of their tiny kitchen.

Ellie hands him the bag of LED lights that Delil gave her and picks up a figure sculpted from plasticine, a smiling man in jeans and a T-shirt. She looks at James. 'Dad?'

He nods and stands up three more figures. 'You. Me. Nan.'

Ellie inspects each of them in turn. 'These are really . . . wow. You've done a really good job here, James.'

'I'll show you how it works,' says James, taking the figures back. He places Nan lying down in her bed, Ellie on the sofa and James in his room. 'You'll have to imagine that I've got the LED lights mounted on the outside of the wall, near the door. They wouldn't be there really, obviously, they'd be in some police station or something. But it's just to show the judges at the competition.'

'Go on, then.'

'OK. So imagine Dad's hooked up to some tracker or, what do you call it, a tag. An electronic tag. It works out whether he's doing something good or bad. If he's doing something bad then he doesn't get any time knocked off his sentence. In fact he might get time added on. But if he's doing something good, they make his sentence shorter, so he'll be free quicker. But this way he gets to be at home. Just under house arrest.'

'Could that happen?'

James nods. 'I looked into it. It's called Home Detention Curfew. They can release you with a tag when you've served a quarter of your sentence.'

Ellie nods. 'Show me. Pretend you've got the lights set up.'

James places the figurine of Darren Ormerod in Gladys's easy chair. 'So, say you've got homework and you've asked Dad to help you, but he just sits here watching the football or something. The red light flashes. That's bad.' He places the Darren figure in his bed. 'Or say it's Saturday morning and he's promised to cook us breakfast, but he just lies in bed all day.'

'Red light. But you do remember how crap Dad's breakfasts are, right, James?'

James takes Darren and Gladys and puts them in the kitchen. 'But this is Dad talking to Nan about the old days, making her feel good. Green light.'

'He is good at that. Always makes her laugh.' She feels tears prickling the backs of her eyes.

'And here he is sitting on the sofa with you, looking at your homework and telling you that you're miles cleverer than he is and you must get your brains from Mum. And he's telling us how much he misses Mum but we're all going to be all right.'

James sniffles and wipes his nose with his shirt sleeve again. Ellie can feel the tears running slowly down her cheeks. 'Yes, he was good at that as well. Telling us everything would be all right.'

James moves Darren to the side of his bed and puts the plasticine model of himself in his bed. 'And this' – James stifles a sob – 'this is Daddy reading me a bedtime story.' He takes a big, ragged breath. 'He's reading me a bedtime story and it's that book about the rabbit who loves his daddy to the moon and the daddy rabbit says he loves the little rabbit to the moon and all the way back again and you just know the daddy rabbit will never leave the little rabbit and never go away and never not be there to read him a bedtime story.'

James's face crinkles up. 'Green light.'

'Green light times one hundred,' says Ellie and she reaches over and gives James a hug and they sit there at his desk, gently rocking together.

✳ 51 ✳

NOT WITH A WHIMPER

The closer it gets to Friday, the more nervous Ellie feels, though she tries not to show it in front of James. What if he doesn't do this? What then? What if he really is just being sent on this competition as some sort of sympathy vote, fulfilling the quota for disadvantaged kids? After the contest there will be just one week for them to pay the arrears or be evicted. Ellie feels as though they haven't made any contingency plans, they've been so wrapped up in the idea that James will win. It is the conversations with Major Tom; they've added a weird sort of sheen to life, made everything feel unreal. But ever since that Claudia came to the house, reality feels as though it's weighing down on them. Without Major Tom's phone calls it all feels like it was a stupid dream that only Ellie is properly waking up from.

Her dad has been calling, every week as usual, just to hear their voices, and Ellie has instructed them all to say nothing about anything.

'There must be *something* going on you can tell me?' he says, his voice echoing in the stark metal emptiness of the prison.

'Just the usual,' says Ellie. 'Can't wait to see you. Love you.'

James, of course, wants to know why they can't tell Dad everything.

'Because he'll worry, and there's nothing he can do in there,' says Ellie. 'And the last thing we want is for him to go to the prison officers in a panic. We'll sort this. We will.'

But just to be on the safe side, she takes as many hours as possible at her jobs, trying to build up as much of a safety net as she can. She is at the Polish shop, stacking tins of kidney beans on to the shelves from a big wire cage when she hears someone clearing their throat behind her. Someone wanting directions to the nappies, or sugar, or toilet roll. Nobody ever needs directions to the booze, though. Ellie turns round and Delil is standing there, grinning.

'I'm not supposed to chat,' she murmurs, continuing to grab tins from the cage. 'I don't want to get sacked from this job as well.'

'That's OK,' he whispers. 'I'll pretend to be a customer.' Then he says loudly, 'Excuse me, miss, can you attest to the veracity of these kidney beans in relation to their performance-enhancing sexual properties? I read an interesting article about them online.'

'Shut up,' she hisses, though she can't help herself laughing. 'What do you want?'

'I am actually here to buy something. My mum's making macaroni pie and I have to get some elbow macaroni. Do you know where that is?'

Ellie narrows her eyes at him. 'This is miles from where you live. There's loads of shops closer.'

Delil shrugs. 'I knew you were working. Thought I'd come and say hello. Were those lights I nicked from school all right?'

Ellie nods. 'He's done a really good job. He was fitting them last night. He has to take it in tomorrow and then he's going down to London on Saturday morning.'

Delil crosses his fingers on both hands. 'He'll ace it, I know he will.'

'He'd better.' A supervisor walks past the end of the aisle and Ellie busies herself with the tins while Delil pretends to read the back of a packet of couscous. When he's gone she says, 'It's our last chance.'

Delil puts the couscous back. 'Are you going to tell me why it's so urgent?'

She shakes her head tightly, then feels tears spring from the corners of her eyes. Stupid stupid tears. She seems to be crying all the time recently.

'Hey,' he says, putting a hand on her shoulder.

'We're going to get kicked out of the house,' says Ellie. 'If he doesn't win, we're going to get evicted. Next week.'

Delil puts his hand over his mouth. 'Shit.'

Ellie nods. 'Yeah.'

'Why, though?'

'Long story,' says Ellie. 'Look, you'd better go before I get in trouble.'

'Look, why don't you come to the party tomorrow night? You wouldn't have to stay long. I think it would do you good.'

She shakes her head again. 'I can't. Even if I could leave James and Nan alone, I have to be up at the crack of dawn to get him to school on Saturday. I just can't.'

'OK. I'll see you at school tomorrow.'

She nods and turns back to the tins. Two minutes later she feels a tap on her shoulder. It's Delil. 'Erm, do you know where the elbow macaroni is?'

'Are you sure you're going to get this to school safely?' says Ellie doubtfully on Friday morning. The model of the house is wrapped in a black bin bag and placed on the sideboard. 'You're not going to drop it or anything on the bus?'

'I'll be fine,' calls James from the kitchen where he's getting his sandwiches from the fridge.

'Maybe we should get you a taxi.'

'I'll be fine,' says James again. 'We're getting a taxi to school tomorrow morning. We can't afford two.'

He comes out of the kitchen and looks around for his schoolbag. Ellie says, 'Nan? Will you be all right today?'

Gladys is sitting in her chair, listlessly watching the breakfast news. James knows why Ellie sounds concerned; Nan seems quiet this morning.

'Don't worry about me,' sighs Gladys. 'I'm all right. Just got a bit of belly ache. I knew I shouldn't have had that fish butty last night. But Bill did insist. He likes a fish butty on the way home from the pub.'

James and Ellie share a glance. 'Maybe I'll pop home at dinner-time, just make sure you're all right.'

'Got to go,' says James, slinging his bag over his shoulder and picking up the model with both hands. 'Get the door for us, Ellie.'

'Be careful!' she shouts from the doorstep.

'I will.'

James finds a seat on his own on the bus and sits with the model across his knee. The LED lights worked a treat, one red, one green. He feels nervous and excited all at the same time about tomorrow. He's never been to London before. The print-out of the talk he's going to give to the judges about the experiment and why it's so important is at school. Mrs Britton says he can have all afternoon to practice it and she's going to get a few of the teachers together so he gets used to talking in front of an audience. He wonders what it'll be like. He imagines a stage and a row of people with serious faces. He hopes he doesn't get too nervous. His palms feel sweaty already and he takes deep breaths to calm himself down. There's a whole day and a night and a train journey to London to get through yet.

When the bus pulls into the turning circle at school James waits until everyone else gets off and then gingerly carries the model down the aisle and carefully negotiates the steps. Mrs Britton said he can leave the experiment in her office and she'll lock it overnight. Not that he expects anyone would break into the school to steal it.

Then he spots Oscar Sherrington.

He's lounging on the metal barriers at the turning circle, with his little gang. James puts his head down and starts to cross the road towards the gates but they move quickly to intercept him. James has kept out of their way all week. Why are they bothering him today of all days, when his hands are full?

'Want a word with you, peasant,' says Oscar.

'I'm busy,' says James. He can't keep his voice from wavering in mild panic.

'What's that you're carrying?'

'Maybe he's made a cake for Britton,' says one of his friends. 'Him being teacher's pet and all that.'

Oscar blocks his path across the road and James looks around for a teacher. There's one near the gate, wearing a high-visibility vest, but she seems to be tending to a reception child who's slipped and grazed her knee. James gasps as Oscar whips the box out of his hands and gives it a vicious shake.

'Doesn't sound like a cake. Help me get this off.'

His friends tear at the black bin bag, exposing the model. 'Aww,' says Oscar. 'It's a doll's house.'

'It's my experiment,' says James.

'Look, it's his family,' says one of the gang, grabbing at the plasticine figures. 'This must be his jailbird dad.'

'And that's his sister,' says another. 'Heard she's a right slag.'

'And this must be Super Gran,' says Oscar, balancing the box on one hand and lifting up the model of Gladys. He brings his face close to James's. 'That old bat made me look a right idiot in front of my dad. Nobody does that to me, peasant, you got that?'

James nods. 'Just give me the box back, Oscar.'

'What? This box?'

Then he drops it on the tarmac. 'Oops.'

James looks dully at it on the ground. It's all right. It's not damaged.

'Oops,' says Oscar again, standing hard on the model.

Then his friends are joining in, frenziedly kicking and stamping the box, until it's just a pile of torn and bent cardboard. Oscar holds the model of Nan in James's face, and slowly squeezes it until it's just a multicoloured mangled mess. Then he drops it on to the wreckage of the experiment.

'Good news is, that makes us even, peasant,' says Oscar with a vicious grin. 'Now keep out of our way.'

They walk, laughing, towards the school gates, leaving James staring numbly at the remains of their last hope to save the family.

'They did what?' says Ellie with a calmness that belies her barely contained fury.

'Threw it on the ground. Then jumped on it until it was wrecked.'

Ellie closes her eyes and counts to ten in her head. When she opens them again James is still sitting there, his cheeks stained with tears. Everything is still lost.

'Did you tell a teacher? Mrs Britton?'

James shakes his head.

'Didn't she ask where your entry for the competition was?'

'I told her I'd bring it in tomorrow. I said I'd forgotten it. She looked a bit disappointed.'

Ellie lets loose a ragged breath. 'And . . . what? You can do it all again tonight?'

James's face crumples and he shakes his head. 'I haven't got time. I don't want to do it. I just want to forget it.'

'James.' Ellie's voice is rising with mild hysteria. 'James. You do realise this is our only chance?'

He nods sadly. Gladys clears her throat. They both look at her and she says, 'The light of the righteous rejoices, But the lamp of the wicked goes out.'

'What?' frowns Ellie. 'What are you talking about, Nan?' She turns to James. 'You've got to. You've got to try. I can help you . . .'

'Through insolence comes nothing but strife,' says Gladys. 'But wisdom is with those who receive counsel.'

'I can't!' shouts James. 'I don't have any paint or plasticine or LEDs! We don't have a box! We can't buy anything because we're always skint! I just can't.'

'Wealth obtained by fraud dwindles. But the one who gathers by labour increases it.'

'Shut up!' shouts Ellie, standing up from the sofa. 'Shut up shut up shut up!'

'Don't shout at her!' yells James. 'It's not her fault!'

Ellie clamps her hands to her head.

And screams.

Everyone falls silent.

'I have had it up to here,' shouts Ellie, banging the side of her hand against her forehead. 'Up to fucking here! With the lot of you! I try my best to keep this stupid family afloat and none of you do anything to help. *You* go and get yourself bullied and *she's* completely losing her mind. I. Have. Had. Enough.'

'Ellie,' says James, his eyes wide. 'You're scaring me.'

'You *should* be scared!' she screams. 'We're going to lose the house and we're all going to get split up and Nan will be put in care or hospital and we'll end up in some scratty, horrible kids' home and if you think that bunch of overprivileged wimps at your school are bullies you haven't seen anything yet, James. We're ruined. Totally ruined.'

Ellie casts around for her school bag and begins to scrabble in it, emerging with her phone.

'What are you going to do?' Are you calling Major Tom?'

'No, I am not.' Ellie jabs at the keypad. 'That's what got us into this mess in the first place. We should never have listened to him. We should have sorted out something properly.'

'Then who are you calling?'

'I nearly had it, then,' says Gladys. '*Proverbs*. I'm sure of it.'

'Ellie, who are you calling?'

She ignores him and when the call is answered Ellie says, 'Delil? It's me. I'll meet you somewhere, you say where. Eight-ish. I'm coming to your party.'

She listens without taking her eyes off James and says, 'What's changed? Everything. But nothing, at the same time. I just decided that if this is really it, if this is how it's going to end, then I want go out with . . . what do they say? A bang and not a whimper.'

52

THE MARRYING KIND

'I must say, I can't really imagine you being married. You don't seem that sort of person.'

Claudia and Thomas are talking via the Iridium phone, but the connection is crackly and hissy, with the faint echoes of what Thomas briefly fancies are the lost ghosts of space. That morning Director Baumann contacted him to say that the link between his computer terminal and Mission Control was unlikely to be re-established. There would be no more Skype, no more internet. It was of the utmost importance that Thomas carried out the EVA and fixed the comms dish.

'We still have the Iridium phone,' Thomas had said.

'Not for long,' says Director Baumann. 'You are simply going to have to do the spacewalk. And soon. We cannot lose contact with you. It would be a disaster for the mission. It would be a disaster for BriSpA. And it could be a disaster for you. You must know this in your heart. You must accept that you simply have to get out there and fix the comms dish.'

'I'll think about it.'

Baumann crushes his eyebrows together, the effect making them look like two moles making love. 'This isn't up for discussion, Major. You have to do it. The end.'

To Claudia, later, Thomas says 'You have no idea what sort of person I am.'

'Oh, I think I have a good idea by now.' There's a pause and a distinct liquid gulp.

Thomas says, 'Are you drinking wine?'

'Of course I am. It's ten o'clock at night.'

'So, what do you want to know tonight?' Over the course of the week he has told her everything – Peter, his father dying, the incident in the cinema. He finds it strangely cathartic, laying out his life like this as though the events are stories, with beginnings and ends, rather than just formless, messy things that have happened to him.

'Pick up where you left off on the first night, Scheherazade. Don't think I didn't spot that you've left that one dangling. Tell me why your marriage failed.'

To be quite honest, Thomas can't really imagine himself being married, not until it happens. And it all rather seems to be out of his hands, from Janet's decision they should do it to the organisation of the day to the booking of the honeymoon. All Thomas has to do is get himself dressed to a suitable standard and turn up on the day, which he manages to do. They get married at York Minster, which daunts Thomas somewhat. Janet's family daunt him as well – her father has fingers in several York pies, which accounts for him securing the minster for the nuptials. Her mother looks on Thomas with the undisguised air of someone resigned to her daughter marrying beneath her. Robert, the brother who was on the stag do, regards him with contempt. Standing at the altar he feels dwarfed by the vaulting beams and flying buttresses of the largest Gothic cathedral in Europe, the breath squeezed out of him by the centuries of tradition pressing down from the impossibly high ceilings, and by the prospect of what is to come. One side of the cathedral pews are filled with Janet's family and friends, her father's golf club buddies and business associates, her mother's ladies who lunch and book group harpies. Thomas has no family, no real friends, just the handful of colleagues he barely knows who sit together like gargoyles on the front pew, Kevin, still wracked with guilt over what happened on the stag do with the marker pen, standing beside him as his best man.

The wedding goes pretty much as Thomas expects, and after honeymooning in the far east, somewhere hot and busy and all rather unpleasant, they begin their married life, moving in to Janet's flat together as it is bigger and more presentable and altogether more homely. Thomas turns up with his possessions. Janet raises an eyebrow at the piles and piles of vinyl records and makes the horrifying suggestion that they could put them in storage somewhere, if he's not yet willing to go to the trouble of selling them.

They are expected to spend significant dates – Christmas, Easter, birthdays – at the Eason family home, a sprawling, red-brick mansion in a pretty village on the outskirts of York. After Christmas lunch the first year Thomas is flicking through Janet's parents' record collection – Daniel O'Donnell and interminable CDs of military marching bands – when her father instructs him to come to the village pub while the 'girls' tidy away the remains of the dinner. Over some pints of meaty beer Janet's father interrogates him as to his prospects.

'I can put some feelers out around here,' he decides. 'Be nice to have you and Jan living in York. There are plenty of opportunities in your field . . . what is it you do again?'

'He's a science nerd,' says Janet's brother, punching Thomas hard on the arm to show he's just joking.

'Science,' nods Janet's father. 'Well, everybody needs scientists, don't they? Sure there's lots for you up here.'

'We do quite like living in London,' says Thomas.

Janet's father harrumphs into his beer. 'Well, it's all right when you're young, I suppose. But it's no place to raise a family.'

The following year Thomas turns thirty-three. Janet reaches the milestone of thirty, which is of course celebrated at the Eason home. Over a sumptuous dinner in the dining room that overlooks the long, flat fields beyond the house, Janet's mother says, 'Everyone is asking when we're going to be grandparents . . .'

'I'm sure Robert has a few little Easons scattered about the place, I saw him in action on my stag night,' jokes Thomas. It falls precisely as flat as he would have expected it to had he thought a little more before opening his wine-loosened lips.

'Mummy,' protests Janet. 'We're having fun in London at the moment.' She gazes at Thomas across the table. 'But I'm sure we'll get round to it.'

Thomas is thankful for the dim light from the candle which he is pretty certain hides the fact that he has gone as white as the pieces of chicken he is pushing around his plate. He and Janet have never spoken about children. It never occurred to him to mention it.

53

THE MARRIED YEARS (2003-2011)

Late in 2003 Janet is given a rather large promotion at her law practice while Thomas finds himself out of work. The papaya from Hawaii experiment has been a great success but the company, finding that there isn't actually much of a market for genetically modified papayas, closes down the research facility.

'I think I might like to try to write a novel,' says Thomas, pondering his new-found freedom. 'Or maybe learn to play the guitar.'

Janet laughs and passes him the jobs section of the *Evening Standard*.

Two months later he is commuting to a single-storey building off the Newbury Bypass where the primary objective seems to be trying to breed chickens with four legs. Janet is now spending more and more time representing clients in court, and has to work long hours preparing for cases. Thomas begins to sneak his vinyl collection, in twos and threes, back from the lock-up where Janet has insisted he store it.

'Ah ha,' says Claudia.

'Ah ha what?'

'She had an affair, didn't she? That's what happened. She met some hunky, thrusting young lawyer and he whisked her away from you.'

'She did not!' says Thomas, scandalised. 'Janet would never have done that. For all her faults, she was loyal. You couldn't say anything about her on that score.'

'Her faults?' says Claudia. 'What were her faults?'

Thomas goes silent for a minute. 'Well, there was only one, really. Her frankly untenable expectation that I was ever going to be anything approaching the husband she deserved.'

The following year Thomas has approximately three times more sex than he's ever had in his entire life before that. Janet is ravenous for him, insisting on early nights, waking him with kisses, dragging him to bed as soon as he walks in from work. He is utterly exhausted and sleeps on the train to and from work every day. He can barely summon up the energy to go running. One evening he arrives home with a story which he can't quite decide is funny or horrifying – about a three-legged chicken that could only run around in circles – and Janet is waiting for him at the door to their flat. She is holding a small white stick. She stands there and bites her lip while he stares dumbly at it for a second, then shrieks and throws her arms around him.

It appears they are having a baby.

They stop having sex almost immediately. Thomas is almost grateful. He finds the time and energy to go running again, pounding the pavement and thinking furiously about what exactly this will mean. A baby. A tiny human being. *Their* tiny human being. His experience of babies is, he has to admit, slim to nonexistent. In fact, the only baby he has really had any experience of was when his brother Peter was born, when Thomas was almost nine.

Thinking about that makes his thoughts dark and shadowy. He realises with a shock that having a baby will mean Thomas has to become a *father*.

The Easons are, of course, delighted. Somewhere along the line it is decided that now is the perfect opportunity for Janet and Thomas to relocate to York. Janet's father has arranged for Thomas to have an interview at the multinational medical corporation Smith and Nephew, which has a research facility near the city. In fact, there is an entire Science Park there. Thomas would, laughs Janet's father, have to be a complete and utter moron not to be able to get a job there.

They spend almost every weekend in York. Thomas is dragged around shops selling baby clothes and hideously expensive prams that appear to have been designed by the same people who make Formula 1 cars. Janet's brother, Robert, punches him on the shoulder and says, 'I never knew you had it in you, Spock,' and everyone laughs. Every time they arrive in York Janet's mother pats Janet's stomach and says, 'And how's the little grandchild doing?'

'Mummy,' says Janet, though indulgently. 'I'm not even showing yet. It's the size of a walnut.'

That night, in the crisp, clean bedsheets of the guest room, Thomas dreams of a zombie apocalypse where the undead all have faces like shrivelled walnuts and chase him into the York branch of Mothercare where he has to sit out the end of the world.

Also greeting them at the Eason household every weekend is a stack of documents from local estate agents. 'You'll be wanting something near us, of course,' says Janet's mother. 'Then we can pop in all the time.'

'Babysitters on tap would be handy,' nods Janet to Thomas.

Janet's father harrumphs. 'Well, it's not as though you'll be going back to work, is it?'

'I do have a career,' protests Janet mildly. 'I was thinking of applying to some law practices in York.'

'Nonsense,' says her father. 'A wife and a mother, that's what you are now. Never did your mother any harm, did it?'

Thomas glances at Janet's mother, who has just that day taken delivery from Amazon of twelve copies of *The Da Vinci Code* and is tying them up, rather inexplicably, in blue and pink ribbons to give to the members of her reading group, pausing only to pour herself another brandy.

Janet smiles. 'You're right. I could do far worse than being just like Mummy.'

Thomas excuses himself to go to the bathroom to hyperventilate and wonder what happened to the woman who almost ran him over on the first day of the new millennium. He begins to suspect that it might have been better if she had.

On Valentine's Day Thomas has the day off work and is preparing a meal he has bought from the supermarket for when Janet gets home. Late in the afternoon he gets a telephone call from her. She is in hospital. He gets a taxi there to find her in the Early Pregnancy Unit, sitting in a bed with the blankets drawn up to her chin, her face streaked with mascara.

'Thomas,' she says flatly. 'I lost the baby.'

Thomas says and does what he hopes are all the right things. When she comes home from hospital, she lies in bed for a week. Thomas brings her food and hugs her and cries with her. He quietly takes all the baby clothes and books and blankets to a charity shop, clears the house of any thing that might remind Janet of what she's lost . . . of what *they've* lost. On the day Janet decides she's ready to go back to work, Thomas takes the day off in case she decides she can't cope. But she does, admirably. Thomas is washing up at the kitchen sink when he sees a man walking with a tiny child, no more than two, holding his hand as the boy takes tentative, wobbly steps down the street. Quite unexpectedly, Thomas dissolves into dry, wracking sobs.

But the next year, against all Thomas's expectations, is rather wonderful. Janet seems to make a decision to put the pregnancy behind her and almost pretend it never happened, and to throw herself into both work and enjoyment. She and Thomas take two holidays, he is instructed to decline the job offer from Smith and Nephew, the house-hunting in York is abandoned. They spend money on decorating the apartment and Thomas is invited to join the residents' committee in the block of flats where they live. He takes to his new role with relish, putting Post-it notes on the windscreens of tenants who fail to park their cars in the few spaces provided without edging over the lines, he knocks on the doors of flat-owners to remind them that extra rubbish bags put out with the bins should not contain foodstuffs for fear of attracting vermin. He is at the vanguard of the campaign to get Transport for London to install a bus stop closer to the block. He and Janet spend more time together, they attend the theatre once a month, they spend summer evenings drinking by the river, she even allows him to try to tutor her in the ways of proper music. To his mild dismay, she seems unable to take to David Bowie, but that is a wrinkle he feels he can live with. They have sex again, but not as frantic and weighed with need as before. Thomas runs every morning, getting leaner and fitter, revelling in a complete lack of responsibility other than to make Janet happy.

Had Thomas not felt such utter relief that things seemed to be on the same track as he imagined they were supposed to be, he might have considered that Janet was, in fact, in a measure of denial about what had happened.

On New Year's Eve that year they are, as usual, at the Eason household for the festive season. A small party has been arranged, with one or two of Janet's parents' friends and neighbours. The subject of the miscarriage is notably absent from conversation, as though it has all been wiped from recent history. As the chimes of Big Ben issue from the TV screen, Janet throws her arms around Thomas and gives him a long, drunken kiss.

'Not sad to see the back of this year, to be honest.'

'It had . . . well, it had its moments,' he says. 'But apart from the . . . you know . . . we've had . . . well, it's not been bad . . .'

Janet nibbles on his ear, which he finds quite agreeable. And then she whispers, 'I'm ready to try again.'

For one crazy moment he thinks she is talking about David Bowie. Then she says, 'For a baby. I'm ready to try again.'

'Well, we don't want to rush into it,' cautions Thomas, reasonably.

'I want to make a baby.' Janet presses her body against his.

Thomas laughs nervously. 'What, right here in your parents' living room?'

Janet stands back, holding him at arm's length, searching his eyes. 'You do want to try again, don't you?'

He doesn't know quite what to say, and by the time he's found the right words, he doesn't get the chance to use them. Janet is shouting at him, throwing her glass against the wall, everyone in the room stops and stares. Thomas doesn't get half of what she's screaming, not a quarter, but the gist is clear. He never wanted children. He wasn't even upset when she lost the baby. He's an emotionally stunted man-child who thinks he can go through life at his stupid, pointless Frankenstein job and listening to his stupid, pointless music and doing his stupid, pointless runs and typing up the minutes of his stupid, pointless residents committee.

His stupid, pointless life, says Janet, is utterly, utterly worthless.

She is taken sobbing into the kitchen by her mother and a coven of friends. Janet's father cleans up the broken glass and glowers at him. 'New Year ruined,' he says, and Thomas is left standing in the middle of the room, everyone pretending not to talk about him, wondering if he should just cut his losses and smash the CD player and its relentlessly chirpy Daniel O'Donnell Christmas album that's driving into his brain like a sledgehammer.

Thomas has no idea how they limp on for the remaining years, and is not inclined to give Claudia the gory details of the progressive shrivelling of their marriage until they are two people who share a flat but barely speak, edging past each other like strangers, him sleeping in the spare bedroom for so long that it simply becomes his room, where he installs a record player and floor-to-ceiling piles of vinyl. One day, Janet sighs and says what they have both known for a long time. It's over.

'Is there anyone else?' he asks, because that seems the right thing to say in this situation.

'No,' she says. 'And there never will be while we're together. But in the future, who knows? I'm thirty-eight. I'm not over the hill yet. I can still be happy. So can you.'

'I am happy,' says Thomas, his eyes filling with tears.

'If you are, it's in spite of me, not because of me,' says Janet. 'I've booked a week off work. I'm going to stay with my parents. I'd like it if you had moved out by the time I get back.'

'Can we stay friends?' says Thomas, though he knows it sounds a wretchedly daytime-movie sort of thing to say.

Janet looks at him, and he wonders what happened to that twinkle in her green eyes that so arrested him when they first met, wonders when she lost it, wonders why he never noticed it had gone.

'Were we ever?'

✳ 54 ✳

EVERYTHING IN MODERATION

Ellie meets Delil in the burger place where she works and he's waiting for her at a table near the door, food already on the Formica surface.

'I got you a chicken burger, fries and a chocolate milkshake.' He stands when she walks in and waves his hand to the plastic chair for her to sit, as though they're on a dinner date in a fancy restaurant. Then, seeing her face, he says, 'Don't you like chicken burgers?'

'I suppose.' Ellie slides into the chair. 'I just don't like people making my mind up for me.'

Delil sits down and regards her critically. 'You look nice,' he decides.

'I didn't know what to wear.' She self-consciously pats her jeans and the black vest under her hooded zip-up.

'That's great. Perfect.' He cocks his head on one side. 'You look different when you put your hair up. And you know how to do your make-up. Most girls at school look like they're auditioning for the circus. Or for Stephen King's *IT*. Or maybe for that clown on the poster over there.'

'Where is this party, anyway?'

'They've got a unit on the industrial estate, you know, that goes up to the motorway. We'll have to get a bus. Do you want me to get you something else to eat?'

'No, it's fine,' sighs Ellie, looking around the burger place, careful to avoid the mirrors that always make her look washed out and tired under the sterile white lighting. She sees someone she knows emptying the bins and nods at them. Not that she has what you might call friends, not at any of her jobs. Not even at school. She looks at Delil, wearing a wide-collared white shirt with a swirly brown pattern which he could have pinched from his dad's wardrobe. For some reason, it looks good on him. He's wiping condensation off his glasses and blinking at her. With a shock she realises that Delil might actually be her only friend in the world.

'Do you like grime, anyway?' Delil puts his glasses back on. 'I can take it or leave it, to be honest. I do like some of the more political stuff. I like Skepta. "Shutdown". D'you remember that from a couple of years back? *Me and my Gs ain't scared of police, we don't listen to no politician.* I'm not into it like my brother Ferdi though. He's mad for it. Do you know what I like? All sorts of stuff. The Carpenters. "Calling Occupants of Interplanetary Craft". I love that one, me. Ha, that reminds me. Your little brother said he'd been talking to that Major Tom on the phone. Cracks me up that. He was on the news, you know. Well, not him. It was about him. Something about him having to do a spacewalk to fix some broken dish or antennae or something.'

Ellie eats while Delil talks, and she envies him the easy, almost off-hand manner in which he speaks on anything and everything, bobbing from topic to topic like a bee in search of pollen. She wonders what it must be like to be so carefree, not to have to worry about grown-up things like Ellie does. She realises he's paused and is looking expectantly at her.

'Am I boring you already?'

'Sorry.' She takes a slurp of milkshake. 'Did you say something?'

'I asked you what music you were into.'

Ellie shrugs. 'Whatever's on Radio One, I suppose.'

'Radio One's the work of the devil. It's so . . . anodyne.'

'What does that mean?' Ellie bunches up the last of her fries and pops them in her mouth, then licks her salty fingers.

'Dunno. I read it in the *Guardian*. I don't think it's good. It might mean boring or something. I like it though. I think it's my new favourite word. Do you have a favourite word?'

On the bus Delil pays for both of them and then pauses halfway down the aisle, indicating the window seat for Ellie. She giggles. 'My carriage awaits.'

'You be Cinderella and I'll be Prince Charming,' says Delil.

Ellie wipes the window with her sleeve and looks out at the orange streetlights. 'I think my fairy godmother's missing in action,' she murmurs.

'Do you want to tell me about the problem with the house?' says Delil gently.

She decides that she does, and it takes as long as the bus journey. Delil presses the bell and stands up. When they get off the bus, on a long dual carriageway that's lined with shuttered factories and business units, the rain-slicked tarmac shining in the glow of the tall lamp-posts, he says, 'That could almost be funny if it wasn't so serious. You should go to the police, you know. That's fraud, that is. They could track this fake prince down and get your money back.'

'Not in time. And if we went to the police everyone would find out about Nan not being able to look after us properly.' She feels fed up of having to explain this to everyone.

'But what are you going to do?' presses Delil. 'You've only got a week. I know your brother's a genius and everything, but what if he doesn't win this competition?'

'He isn't going to win the competition because he isn't going.' Ellie feels a spot of rain on her nose. 'Those kids that were bullying him? They did it again. He was right about Nan making things worse when she took them on.'

Delil clicks his fingers. 'Wait. The masked ninja you were going on about to your brother's teacher. That was your *nan*?' He whistles. 'That is safe.'

'To be honest, I don't want to think about it, I don't want to think about anything, just for one night,' sighs Ellie. 'Where is this place, anyway? It's going to chuck down.'

'Over there.' Delil indicates an access road that slopes down to a series of single-storey units, cloaked in darkness. 'Can't you hear it?'

As the rain starts to fall, they hurry towards the thud-thud-thud of the bass.

'Is this actually legal?' shouts Ellie as they are enveloped by the warmth of the interior of a unit buried in the middle of the industrial estate, three big men in black bomber jackets waving them through after seeing Delil. The unit is so dark Ellie can't tell how big it is, flashing strobe lights painting the bodies of dancers crushed into the centre before a scaffolding stage on which three men in black jeans, white tops and baseball caps are thunderously issuing staccato rhymes.

'I very much doubt it!' shouts Delil cheerfully back. 'I imagine the feds'll be here to close us down before dawn.'

'Feds?' Ellie smiles. 'You've gone awfully street all of a sudden.'

'Hangin' with my homies, innit?' says Delil.

'Is that your brother?' says Ellie, pointing to the stage. It's awfully hot in the unit and she takes off her hoodie and ties it around her waist.

'Nah. Ferdi won't be on until after midnight at the earliest. Come on, I'll show you where the loos are and everything.'

'There are toilets? I'm impressed.'

'My cousin Rodge owns this place,' yells Delil. He takes her by the hand to lead her through the throng of dancers, and Ellie doesn't protest. 'Uses it as a body-shop most of the time, you know, to do cars up. Every few weeks they have a party here.'

By the toilets are two trestle tables bearing big rubber garden buckets in bright colours, filled with ice that's already melting in the heat and loaded up with bottles of beer and soft drinks.

'Help yourself,' shouts Delil. 'Drinks are included in the ticket price. Which was free for us, so you can fill your boots.'

Delil and Ellie reach into the same tub together. He pulls out a can of Coke; she has a bottle of Red Stripe. They look at each other.

'Don't you drink?'

'Do you drink?'

'Nah, take it or leave it, me,' says Delil. 'I might have a beer later. Everything in moderation, like they say. Did you know in France there's no minimum age limit for drinking? They love it over there. But they don't have this piss-head problem we have. Binge drinking and all that. Throwing up in your kebab. Ugh. Not for me.'

Ellie looks at the beer. Delil takes a bottle opener tied with a bit of string to the trestle table and flips the top off for her. 'You sure you're OK with that?'

Ellie has never had alcohol before in her life. She puts it to her lips and is at first shocked by how cold it is, and then at how icily bitter it tastes. 'Great,' she says, wiping her mouth with the back of her hand to hide her involuntary grimace. 'I'll probably only have one or two. I'm like you. Take it or leave it. Everything in moderation.'

Delil nods and cracks the tab open on his Coke. 'Safe. Do you fancy a dance?'

'CALLING OCCUPANTS OF INTERPLANETARY CRAFT'

Delil dances exactly as Ellie expects him to, arms flapping like a chicken, knees and ankles flying off in random directions, his smile beaming like a lighthouse. But he pulls it off with the aplomb of the naturally cool. He is so geeky he's gone completely across the spectrum and come in again at the other side of effortlessly stylish. More to the point, he actually looks like he's having a good time.

'Come on!' he yells. 'You want fame? Well, fame costs. And right here is where you start paying . . . in sweat!'

Ellie yelps as he grabs her arm and pulls her deeper into the mass of gyrating bodies. 'What's that off?' she shouts.

Delil throws back his head and waves his arms in the air. 'Fame! I'm gonna live for ever! I'm gonna learn how to fly!'

As Ellie tips up her beer bottle and is surprised to find it empty, she thinks that he just might, at that.

After her second beer, Ellie realises she needs to pee very, very badly, and when she comes out of the toilet she can't find Delil, so she stands by the trestle tables and helps herself to another bottle. It's actually not that bad when you get used to it. As she looks at the people dancing, she realises that not everything about growing up is actually that bad. Some of it is quite fun. It's just that all the things she's done – looking after her brother, caring for her nan, cooking everyone's meals, making sure everyone gets here on time or there when they should – all that's the boring stuff. She's just been doing the boring stuff all this time without having any of the fun. Ellie is startled to realise she needs to pee again, and wonders if she's got an infection or something. She puts down the empty bottle and weaves unsteadily towards the toilet.

When she comes out Delil is waiting for her, cracking open another Coke. She grabs on to his arm and shouts, 'Stop being so boring! Have a beer!'

He raises one eyebrow. 'I will, after this. Do you want to dance again?'

On the dance floor, Ellie swings around her half-empty bottle. Is this her second? Her third? Fourth? 'Who's counting?'

'What?' shouts Delil over the thudding bass and the MCs.

'Who's counting?' she shouts back.

'Who's counting what?' he yells.

'Beers!'

Delil looks at his empty Coke can and crushes it in his hand. 'OK, I'll have one with you. Come on. My glasses are steaming up anyway.'

'It's all those girls on the dance floor,' says Ellie, swinging on Delil's arm as he tries to take the tops off two bottles. 'That's what's making your glasses steam up. Some of them are *gorgeous*. Like models.'

Delil shrugs. 'No nicer than you.'

Ellie laughs wildly. Delil hands her the bottle, running with condensation. Their fingers touch and she looks up into his eyes, or at least into his steamed-up glasses. Her heart is beating faster than it ever has before. She doesn't even know how or why, but her body is pressed up against his, moulded to him.

'Give us a kiss,' she says.

Delil puts down his bottle on the table and takes her elbows in his hands, then laughs and gently pushes her an inch or two away from him, breaking the hot contact of their bodies.

She feels her eyes prickle. 'Don't you fancy me?'

'I have a policy not to get off with girls when they're drunk,' he shouts.

Ellie raises her eyebrows. She counts off on her fingers. 'One, Delil Alleyne, I am not drunk. I've only had two. Or three. And two . . . you get so much action that you have a *policy*?'

'Every gentleman should have a policy,' nods Delil. 'But, to be honest, this is the first time I've ever had chance to put it into practice.'

What feels like some considerable time later Ellie is sitting on the concrete floor with her back against the breeze block wall. She's crying and she doesn't even know why.

'Can you lend me five thousand pounds?' she says.

'I would if I could. I'd give it to you if I had it.'

'What about your parents? Can they lend it to me?'

Delil laughs. 'My dad's a bus driver and my mum's a cleaner. We get by, but only just. I'm sorry, Ellie.'

'If your dad's a bus driver and your mum's a cleaner why are you such a weirdo genius?'

He shrugs. 'We're only condemned to repeat the past if we don't learn from history. I read that—'

'In the *Guardian*, I know.'

'It's true, though. Not that I think my parents have made mistakes. They're brilliant. And we're all weird in our family, in our own way. It's like it says at the beginning of *Anna Karenina*. But it doesn't just apply to unhappy families. You can't make assumptions about anybody. My brother's big thing is MCing; my dad paints these brilliant pictures of Barbados, but he's never even been. He just uses photos. My mum sings like an angel. We all do our own thing. Like any family. Like yours.'

'There's nothing special about the Ormerods. We just balls everything up.'

'No, you don't,' says Delil kindly. 'And even if you do, you don't have to balls everything up for ever. I read this thing that Einstein said once. *Learn from yesterday, live for today, hope for tomorrow. The important thing is not to stop questioning.* That's me, that is. Hope for tomorrow. That's why I'm going to be a writer, or a journalist, or a detective. Or all three. You can't stop hoping for tomorrow, or you might as well be dead.'

'It's the living for today that's the problem,' says Ellie. 'I don't even want to have to worry about this stuff. I just want to be a kid.'

Delil takes the empty bottle from her. 'Kids don't drink their bodyweight in beer.'

'They do in France.' Something is vibrating in her pocket. 'I'll move to France and get adopted by a French family and we'll sit on our balcony in Paris and I'll drink wine and read *Anna Karenina*.' She tries to wriggle her phone out of her jeans but can't. 'What time is it, anyway?'

Delil looks at his wristwatch, which is an old digital one of course. 'Nearly one.' There's a cheer from the crowd and he looks up. 'Oh, Ferdi's come on stage.'

Something shifts inside Ellie. She gives a liquid belch and looks at Delil with wide, teary eyes. 'I think I'm going to be sick.'

In the corrugated steel toilet cubicle Ellie is on her knees, hands gripping the toilet bowl, throwing up relentlessly. Someone is banging on the wooden door shouting they're dying for a slash. Delil holds her hair out of the way of the seemingly endless stream of vomit.

'I'm sorry I'm sorry I'm sorry,' gasps Ellie between vomiting and sobbing.

'I shouldn't have let you have so much beer, it's my fault,' says Delil, rubbing her back. She can't decide whether she finds it soothing or annoying.

'Yes, it is your fault,' she says, retching again. 'You shouldn't have let me have so much beer. Why don't you have a policy on that?'

She's sweating and freezing all at the same time, and with each heave her stomach muscles convulse and knot. This has ceased to be fun. They were only supposed to be here to see—

'Oh, God.' She dissolves into sobs. 'We missed your brother. Oh, God. I'm sorry I'm sorry I'm—'

'It's fine, it's fine,' says Delil softly. 'I've seen him before. He's not all that.'

Ellie leans forward to heave again. There can't be anything left in her stomach, but that doesn't seem to stop it wanting to empty itself. She crouches forward to relieve the agony in her muscles, and feels something separate and drop, and clatter to the floor. Her phone.

Delil picks it up. 'Um. Ellie. You've got thirteen missed calls.'

She wipes the beads of sweat from her forehead. She actually feels like she might have stopped vomiting. 'Who from?'

'Twelve from your nan and one from . . .' The phone bursts into life in his hand. She looks at him. 'Who's the other one from? And who's that now?'

Delil looks at the phone as though he can't quite believe it, and hands it to her. 'It says *Major Tom*.'

Ellie sits back against the steel wall of the cramped cubicle and takes the phone. It hits her that Nan has tried to call her *twelve times*. Oh my God. What's going on? And why is . . .

'Hello?' she says.

'Ellie,' says Major Tom.

'We're not allowed to speak to you,' she mumbles, wiping spit and vomit from her mouth.

'Gladys has been trying to get you for the last hour,' he says. He sounds indistinct and crackly and very far away.

Delil says, 'That's not really . . . is it?'

'What's happened?' says Ellie into the phone, the fog in her head clearing. 'Is it Nan? Is she hurt?'

'It's James,' says Major Tom distantly. 'You need to get back. Gladys phoned me in a right state. James has run away from home.'

✳ 56 ✳

STICKING TOGETHER

It is almost two in the morning by the time Ellie gets Delil to persuade a taxi to come out to the industrial estate and take them to Santus Street, where Gladys is pacing up and down the hearth rug in her long dressing gown and her slippers.

'At last,' says Gladys as Ellie and Delil spill in through the front door. 'I've been trying to get hold of you half the night.'

'We came as soon as we could, Mrs Ormerod,' says Delil. 'Ellie didn't get your calls at first—'

Ellie puts up her hands for silence and everybody quits speaking. 'Right. Nan, what happened?'

'I put James in bed about nine and then I watched that thing with the people talking, a bit like Parkinson but with more shouting—'

'Nan,' says Ellie. 'After that. What time did you notice James had gone?'

Gladys takes a deep breath. 'I got up for a wee and a glass of water and I think it had just gone twelve. I saw a light under James's door and thought he'd fallen asleep with his lamp on so I went in to turn it off. The lamp was on but he wasn't there. His bed hadn't been slept in. He'd left this note.'

Ellie snatches the piece of notepaper from Gladys and scans it. There isn't much to read. She passes it over to Delil, who reads it out:

Dear Ellie and Nan,
Everything's a mess and it's all my ~~fualt~~ fault. I was supposed
to make everything OK and I've just made it all worse. I have
gone to find Dad and make them let him go from jail. I will
spring him from his cell like in the films if they won't let him
go. Don't worry about me. I have some cheese sandwiches and
some Lucozade and I have got the £20 from your knicker
draw Ellie that you didn't know I knew you had. I hope this is
OK.
James

Delil looks from Ellie to Gladys. 'Where's the prison?'

'Oxfordshire.' Ellie rubs her face with her hands. 'Bloody miles away.'

'It's near a place that looks like it should be Bi-Sess-Ter when you read it,' says Gladys. 'But you say it 'Bister'. Like Bisto.' She takes a deep breath through her nose. 'Ah, Bister.'

Delil looks at his watch. 'So he's got . . . at least two hours' start on us. But he's a ten-year-old kid. He's can't have got very far. He won't get a train at this time of night, and not for twenty quid.'

'He might get a coach, though. He could be hitchhiking.' Tears spring from her eyes and her hand flies to her mouth. 'Oh, God, anything might have happened to him.'

She takes out her phone and jabs at it, saying to Gladys, 'Haven't you tried to phone him?'

'Course I have,' says Gladys, affronted. 'I'm not stupid. He didn't answer the phone, same as you. That's why I had to call Major Tom.'

Ellie listens to the phone ringing out and when it clicks on to the answer phone she shouts, 'James! Pick up! Call me back! We're worried sick! You're not in trouble!'

As soon as she kills the connection she says to Delil, 'I'll strangle the little bastard when I get my hands on him.'

'Ellie, I know it's not what you want to do, but . . . I think you might have to ring the police.'

Ellie nods and puts her hands over her face, sitting down heavily on the sofa. 'I can't believe it. After all this time doing my best to keep us together, I can't believe it's all unravelled like this at the last minute. Even if I don't call the police James is going to get himself picked up by the authorities at some point, so whichever way it falls we're done for. And what if some . . .' She can't bring herself to say the word, and swallows back her sobs. 'What if some bad guy gets hold of him?'

Ellie's phone buzzes into life and she almost drops it. She glances at the display and says, deflated, 'Major Tom.' She opens the connection. 'Hello?'

The line hisses and crackles. 'I can hardly hear you.'

'I know, I'm . . . etting out of range . . .' says Thomas. 'Have you . . . him yet?'

'No. Have you?'

' . . . been trying but can't get through. But two minutes ago . . . alled me . . . lost the connection.'

'What?' shouts Ellie. 'What? He tried to call you?'

'I think . . . was him. But the line   crackling and I lost . . .' says Major Tom. The line hisses and clears. 'It keeps coming and going. I'm getting out of range fast, but I've got a couple of hours left. I think he's all right. I just need to get back in touch with him.'

'I'll text him!' shouts Ellie. 'I'll text him and say if he won't speak to me, at least for him to talk to you. He'll do that.'

'Right,' says Thomas. 'I'll try him again. You sit tight. I'll call you back.'

Ellie furiously texts and looks up at Delil. 'It's going to drive me mad just sitting here. I hope Major Tom gets back in touch with him.'

'There was something on the news earlier,' says Delil. 'There's a problem with his communications system on the *Ares-1*. That's why the signal's bad. They were saying he has to get out there and do a spacewalk to fix something.'

'I wish *we* could do something. We need to be looking for James ourselves.'

'We could,' says Gladys.

Delil is looking at his phone. 'If he has got a lift or a bus, he'll be heading south. We could get on the M6 if we had a car.'

'We do,' says Gladys.

Ellie sighs. 'It's pointless. We're fifteen. Even if we had a car we don't have anyone to drive it.'

'We have,' says Gladys.

'Nan. Maybe you should go back to bed.'

'Wait.' Delil waves his hands. 'What did you say, Mrs Ormerod?'

'I said, we could, we do and we have,' says Gladys. 'We could go looking for James. We do have a car. We have got someone to drive it.'

Ellie looks at Delil. 'No, no, we don't. Don't be ridiculous.'

Gladys goes into the kitchen and comes out holding a set of keys. 'We've got your dad's van parked outside. And I can drive.'

Ellie stares at her. 'No, you can't.'

Gladys gets her purse from the arm of the easy chair, delves into its pockets, and says, 'Yes, I can. Look. Here's my driving licence. I passed my test in 1966.'

Ellie stares open-mouthed for a moment. 'But you're . . . you know.'

'I'm fine,' says Gladys crossly. 'Look, Ellie, I'm not stupid. I know what's wrong with me. But you're going to have to help me, all right? You and Delil. You might be drunk, he might be crackers and I might be losing the plot, but if we stick together we might be all right. That's what makes us strong, right? Sticking together. That's how we've always done it round here. They might put fancy names on it every few years, like community spirit or big society or something else that they've paid someone a fortune to come up with, but it doesn't really need a label. It's just about people looking out for each other. That's the way we do things. That's the way we've always done things.'

'Grassroots socialism in action,' says Delil with admiration.

Gladys points her finger at him. 'Oi. You. I said no labels or fancy names, all right?'

'So what are we waiting for?' says Ellie. 'Come on!'

Gladys frowns at her. 'I need to get dressed first. I might be losing the plot, but I'm not going to Bisto in my nightie.'

'Can she really drive in her . . . condition?' whispers Delil as Gladys goes upstairs.

Ellie shrugs. 'I don't suppose she's meant to. But with us looking out for her, acting as her eyes and ears . . .' Ellie puts her hand to her mouth. 'Oh. But you don't need to come. You should probably get home.'

'Are you kidding? I knew you were a dark horse, Ellie Ormerod, but one night with you's like falling down the rabbit hole. You try and stop me.'

Ellie has the phone at her ear again, muttering, 'Come on, come on, come on, James. Where the bloody hell are you?'

✳ 57 ✳

GOING SOUTH

The decision to go and find his dad at Bullingdon Prison was one that James made around an hour after he had gone to bed, where he lay wide awake in the darkness, listening to his nan snoring in her room. He couldn't quite say why it was a good idea, but he didn't have anything else. Everything was ruined and they were going to lose the house anyway; at least Dad should know what was going on. So he gets up, gets dressed and goes quietly downstairs to make some sandwiches and pack a bag. He goes into Ellie's room and borrows the £20 he knows she keeps in her underwear drawer for emergencies, then rips a page out of his school book and writes a note, which he leaves on his pillow. It is eleven-thirty when he lets himself out of the house and sets off in, according to the compass app on his phone, a westerly direction towards, he is sure, the motorway that will take him south towards the prison.

It takes an hour of walking along the wide Ormskirk Road, putting his head down and hurrying past the pubs with their boozy, shouty groups spilling out on to the pavement, before he gets to the bridge over the M6, where traffic whispers by in both directions. The M58 continues west, but he is sure he doesn't want that. James crosses bridges over a knotted spiral of slip-roads and junctions to the cheap hotel car park and ponders his next move. There are a couple of lorries in the hotel car park, and James sees one man walking across from the hotel towards a truck with the name of a haulage company from Scotland on the side. He hurries after the man, catching him up just as he is pulling himself up into his can.

'Hello, mister,' says James. 'Are you a paedophile?'

The man frowns with one eyebrow, and says in a deep burr, 'No, lad, I'm not. Why, are you looking for one?'

'No. I'm trying to avoid them. Are you going south?'

The man frowns with his other eyebrow. 'Aye. Why?'

'Can I have a lift?' says James.

The man gets down from the wide step into his cab and assesses James. 'What's your name?'

'James Ormerod,' says James, then realises he should probably have said something else.

'And how old are you, James Ormerod?'

'Eighteen,' says James, making his voice as deep as possible.

'Of course you are,' says the driver. 'Just short for your age. Very short. Running away to join the circus, are you?'

'Will you give me a lift or not? I can give you some money.'

The man rubs his whiskery chin. 'Aye, you can have a lift, lad.' He holds out his hand. 'Rab Collins.'

James cautiously takes it. 'You're definitely not a paedophile?'

'Definitely,' says Rab. 'Get up here in the cab. We're going south.'

Ellie is shouting into the phone, trying to make herself heard above the hissing and static. 'We're setting off. In the van. Going to get on the M6 and head south. Call me as soon as you get through to James.'

'I still can't believe you've been talking to Major Tom all this time,' says Delil, helping Ellie into the front of the van. Gladys is already there, in her brown Nylon trousers, her fur-lined boots and her best cardigan. 'James tried to tell me and I didn't believe him.'

'You're sure you can do this, Nan?'

Gladys closes one eye and bites her tongue as she tries to get the key into the ignition. 'It's like riding a bike, you never forget.' She looks up. 'Though I'm not sure I could actually remember how to ride a bike.'

Delil pulls the door closed and Gladys says, 'Here we go!' The van smells musty and vaguely of cement. Behind the three seats the back is piled high with tools and off-cuts of wood. Gladys turns the key in the ignition.

Nothing happens.

She tries it again. It clicks and whirrs, but with a rather sickly air.

'It's been left too long,' says Ellie. 'The battery's dead or something.'

Gladys pumps the clutch with her foot. 'Once more for luck!' She turns the key and the engine coughs, pauses, then staggers into life. Gladys stamps on the gas pedal until the engine roars, then puts the gearbox in neutral and lets the engine warm up, along with the heater that begins to blow brackish air across the windscreen.

'Safe!' says Delil.

Gladys reaches into her coat pocket and pulls out a pair of sunglasses, slipping them on. Ellie says, 'Nan, what are you doing?'

Gladys turns on the stereo and slams in the tape that's poking out of it like a clear plastic tongue. Sirens are screaming. Fires are howling. 'Bat Out of Hell', by Meat Loaf. Ellie says, 'Dad did always have godawful taste in music.'

Gladys looks across Ellie at Delil, over the top of her shades. 'It's one-hundred-and-six miles to Chicago, we got a full tank of gas, half a pack of cigarettes, it's dark . . . and we're wearing sunglasses.'

'What?' says Ellie crossly.

Delil laughs delightedly, and shouts, 'Hit it!'

Gladys rams the van into gear and lets out the clutch with a whoop.

Five minutes later they get to the end of Santus Street. Delil says, 'Um, Mrs Ormerod? If you don't mind me making a suggestion . . . we might actually get there a bit quicker if you get out of first gear . . .'

Trevor Calderbank is far too old to be pulling late-night shifts. But that's what happens when you're content to be a PC all your life and never bother to try for promotion. But he likes being a constable, likes being a community bobby. He gets to know people, gets to recognise the same faces, gets to know the villains and the victims. He has what they call local knowledge.

He only has an hour to go on his shift when the call comes in that there's an illegal party underway on the Orwell Road industrial estate. Same mob as do it every couple of months, probably. PC Calderbank drives up there, though he knows there are two other units on their way, just in case. When he gets there the other cars have everything in hand and the party-goers are trooping out of the unit in a fairly good-natured manner. They don't need PC Calderbank. He gets back in his car and glances at the time. Hardly worth going back to the nick now. He reckons he'll just take a couple of turns around the patch, make sure all the bad lads are tucked up nice and cosy in bed. He idles at the access road to the industrial estate, waiting until a filthy white van heads past him towards the motorway, then starts to pull out.

Almost immediately, Trevor Calderbank pulls in to the kerb. Was that Darren Ormerod's van? It said so on the side, he is almost sure of it. Darren Ormerod who's banged up for that robbery. Darren Ormerod whose mother Trevor Calderbank had to go and see about those kids getting rolling-pinned at the school. Would have made a good story for the lads in the nick, that, but for some reason Trevor held it back. Didn't even bother writing it up. There was something about Gladys Ormerod, he could tell she wasn't quite the full shilling. Something about the whole family set-up . . .

Trevor Calderbank dithers, not sure whether he should follow the van or not. What if he was mistaken? He only caught it out of the corner of his eye. It wasn't speeding or being driven erratically.

In the end he decides to take a detour via Santus Street. If the van's outside number twenty-three, he was mistaken. If not, he'll call it in.

The cab of the truck is warm and cosy and James feels his eyes drooping. Rab Collins doesn't say much, just listens to a talk radio station where people phone in to rant about politics. James tries to keep himself awake by staring out of the window, but the dark countryside stretching out beyond the hard shoulder offers nothing stimulating enough. He jerks himself awake twice, and the third time it is only the loud tick-tick tick-tick of the lorry's indicators that pierce his sleep.

'What are we doing?' says James blearily

'Just pulling off at the services,' says Rab. 'I need to pick up a few things from the shop. For breakfast, like.'

Rab negotiates the truck into the lorry park and turns off the engine with a shudder. It's pitch black outside and there are just two or three other HGVs in the park. Rab turns to James. The lights from the dashboard light up his face in a sickly greeny-yellow colour. 'Do you need the toilet or anything?'

'I'm good.' He is wishing he had never got into the lorry now. Nobody knows where he is. He's kept his phone switched off because he knows Ellie will have found out whenever she gets home from her party that he's gone and will be trying to get in touch with him. Now he feels isolated and alone and out of contact.

'OK. I'm going to go to the shop, take a leak. You be a good lad and wait here until I get back, right? You won't go anywhere? Promise?'

James nods as Rab climbs out of the cab and down to the tarmac. He sets off on a path through some bushes towards the low buildings of the service station. Before he goes out of sight, he turns back and casually presses his key fob, locking the cab doors.

James feels scared now, wishing he was in his bed. He gets out his phone and turns it on, and the missed calls from Ellie and

Nan make his stomach flip. Then he sees a missed call from Major Tom. Hands shaking, James returns the call.

'. . . ames?' says Major Tom. He sounds crackly and indistinct. 'James is that . . .? Are you all right?'

'Major Tom!' shouts James. 'I'm in a lorry but he's locked me in and I'm scared!'

But there's just hiss on the line, and eventually it goes dead. James is trying to redial when he looks up and sees, silhouetted against the lights of the main service station car park, the shape of Rab Collins returning to his lorry.

James's eyes widen and his heart sinks to his stomach as he realises the trucker isn't alone. Two other outlines flank him. All this stopping for food and toilets . . . it was all a ruse. Rab and his mates . . . They've got him where they want him, and he's trapped, and he's no idea what they're going to do. Oh, God, thinks James, and clutches his bag to his chest, and starts to cry.

✳ 58 ✳

THE ORMEROD WAY

PC Calderbank stands in the rain outside 19 Santus Street, in the space previously occupied for long months by Darren Ormerod's van. If it has been stolen, he can't imagine why, given the state of it, unless it's for the tools in the back. The house is in darkness, which he would expect given the hour. He goes to the window and peers through a crack in the curtains, and then hammers on the door for the third time. A light comes on in the bedroom next door, but nothing in the Ormerod household. Which suggests they are out. And also, he reasons, if they are out and the van is gone then they are out in the van. But the children are obviously too young to drive, and if Gladys Ormerod is at the wheel . . . well, he doubts that she should be. He decides to call it into the station.

'Sue,' he says when he gets through. 'Need you to run a check for me on a Ford Transit. The number should be in the computer already. It's registered to an Ormerod, Darren, of 19 Santus Street.'

'Will do,' says Sue. 'Ormerod, did you say? Funny, that.'

'Why?'

'Something's just come in from Cheshire. The motorway unit at Knutsford services. Suspected runaway with the same surname.'

'Was there a first name?' says PC Calderbank. 'Have they picked him up?'

'Possibly James. And no, they haven't got him. Believed to be in the vicinity, though.'

Although his shift is all but over, PC Calderbank thinks it would be a good idea to get back to the station.

Rab Collins looks at his watch. He really needs to be on the road. These sprockets won't get themselves to Bristol.

'Almost done, sir,' says the policeman, flicking through his notes. His colleague is away to one side, on the phone to the Wigan nick. 'So, to summarise . . . you picked up this boy at Junction 27, near Wigan, and he indicated only that he was heading "south". Given his age – you estimate between nine and twelve – and the time of night, you surmised he was running away.'

'Aye,' says Rab. 'I thought I'd just spook him if I asked him too many questions and I didn't want to leave him there in the middle of the night. So I pulled off here because I know you guys have a base at Knutsford. I told him to stay put told him I was away to get some food. I locked the cab but he must have squirrelled out through the window.'

The other policeman heads back to them, tucking his phone in its holster across his hi-visibility vest. 'Wigan haven't got anyone reported missing from home with that name, but there's a PC there who might know the lad. They're getting him to give me a call.'

'Can I go now?' says Rab.

The traffic officer nods. 'Yes, sir, you can be on your way, soon as we've looked inside the trailer.'

'I haven't got him tied up in the back,' protests Rab. 'I'm not Hannibal bloody Lecter, you know.'

The search of the sprockets takes another fifteen minutes, then Rab is finally allowed on his way. He shakes his head as he noses the truck towards the exit slip road. Bloody kids.

From a tangle of bushes near the exit to the M6 carriageway, James watches Rab's lorry gathering pace and disappearing out of view. He looks back to the car park, at the two policemen. That's torn it. They'll be after him now. Then they'll take him home and the social services will come and everything'll collapse and it'll all be his fault. He'll probably be sleeping in some horrible kids' home this time tomorrow.

His phone chirps in his backpack and he wipes the tears from his eyes and digs into it. It'll be Ellie again. He's going to have to tell her what's happened. He feels his insides turn to water.

But it's not Ellie, or Nan.

'Major Tom!' gasps James into the phone.

There's a squall of static and then Major Tom says, 'How many times have I told you not to call me that?'

James bursts into tears again. 'I thought we were banned from talking to you. That woman—'

'Forget her. James, where are you? Ellie and Gladys are worried sick.'

'I can hardly hear you,' says James. 'You sound far away.'

'That's because I'm on my bloody way to Mars!' says Thomas. 'But where are *you*?'

'I'm at a motorway services,' sniffs James. 'I think it's called Knutsford. I don't know where it is though.'

'What the hell are you doing there? Shouldn't you be in bed? Christ, shouldn't you be getting up in a couple of hours to go to London?'

'I'm not going.'

'But the competition?'

'I'm not going! Those idiots smashed up my experiment. Everything was ruined. Then Ellie said she'd given up and she went out to a party and Nan was singing Sunday School songs all night and when she went to bed I decided I was going to go and find my dad.'

238

'Your dad?' says Thomas through the hiss. 'But he's in prison.'

James shifts in the bushes, feeling the patter of rain on his head. 'I know! I'm not stupid! I was only ever stupid to listen to you!'

There's a pause, then Thomas says, 'What have I done?'

'You made me think I could do this science thing and I can't because I'm just a kid and I can't do anything and everybody was relying on me and now the police are going to get me.'

'Where are you, exactly?' says Thomas.

'Hiding in some bushes. Near the road that goes back down to the motorway.'

'The slip road. Right. Wait there. Don't move. I'll call you straight back.'

Gladys has the wipers batting to and fro and is peering over the steering wheel at the road ahead. Delil says, 'Straight up here and you can get on the M6. We need to go south.'

'This is ridiculous,' says Ellie, sandwiched between them. 'We have no idea where he is. He might not have even left Wigan. Maybe we should just go to the police.'

'No,' says Gladys resolutely. 'We're going to sort this out the Ormerod way.'

Ellie glances at her. 'You mean go off half-cocked with absolutely no plan and no idea what's going to happen and no actual thought for how serious it all might turn out?'

'Yes,' says Gladys. 'Exactly that.'

Ellie's phone buzzes. 'It's Major Tom! Hello! Hello! Have you found him?'

She grips Delil's arm with her free hand and bursts into tears. 'Oh, God. Oh, God, he's found him. He's got through to James.' She listens carefully and nods. 'OK. Thank you. I'll call you when we get there.'

'Where is he?' says Delil.

'Knutsford services. It's on the M6 apparently.'

Delil consults his phone. 'It's not far. Maybe half an hour? Forty minutes?' He glances at Gladys then at the speedometer. 'An hour. Mrs Ormerod, I hope you don't mind me saying, but I think this van has a fourth gear . . .?'

239

59

THE MARTIAN SUNSET

'James?'

'Major Tom!'

'Listen,' says Thomas. 'I've spoken to Ellie. They're on their way. You just have to stay put, all right? They're going to call me when they reach Knutsford.'

'OK. Will you talk to me, though? It's dark and I'm scared and I don't want the police to get me.'

Thomas pauses. 'All right. But listen. You hear the crackling on the line? This phone's going out of range. It could cut out at any time.'

'Then this is the last time I'll speak to you?' says James.

'Yes, probably.' He pauses in the cabin, and looks through the porthole at the receding Earth. 'Unless I go outside and do a spacewalk, this is the last time I'll speak to anyone.'

'If I was there I'd do a spacewalk,' says James.

'If you were here, I'd bloody let you.' Thomas listens to the hissing for a while. 'I can't believe you're not going to the competition. After all the work you put in.'

'I wouldn't have won anyway,' says James. 'It was a stupid idea.'

'It was a great idea. I can't believe you're just giving up. This could be the start of everything for you, James. It could open doors. You could be whatever you want in life.'

'I'll never be anything. I'm just James Ormerod from Wigan. I'm not like you. I'll never go to Mars.'

Thomas says nothing for a moment. 'No. You're not like me, James. You could actually have a successful life. A happy life.'

'But you're going to be the first man on Mars! You'll be the most famous person in the world. How can you not be happy?'

'James,' says Thomas quietly. 'Why do you think I'm here? I went to space because I couldn't stand another moment on Earth, couldn't look for one more second at the complete mess I've made of my life. Ever since I was a child, things have gone wrong around me. I failed at being a son, I failed at being a husband, I failed at everything. I even failed at *not* being the first man on Mars. It wasn't even meant to be my job. I only got it because someone dropped dead in front of me.'

James giggles.

'It's true!' says Thomas. 'And not actually funny.' He pauses. 'Well, a bit funny. If you've got a very dark sense of humour. The thing is, James, I made everyone's life around me worse. I never meant to, but I did. If I'd never existed life would have actually been *better* for everyone else.'

The silence lasts so long that Thomas thinks the connection has finally given up the ghost, then James says, 'It wouldn't have been better for us if you'd never existed. For me.'

'But what have I done, really? All I did was give you false hope.'

'It's better than no hope at all,' says James quietly. 'I don't think you're what you say. I think you must have made some people happy.'

'Not really. In fact, you could go as far as to say I've ruined people's lives in my time. My dad died when I was young, James, and I could have been a bit nicer to him. There was a girl I really liked, and I spoiled everything with her. And my brother . . . I could have saved him. That's what everybody thinks. I could have saved him. But I didn't.' Thomas goes quiet for a moment. 'And I was married once and all that I had to do to make her happy was to let her have children, but I couldn't even do that.'

There's a crackle and hum and James says, 'I bet you would have made a good daddy.'

Thomas can barely believe he's heard correctly. 'I would have been an *awful* father!' he hoots. 'How could I have been a good father with the example that was set to me? You know what my dad did, James? He took me to watch *Star Wars* for my birthday and left me there while he went off to have an affair.' Thomas pauses. 'And I swear to God, if you ask me what *Star Wars* is I'm going to do the spacewalk right now but without a spacesuit.'

'At least he didn't get himself sent to prison.'

'Your father's in jail because he tried to do the best by you, as misguided as that was,' says Thomas. 'Mine just couldn't keep his trousers fastened. I couldn't save my own brother from drowning

241

even though I was right there, James. With a pedigree like that, how could I be expected to be any sort of dad?'

'Is that why you decided to help us?'

'What?' says Thomas, though he's heard full well.

'Because your brother died. Because you never had a family. Because you let everyone down. Is that why you wanted to help us? To make yourself feel better?'

Was it? Thomas rubs his hand over his mouth. A shot at redemption? At this late stage? Is that all this is? Just something to . . . what? To make himself feel better, as James so succinctly puts it? He looks out at the dwindling Earth again, and feels a sudden jolt. James is down there, somewhere, in the dark. James and Ellie and Gladys and Laura and Janet and all those people whose lives his intersected with. All those people. Claudia. And up here . . . nothing but Thomas. Not a single human being beyond him. Six billion of them on Earth, and he couldn't find it in him to be friends with a single one? The void is empty and weightless but abruptly he feels it pressing down on him from all sides.

And for the first time since he sat on top of a big Soviet firework and was shot into space, he feels terribly alone.

'I thought I could survive in a vacuum,' whispers Thomas. 'But I was wrong.'

'You are surviving in a vacuum,' points out James.

'I'm speaking metaphorically. Don't they teach you anything at school? I mean, I thought I could live without other people. I was wrong. We need other people. We all need other people.'

'I don't like to say this,' says James. 'But isn't it a bit late to realise this?'

'For me, maybe, but not for you. You've got to have a good life, James. You've got to be better than me. Better to other people, and better to yourself.'

The boy says nothing.

'James. I'm going to tell you something now that I've never told anyone else, was never planning to tell anyone else. You know this ship, the *Ares-1*? It's got a cargo of habitation modules and light plant machinery. I have a job to do on Mars.'

'I know. You have to set up the landing site for the first settlers.'

'Yes,' says Thomas. 'I also have to keep myself alive until they get here. That was the attraction of all this. That's what drew me to come to Mars. The idea of being alone.'

'So what's the big secret?'

Thomas pauses. 'I wasn't going to bother. With the survival bit. I was going to set up all the habs, dig the irrigation ditches, lay out the welcome mat, all that. And then . . .'

'Then what? What do you mean?'

'I don't know. Hadn't planned it through. All I can say is that I haven't bothered reading the three thick manuals on how to plant potatoes and keep the breathable air flowing. I have a vague idea of walking off into the Martian sunset, but that's about it.'

'Oh my God,' breathes James. 'You're going up there to *die*?'

'Only because I have nothing to live for,' says Thomas. 'Unlike you. Do you understand?' The phone squawks and crackles. Thomas says, 'Hang on, the phone's beeping. I think it's Ellie.'

'Don't go —!' says James, but the line goes dead. He cradles his phone, pulling up the hood of his anorak against the rain, and watches the occasional car negotiating the slip-road. Five minutes later it rings again.

'Major Tom!'

'Stop . . . me that,' says Thomas. '. . . nan and Ellie . . . here. Told them where . . . are. Losing the connect . . , Listen carefully. This is the last time we'll speak.'

'Major Tom!' says James, stricken. 'Don't go! Wait.'

'. . .orry. Going out . . . range. Now shut up , , , listen '

James nods and feels the tears on his cheeks mingling with the rain, and listens very closely to what Thomas is saying, not asking questions even though he wants to because there's no time. He isn't even sure that Thomas has finished speaking when the line hisses for a long time then goes dead, but he knows the call is over. He stands up in the bushes as a pair of headlights sweep over him, and he squints at the dark shape of the van. He thinks he's understood everything Major Tom said, but there's one thing he's certain of that's wrong. Major Tom would have made an *excellent* daddy, no matter what the grumpy bastard says.

60

MAJOR TOM HAS A PLAN

Ellie has a dim knowledge that it's a cliché, played out in a thousand films and TV shows, but as soon as she jumps down from the van she embraces James, standing like a sodden little terrier by the side of the motorway slip road, and then shakes him by the shoulders.

'You stupid little brat!' she yells. 'What do you think you're doing? You've had us worried half to death.'

James blubs an apology and looks at the van, Dad's van. He goggles at the sight of Nan at the steering wheel, and Delil gives him a little wave. He rubs his face, and says, 'I just wanted to see Dad.'

Ellie sighs and hugs him again. 'Dad can't help us. Nobody can help us.'

'You're wrong!' says James excitedly as Ellie helps him into the van. 'Major Tom can help us! I've spoken to him. He says we've got to get ourselves to the competition.'

Ellie looks at her phone. 'But it's gone three in the morning. We'd have to get to London.' She squeezes in at the end, pushing Delil and James up against Gladys. 'Nan shouldn't even be driving as it is. Perhaps we should go back to Wigan. Meet up with James's teachers.'

'I don't want to go with Mrs Britton,' says James. 'Can't we just go ourselves? What if she's cancelled the train tickets?'

'I can get us to London,' says Gladys. 'I had a nap this afternoon. I'm fine. How far is it, anyway?'

Delil consults Google maps on his phone. 'About two hundred miles. We could do it in three, maybe four hours. Depending on traffic once we get on the M40 and then into London.'

'Bags of time,' says Gladys. She rams the van into gear. 'Everybody set? We can sing songs to keep us awake.'

'But I don't understand,' says Ellie. 'You don't have an experiment. What's the point of going?'

'I don't know But Major Tom has a plan. I don't know what it is because the phone went dead. But he said we just have to get to London and it'll all become clear. Oh, and we have to have a telly. That's very important. We need a telly and the BBC News on.'

'Maybe he's done a version of your experiment up on his space-ship,' says Delil. 'That would be dead safe.'

James looks at Ellie. 'He's really sad, you know. That's why he's so grumpy. He's had all this awful stuff in his life. He's going to Mars to get away from it all. He's going to Mars to . . . well, to die. But I think he feels like he's made a mistake. He realises not everybody's bad or hates him.'

Ellie bites her lip. The sensible thing is to go home. But there might be a chance to save them all . . . Could she ever forgive herself if she stopped them taking it?

'Can you do this, Nan? It's a long way.'

'I've had my vitamins.'

'Look,' says Delil. 'We've only been on the road an hour. What if Mrs Ormerod does another half an hour, then I'll take a turn.'

'You're only fifteen,' says Ellie.

'But I can drive. It's one of my many talents. Ferdi taught me. And I think we're probably past the point where we have to worry about whether we're doing anything illegal.'

'Did you learn on Southport beach like me?' says Gladys.

'I did!' beams Delil.

Ellie thinks about it. What was it she said to herself? She's not going out with a whimper. But a bang.

'Drive,' she instructs Gladys.

Gladys whoops pulls the van out on to the slip road. The engine whines and protests as she gathers speed and joins the carriageway.

'Second gear,' murmurs Delil.

Gladys crunches the gears and starts to sing. 'She wore! She wore! She wore a cherry ribbon! She wore a cherry ribbon in the merry month of May! And when! I asked! Her why she wore that ribbon! She said it is for Wigan and we're going to Wem-ber-ly!'

Precisely what the two officers of the Cheshire Constabulary Motorway Division do not need at three o'clock on a Saturday morning is a ten-year-old boy missing from home. They have conducted a sweep of the services buildings and are standing in the pale light of the petrol station near the southbound exit slip road.

'We're going to have to call it in, Gary, get some uniforms here.'

Gary nods. 'What did Wigan say?'

The other officer, who is called Adam, consults his book. 'Definitely not reported, but there is an Ormerod family with a kid called James matching the description. This PC Calderbank's been round to their house; there's nobody in and the van belonging to the dad's missing. He's banged up down in Bullingdon, by the way.'

Gary nods again, as though the son of a convict is going to be exactly the type to hitchhike to his patch and go missing in the middle of the night. Adam goes on, 'Calderbank thinks the family might be out looking for him. He also suspects the vehicle is being driven by a pensioner who might not have all her jam jars lined up in the pantry, if you know what I mean.'

A bleary-eyed motorist pulls up to the petrol pump nearest to them and gets out. Gary, following procedure more than in hope, says, 'Excuse me, sir, I don't suppose you've noticed a white van with . . .' He looks to Adam.

'Darren Ormerod, Builder, written on the side. Ford Transit, 99 plate,' says Adam.

'Possibly being driven by an elderly woman,' adds Gary.

The driver, unscrewing his petrol cap, nods towards the slip road. 'You mean that one?'

Gary peers through the rain. There is indeed the outline of a white van pulling away from the side of the exit road, heading towards the M6. He looks at Adam.

'I'll drive,' says Adam. 'Come on.'

They are only five minutes from Knutsford when disaster strikes. Gladys is several verses into the song now, and it makes her feel that Bill is with her, egging her on. He did like to sing that song when he went to the rugby, did Bill. There were a couple of saucy verses as well. She's not sure if the kids are ready for those.

'Mrs Ormerod,' says Delil.

'Oh, don't worry,' says Gladys. 'I know they don't play the rugby at Wembley in May any more. But August doesn't seem to fit the song quite as well—'

'Mrs Ormerod,' says Delil urgently, looking into the flashing blue lights filling the wing mirror on the driver's side. 'It's not the song. It's the *police*.'

✳ 61 ✳

ONE MORE CALL

Thomas has spent the past twenty minutes sorting through the foil-wrapped dried food packages in his larder. He is stuffing them into a bag which he keeps tight hold of around the opening to prevent them floating away as he sorts through, selecting those meals that have beans and pulses, vegetables such as cauliflower and cabbage, dairy products, cereals. He shuts the rest of them away and pushes himself to the desk, clipping the bag to the wall and ripping open one of the meals. It's supposed to be mixed with water and blasted in the microwave oven, but he begins to eat it down, squirting water into his mouth to offset the dryness. Then he picks up the phone and closes his eyes. He's not exactly praying, because he's never had any truck with that, but he's certainly trying to access some thread of good luck running through the universe, something he's never been able to get a hold of before.

'Please,' he whispers. 'One more call. That's all I need. One more call.'

He dials the number and waits while it rings once, twice, three times. It rings again. He glances at the clock on the wall; it's late. Or early, depending on your point of view. It rings. And rings. Then she answers.

'Hello. What. Hello?' says Claudia blearily.

'It's me. Thomas,' he says. There's a wall of static and he doesn't catch her reply, and says again, 'I've not got much time. Seconds.'

247

'Do . . . what time . . . is?' says Claudia.

'Listen very carefully, I need you to do something for me. Call Baumann. Now. Tell him I'm going out to do the EVA. The spacewalk. In the next half hour. Make sure there's a team in at Mission Control.'

Claudia is alert now. 'What? You're doing the spacewalk now? But there needs . . . preparation . . .'

'No time,' says Thomas. 'And I need you to do something else for me. You need to get me on the BBC News channel at eleven o'clock.'

'Tomorrow?' says Claudia. 'I mean, today? Eleven o'clock in the morning? But why?'

'You just need to do it,' says Thomas. 'Look, I can hardly hear you.'

'I can't just . . . it's the . . . BBC,' says Claudia.

'You can. I know you can. I have every faith in you. Eleven o'clock. On the nose.'

There's a long hiss. The connection's lost. But then her voice comes back, just for a moment.

'Be careful,' she says, then is gone.

Thomas discards the foil wrapper, which floats off behind his head, and digs in the bag for another one. Then he takes the manuals with weighted covers from the shelf into which they're snugly fitted and starts flicking through them for the Extra Vehicular Activity procedures, and when he's found it he sits back to read and helps himself to a packet of processed cheese. He pauses for just one moment, thinking about what James said.

I bet you would have made a good daddy.

Three weeks before he is due to go back to Star City for the final time, Thomas goes to visit Janet. He has given up the lease on his flat, said goodbye to the handful of people he considers as little more than strangers. He will spend some time in final training at Star City, then he will be transferred to the Baikonur cosmodrome in Kazakhstan for the blast-off, which is considered an ideal launching spot for of two reasons. One, the weather conditions are extremely temperate and barely fluctuate, ensuring no delays to the launch. Two, it is so remote that if the clunky old Soviet tech from which the *Ares-1* has been jury-rigged decides to explode and crash to Earth in a ball of flame, nobody will be killed. Apart from Thomas.

Of course, he doesn't say that to Janet. He had been surprised to get her letter a couple of weeks before, saying that she had, of course, seen him all over the news and wondered if he might want to visit her before he went to tell her what the hell he thought he was doing.

She lives in London, still, in a nice townhouse with a long garden at the front. The parallels with his visit to Laura many years before are obvious, even down to the butterflies in his stomach as he walks up the garden path, but of course he doesn't say that to her either. He doesn't really know what he's going to say to her, until the point where she opens up the front door.

'Oh,' says Thomas. 'You're pregnant.'

'I am.' She hasn't changed much since the last time he saw her. She is still slim and pale and red-haired, and is holding a tea-towel that says Scarborough on it. 'Which is a good job, because you shouldn't really just say that to women, Thomas. Not until you know for sure. I might have just put weight on. Then this would have got off to an awfully bad start.'

She shows him into the hallway, with its tall ceilings and stripped staircase, and through a white door into a living room.

There's a man there.

He's sitting on the chair reading the *Telegraph*, tall and dark-haired. Handsome, Thomas supposes. He wears jeans in a way that Thomas could never pull off, and a polo shirt that shows off toned arms. He folds his paper and stands up. 'Hullo. You must be Thomas.'

They shake hands and Thomas perches on the edge of a sofa. Janet says, 'This is Ned.'

'The father?' he says, without thinking.

'I hope so,' says Ned with a laugh.

Janet rolls her eyes and throws the tea-towel at him. 'Go and make some tea.'

Ned ducks into the kitchen. Thomas stares at his hands. He says, 'I was surprised you wrote to me.'

'So was I,' says Janet. 'It was Ned's idea. He said maybe we had things to discuss before you . . . before you went.' She shakes her head. 'Mars. I can't believe you're going to Mars.'

'You always said I should, you know. Be more dynamic. Do more stuff,' says Thomas.

She laughs. 'I meant put your socks in the laundry basket and maybe put a couple of shelves up. Not go to Mars.'

Thomas points at her stomach. 'And you've been doing . . . stuff, too.'

Janet lays her hands on her belly. 'Yes. About four months ago.'

'I'm . . .' Thomas searches for the right words. 'Um. Congratulations.'

'Thanks,' she says. 'It's still early days yet, and I'm over forty, so there are a lot of considerations. We know there are risks and I might not . . . well. Given my history and everything.'

'I'm sorry.'

'No, you're not.'

He feels himself tense. 'I didn't come here for an argument.' Thomas is not quite sure whether or not she's being passively aggressive here, but he decides to let it go. He says instead, 'I'd have been an awful father.'

Janet shrugs. 'Why do you say that?'

'Because my father was a shit,' says Thomas. 'Because I couldn't look after anybody. My mother, my brother. I never think about anyone else. You said yourself on many occasions I was like an overgrown child. I couldn't have done it.'

Janet looks at him for a long time. 'I think you're wrong.'

Thomas raises his eyebrows. 'What?'

'I think you're wrong,' she says. 'All those reasons you give, they're exactly why you *would* have been a good father. We're not trapped by mistakes, Thomas, whether they're ours or other peoples. We learn from them. What doesn't kill us makes us stronger, and all that.'

Thomas doesn't quite know what to say, and perhaps taking his cue from the silence in the living room, Ned emerges with a tray of tea. He sets it down on the coffee table and says, 'I'll be in the kitchen . . .'

'It's fine. I think we've said everything that needs to be said in secret. Oof. If you'll excuse me I need the loo.'

Janet creaks up the stairs and Thomas and Ned regard each other warily for a moment. Ned pours the tea and says, 'I should thank you for letting the divorce go through without any problems.'

Thomas shrugs. 'Couldn't see the point in causing a fuss. To be quite honest, if I hadn't got those papers through on that day, I wouldn't be going to Mars right now. So it all worked out all right.'

Ned looks at him curiously. 'And you're good with all this? All this going to Mars on your own, not potentially seeing another living soul for twenty years or something?'

Thomas smiles. 'It's brilliant. I've done Earth. I've done people. I can't think of anything better.'

Ned pulls a face. 'Wouldn't do for me.'

'Well, no, especially not with a baby on the way. Congratulations.'

'Thanks,' says Ned. 'Though I can see there might be some benefits in not having to see certain people ever again . . .' He raises one eyebrow in invitation.

Thomas takes a chance. 'And how's spending every Christmas and birthday in York working out for you.'

'Nightmare,' says Ned, and they both laugh. Hearing Janet's tread on the stairs, Ned hurriedly changes the subject. 'So. Chelsea's chances this season . . .?'

At the door, Janet gives him a chaste kiss on his cheek. 'I'm glad we had the chance for a chat. To clear the air, I still can't believe you're doing this.'

'Neither can I, sometimes,' says Thomas.

They both look up at the sky, imagining life beyond the blue. Janet shakes her head. 'God. Who'd have thought it. Mars.'

He searches for the right things to say. In the end he settles on, 'I'm glad you're happy.'

She smiles. 'And I am happy, Thomas. Happier than I've ever been in my life. I hope that doesn't sound harsh.'

'A bit,' he admits. 'But fair.'

'I believe things happen for a reason. In a way it's for the best that I lost the baby, that I didn't try again. We'd have been miserable.'

'We'd also have been miserable with . . . God. With a teen-ager, practically.' He pauses. 'Can we talk again? Maybe before I go?'

Janet gives a small shake of her head. 'Probably not a good idea.' He isn't expecting her eyes to fill with tears, and she gives him another quick kiss. 'Stay safe, if you can. And if you're allowed to change your mind before you go . . . well, the world's not as bad as you think it is, you know. You could be happy, too, if you'd let yourself.'

Thomas smiles ruefully. 'I'm not really sure I'd know how to,' he says, and walks away without looking back.

Helping himself to another dried meal, Thomas realises he has been thinking of that last meeting with Janet rather than reading up on the EVA procedures. He still doesn't know why he called what he thought was her number, the one that got him through to Gladys Ormerod. He'd said his goodbyes. He'd made his peace. He thinks about it for a while, and decides that what he'd wanted to tell her was that she was wrong, he did know how to be happy, and this was it: leaving Earth, leaving them all behind, that was what made him happy.

And now he realises that he is glad he never made the call, glad he got through to the Ormerods rather than her. Because otherwise, how would he know? How would he know that he was wrong? That suddenly, and crushingly, he wishes with all his heart that he'd never left at all.

✳ 62 ✳

BROTHERS

Mission Control is staffed throughout the night, of course, but mainly – especially since the comms went down on the *Ares-1* – with a skeleton team. But within half an hour of Thomas's call to Clau-dia the place is filled with technicians and BriSpA staff. Baumann shouts at someone to bring him another pot of coffee and stares at the screens. With no views of the spaceship to be had, they are a combination of diagnostic diagrams, fuzzy images from the satellites in orbit around Earth and Mars, and one wall of static. That is supposed to be the direct comms link to the *Ares-1*, and if Major does as he says he will it will shortly be filled with his miserable astronaut mug.

'What exactly did he say?' says Baumann crossly. 'Are you sure you weren't just dreaming about him?'

Claudia ignores that and repeats what Thomas told her. Baumann strokes his unshaven chin. 'He can't just suit up and go out,' he says. 'It's not like . . . like putting on a bloody onesie and popping out to water the hanging basket.'

'What is it like, then?' says Claudia.

Baumann glares at her. 'He's supposed to acclimatise for, well, for *hours*. Sit in the spacesuit and breathe nothing but pure oxygen. If he doesn't do that he doesn't get rid of the nitrogen in his body.'

'And what if he doesn't get rid of the nitrogen in his body?' says Claudia. She is beginning to wish she'd talked Thomas out of this.

'He could get decompression sickness. The bends.'

'Like divers get?'

'Exactly like divers get. Air bubbles trapped in his body. It can cause severe pain.'

'Can't that . . . can't it kill you?'

Oh God that it would, thinks Baumann. He knows that is not the thought of a rational man. But he has to admit to himself that it would be an attractive proposition. Of course, billions of pounds of equipment and flight-plans would be lost but . . . He fantasises for a moment about Thomas Major, contorted in agony, slowly dying on the big screen. Claudia would shed a tear and then wrap herself around Baumann, whispering, 'I thought it was Major I fancied but really I was just projecting my suppressed feelings for you on to him.' Baumann frowns; would Claudia talk like that? Well, he'll just have to work on what she would say later.

Baumann turns to grab the coffee from the technician who's hovering close by. 'I just wish we knew what had possessed him to do the EVA in the middle of the bloody night.'

253

Claudia is aware of Craig standing beside her, the only person in Mission Control who doesn't look like he's just stumbled out of bed. He murmurs to Claudia, 'I might be able to help with that. Over here.'

She follows him out of earshot of Baumann, and Craig says, 'I've been looking through the transcripts of his calls. The kid he was helping . . . this school science competition is supposed to be today. At Olympia, in London.'

Claudia looks at him. 'You think that's what all this is to do with? Why he wants to go live on the BBC at eleven?'

Craig shrugs. 'Did you get that sorted?'

'I'm still working on it,' says Claudia tightly. She clears her throat and says to Baumann, 'I'm just going to go to my office. Work on some announcements. Call me on my mobile if anything happens.'

Baumann nods without looking at her. 'Let's just hope you're not putting out a press release saying the poor bugger's floating halfway to Venus without a spaceship.' He shakes his head. 'I just knew Thomas Major was going to be trouble. Knew it. But would anyone listen to me?'

Thomas is, of course, fully aware that he's meant to spend a good four hours breathing nothing but oxygen before attempting a spacewalk. The air mix on the *Ares-1* is twenty per cent oxygen and eighty per cent nitrogen, and a pressure roughly the same as sea-level on Earth. If he climbs into the Extra-Vehicular Mobility Unit – or 'spacesuit' as he likes to call it – at the same pressure, he'll look like the Michelin Man. So the pressure has to be drastically reduced, which means upping the oxygen to near 100 per cent.

So says the manual, which also suggests the four hours pre-breathing on a respirator. Thomas figures if he exercises constantly on the treadmill, he could half that. Eventually, he allows himself sixty minutes, and that's going to be pushing it if he's going to get outside, fix the dish, get back in, re-pressurise, and get the comms link up and running in time for eleven.

It is, he admits, a very big ask.

It is also, when it comes to going out there, a very big if.

So he runs on the treadmill, breathing deeply through the respirator mask connected to the oxygen tanks on his back, and remembers.

The Hydrolab is a vast, circular pool in Star City, the water twelve metres deep. For the past five hours Thomas has been sitting in an Orlan spacesuit, which is a fetching shade of Soviet beige, while his heart rate and vital signs are monitored by a trio of white-coated doctors via a series of sensors taped to his skin. Insulated in the suit and helmet he can only converse with the doctors and his old friend The Meerkat via short-wave radio.

The Meerkat, stripped to the waist, proudly baring his hairy, broad chest, grins at Thomas. 'Maybe twenty more minutes, then in you go.'

In the pool has been submerged a Soyuz TM orbital module, which is the nearest thing in Star City to the hybridised *Ares-1*. The Hydrolab is designed to ape the effects of weightlessness to train cosmonauts for Extra-Vehicular Activity.

Thomas nods. He isn't sure if it is the steady flow of oxygen that is rushing through his system, but he feels a little unusual.

One of the doctors says something to The Meerkat, who thumbs his radio handset and says cheerfully, 'Your heart is banging like the shithouse door in a Siberian gale. What is being your problem?'

'I don't see the point of this,' says Thomas, his voice sounding tinny and echoing in the helmet. 'I thought this movie was *Journey into Space*, not *Voyage to the Bottom of the Sea*.'

'Imperialist American clap-trap!' declares The Meerkat. Thomas decides not to point out that *Journey into Space* is a BBC radio programme. 'We are *Battleship Potemkin*! We are brave Russian sailors rising up in revolution!'

'I fail to grasp the analogy.'

One of the doctors nods at The Meerkat, who says into his radio, 'Heartbeat all okey-dokey. Get in.'

Thomas stares at the winch that The Meerkat brings over to fasten to the harness on his spacesuit. 'I'm not sure I can.'

'Nonsense!' says The Meerkat, slapping him on the shoulder, which stings even through the thick suit. 'Meerkat once swam entire width of Lake Topozero . . . in January! What is the problem, Thomas? You cannot swim?'

Then the winch is lifting him off his feet and he's being swung out over the blue water of the pool, dangling stupidly until he starts to be lowered towards the shimmering image of the Soyuz.

'Imagine you are stepping out into the void!' The Meerkat says in his ear. 'The vastness of infinity!'

Pete's not come out!

The water is up to Thomas's waist now.

'The endless beauty of space!' cries The Meerkat.

Pete's in The Pond!

'Nothingness! All around! For ever and ever!'

He's drowned! He's drowned!

The water laps at the faceplate of the helmet. Thomas closes his eyes tightly.

He's got to go in!

'Peter!' calls Thomas, his voice cracking.

'What?' says The Meerkat. 'Who is this Peter?'

Thomas feels himself submerge, the Soyuz swimming into view. He feels faint.

Why's he not doing anything!

He could have gone in. He waited too long. He could have gone in but he was hesitant. He was scared. Scared of going in The Pond. So frightened that he let his brother die. Fear conquered him, and took Peter.

He's got to get him.

Fear claimed him and the life of his brother. Fear snatched Peter from under Thomas's watch, and left his mother a living corpse.

Thomas floats in the deep blue, the heavy stain on his soul momentarily and deliciously weightless. A millstone no longer dragging him down. He is, momentarily, without his burden.

'Peter,' he whispers. 'I'm sorry, I'm so sorry.'

Then he can hear beeping and buzzing in the radio, and the perfect moment is gone, and he is being winched up and out, the bright lights of the Hydrolab flooding his vision. The Meerkat is on his radio, crouched by the poolside, saying, 'Thomas, Thomas, we are bringing you in.'

Later The Meerkat stands him several vodkas in the Star City bar. 'No training for a week,' he says, directing Thomas to a dark booth with a dark leather sofa curving around a round table. 'Only drinking. Thomas, what happened down there?'

'Ghosts happened,' says Thomas.

The Meerkat nods. 'Many ghosts in Russia. Mostly wanting alimony cheques.' He barks a laugh and claps his hand on Thomas's shoulder.

'My brother died,' says Thomas quietly. 'He drowned. I could have saved him. I didn't. It was my fault.'

The Meerkat slams down the vodka bottle, moves round to Thomas's side of the booth, takes his head in his big, meaty hands, and plants a kiss on Thomas's forehead.

'I too lost my brother,' says The Meerkat. 'He died from alcohol poisoning. It too was my fault. I made him drink until he fell over.'

The Meerkat fills both their glasses from the bottle. 'Thomas, this makes us brothers. And you know what brothers do?'

'Drink until they fall over?' hazards Thomas.

A huge smile breaks out on The Meerkat's face. 'Simples!' he says, and throws back his drink.

⁂ 63 ⁂

FEAR OF FLYING

Thomas has climbed into the Extra-Vehicular Mobility Unit – the EMU – and completed his checks, then double checked, then triple-checked for good luck. Then checked again. The suit is sound. All he has to do is walk to the airlock at the front of *Shednik-1* and step out into space.

Simples.

He walks slowly and deliberately towards the airlock. He is not yet convinced he can do this. He pauses when he reaches the door and its central wheel lock. Thomas unlocks the airlock door and steps inside a cabin the size of a large wardrobe, and turns and closes the door, locking it from the inside. He gives it a tug; it is sound.

Now Thomas turns and faces the exterior door. All that stands between him and the endless infinity of space. He checks the oxygen gauge on the arm of his suit for the tenth time, then hits the switch on the wall to equalise the pressure inside the airlock with that of outside. He watches the red light on the switch blinking until it turns green. On the wall of the hull beside the switch-operated sliding door is a tether that clips to his belt, alongside the array of tools attached there for the purposes of fixing comms dish damage. The tether is coiled round a steel column fixed to the floor, his lifeline to the ship.

Now all he has to do is hit the door control. And step outside.

Thomas closes his eyes and takes a sip of water through the straw in his helmet. Eyes still closed, he leans forward, and hits the switch.

When he opens them again, he is looking at infinity.

'My God,' says Thomas. Nothing had prepared him for this. At first it's like looking at a piece of black velvet, perfect and flawless and all-encompassing. Then the stars emerge, shy pin-pricks of light that intensify before his very eyes, blazing suns billions of light years away, some so far that they have long since died, their light the mere ghosts of their past lives. He edges towards the lip of the door, and grabs with both gloved hands on to the hull. There is not, as he'd feared, a sense of vertigo. It's much, much worse than that. There's no fear of falling because there's nothing to fall to; it's a fear of *flying*, of flying for ever and never being able to stop. It's a horror of scale, a terror of scope, a crushing sense of insignificance in front of all that emptiness.

But it is, of course, not empty at all. This black night is haunted by ghosts. The blackness of space wavers and here they come, three of them, swimming like pale fish out of the darkness, where they have been waiting for Thomas all this time.

Peter, his brother, the boy who died.

His and Janet's unborn child, who Thomas sees for the first time is a boy, the boy who never lived.

And finally, a small boy who looks around at the blackness, the stars fattening and resolving into the light-painted faces of a cinema audience, and who wonders just where his dad has gone.

Thomas Major, the boy who didn't die, but didn't truly live either.

Thomas regards his eight-year-old self. 'It wasn't your fault,' he whispers. 'None of it was your fault. None of it is my fault. I couldn't save any of you. It's taken me until now to realise that. But there is a little boy I can help. Down there, on Earth. A little boy and his family. I can save them. Is that enough?'

Thomas closes his eyes. When he opens them, the ghosts have gone. Yes. It's enough.

He takes a deep, long breath of oxygen and launches himself out into forever.

Thomas has never seen the *Ares-1* in all its glory. He was within the main capsule which was encased in the nose of a rather large rocket that blasted him off from Kazakhstan, almost crushing the life out of him with the G-force as it broke free of Earth's gravitational grip. The sections of the rocket boosters fell away one by one until he achieved orbit and then it unfurled like a pupating insect. He feels bad that he refers to the ship as *Shednik-1*.

It's beautiful.

It looks like a dragonfly, its shimmering solar panel wings spread out, lazily harvesting the fiery energy of a sun that never sets. A further three modules, all containing everything he and future settlers will need for life on Mars, are linked to the main section like a train, ending in the engine block that pulses him relentlessly on in a huge curve towards the red planet.

Thomas remembers another dragonfly, lazily skimming the surface of a pond.

His breathing is loud in his helmet. The *Ares-1* is skimming the surface of the universe, of everything there is, there was, there will be. He feels so small.

One man against infinity. Perhaps a year ago that would have made him afraid.

One man against infinity. Now, it makes him fierce and proud.

He is that man.

He is Major Tom.

And he's got a job to do. The comms dish is situated on the hull of the second module in the train-link, and tugging on the tether Thomas brings himself back towards the main module and begins to drag himself, hand over hand, along the rails mounted on the exterior, towards the second module and the dish.

Thomas is just crossing the thick coupling that links the first and second modules when he jerks backwards, losing his grip. He panics, his arms flailing, and manages to get a thick-gloved hand on the rail again. The tether is taut. It must be caught on one of the exterior nodules on the hull, or someone at BriSpA cut some corners and didn't put enough cable in. He gives it a tug, and then another one, and it loosens. He's negotiating his way on to the second module when he glances round and sees the tether not spooling out as he had expected but floating free behind him, like an umbilical cord cut way too soon.

'Shit,' says Thomas. He can go back, couple up to the second tether in the airlock, or carry on. He looks at the oxygen gauge and the clock on his forearm. No time. He has to do this. He'll just have to be careful not to let go.

Gingerly he crawls up and over to the top-side of the module, though he knows of course there's no up or down in space. The comms dish is bigger than he'd expected, seven or eight metres in diameter. The problem is obvious; the micrometeoroid shower did a number on it, its concave dish is pocked and pitted with tiny holes. More than that, it's come away from its housing, almost floating free, kept in check by just one of the several cables that connect it to the electronic infrastructure of the *Ares-1*. He mentally draws up a checklist. One, refasten the dish to the hull. Two, repair and reconnect the severed cables. Three, get himself the hell back inside.

Clipping himself to the rails around the dish, Thomas pulls out the tools tethered to his belt and gets to work.

It's perhaps three hours later that he reckons he's finished. The dish is reconnected and fixed to the hull. There's no way of testing it until he gets back inside the module, though. Gathering his tools into his belt, he gives the dish one more check and begins to pull himself back towards the main section.

He's not sure what happens, but as he reaches across the gap between the second and main module he misses the rail, his momentum spinning him around and disorientating him. He sees a whirl of stars, a flash of the sun and he's out there, ten feet from the *Ares-1*, fifteen, twenty.

He panics and a light flashes on his forearm. The oxygen is getting low. He needs to get back, and now. Think. Think. Thomas calms himself. Thirty feet from the *Ares-1* now. Still moving. This is, of course, a situation that has been legislated for. Bolted on to the oxygen tank is SAFER – Simplified Aid For EVA Rescue. They do like their acronyms in the space business. There's a tiny flap on his other forearm covering a joystick and ignition button. Short, controlled thruster bursts that can get him back to the ship. Thomas orientates himself in space, facing the *Ares-1* (forty feet away! Forty-five!) and hits the thruster ignition.

Nothing happens.

The sun is rising dully over Slough and Director Baumann is peering into the bottom of the coffee pot when a cheer goes up from the technicians. He blinks and looks up to the main screen, which fizzes and resolves itself into a rather clear picture of the interior of the main module of the *Ares-1*.

'Bloody hell,' says Baumann, somewhat sourly. 'He's done it!'

A technician appears at his shoulder and says, 'All comms systems back online, sir!'

Baumann stares at the screen, at the interior of the ship. He can't quite believe Major had the balls to do the EVA, nor the wherewithal to actually fix the dish. Grudgingly, he suspects he might have underestimated the man.

'But where is he?' says Baumann, looking at the empty cabin.

Then a shape moves across the camera. Baumann exhales, then frowns. 'Wait. What *is* that?'

The technician peers at the object moving with stately grace across the screen. 'Er, it appears to be a book of crosswords, sir.'

*

WELL?

Delil nudges Ellie, who has just dropped off, and points at the blue flashing lights reflected in the wing mirror. She groans and puts her head in her hands. Gladys winds down the window, letting in the rain and the roar of the wind, and shouts, 'You'll never take me alive, coppers!'

'Nan,' says Ellie, deflated. 'Pull over. We're done for. I knew this was a stupid idea.'

The tick-tock of the indicator wakes James, who looks around, red eyed. 'Are we there yet?'

Gladys brings the van to a halt on the hard shoulder and Ellie says, 'It's the police, James. They've got us. We're properly done for now.'

He begins to bang his fists on his thighs. 'No. No no no. Not when we're so close. It's not fair.'

Delil watches the approach of the two officers from the car in the mirror. 'Let me do the talking.'

'No,' says Ellie. 'I'll handle this.'

The officer pokes his head into the open window and looks at them all in turn. 'Good morning. Going anywhere nice?'

'London!' says Gladys. 'Olympia. Do you know it?'

The officer looks at his notebook, and then over his shoulder. 'Adam? Are you on to Wigan? Have you got him?' Then he says into the van, 'Do I happen to have Gladys, James and Ellie Ormerod here?'

They all glance at each other and nod. Gary says, 'And you, young man?'

Delil leans across Gladys and holds out his hand. 'Mr Delil Alleyne. I'm the legal representative for the Ormerod family. They're saying nothing until you arrest them.'

Gary raises an eyebrow and sighs. 'We had a report of a James Ormerod missing from home. Is that you, son?'

James nods tearfully. Gary says, 'And where do you all think you're going?'

'To the National Schools Young Science Competition,' says James quickly. 'If we don't get there before eleven I can't win it and if I don't win it we'll lose our house.'

'Right,' says Gary. 'Mrs Ormerod, can I look at your driving licence?'

'Of course, officer,' says Gladys and digs in her purse. Gary gingerly opens out the folded paper. 'Mrs Ormerod, are you aware this licence expired in 1996?'

'Did it? Oh dear.'

'Oh, God,' says Ellie.

Adam appears and whispers into his ear. Gary takes the phone from him. 'I'll just be a moment. I have to consult with a colleague in Wigan.'

'They've got an all-points bulletin out for us,' hisses Gladys.

Gary returns a moment later and says, 'Mrs Ormerod, can you hand the keys over, please? I'm afraid we can't let you drive any further. My colleague here is going to drive your vehicle back to Wigan.'

James punches his thighs again. 'No! No! It can't be over. Not now!'

The wind is cold on the hard shoulder of the motorway, and as they watch Adam driving Darren Ormerod's van back on to the carriageway, to turn around at the next roundabout, Ellie wraps her arms around James.

'We gave it our best try,' she says softly.

'But it wasn't good enough, was it? It's never good enough. We always nearly make it and then it all collapses.'

Elle puts a hand on his shoulder and says to the policeman. 'What's going to happen to us?'

'First things first. I need you all in the car. It's not safe standing on the carriageway.'

Delil, Gladys and Ellie climb into the back seat and Gary motions for James to ride up front. James says, 'Don't think me getting a ride in a police car makes up for anything. I'm not a little kid.'

Gary sighs. 'I have just been speaking to a PC Calderbank in your hometown. He has given me something of a quick rundown of your situation.'

'So what happens now?' says Ellie. 'You take us back to Wigan? Do we get arrested? Are social services waiting for us?'

'Precisely none of those things,' says Gary. 'I'm not sure why, but you have PC Calderbank to thank for this. It appears I am now going to spend the rest of my shift driving you to London as a matter of urgency.'

Ellie looks at Delil and James, and they break out into a small cheer. Gladys throws her hands in the air and sings happily, 'One man went to mow, went to mow a meadow!'

'We're here,' says Gary, pulling the police car up outside the red brick façade and curved glass room of the Olympia Conference Centre. Delil, Ellie and Gladys have been dozing in the back seat; James has been watching wide-eyed as his first view of London rolled past the car window.

Ellie blinks and yawns and says, 'Thank you. Thank you so much. What time is it?'

Gary leans over the back of his seat. 'Nearly ten-thirty. Bang on time. How are you getting home?'

'Hadn't thought that far ahead,' says Ellie. 'We'll organise something.'

The policeman shrugs. 'I have to go back up north anyway. Might as well see this through. James has been telling me all about it.'

Ellie glares at James. Even if they win the competition, they still can't risk anyone finding out about their situation. Delil breathes on his glasses to clean them and says, 'Urgh. My breath stinks.'

'Lovely.' Ellie nudges Gladys. 'Nan? Nan, we're here.' She pauses. 'Nan?'

James looks over. 'Is she all right? She looks . . .'

'I'm just resting my eyes,' snaps Gladys. 'I wasn't asleep.'

'We'll leave the car here,' says Gary as they climb out and stretch. He grins. 'Perk of the job.'

Inside, Olympia is vast and cavernous, like an aircraft hangar. In the main hall there is a stage with several smaller platforms around

264

the edge of the huge space. Banners proclaiming the National Schools Young Science Competition hang from the vaulted glass ceiling, past mezzanine floors from which people lean. The place is packed with people.

'Woah,' says James. Ellie glances at him; the last thing they want is him taking fright now, especially since no one seems to have any idea what he's going to do.

There's a long registration desk at the back of the hall and they go over to tell them James is here. Ellie says, 'James Ormerod, St Matthew's Primary School, Wigan.'

A woman looks through a list and tuts. 'We had word from your teacher that you weren't coming. She phoned this morning to say she couldn't get hold of you.'

Ellie says, 'We decided to come down on our own.'

The woman looks them all up and down with a critical eye. 'Have you slept in a car or something?'

Gladys glares at her. The woman looks at her watch. 'We did leave your entry open because your teachers asked us not to formally withdraw it just in case you were making your own way down. But I'm afraid I'm not sure we can allow you to participate now. We really needed your teachers here and you should have registered properly by nine.'

James's shoulders sag. 'I told you. Every time we get close we take ten steps back.'

'Please,' says Ellie. 'You don't know what we've been through to get here.'

'Leave this to me.' Gladys elbows Ellie out of the way. 'Look, love, this little lad's worked his socks off to be here. I've driven a van down the M6, I've sung sixteen verses of "She Wore a Cherry Ribbon" and I've been pulled over by the police. I'm seventy-one next birthday and you really don't want to make me mad.'

The woman taps her pen on her table. 'Well, you're here now, I suppose.' She indicates the main stage, before which are rows and rows of chairs, all filled. 'James is on in ten minutes. The big stage. Good luck.'

They wander down the aisle between the rows of seats. On the stage is a judging panel of four people sitting behind a long table.

One of them Ellie vaguely recognises from the telly, a woman who from a science programme. Behind the judges is a huge monitor, showing in close-up what is happening on the stage. There is a girl standing in front of the judges with a small table. She is wearing a white lab coat and goggles. She does something and there's a loud bang and a puff of green smoke. Everyone gasps, then laughs, then applauds.

'I'd have brought some potassium if I'd known,' mutters James.

'Amazing!' says one of the judges, a young man with wild hair. 'A round of applause for Kayleigh Harrison-Butler from Bristol!' He looks at his clipboard. 'And next we've got . . . James Ormerod of Wigan!'

'Go on,' says Ellie, pushing him forward. She finds a seat on the end of a row, indicating two chairs behind her for Delil and Gladys.

'Good luck, love,' says Gladys.

Delil winks and punches him lightly on the arm. 'Go get 'em, tiger.'

The colour drains out of James's face. 'Ellie. I'm scared.'

'Me too,' she says. 'But you give me strength. You don't give up. Even when things were at their worst, you went off to find Dad. I believe in you, James.'

The man on the stage says into his mic, 'Ah, James Ormerod? Is James here?'

James puts up his hand and says in a small voice, 'Here, sir.'

Ellie kisses him on the top of the head. 'Do your best. That's all anyone can ask.'

And James starts the long walk down the aisle to the steps at the front of the stage.

'Here he comes,' says the man. 'James Ormerod, everybody.' There's a smattering of applause. 'Now, which school are you from, James?'

'St Matthew's,' mutters James into the microphone.

'Excellent,' says the man. He looks around. 'And your experiment to show the panel of judges . . .?'

James swallows. 'What time is it?'

The man blinks and looks at his watch. 'Almost eleven. Why, do you have to be somewhere?'

The audience laughs. James points at the big screen and says, 'Can you get the telly on that?'

The man raises an eyebrow and looks towards the wings of the stage. He says, 'Apparently we can. Is this part of the experiment?'

James nods. 'Can we have the BBC News channel, please.'

There's a slight pause and Ellie puts her hand to her face. What if this doesn't work? What is it even supposed to be? Her heart breaks into two at the thought of James standing there, nothing happening, no idea what to do.

The image of James and the man dissolves off the big screen and the image of Clive Myrie in the BBC news studio appears. The clock in the corner says 11 a.m. He is talking about a landslide in Peru.

The man leans forward and puts his mic under James's nose. 'Well?' he says.

⋆ 65 ⋆

BREAKING NEWS

'Thank Christ,' says Director Baumann, and the technicians give another cheer. Thomas has just slid into view in front of the monitor. He has an oxygen mask to his face, alternately taking deep breaths from it and then from the air mix inside the cabin. He's acclimatising back to the module atmosphere.

'*Shednik-1* to Ground Control,' says Thomas between breaths. 'Are you receiving me?'

'Bloody good to see you, Thomas,' says Baumann. 'And I never thought I'd be saying that.'

A technician holds out a phone for him. 'Claudia Tallerman,' he says.

Baumann waves it away. 'You fixed the comms link. Good work. No problems?'

'Apart from the fact that the tether snapped and the SAFER back-up thrusters didn't fire for seven goes, yes, everything was hunky dory,' says Thomas. 'I thought I'd be floating to Mars on my own. I was nearly a hundred bloody metres from the ship before I got it working.'

'She says it's urgent,' says the technician. Baumann glares at him and takes the phone.

On the screen, Thomas is looking at his clock display. 'Christ. It's eleven. Patch me through.'

'Where to?' says Baumann.

'The bloody BBC. Quick. I fixed it with Claudia.'

Baumann looks at the phone in his hand and puts it to his ear. 'Claudia? Where the bloody hell are you?'

'Oxfordshire,' she says.

'What the hell are you doing there? Shopping trip?'

'Shut up, Bob. You need to connect Thomas through to the BBC. Usual protocols we've got stored in the system, apparently. And you need to do it now.'

Baumann looks at the phone then at Thomas's image. 'Is anyone going to tell me what's going on?'

Thomas doubles up, his face twisted with agony. Baumann shouts, 'Decompression sickness! You've got the bends!' He tries to keep the joy from his voice.

Thomas shakes his head. 'Not the bends. I've been eating cabbage for ten hours. I really need to go. Put me through to the BBC, quickly!'

A technician waves at Baumann and shouts, 'Link established, you can patch him through when you're ready.'

Baumann shakes his head. 'No.'

There's an expectant silence in the Olympia, all faces turned to James. He is watching the TV screen intently, biting his lip. The judges are looking at the screen but turning back to James. Then Clive Myrie pauses and glances off-screen, then says, 'Apologies, I thought we were getting some kind of message in there. But . . . now, it's back to Cumbria where we've got the first of our in-depth reports on what leaving the European Union will mean to sheep farmers.'

The judging panel glance at each other as the screen cuts to a reporter standing in a field, wind whipping her hair around her face. James looks at Ellie, his eyes wide. She pulls a face back; she doesn't know what's going on either.

Other than it appears there's nothing from Major Tom.

'Is your experiment about sheep?' says the female judge encouragingly.

James opens his mouth to say something but then the windswept report disappears and Clive Myrie is back on the screen. 'Ah, and it appears we are interrupting this report . . . we'll be back in Cumbria after a short while . . . but this just in . . . it appears we're going live to . . .' Clive frowns. 'Ah, and perhaps not. We were . . . we're going to return to Cumbria now . . .'

James looks at Ellie, who shakes her head mutely.

'Yes,' says Thomas.

'No.'

'I swear to God,' says Thomas, 'if you don't patch me through to the BBC right now I'm going to go back out there and smash that bloody comms dish with a hammer.'

Baumann's eyebrows seem to grow and assume menacing proportions. 'Major. You need to get one thing into your head. You might be the man whose name's on everyone's lips, you might think you're something *special*, but believe me, you're no more valuable than the rest of the kit on the *Ares-1*. Less valuable, in fact. You do know we can run this mission without you? That having a human being up there is nothing more than a bloody PR exercise?'

Thomas stares at him. 'What do you mean? I don't need to be here?'

Baumann laughs unpleasantly. 'Everything could be automated. We have robots that can do what you're doing, which at the moment seems to be disobeying direct orders and spending half your time doing bloody crosswords. I didn't even want this to be a manned mission. Put humans into the mix, I said, and things are more likely to go wrong. But oh no. I was overruled. What a great honour this would be for Great Britain. Send the first man to Mars. On a mission that didn't even need a man, let alone a man like *you*.'

Thomas is silent for a while. 'Baumann . . . Director. Bob. Put me through. Please.'

Baumann shrugs. 'Why should I?'

'Because if I am just a walking PR exercise, then this is going to be the best publicity you'll ever get.'

'Fine,' says Baumann. 'Whatever. I'm only the bloody director here.' He turns to the waiting technicians. 'Do it.'

James stands on stage at Olympia, feeling small and afraid and alone, staring at pictures of sheep on the big screen. Then, suddenly, Clive Myrie is back.

'Ah, apologies once again for interrupting that report but . . .' He smiles. 'It seems that now we're going live for an unscheduled broadcast from the *Ares-1* which is currently carrying the British astronaut Thomas Major on the first manned mission to Mars.'

The expectant silence turns into a stunned one. James breaks out in a wide smile as the picture changes to a full screen image of Major Tom, leaning into the camera. 'I hope you can hear me down there,' says Thomas. 'This is Major Tom in the *Ares-1*. Hello the National Schools Young Science competition!'

There's a heartbeat and then the audience starts to shout and applaud. Across the bottom of the screen a banner says: *BREAKING NEWS: Astronaut Thomas Major in unscheduled live broadcast to the nation.*

Thomas says, 'You might be wondering why I'm making this surprise broadcast to you. Well, I'm hoping, if everything's gone according to plan, that right in front of you at this minute you've got James Ormerod . . . I can't see you, so if he's not there you're just going to have to pretend he is.' He waves into the camera. 'Hello, James.'

James waves back and shouts, 'Hello, Major Tom!' though he knows he can't hear or see him.

'Right,' says Thomas. 'Down to business. Now, I imagine you're thinking, where's James Ormerod's experiment? And why's Thomas Major involved in this anyway? Well, the fact is that just yesterday James's entry for the competition was smashed up by bullies at his school.' He waits for the inevitable gasp from the audience, and leans into the camera with a stern look on his face, then sits back. 'So. What's it got to do with me. Well, as James is such an exemplary young scientist, we have been conversing over the past couple of weeks. And in the event of such a problem, we came up with a back-up experiment.'

'We did?' says James, largely to himself.

'Yes, we did,' nods Thomas. 'James. Tell them about *flatus ignition.*'

James opens his mouth and closes it again. Then his eyes widen. His mouth drops open. And all he can think is *Oh. My. God.* He takes a deep breath and clears his throat. The man hands the mic to him. James turns half to the judges and half to the audience. '*Flatus ignition,*' he says. 'That's the scientific name for, uh, lighting your farts.'

There's laughter from the audience, and James grins. 'Farts are caused by what we eat being broken down in our stomachs by bacteria. Most of our food's all processed or complicated, and we need it to be in simpler chemical compounds. Most farts have' – he counts on his fingers – 'six main gases. Carbon dioxide, hydrogen, hydrogen sulfide, methane, nitrogen and oxygen. But did you know everybody's farts are different? It depends on their biochemistry and what they've been eating. That's why mine are dead loud but don't smell much, but my Nan's are quiet and whiffy. Silent but deadly we always say.'

There's more laughter and James sees Gladys waving around at everyone in the audience.

James frowns. 'But even though they pong I wouldn't want her to go into a home. That's what'll happen if we lose the house. They'll split us up. We love our Nan even if she is going a bit daft. But our Dad's in jail and Ellie's doing everything. She's my sister. She's brilliant.'

There's a silence and James catches the stricken look on Ellie's face. He clears his throat. '*Flatus ignition* occurs when you fart on a naked flame. Hydrogen, hydrogen sulfide, and methane are the most flammable gases. There's mostly hydrogen, and that makes a yellow flame. If you have a lot of methane it burns blue. I've never been able to do that. It's really rare. They call it the Blue Angel.'

Thomas coughs and starts to speak again. 'Now I don't know how long the BBC is going to keep us on air, so we're going to have to speed it up. I imagine you're pretty fed up of the word fart by now, but bear with us just a bit longer.' Thomas steeples his fingers beneath his chin. 'Look. I had a brother once and he was always trying to light his farts. Little boys, they're just horrible, aren't they?'

271

The audience laughs again. Thomas looks down. 'He died, my brother, when he was the same age as James is now.' Silence descends on the hall. 'I always thought it was my fault, but now I don't think it was. But if I could go back and do anything, I'd help him light a fart.' Thomas shakes his head. 'When I was talking to James he asked me a question. He said, what would happen if you set fire to a fart in a spaceship? Do you remember that, James?'

James nods. 'It was the first time we spoke.'

Thomas says, 'I thought it was a ridiculous, stupid thing to ask. Nobody had ever done that. Nobody had even wondered about that. Why would they?'

He leans forward. 'But that's what science is about, isn't it? Asking the questions that nobody's ever thought of asking before, or everyone's been too scared to ask before, or been told it's too stupid a question too many times before.'

Thomas sits back and puts one foot, and then the other, splayed on the desk. There's a gasp as everyone realises that beneath his BriSpA branded red T-shirt, he's only wearing boxer shorts. They are *Star Trek* boxer shorts, with the words To Boldly Go emblazoned across the front.

'Uh, apologies for these,' says Major Tom. 'They're my lucky pants, and I thought we might need a bit of luck today. They were a present. From my best man.' There's a pause, then Thomas says, 'Anyway. What would happen if you set fire to a fart in a spaceship?' He reaches to one side and picks up a cheap disposable lighter. 'In the name of science, shall we find out?'

✳ 66 ✳

WHAT'S THE WORST THAT COULD HAPPEN?

'Oh sweet Jesus,' says Director Baumann and puts his head in his hands. 'Please someone tell me I'm dreaming.'

No one offers that comfort, so Baumann peers through his fingers. 'Did I not say something like this was going to happen?

Did I not say *no*? Can you all remember this when the shit hits the fan?'

He takes a deep breath and clicks his fingers in the general direction of the techies. 'Someone. Quick. Give me a sit-rep vis-a-vis likely negative outcomes here.'

One of the technicians says, 'Do you mean what's the worst that could happen?

'Precisely that, yes,' says Baumann testily.

The technician considers this. 'He ignites all the oxygen on board the ship and blows it to smithereens.'

'And the best-case scenario?'

The technician shrugs. 'The flint on his lighter doesn't work?'

Baumann can feel his chest tightening. 'There must be something in between.' He looks up at Major on the screen, legs akimbo, undercarriage lowered.

Another technician raises a hesitant hand. 'NASA has done controlled experiments with fire on spaceships to see what would happen. They went off without incident.'

Baumann glares at him. 'And would you call this a *controlled* experiment?'

He puts his head in his hands. Someone else is at his elbow. 'Director Baumann? I have the *Guardian* on the phone. And the *Mail*. And the *Sun*. Pretty much everybody, really. Where's Claudia?'

'That's what I'd like to know,' he growls, jabbing at his phone. 'Claudia! Where the bloody hell are you? Still in Oxfordshire?'

'Just walking into Olympia,' she says.

'What's on there? Come on, woman! This is an emergency!'

'You're a rude, sexist boor with no imagination!' shouts Claudia.

'Have you *seen* this? Have you bloody seen it? Do you think Terence Bradley would be . . . would be lighting his own farts halfway to Mars? Do you?'

'Do you think Terence Bradley would be live on every single news channel in the entire world right now?' yells Claudia back. 'He was a rude, sexist boor too. I can see why you had a hard-on for him!'

Baumann feels faint. His head is pounding. His heart is pounding. He can't feel his thumbs. 'He's going to blow up the

273

Ares-1. Live on television. All those people watching this . . .' He pauses. His eyes widen. He laughs. 'What am I thinking? Nobody has to watch this!' He shouts over to the technicians. 'Kill the feed.'

'No!' shouts Claudia. 'You can't! Not now!'

'Kill the feed!' screams Baumann. The techies look at each other uncertainly. 'KILL THE FUCKING FEED! He's not doing this! Not on my watch!'

'Don't touch anything,' booms a voice.

Baumann turns in astonishment to see Craig looming over him. 'What the *fuck* do you want?'

Craig points at the technicians. 'You leave this running, all right? Think of that little lad.'

'I'M THE DIRECTOR,' screams Baumann, throwing the phone on to the floor. 'You're not the boss of me.'

'Director Baumann, I am hereby relieving you of your command,' says Craig. 'You're not of a fit mental capacity to make decisions any longer. You're stressed and you've been up all night.'

Baumann sneers 'What do you think this is, the *Good Ship Lollipop*? You can't relieve me of command.' He brings his face close to Craig's. 'I'm going to have your balls for this, you pansy.'

Craig smiles. 'Don't let your mouth write cheques your arse can't cash,' he says, then delivers a swift, hard uppercut to Baumann's stomach.

The director staggers and falls on to his backside. He stares uncomprehendingly at Craig standing over him, then shrugs and crosses his legs. 'Fine. Fine. You have your *Apollo 13*. I don't care any more. I didn't even want this job.' He giggles. 'I always wanted to be . . . a lumberjack.'

Craig leaves him sitting there, whistling to himself, and picks up the phone Baumann discarded. 'Claudia? It's Craig. We're still on the air.' He looks up at the screen. 'And a good job, too. I think our boy's gonna blow.'

'I've been eating dried cabbage all day,' says Thomas. 'You can probably be quite thankful you're not up here with me. Oops. I think something's happening. Are you all ready down there?'

Though they know he can't hear them, the crowd shouts, 'Yes!' Thomas smiles.

His stomach gurgles.

He holds the lighter around his thigh and under his backside, gives a thumbs up with his other hand. He says, 'How about we have a good, old-fashioned space-style countdown? Here we go . . . Ten! Nine! Eight!'

'James,' says the lady from the science show. 'Do you think you could tell us what's happening?'

The audience is joining in. 'Seven! Six! Five!'

Transfixed by the screen, James begins to speak into the microphone. 'When we light a fire on earth, like a candle, it's gravity that makes the flame look like a pear-drop. That's because hot air rises up and pulls cold air behind it, and that's what makes the flame stand up and flicker.'

'Four! Three!'

'But on the spaceship . . . it's not got the same gravity. It's got microgravity. So the flame doesn't stand up. It does something different. There's no pull so it won't be pear-shaped.'

'Two! One . . .'

'Blast off!' shouts Major Tom and everyone in Olympia.

And then there is a low rumble that builds to a trumpet-like *parp* as Major Tom breaks wind.

The tiny flame on the lighter clicks into life and then blos soms and expands like an oil slick, but quickly resolving itself into what can only be described as a bubble of fire that, borne on Major Tom's exhaust looms over the edge of the desk like an alien sunrise.

Everyone gasps as a perfect sphere of flame the size of a cricket ball rises slowly from between Major Tom's legs, as he kicks backwards against the desk, getting away from it. It is glowing blue on the outside and burning pink in the middle.

It is quite, quite beautiful.

'It's not spreading like a fire would on Earth,' says James slowly. 'It's not . . . not lapping up oxygen. It must be . . .' He looks to the woman, who nods encouragingly. 'It's pulling the oxygen into it, keeping it fuelled.'

Thomas is sitting, transfixed by the ball of fire that bobs in front of him, painting his face with deep blue light. It floats and glows like something otherworldly or divine, a thing not of Earth. It's the colour of the sea, of the sky, of distant horizons. James whispers, 'He did it. The Blue Angel. He did it.'

The crowd goes wild.

Thomas leans forward to the camera, not taking his eyes off the shimmering ball of blue flame. 'And that's what happens if you light a fart in a spaceship,' he says. 'And now, I think I'd better get the fire extinguisher on this before it gets into the ventilation system and really gets me in trouble.' He looks into the camera. 'I now return you to your regular programming. Good luck everybody – well, James, really, and, um . . .' He looks like he's trying to think of something useful to say. 'Be good at school.' He reaches for the monitor, then pauses. 'And don't do drugs.'

Then the screen goes momentarily black and then Clive Myrie is there, looking somewhat nonplussed, and the banner across the bottom of the screen says, *BREAKING NEWS: British astronaut first man to light fart in space.*

The big screen switches back to the National Schools Young Science Competition logo and the man with the mic waves his hands for quiet. 'Wow. Well. That's our final entry of the day so the judges are going to retire for a few minutes to consider what they've seen. Back with you all in a short while.'

✴ 67 ✴

IS IT OVER?

James runs down the steps and along the aisle, people standing and clapping, patting him on the back, and he throws himself at Ellie, hugging her.

'I am so proud of you,' she says, holding him tight.

Delil punches him lightly on the arm again. 'That was double-safe, little dude.'

'Is Nan all right?' says James. Gladys is sitting quietly, her eyes closed.

'She's just tired, I think,' says Ellie. 'She was complaining of a headache.'

James looks at her curiously. 'Ellie? Have you been crying?'

She wipes her face with her hand. 'It's nothing, silly.'

'Tell me,' he says.

She takes a deep breath. 'It's just . . . when you were talking . . .' She bites her lip. 'You told them everything, James. About us. And Nan. And dad being in prison. You told them everything. The whole world was watching.'

His hand flies to his mouth, and he bursts into tears. 'I've properly ruined it now, then, haven't I? Even if I win they'll take us away from each other.'

'Hush,' she says, hugging him again. 'Hush. It's not your fault. Look. The judges are coming back on stage.'

The judges troop on and stand in front of their table. The man with the mic says, 'And have you reached a decision?'

The woman from the TV show takes the mic and says, 'We have. Firstly, we want to say congratulations to all our finalists. We've seen some marvellous entries and it feels like the future of science is in safe hands with the young people of today.'

There's a round of applause. Gladys opens her eyes and mutters, 'Get on with it, woman.'

'I'd like to say the decision was a difficult one,' says the woman, and pauses. 'I'd like to, but to be honest, there was a clear winner here today. There's something called Occam's Razor, which is more to do with philosophy than hard science, but really it means that sometimes the simplest choice is the obvious one. And when it comes to originality, a sound grasp of scientific principles, bringing something new and practical to theory . . . well. What can I say? It's James Ormerod, everyone.'

There's a thunderous clapping and the woman beckons James up to the stage. 'Bring your family, as well.'

Holding hands, Ellie, James, Delil and Gladys march up the steps and stand in a row. James blinks as a photographer takes pictures. The woman hands him a trophy and an envelope. She says, 'There'll be a contribution to your school as well, but this is for you. Five thousand pounds! How are you going to spend it, James? It's a lot of money.'

'Probably pay our phone bill,' says James. 'It must be astronomical by now.'

The crowd laughs again, but then there's a disturbance at the back of the hall, and Ellie can see a group of people marching down the aisle. A lot of them seem to be carrying cameras and notebooks. At the head of them she recognises that woman who came to their house. Claudia. So this is it, then. She's getting her bit of PR. Now they'll be expected to tell their stories to the papers and the TV.

Ellie shouts at Claudia, 'Is this it, then? Have you come to take your pound of flesh?'

Gladys squints at Claudia. 'It's that woman from the space place. And, look who's with her.'

Claudia stands to one side and the press pack parts. There are two men in security guard uniforms, flanking a man with dark hair, wearing a blue shirt and black trousers. He smiles at Ellie. She staggers and thinks she might faint.

Gladys says, 'It's our Darren.'

'Daddy!' yells James. He drops the envelope and the trophy, which Delil manages to scoop up just before it hits the stage. James lunges forward and runs down the steps, hurtling along the aisle and into the arms of Darren Ormerod.

Ellie closes her eyes.

Is it over?

They are taken into a private room on the upper floor, Claudia, the Ormerods, the security guards and Delil. James cannot stop hugging Darren; Ellie regards him a little warily. She says to Claudia, 'Did you do this?'

Claudia smiles. 'Ever since I met you I've been in talks with the Probation Service. I outlined the situation and, given that your father has been an exemplary inmate, they agreed to let him out on licence, due to the time he's already served. He's essentially still serving the rest of his sentence, but instead of being in prison he can do it at home. With you. So long as he keeps his nose clean, he won't go back.'

Darren extricates himself from James's grip and looks at his daughter. 'Ellie,' he says. 'Don't I get a hug.'

Ellie looks away. 'I haven't forgiven you for what you did.'

'You should have told me,' he says. 'About the trouble you were in. I could have done something.'

'You couldn't have done anything,' she says. 'Not inside. We couldn't come to visit you because Nan was getting worse and when you phoned . . . well, I didn't want to worry you. You'd have just made a fuss to someone and that would have got us split up quicker.' Ellie folds her arms and looks at her feet. 'I've been coping. Maybe we don't even need you any more.'

Darren's face creases with anguish. 'Don't say that. I know you're angry with me, but don't say that. I'm back. We can do this. But we have to do it together.'

Ellie feels one tear roll down her cheek then drop on to her forearm. She looks at her dad, then runs towards him, throwing her arms around his neck. He holds her tight, and Ellie feels like a child again, and cries like a child, and hugs her dad. And, for the moment, she lets herself believe that it's all going to be all right.

Gladys goes over to that Claudia, who's crying like a baby herself, and says, 'Can I speak to Major Tom?'

Claudia dabs at her eyes and says, 'What, Mrs Ormerod? Now?'

Gladys nods. 'It's quite important. Very important, I think. Can't you phone him?'

Claudia shrugs and punches a number into her phone. She says into it, 'Mission Control? Craig! Where's Baumann? What? Whistling? Never mind. Can you ask if the techies can patch this call through to Thomas? Is that possible? Yes, I'll hang on.'

Gladys has a headache, and she feels like she should go for a lie down. While she's holding, Claudia frowns at her. 'Mrs Ormerod? Are you all right? You look a little pale . . . Oh, hang on.' She hands the phone over. 'You're through to the *Ares-1*.'

Thomas sits in front of the monitor through which the audio is being routed. 'Gladys!' he says. 'Lovely to hear from you! How did he do?'

'He won, of course,' says Gladys. 'Though farting on live telly . . . I don't know what the world is coming to. Anyway, it wasn't that I wanted to talk to you about. I was resting my eyes before James went on and I had a little dream about Mr Trimble.'

'Trimble?' says Thomas, at a loss. He'd almost forgotten what conversations with Gladys were like.

'Yes,' says Gladys crossly. 'Mr Trimble. He was one of my Sunday School teachers. Keep up. I've been thinking about Sunday School all the time since you gave me that crossword clue. I think I've cracked it.'

Thomas pauses, then says, 'Bloody hell. Have you?' He looks around for his book and pencil, finds them hovering near the window. 'Hang on. I've got it. Here we go. *18 Down: If put off, can encourage angina, say – proverbially.* Four letters. It's the last clue. I'm stumped.'

'Well,' says Gladys. 'Angina. That's like heart disease, isn't it? That's what did for my Bill, in the end. And when you put something off, you defer it, don't you?'

Thomas stares at the grid. 'I still don't get it.'

'It's the proverbially that does the trick. *Proverbs.* From the Bible. Chapter thirteen, verse twelve.'

'You're going to have to help me out,' says Thomas. 'I never did Sunday School.'

Gladys sighs. '*Hope deferred makes the heart sick,*' she says. '*But a longing fulfilled is a tree of life.* If put off it can encourage angina. If deferred, it can make you heart sick. You see?'

He does. With a flourish of his pencil, Thomas fills in the four blank squares.

'Hope,' he says. 'It's hope. I've got it.'

Gladys looks at Darren, embracing Ellie, James standing beside them with his arms stretched around them both. Delil and Claudia are standing together, crying. Gladys smiles. 'We've all got it, Major Tom,' she says. 'At last, we've all got hope.'

FEBRUARY 11, 2017

'This is Ground Control to Major Tom, come in, Major Tom!'

Thomas anchors himself at the desk and smiles into the camera. It's Claudia, standing in Mission Control. 'This is the *Ares-1* receiving you loud and clear,' he says.

'Not *Shednik-1?*' says Claudia with a raised eyebrow.

Thomas shrugs. 'After I saw her in her entirety for the first time, I thought she deserved a little more respect, that's all.' He pats the desk. 'She *is* getting me to Mars.' He pauses. 'Where's Baumann?'

'Yes, well . . . Director Baumann is taking some leave,' says Claudia. 'He's going to be away for some time on long-term sick. We have a new interim director of operations.'

'You?' says Thomas.

Claudia laughs. 'Thomas, of course not. I wouldn't have the job for all the shoes in Jimmy Choo.' She looks to one side and beckons with her head. 'The BriSpA board thought that someone with some space experience might be useful for the rest of your journey.'

The new interim director steps into view grinning broadly. '*Privyet*, Thomas,' he says in greeting.

Thomas goggles at the screen. 'The Meerkat!'

'Maybe just call me Sergei,' says The Meerkat. 'Or Director. Whichever you are feeling the most comfortable with.'

'The Meerkat,' says Thomas. 'It's how I know you.'

The Meerkat winks. 'Simples,' he says.

'There's someone else to see you as well,' says Claudia.

'I'm still not recording "Space Oddity" for that man,' says Thomas, but Claudia ushers three people in front of the camera, a tall man with dark hair, in a T-shirt and jeans, a teenage girl and a small boy with unruly hair.

'Ellie and James I think you know,' says Claudia. 'And this is their father, Darren.'

Thomas leans forward on the desk and smiles. 'You're nothing like what I thought you'd be.'

'What were you expecting?' says Ellie.

Thomas shrugs. 'The Simpsons, I think.' He scans Mission Control. 'Where's Gladys?'

Ellie looks off-camera and hisses, 'Nan!'

Then a small, white-haired woman joins them, peering at the screen. 'Ee, he's bigger than he sounds on the phone.'

'It's a large screen,' explains Claudia.

Thomas says, 'Gladys. We meet at last.'

'Major Tom! It sounds like you're in the next room. Did you finish the crossword?'

'I did, thanks to you. That was brilliant.'

'There's nothing worse in life than an unfinished crossword,' says Gladys.

There's a momentary silence, then James says, 'Ellie's got a boyfriend.'

She punches him on the arm. 'I have not! We're just friends! God!'

'Ow,' says James. 'She has. His name's Delil. He's weird but nice. And she's staying on for another year at school because she's missed so much looking after us.'

'Good,' says Thomas. 'You're a bright girl, Ellie. You need to take all the chances you can. And so do you, James. What are you going to do to capitalise on your success in the science competition?'

James says, 'You know what we were talking about? In the motorway service station? When you said . . . about setting up the hab modules? And the Martian sunset?'

'I remember,' says Thomas.

James smiles. 'Well, you can't do that. Because I'm coming to see you. I'm going to be an astronaut. Mr Meerkat says I can.'

Claudia smiles. 'We've pledged to sponsor James's university education if he can commit to getting good grades in science subjects, and after that we can guarantee him a place at our training academy. I know he's only young, and might change his mind . . .'

'I won't!' says James fiercely.

'. . . but,' says Claudia, 'there's every chance he might well be coming to see you in ten or fifteen years.'

Thomas rubs at something in his eye. 'I'll be waiting,' he says quietly.

'Do you mean it?' says James.

'I mean it,' says Thomas, and to his mild surprise he realises that he really does.

'Uh, Mr Major?' says Darren. 'I just want to thank you, if that's all right. I let my family down and you stepped in to help them when I couldn't.'

'They did it themselves,' says Thomas. 'Ellie held them together and James worked hard to win the competition. And you made a mistake; we all make mistakes. I should know about that.'

'That's true,' says Darren, looking at his children proudly. 'But if it hadn't been for you . . . Well, I just want to say thank you, Mr Major.'

'Don't call me Mr Major,' says Thomas. 'You make me think my father's in the room.' He smiles. 'Call me Major Tom.'

After he's had his dinner – avoiding anything with cabbage – Thomas does an hour on the treadmill then starts a new crossword. There's months to go before he makes Mars orbit, after all. After a while he leaves it and fishes out the manuals. He's going to have to study them carefully if he's going to set up the hydroponic growing systems.

If he's going to survive on Mars.

Which, he is still rather surprised to realise, he intends to.

He looks at the calendar, at the days already marked off. Then he notices the date. February 11. Already, February 11. He flicks through his music library and hits play.

He's lost in the intricacies of growing root crops when the monitor pings and Claudia's face appears. She's in her office, patched through to him via the comms link.

'Working late?' he says.

She shrugs. 'Just wanted to give you a call.' She pauses, and cocks her head to one side. 'What's that godawful noise?'

Thomas says, 'It's the *Star Wars* soundtrack by the London Philharmonic Orchestra.'

'I thought you were supposed to have quite cool taste in music,' says Claudia.

'Yes, well,' says Thomas. 'I play it every year on this date. It's the day my father took me to the cinema and abandoned me.'

Claudia nods thoughtfully. 'Do you hate him?'

'I did,' admits Thomas. 'For a while I thought I hated everybody. Every single person on Earth. Including myself. That's why I'm here.'

'We're not all bad,' says Claudia.

'No. It's almost funny that it took for me to leave it all behind before I could realise that.' He pauses. 'The thing is, I only remembered the bad stuff. It blotted out the good stuff to the point where I didn't even know it had happened. There was good in everything. In everybody. I just chose not to see it.'

'Even that day at the cinema?' says Claudia.

It's only the afternoon but already the sky is deep blue, a full moon low on the horizon above the black rooftops. 'Like a ten-pence piece,' says Dad. Thomas closes one eye and puts his thumb and forefinger around the disc of the moon.

'I got it, Dad! I got the moon!'

'Put it in your pocket, son,' he says. 'You never know when you might need it. Come on, we're going inside at last.'

'Yes,' says Thomas. 'Even that day at the cinema.'

They sit in silence for a while, each one looking away when they catch the other's eye. Eventually Thomas says, 'What sort of music are you into, anyway?'

Claudia shrugs. 'This and that. Stuff on the radio. I don't know much about music.' She pauses. 'Why don't you educate me?'

Thomas nods. 'Good idea.' He kills the *Star Wars* soundtrack and scrolls through his music. 'Here we go. Why not start with a bit of Bowie?'

As the music begins, Thomas looks through the window at the Earth, which is now just about the size of a ten-pence piece. He closes one eye and with his thumb and forefinger plucks it from the blackness.

'What are you doing?' says Claudia, puzzled and amused.

'I got the Earth, and everyone on it,' says Thomas softly.

He puts it into his pocket, next to his heart. 'You never know when you might need it.'

'You're funny, Thomas. I actually think I miss you. But I didn't even know you properly until you went away.'

Thomas says nothing, but instead closes his eyes and listens to the music. And then he starts to sing, as the *Ares-1* moves slowly yet inexorably, like a beautiful dragonfly on its one-way journey through the void.

There's a starman.

And he's waiting in the sky.

THE END

Acknowledgements

As Thomas finds out in this novel, no one can truly exist in a vacuum, and that goes for writers as well. It might seem a lonely, introspective job, being an author, but a book like this does not come into being without a huge effort from a great many people.

Indeed, this book would not exist were it not for Sam Eades, editor extraordinaire and tireless champion of not only this novel but all the titles which form the launch books of the new imprint Trapeze, of which I am proud and honoured to be a part. Sam has seemingly acquired the secret of squeezing more hours out of the day than anyone else; either that, or she uses them more wisely than the rest of us. Her ideas, input, encouragement and suggestions have made this book what it is.

Thanks also to my agent John Jarrold, for his unwavering support of my work over more than a decade, even – especially – when it's taken us into areas neither of us were expecting.

CALLING MAJOR TOM is, of course, a work of fiction, and for reasons of continuity I've pretty much made everything up rather than trying to get some things completely accurate. I expect I owe an apology to any scientists or even astronauts who have read it; hopefully I haven't got you seething with fury too much, but I've drawn on my journalistic background quite substantially in terms of research to ensure the facts don't get in the way of a good story.

The British Space Association is, of course, a complete invention, and should we get to the point where Britain is indeed involved in organising, financing and operating manned missions to other planets, I'm sure it won't be as shambolic as what's been portrayed on the preceding pages. Fairly sure, anyway. Well, it probably won't . . .

I suppose a lot of CALLING MAJOR TOM is played for laughs. I've been asked more than once where the inspiration for the more comic side of the Ormerods has come from; all I can say is that I grew up in a working class household in Wigan. As a very wise man named Ted Bovis once said, 'The first rule of comedy, Spike, is reality.'

That said, there are a couple of aspects of the Ormerods' lives that are no laughing matter. Gladys suffers from, we understand, some form of dementia. These are terrible diseases that rob people of their loved ones even as they continue to live. If, as they say at the end of a particularly harrowing episode of EastEnders, you have been affected by anything in this book on that score, you'd do worse than checking out the websites alzheimers.org. uk and alzheimersresearchuk.org for a wealth of information and support.

Similarly, the situation Ellie finds herself in, as the carer for her family due to circumstances beyond her control, is sadly not one confined to fiction. A BBC survey a couple of years ago estimated there are 700,000 young people caring for other members of their families, the majority of them without any support whatsoever. carersuk.org and childrenssociety.org.uk can offer help and advice.

Finally, this book is dedicated to my wife, Claire, and our children, Charlie and Alice. If I've learned anything about life, it's probably been from them.

And, ultimately, thank you to you for reading this far (unless you're the sort of person who reads the acknowledgements first; in which case SPOILERS. Oh, I suppose it's too late now . . .). I hope you enjoyed CALLING MAJOR TOM. If you did, you can generally find me procrastinating on Twitter at @davidmbarnett. In fact, even if you didn't enjoy it, you'll still find me there. Angry astronauts and scientists might end up blocked, though, purely to save my own blushes . . .

David Barnett
Somewhere on Earth
2017

Reading Group Guide

Topics for discussion

1. What do you think about our first introduction to the Major family? How different are they in their relationships from the Ormerod family?

2. When we meet Thomas as a grown man in chapter one, how much has he changed from that opening scene? Can you recognise that little boy as an adult?

3. As a grown-up, Thomas is incredibly grumpy. Do you like him as a character from the beginning? Do you know other curmudgeons like Thomas?

4. As readers, Thomas's past is revealed piece by piece. What surprised you about Thomas's early years? Why do you think the author decided to tell his story in this way?

5. What are your first impressions of the Ormerod family? Are they a happy family? Or are they as dysfunctional and unhappy as Ellie believes?

6. What pressures and fears might someone in Ellie's position have? Do you think she does a good job of keeping the family together? Or should she seek help earlier?

7. Director Baumann talks about the 'expectations' placed on Thomas as the first Briton to head to Mars. Does he live up to these expectations by the end of the novel? How does Thomas

compare to other astronauts from popular culture such as Mark Watney from THE MARTIAN?

8. How does Darren Ormerod compare and contrast to Frank Major? Are they both bad fathers? Or did they make bad choices?

9. Thomas fears he will follow in his father's footsteps. Is he like his father? Does his decision to be different prevent him from making meaningful relationships?

10. A number of characters – Claudia, Thomas, Delil – are changed by their interactions with the Ormerod family. Are they changed for the better?

11. Do you like Thomas at the end of the book?

12. Does Director Baumann get his comeuppance?

13. Would you like to see CALLING MAJOR TOM made into a movie and, if so, who do you see playing the main roles?

14. Is the ending hopeful? Do you think James will join Thomas in space?